DEATH OF A
CHEF

Also by Alexander Campion

THE GRAVE GOURMET

CRIME FRAÎCHE

KIILLER CRITIQUE

Published by Kensington Publishing Corporation

DEATH OF A CHEF

ALEXANDER CAMPION

KENSINGTON BOOKS
www.kensingtonbooks.com

KENSINGTON BOOKS are published by

Kensington Publishing Corp.
119 West 40th Street
New York, NY 10018

All Kensington titles, imprints, and distributed lines are available at special quantity discounts for bulk purchases for sales promotion, premiums, fund-raising, educational, or institutional use.

Special book excerpts or customized printings can also be created to fit specific needs. For details, write or phone the office of the Kensington Special Sales Manager: Attn. Special Sales Department. Kensington Publishing Corp., 119 West 40th Street, New York, NY 10018. Phone: 1-800-221-2647.

Kensington and the K logo Reg. U.S. Pat. & TM Off.

First Kensington Hardcover Edition: July 2013

eISBN-13: 978-1-61773-291-1
eISBN-10: 1-61773-291-5

ISBN-13: 978-0-7582-6882-2
ISBN-10: 0-7582-6882-3
First Kensington Trade Paperback Edition: June 2014

10 9 8 7 6 5 4 3 2 1

Printed in the United States of America

Per T., duo da capo per sempre

Acknowledgments

For my daughter Jessica without whose help this volume would not have blossomed.

Many thanks to my editor Martin Biro who masterfully took charge of a very difficult situation when I was flat on my back in the hospital.

"Lifelong enemies are, I think, as hard to make and as important to one's well-being as lifelong friends."
Jessica Mitford

CHAPTER 1

"*Putain!* Shit! What's in this goddamn thing? More sodding gold ingots for their collection?"

The stocky man in blue workers' overalls let his end of the trunk drop on the stair tread with a loud thud. Panting, he mopped his brow with his sleeve, shook his head in disgust, took the dead Gauloise out of the corner of his mouth, spat, replaced the cigarette. "It's going to come, Jean," he said to his partner, "the day we put all these fat-assed bourgeois that live off our sweat up against a wall and take care of them for good. You'll see."

Cécile smiled down at them sweetly. The men had just started up the third flight of gently sweeping oak stairs. The trunk, a pre–World War I Vuitton portmanteau, was absolutely precious. True, it had cost a small fortune, but transformed into a bar, it was going to absolutely make her new sitting room. As the two men lifted their burden with a grunt and renewed their climb, she smiled blissfully. It was going to be too, too darling.

Grumbling, the deliverymen wrestled the trunk into the apartment. Cécile led them into the sitting room, hesitated, and finally elected to have them set it up vertically in a corner by the window. Théophile, her husband, stared myopically through wire-rim glasses and wrinkled his nose.

"Is that what you bought?"

"Yes, dear. I told you. It's going to be a bar. You'll be able to serve our guests cocktails, and that way they won't drink your precious wines before dinner. You remember, don't you? We discussed it."

Théophile seemed mollified. "Of course. Drinking wine without food is an egregious solecism. Yet another thing we have to thank the Americans for—"

The man called Jean glowered at them as he mopped his face with a grubby handkerchief. "Listen, pal. We're not all members of the leisure classes. Some of us have a day's work to do, so sign the goddamn receipt and let us get out of here."

Théophile ignored him and looked quizzically at his wife. "But if it's just an empty steamer trunk, why is it so heavy? Did you buy something else at the flea market?"

"Nothing. Just this fabulous piece. Don't you just love it?" Cécile said, scribbling her signature on the form.

The deliveryman tore off the strip that bound the three copies, handed the bottom copy to Cécile, hovered for a few seconds, demanding a tip with surly glances, and then lumbered out of the apartment with his partner, shaking his head in disgust at the stinginess of the rich.

The trunk was chest high. Over the century it had been in existence, the famous Vuitton-monogrammed brown oilcloth had mellowed to sepia, and the leather trim and strengthening wood battens had darkened to mahogany. The piece radiated the gravitas of a serious antique. It was so going to be the pièce de résistance of the room.

"Wait 'til you see the inside," Cécile said. "It doesn't have any of the usual drawers, just a wooden rod and those wonderful wood hangers. Wouldn't it have been sublime to find all your clothes waiting for you, hanging

up in your own private little closet when you arrived in
your stateroom?"

Cécile snapped open the two brass hasps and struggled
to open the trunk. The thick pile of the carpet resisted.
Théophile stepped in to help and, with a sharp wrench,
opened it wide. His hand went to his mouth, and he
gagged. By his side, Cécile leaned in for a closer look.

As Théophile ran to the bathroom, retching, Cécile picked
up the phone and punched in a number.

"Police Judiciaire," a voice answered crisply.

"Commissaire Le Tellier, please. Could you tell her that
Madame de Rougemont is on the line and that it's urgent,
extremely urgent?"

After a very short pause a new voice came on the line.

"Urgent?" There was amused sarcasm in the tone.

"Absolutely. I really need you to see something I bought
at the Biron flea market yesterday."

"Cécile, you're sweet. But I'm completely up to my eye-
balls today. Why don't Alexandre and I drop by on Saturday to see your treasure? We could take you out to lunch
after."

"*Ma chérie,* we can do that, too, of course. But I'm
afraid you really *do* need to come right away, and with
some of your police people, or whatever they're called. My
treasure was delivered with something absolutely horrible
inside."

CHAPTER 2

Half an hour later Commissaire Capucine Le Tellier rose, swayed back and forth in the rattling, glass-paneled, coffin-sized elevator of Cécile's building with one of her detectives, Brigadier-Chef Isabelle Lemercier, a close-cropped, muscular blond woman whose face was heavily studded with piercings. Capucine knew the elevator well. One tenth of it belonged to her best friend, and she had been in it countless times. The building refused to modernize the ancient unit, still equipped with a folding wooden seat to ease the journey for the aged and infirm and a RENVOI button to send the elevator back to the ground floor once the passenger had alighted. Through the glass panels they could see two other detectives. One, svelte, elegantly dressed in a linen suit, with long, glossy auburn locks—Brigadier David Martineau—raced up the circular staircase wrapped around the elevated shaft two by two, a small boy trying to beat the elevator. The other, a huge olive-skinned North African—Brigadier Mohammed Benarouche, known to everyone as Momo—lumbered up slowly, nearly a flight behind.

A pale and tight-lipped Cécile waited for them on the landing. Mechanically, she kissed Capucine on both cheeks.

"It's in here," Cécile said, ushering the four detectives into the sitting room, hesitating nervously, then disappearing into the back of the apartment.

Inside the trunk, a male cadaver, completely naked, huddled in a tight fetal position. The body was stringy and muscular, no longer in the flush of youth but not advanced into middle age, either. It was impossible to be more precise since he had no face. A double-barreled shotgun rose from between his naked legs like an overlong phallus. The right hand hung limply, fingers grazing the bottom of the trunk as if they had fallen away from the trigger.

As the detectives examined the body without touching, a dull metallic aluminum clatter behind them announced the arrival of the PTS forensic squad—the *Police Technique et Scientifique*—clamorously pushing a clattering foldable aluminum gurney.

A young man energetically approached Capucine. "Commissaire Le Tellier?"

Capucine nodded.

"Ajudant Challoneau, PTS." He shook her hand with the vigorous one-two pump of the business world.

Snapping on latex gloves with the exaggerated joy of a TV-comedy proctologist, he poked, prodded, and fiddled with the limbs of the body, then finally reaching up, grasped the morning-after-pizza remains of the face and turned it toward the room.

"A perfect Janus," he murmured. "The other side is intact, Commissaire. Have a look."

The entire blast of the shotgun had hit the right side of the face. The other side, untouched, presented the countenance of a Roman senator, aquiline nose, slim lips, receding hair line accenting a high, intellectual forehead.

"Of course, you can never be sure before the autopsy, Commissaire, but it certainly looks like a suicide. The wound certainly could have come from the shotgun in that position. Look. Here's the hole where the shot exited—"

"Yeah," interrupted Isabelle. "When the trunk was tipped on its side, the hole would have been on the bottom. That's why the delivery guys never saw it."

Capucine noticed that the brass corner reinforcements of the trunk were deeply scored with bright scratches, as if the trunk had been recently dragged over a rough surface.

"And he managed to snap the latches shut before he shot himself?" David asked.

"No, dummy," Isabelle said with curled lips. "Obviously, the delivery guys did that. They're not going to try to haul a trunk that pops open at every step, now are they, asshole?"

As the two detectives bickered, the PTS *agents techniques* took photographs, then extracted the body from the trunk and laid it on an open black plastic body bag on top of the now fully deployed gurney.

During the maneuver, Challoneau commented, "The problem with cases like this is that it takes forever to get an identification of the body. Unless someone reports someone missing, we have nothing to go on. Unlike the rest of the civilized world, we have yet to create a centralized computer database for dental work. Sure, we can get a guy's dentist to identify a stiff, but we have to know who he is first."

Now that the body was stretched out, Capucine noticed a *chevalière,* a signet ring with a well-worn coat of arms, on the ring finger of the left hand.

"Ajudant, what if you printed that and let me have it for a day? I know an expert on heraldry who might be able to identify it and give us the name of the deceased."

One of the agents techniques dusted the ring with dull gray aluminum fingerprint powder, found no prints, pulled the ring off, dropped it into a plastic bag, and handed it to Capucine.

Two of the agents rolled the body out onto the landing and prepared for the difficult descent down the circular stairway. Two others closed the portmanteau trunk, flipped it over on its side, and grabbed the handles, ready to follow the gurney.

Cécile, revivified now that the apartment was hers once again, followed them out onto the landing.

"Don't forget I'm going to need that back. It was irresistible before, but now it's going to be the best conversation piece ever."

CHAPTER 3

"Hubert," Capucine's mother said over-loudly to her husband, "do you hear? Capucine is delighted that her best friend, Cécile, has moved back to Paris." Her parents had spoken about her over her head as long as she could remember. And, true to form, her father showed not the slightest interest.

"I think she found Switzerland as boring as her job there with a giant corporation," Capucine said, faithful to the role of the dutiful daughter. "So she negotiated a partnership in a Paris venture capital firm and is going to be investing in computer-game companies."

"Computer games?" Madame Le Tellier was puzzled. She opened her mouth to ask a question, but thought better of it. Instead she followed the more rewarding path of scolding her daughter. "You see, ma chérie, *you* could be doing something like that. You're much more intelligent than Cé—"

She was cut off by the loud braying laugh of her nephew Jacques, a foppish young man who held a vague, but apparently exalted, position in the DGSE, France's intelligence service. Family lore described him as being "very successful in the Ministry of the Exterior."

"*Ma tante*," Jacques said. "Your sweet little daughter has already modeled her life after video games. Her greatest cultural influence is a game called *Grand Theft Auto*. You get to shoot hoes and moes. And now Capucine has transcended even that, graduating from the virtual to the real. She's a plant that has blossomed."

"Hoes and moes?" Capucine's father asked. Etymology was one of his hobbies.

"Prostitutes and homosexuals," Alexandre explained.

"How interesting," Monsieur Le Tellier said. "It's curious that both terms have different syllabic origins. I wond—"

"Interesting!" Madame Le Tellier interjected. "*On est à table.* I forbid this sort of conversation when we eat." Her eyes shot daggers at Capucine. Her unspoken thought was perfectly clear to everyone at the table. This general abandonment of propriety was the inevitable consequence of a child who had defied her family to join the police.

Alexandre, Capucine's husband and one of the most well-known French food critics, had been examining the pair of partridges on his plate anxiously, clearly waiting for Madame Le Tellier to lift her fork so he could dig into the perfectly browned little carcasses. His impatience with the family squabble was obvious. It had been nearly eight months since he had eaten a game bird. The fall was a glorious time for a gastronome. He knew the plump, round birds came from the Château de Maulévrier, the family seat, currently owned by Madame Le Tellier's brother—Jacques's father—and would be deliciously gorged from foraging through corn stubble. Enough was enough. It was high time to get on with the meal.

"Madame, nothing is more magical than the odor of the first partridge of the season. You're giving us a real treat tonight."

Madame Le Tellier patted the top of Alexandre's hand by way of thanks. She realized she had gone too far with her daughter. The gesture looked like a warm one, but it was no secret at the table that Madame Le Tellier disapproved almost as much of her daughter's decision to marry a food critic nearly twice her age—even if he was wellborn and even titled—as her unconscionable idea of joining the police force. As far as anyone could tell, she would never accept either of her daughter's choices.

Madame Le Tellier lifted her fork. Alexandre beamed.

"So," said Jacques with a Cheshire cat smile, "why don't you tell Tante Coralie about your latest case? You know how she loves Vuitton." He brayed a donkey's laugh in a screeching falsetto.

At the word *case* Madame Le Tellier returned her fork to its place beside her plate. Alexandre's brows moved microscopically closer to each other for an instant; then he relaxed and tucked happily into his partridge. The fork had been lifted. It was not required that the hostesses actually begin to eat.

"Capucine, whatever is Jacques talking about?" Capucine's father asked her.

"Cécile found a body in a Vuitton portmanteau she bought at the Puces."

"A body of what?" Madame Le Tellier asked, perplexed once again. Her daughter's ability to confuse her was endless.

"An actual dead body. Cécile's redecorating her apartment and she bought the trunk to turn it into a bar. When it arrived, there was a dead person inside."

Madame Le Tellier was outraged. She shot a glance at her husband, demanding he intervene and order the conversation back into the norms of propriety. She was dismayed that he, for once, seemed interested.

"A bar?" he asked. "Her husband, Théophile, is one of the foremost amateur oenologists in France. I hardly see him setting up a bar in his living room to serve Bull Shots, or whatever, to his guests."

"Actually, he's all for it," Alexandre said. "It seems he

despises having his *grand crus* lapped up as *apéros* before dinner. Apparently, he *would* rather give them Bull Shots, whatever they may be, and save his wines for dinner."

"Enough about Bull Shots, *ma cousine*," said Jacques. "Tell us about the body. Was it a nubile little creature, completely naked, with stunningly enormous *nichons?*"

"Actually, it was a man, but he *was* completely naked. It seems he committed suicide. The poor fellow shot himself with a shotgun and blew most of his face off. You see—"

"Capucine, that's *quite* enough. We're *à table!* This sort of conversation is entirely inappropriate," Capucine's mother said. She continued, addressing her husband, "Hubert, I warned you our daughter would no longer be *sortable* if you lost control of her development. But you wouldn't listen, would you? And now look where we are."

Capucine crossed her arms, a vexed schoolgirl. It took all her self-discipline not to storm out of the dining room and retreat into her old bedroom, slamming the door behind her. In fact, she was already on the balls of her feet—shod in Jimmy Choo snakeskin slingbacks with a peep-toe she found irresistible—before she remembered she now had her own apartment, a large, rambling affair in the Marais that might have been Alexandre's since time immemorial, but was definitely now her domain. What had ever possessed her to actually suggest to her mother that she come for dinner? She bit her lip. But, remembering her mission, her petulance evaporated.

"You know, Mother, I'm going to ask you to help me on this case."

"Help you on a case? Well, I never! Not at the table, in any case. We'll discuss it after dinner. In private," Madame Le Tellier said, torn between outrage and curiosity.

The rest of the meal was as anodyne as any at Capucine's parents'. Jacques was politely outrageous; Madame Le Tellier clucked; Capucine's father chatted happily with Alexandre, frowning every five minutes or so, when he remembered that he was expected to disapprove of him. Partridge gave way to salad, which in turn yielded to cheese, which surrendered to dessert. Finally, it was time to move to the salon for coffee.

Jacques, pouring Armagnac into dollhouse-size crystal thimbles, followed the ancient, stiffly starched majordomo spurting coffee into elegant Limoges demitasses with only partial accuracy.

"Did you really want me to help you with a case?" Capucine's mother asked.

"Of course, *Maman*. I don't joke about my cases." Capucine bit back her sharpness, kissed her mother on her cheek, reached into her bag to extract the plastic pouch containing the chevalière, removed it, and handed it to Madame Le Tellier, who examined it closely. The ring was highly worn, the crest rubbed almost flat, the engraving almost unrecognizable. Obviously handed down over the generations, it was the quintessential accoutrement of the aristocracy.

"I can't say I recognize the crest. Come with me to the library. We'll look through my books."

The library had once been her father's office, but as he spent more and more of his time at work in a private investment bank, Capucine's mother had taken it over. One by one the leather club chairs had disappeared, to be replaced by pillow-strewn sofas and chintz-covered armchairs. The shelves had gradually filled with best sellers and a comprehensive collection of leather-bound volumes on the French aristocracy.

Madame Le Tellier sat at the desk and turned on the lamp, an ormolu Empire affair originally made to hold candles under a dark green lampshade but now wired for electricity.

She produced an oversized magnifying glass with a brass inlay, delicately carved ivory handle and examined the crest closely.

"Ma chérie, I'm delighted you're finally taking an interest in heraldry. It's so much healthier for you than all those guns and things. Look here. You'll understand immediately. See, this V in the middle of the crest is called a chevron, and the thin lines on the background are a code for the heraldic color, *gueule,* which is a blood-red. The coronet over the crest is a baron's. In antiquity, a baron's coronet was only a gold ring with no embellishment. But these little dots represent pearls. It's the sort of fancy decoration that was added by the horde of barons Napoleon created. You know that he gave a barony to almost all his functionaries. Even the mayors of remote little villages were made barons. Of course, they aren't true aristocrats. That's why I don't recognize the crest. But don't worry. Give me half an hour with my books and I'll tell you exactly who it is."

She picked up a big leather book and began to turn the pages with the excitement of a young teenage boy who has found a pile of *Playboy*s in his older brother's closet. Capucine slipped out, unnoticed, and returned to the sitting room.

Jacques had resorted to his favorite pastime, teasing Alexandre with thinly veiled allusions to his imaginary adolescent sexual peccadilloes with Capucine. He had honed his technique to a point that the slightest innuendo could reduce Alexandre to paroxysms of jealousy.

"So there I was, racing through the commons of the château—you've seen how extensive they are at Maulévrier—with both Capucine and Cécile chasing me and giggling as if they were trying out for a porno film, when I realized I was running into a dead end. Mercifully, there was an enormous haystack in a corner. I tried to burrow my way into oblivion. But I felt silky adolescent female hands grab my ankles and begin to pull me out. . . . Ah, cousine, just in time. I wanted a female voice to do the moaning necessary for the verisimilitude of the story."

Alexandre ground his teeth. Capucine's father sat, oblivious, deep in the recesses of a down-filled armchair, reading *La Croix,* the official newspaper of the French Catholic Church.

"What did you do with Tante Coralie? Do you have her on the street, tailing hoes and moes?" Jacques brayed his laugh.

For a half hour calm was restored. Jacques poured more Armagnac. The two cousins and the cousin-in-law chatted happily, while Monsieur Le Tellier immersed himself in the doings of the mother church. Time bobbed on by as pleasantly as it was intended to in the Sixteenth Arrondissement.

In twenty minutes the door opened with élan and Capucine's mother breezed in, looking very pleased with herself. She made a noise that sounded like a loud, liquid belch. "Brrroooh!"

Jacques sat up in mock horror. "Ma tante, what's come over you? Are you ill?"

"What on earth do you mean? Brault!" she eructated. "The Baron Brault. That's whose arms they are." She held a copy of a thick, clothbound book with the title conspicuous on the cover, *Dictionnaire de la Noblesse Française,* marking a page with a finger. She thumped the book down on a table and opened it.

"Here's the entry. The arms match perfectly. The current baron is Ferdinand Brault. He lives in the family château in La Cadière-d'Azur, a small town in the department of the Var. His issue is two sons. The *aîné,* Antonin, is thirty-seven, and the cadet, Jean- Louis, is thirty-three."

Alexandre sat up straight. "Capucine, did the victim have an aquiline nose and a very high forehead?"

"Yes," Capucine said. "And blue eyes. Or at least one."

Capucine's mother paled. "The victim! Capucine, is this the dead man's ring? This ring was on the body's finger?" She put the chevalière on the table and backed away from it.

"Yes, it was, Maman. You may have shortened the identification process by several weeks. If you're right, think of how much anguish you've saved the family."

"I'm sure she's right," Alexandre said. "The description fits Chef Jean-Louis Brault perfectly."

"Why on earth would Chef Brault commit suicide?" Jacques asked. "I thought he was the boy wonder of the restaurant world."

"He is—or was. The youngest person after Jean-Basile Labrousse to get three stars from the Michelin Guide. But he's always been very high strung. There are rumors that he has a lot of debt. And for the past few months Lucien Folon, the food critic for *Le Figaro,* has been attacking Brault viciously. He's always accused Brault of being a flash in the pan, but a few weeks ago he started claiming that he knew for sure that Michelin was going to take away one of Brault's stars in its next Guide. Obviously, no one thinks Folon has the slightest clue what Michelin's ratings are going to be, but it's not impossible his attacks may have pushed Brault over the edge."

CHAPTER 4

The body, pasty white as a suckling pig in the window of a butcher shop, lay on a slide that cantilevered out from inside a refrigerated cubby. A long, gaping Y-shaped incision had been cut from the shoulders down to the pubic hair. The scalp and the top of the cranium had been removed, leaving an empty brain cavity. The side of the face obliterated by the shotgun blast faced the door and now looked like a *civet de lièvre*—a black-blood hare stew—dried hard and gone bad after it had been left too long in the back of a refrigerator.

Formal recognition of bodies was the purview of the *médecin légiste*—the coroner—and did not normally involve the police. Still, Capucine was intrigued enough to find out if the body in the trunk actually was Chef Jean-Louis Brault's to want to be present at the identification by Delphine Duclos, Brault's live-in girlfriend.

As she stared at the body, Capucine heard the stainless-steel door whine on its spring behind her back. A scrawny blond woman walked hesitantly a few paces into the room. She looked so ill at ease in her expensive dress, it might have been borrowed for the occasion from someone who had been reluctant to lend it. Her face was as scrubbed of emotion as the body on the slide.

She darted a quick glance at the cadaver and then looked up at Capucine.

"It's him, all right. Can I go, or do I have to sign a paper or something?"

"How can you tell it was your fiancé without seeing his face?"

"The scars on his hands and arms are very familiar." She pointed to a scar on the wrist that was still slightly raised. "He got this one last week. He wouldn't put ointment on it because he was afraid it would run into his sauces. So it got infected." She glared at Capucine. "And he wasn't my fiancé."

The backs of the body's hands and its forearms were covered with an extended latticework of burn scars. But any chef's would have been.

"So, can I go now?"

"The form you need to sign requires you to state you recognize his features. Can you come around to this side and look at his face, please?"

Reluctantly, the woman moved to the corner of the slide, shot a quick look at the body's head, and scuttled back to the far side.

"Okay. It's Jean-Louis. Can I go now?"

"You also need to identify his possessions, a ring and a shotgun that might have been his."

A white-coated technician entered and queried Capucine with his eyebrows. She nodded. Without a word he slid the body back into the refrigerated cuddy and led Delphine into the next room. An official form had been set on a stainless-steel table, next to an elegant-looking shotgun and the chevalière, now back in a plastic pouch.

"That's all there was?" Delphine asked. The question came out in a choked gasp.

She picked up the plastic envelope containing the ring, held it up to her eyes, and put it back down next to the shotgun.

"It's his ring. I'm sure of that. I don't know about the gun. He had one like it, I guess, but I really couldn't tell one gun from another. Let me borrow a pen. I want to go," she said, looking away, pale, her eyes filling with liquid.

The attendant produced a ballpoint pen. Delphine scribbled a signature and moved toward the door.

"Can I ask you a few questions?" Capucine asked.

"Can we do it outside? I really, really need a cigarette."

The crisp autumn air and the cigarette's nicotine brought some of Delphine's color back.

"I should have introduced myself," Capucine said. "I'm Commissaire Le Tellier. I'm in charge of investigating your financé's death."

"Look. I keep telling you! He wasn't my fiancé. I work in his restaurant. I live in his apartment. That's it." She paused and took a deep drag on her cigarette and then squeezed her eyes tight in rapid blinks.

"I know I sound like a complete bitch to you. It's just that our relationship was—how do they call it in the women's magazines?—'complicated.' "

"Had you been together for a long time?"

Delphine shot her a hostile glance at the word *together* and then decided to let it go. "Three years. I was out of a job and answered an ad for a restaurant hostess job. I wasn't too excited that it was in Sèvres, but the money was good and I got a generous allowance for clothes." Delphine ran her hands down the front of her dress to demonstrate the generosity of her clothing budget. "I also got free room and board, a small studio in the attic, and all I could eat at staff meals. It was a real good deal except for it being in the boonies.

"The restaurant wasn't open yet, so I helped out wherever I could. Jean-Louis discovered I knew a little about accounting, so he had me work on the books." Her voice trailed away. She made an elaborate production of lighting another cigarette.

"It took him way longer than I expected to make a move on me, and when it finally happened, he was so bad in bed, I thought he was a gay guy trying to prove something to himself. But he wasn't." She gurgled a snort of laughter.

After a few puffs on her cigarette, she picked up her narrative.

"He was a hell of a hard guy to figure out. He definitely wasn't gay, but he sure wasn't interested in screwing me. Pretty quickly I started running the business side of the restaurant, on top of doing the hostess job. So I figured he just wanted a *patronne* to keep the staff in line and thought it would be more credible if it looked like we were living together." She looked searchingly at Capucine, as if she might have an answer.

"So it was only for appearance's sake? You never did anything together, like go off on vacation?"

"Vacation? You've got to be kidding. Jean-Louis only had one thing going in his life—his restaurant. When he wasn't sweating in the kitchen, he was sweating about losing one of his precious three Michelin stars."

Delphine lit a third cigarette and blew out the first drag slowly, shaking her head. "But I see what you mean. Maybe he did want something from me, but I never really did figure out what it was. Too late now. And I guess when you think about it, the poor guy did have one or two interests. He had this collection of old *faïence* that he would poke at every now and then, and look at auction catalogs, stuff like that. And he'd go shoot pheasants sometimes in Sologne." She finished her cigarette and ground it out under the sole of her shoe.

"The whole shooting thing was weird. He'd never come

back with any birds. I used to kid him about it and tell him he had a boyfriend somewhere he didn't want anyone to know about. That really pissed him off. So he made me go with him one Sunday. It was the muddiest place I'd ever seen. Of course, I wanted to make a good impression, so I wore my best pair of heels. I'm a Paris girl, born and bred. I don't know anything about the country. Jean-Louis made me walk around all day with my feet in two five-pound clumps of mud. I guess he was punishing me for the crack about the boyfriend. The odd thing was that he shot more than a dozen pheasants, but he just left them there. I said we had enough to put on the menu, but he told me to mind my own business. He got so mad, he didn't talk to me until we got back to the restaurant."

She dug her pack out of her purse and began to extract another cigarette but thought better of it. "Merde, I don't know why I'm telling you all this. It's not like I'm going to miss him or anything. Did I tell you everything you wanted to know?"

Capucine nodded.

"Good. I'll get going. I tell you, that Jean-Louis was a guy you just couldn't figure out." Her eyes filled with liquid again, and she rushed off just as the first drops rolled down her cheeks.

CHAPTER 5

Capucine awoke from a dream in which her husband was yelling at someone. Easing into the waking world, she realized that Alexandre actually was yelling somewhere in the apartment. Since there were no answers, he must be on the phone. The tin roofs of Paris were washed in watercolor rose and carmine from the dawn sun. Nearly seven o'clock. Alarmed, she slid out of bed and slipped on a silk robe. Something awful must have happened. Alexandre *never* got up before ten.

In the kitchen, Alexandre sat at the long central table covered with bright Provençale tiles, the cordless phone to his ear. He nodded in agreement with whatever was being said. Behind him, the red ON light of the Pasquini coffeemaker was lit, but both long-handled grounds filters lay on the counter. Alexandre's only shortcoming in the kitchen was his inability to operate the complicated machine.

Capucine started to reassemble the Pasquini, creating noise. Alexandre tapped imperiously on a tile on the table with his fingernail; when Capucine turned, he raised an index finger to the vertical and hiked his eyebrows in a cartoon supplication for silence. The gesture was usually reserved for pre-deadline tensions.

"*Paul, parfait. A demain, alors,*" Alexandre shouted and hung up.

"Bocuse?" Capucine asked.

"Yes. He's devastated. Poor man, he's become completely deaf."

The phone rang.

"*Ah, Michel, salut. . . . Oui, c'est demain. . . . Eglise Saint François Xavier . . . onze heures.*"

Capucine walked down the hall to the study and turned on the TV to catch the morning news. So Brault's funeral was set for eleven the next day at the Eglise Saint François Xavier, a huge church in the chic Seventh Arrondissement. The Michel on the phone was bound to be Michel Troisgros. It was going to be a gathering of the eagles of the culinary world.

Five minutes later, Alexandre stuck his head in the study door. "Capucine, *ma chérie adorée,* please come back. If you make some coffee, I'll make you my scrambled eggs."

Back in the kitchen, Capucine finished reassembling the Pasquini and made coffee. Alexandre got started with the eggs.

"That was Michel Troisgros. He's coming with his father, Jean. Both Bocuse and Jean Troisgros will deliver eulogies. They were very close to Jean-Louis. I spoke to Jean-Basile Labrousse. He's going to fly from New York to do a reading at the service. You can't imagine. Every important personality in the cooking world is going to be there." Alexandre's almost childish excitement floated on top of a deep, dark pool of sadness.

"Who el—"

The phone rang again. Alexandre snatched it up. He deflated slightly and handed the receiver to Capucine, who wandered back down the hall to the study.

"Commissaire? Ajudant Challoneau. I hope I'm not disturbing you so early."

"Not at all, Ajudant. Do you have news?"

"Quite a bit. We just finished our post-autopsy meeting. We were ordered to hurry it up so we could release the body for the funeral. The pathologist was furious."

He paused expectantly, waiting for Capucine to make a comment. She said nothing.

"Well, it was murder. There's plenty of evidence. For openers, the blood alcohol content was point-two-eight percent. In other words, he was blind drunk. That's not entirely inconsistent with suicide, but it's very unusual. Also, there was no gunpowder residue on either of his hands. Again, powder residue tests are notoriously inaccurate, but it was another thing that pointed away from suicide. But there's a real clincher. The gun was a side-by-side twelve-gauge shotgun with double triggers. One trigger for each barrel. The spent cartridge was in the left-hand barrel. It's the back trigger that fires the left-hand barrel. There was a nice clear thumbprint of the victim on the front trigger but none on the back one, which had been wiped clean like the rest of the gun. It's obvious that someone shot him, wiped the gun clean, and then afterward pressed his thumb on the rear trigger to leave a print. But whoever it was screwed up and picked the wrong trigger."

"Anything else I should know?"

"He was shot in the trunk, not placed in it after death. The hole was definitely made by the shot, since there are traces of his blood and brain matter. The DNA match is conclusive. My guess is that he passed out drunk and woke up to find himself naked in the trunk with someone trying to put the barrel of a shotgun in his mouth. He was struggling when the shot went off, which is why it only hit one side of his face. The infrared examination showed some bruising that might, or might not, have come from a hand trying to push his head back into the trunk."

"Time of death?"

"Between nine and midnight on Friday."

"The Puces is pretty much deserted after nine. He might well have been taken there and shot. There were no traces of drugs or sedatives in the blood?"

"None. Just a hell of a lot of alcohol."

"And the pathologist will release the body for the funeral even though it's a murder?"

"He's mad as hell about it, but he has no choice. We had a call from the mayor's office very early this morning. The mayor himself is going to the funeral."

Capucine said nothing.

"Commissaire, are you still there?"

"Sorry. I was just thinking about the consequences of what you've told me. Thank you, Ajudant. I've really got to run."

In the kitchen, Alexandre had seen the LINE IN USE indicator extinguish and was pressing in the numbers for another call. When he saw Capucine's expression, he squeezed the OFF button and put the phone down.

"What's the matter?"

"He was murdered."

"Brault was murdered?"

"Without a doubt. The killer pressed Brault's thumb on the wrong trigger of the gun. He was dead drunk, and someone took him to the Puces, squeezed him into the trunk, and shot him." She paused for a few seconds to let this sink in. "The forensics people think Brault was struggling, and that's why the gun hit only half his head."

There was a long pause. Alexandre was visibly shaken.

"I'm going to have to call Bocuse and Troisgros. They'll need to reframe their eulogies." Alexandre thought for a moment and then broke into a sad grin. "The fleck of silver in the lining of this very dark cloud is that I won't have to argue with that insufferable priest anymore."

"What priest?"

"The pastor of the church is a runty, stuck-up little man with a face like a donkey's ass. He's attempting to refuse a church service on the grounds that Jean-Louis committed suicide. I had to imply that I had it on good authority that the police were convinced it was murder."

Capucine raised her eyebrows and made a moue of false astonishment.

"But the silly man insisted on compromising—a memorial service with no mass and coffin waiting outside in the hearse. I was just going to go down there and do battle with him. When are the police going to announce this? I'd love to be able to wave a newspaper in that preening little cockalorum's face and watch him sputter."

"That's for headquarters to decide, but it's certainly not going to happen until I tell his fiancée or girlfriend, or whatever she was. It would be unthinkable for her to find out from a newspaper. I'm going out to Sèvres to see her this morning."

CHAPTER 6

The restaurant Chez La Mère Denis was at the very end of the avenue Gambetta in Sèvres, on the edge of the Parc Saint-Cloud. Even though Sèvres was a busy commercial suburb of Paris, the avenue Gambetta turned out to be a sleepy, tree-lined street so narrow it was almost a country lane. The avenue led to massive lichened stone pillars supporting a large wrought-iron gate, beyond which Capucine could see the endless green acres of the park.

The hotel, across the street from the restaurant, was a nondescript, white-fronted, three-story building, which announced itself demurely in gold letters on a small black marble plaque: L'HOSTELLERIE DENIS.

The interior was as opulent as the exterior was plain. The small reception area had been done up in watered silk curtains and brass-rimmed black-and-white floor tiles with a backdrop of dark seventeenth-century portraits in elaborate gilt frames and ancient-looking blue and white faïence vases on tall stands made to resemble Greek pillars.

A fastidiously coiffed and made-up woman behind an elaborately carved oak desk explained politely to Capucine that she was in the hotel and Mademoiselle Duclos had a flat in the apartment section of the building. Capucine would have to walk around to the entrance at the back.

The rear of the building had clearly not been touched. Paint peeled from the once white façade, and long black streaks ran down from the gutters. There were six buzzers by the side of the unvarnished wooden door, most identified by scrawls on scraps of paper Scotch taped next to the button. Only one—BRAULT—had been cut from an engraved calling card.

Capucine pressed the button. There was a long wait. Finally, a sleepy voice asked, "*Ouais?*" in the coarse accent of the Paris projects.

"Mademoiselle Duclos? It's Commissaire Le Tellier."

The accent morphed into gentility. "*Mon Dieu!* You're early. You said you'd be here after ten. Well, *tant pis*, come on up. You'll have to give me a second to get decent. It's three flights up. Sorry, there's no elevator."

The hallway was even dingier than the façade. Uneven tiles clicked loosely under Capucine's feet. Fading paint flaked on the walls. The stairs were bare wood, three of them unsteady enough to constitute serious violations of the building code. Converting even part of the dilapidated building into a luxury hotel had clearly been a labor of love and a very costly one at that.

Delphine Duclos was waiting on the third-floor landing in a sequined sweatshirt, looking even more gawky than at the morgue.

"I was planning on dressing better, but you arrived way before I expected."

The living room was decorated with nondescript, well-worn furniture that might have come from thrift shops. Incongruously, the room was dotted with a good number of valuable-looking pieces of faïence.

Sitting down, Delphine lit a cigarette and said, "I have to apologize for my rudeness yesterday. It was a very upsetting moment."

A large antique faïence yellow and blue inkstand with three demitasse-sized inkwells sat on the scarred top of a shabby coffee table with wobbly legs. Delphine removed the cap of one of the inkwells and tipped in her ash. She glanced at Capucine apologetically. "Don't worry. The ashes wash right out. Anyway, we don't have any proper ashtrays. Jean-Louis didn't allow smoking."

In the back of the apartment someone turned on the shower. Delphine blushed.

"That's Prosper Ouvrard, our sous-chef. He, you know . . . It's, like, they're fixing the plumbing in his apartment," Delphine said in a rush. "So he has to come down here to shower."

There was a moment of awkwardness.

"Mademoiselle, there's been new information about Chef Brault's death. I thought it would be better if I came to tell you personally."

Delphine took three quick puffs on her cigarette and stared at Capucine, alarmed and puzzled.

"Information? What kind of information?"

"The results of the autopsy indicate he was murdered."

Delphine looked at her, uncomprehending.

"He didn't commit suicide. Do you understand?"

"Yeah. I get it." Delphine paused. "But I don't see what difference it makes." She glanced nervously at the door that led to the back of the apartment. "He's still dead."

"It will excite the press, who will almost certainly badger you. You need to make plans to protect yourself from them. Also, there has been a change in plans for the funeral. There's now going to be a mass at Saint François Xavier in the Seventh before the interment."

"A mass. I don't know anything about that stuff. Do I have to do anything? What am I going to wear? One of those big floppy black hats, like in the movies?"

"You won't have to do anything. Chef Brault's friends

will take care of all that. Anything dark and conservative will be perfect. You won't need a hat."

Delphine drew her lips down in a frown.

"You don't want to go, do you?" Capucine asked.

"Sure I'll go. I had a soft spot for Jean-Louis. More than he had for me, anyway. All he cared about was his cooking." She paused. "It was all he thought about. We'd be going over the weekly accounts and he'd stop and ask me something crazy, like, 'What would pigeon and lobster taste like together?' Naturally, I didn't have a clue. But he could make dishes in his mind that were so real, he could actually taste them. Then he'd go to the kitchen and cook it up and keep cooking it up over and over again, until what was on the plate matched exactly what was in his mind.

"He'd get up in the middle of the night to cook something he'd been dreaming about. Sometimes he'd spend the whole night in the kitchen, and he'd be in there, sweating away, when I came down to breakfast. The poor guy was completely strung out about food, and a whole bunch of other stuff, too, not like Monsieur Calm in there, his sous-chef." Delphine jerked her head in the direction of the back of the apartment.

"What other stuff?"

"You know, money and crap. Everything. His whole life was one worry after another."

"Wasn't the restaurant doing well?"

"Of course it was. But Jean-Louis got it in his head that a three-star restaurant that wasn't in downtown Paris had to have a luxury hotel tacked on to it. I think he picked that up from Troisgros when he was an intern there. Another of his crazy ideas was that true gastronomy only happens in provincial towns. You know, Bocuse in Collonges-au-Mont-d'Or, or Point in Vienne, or Troisgros in Roanne. This place was a compromise. It looks like it's in a small town, but it's only a taxi ride away from Paris."

"I see. And there wasn't enough money to finish the hotel, is that it?"

"You got it. His financial backer staked him with enough to buy the building and do up the entrance hall and a couple of rooms. Then the backer drew the line. I guess the hotel cost way more than he had been told to begin with. So every penny the restaurant made went into decorating rooms." Delphine sighed and shook her head. "And this was when he still only had two stars. He was convinced that Michelin would never give him the third one unless the hotel had eight rooms that the president of the republic would feel at home in." She lit a cigarette and took the lid off the other inkwell on the stand, ready to flick her ash.

"Jean-Louis needed things he could touch. Things that lasted longer than food. I guess that's what his obsession with faïence was, another prop in his life. When the hotel bug was biting him extra hard, he'd look at one of his beloved pieces of faïence and you could hear his stomach growling. He'd be thinking about selling it off to finance another room but wanting to keep it. Choosing between the two would eat him alive. I tell you, he was a complete wreck until he finally got that third star."

"Did he calm down when that happened?"

"Yeah. For all of two weeks. And then that awful Lucien Folon got going. He'd written bad reviews in the past, but he really went to town when we got the third star. He started out with a review saying Jean-Louis's cuisine was *pipo*—bullshit—and that Jean-Louis was just a fake whose gimmicks had conned Michelin. And Folon wouldn't let go. He kept coming here way more often than any other critic. Jean-Louis would make himself sick cooking for the guy. He'd cook everything himself. The line chefs couldn't touch a thing. And every single time Folon would sneer at Jean-Louis and tell him the meal was pure shit. And the reviews he wrote! I felt like crying when I saw how Jean-Louis took them to heart."

She crushed her cigarette out in the inkwell; her eyes filled with tears.

"Folon's last review was the worst. After he panned the cooking, he claimed that he had it on good authority that the restaurant was going to be demoted to two stars in the next Guide and that Michelin was being generous to give him any stars at all. Jean-Louis had a fit and ordered the builder and the decorator to do two more rooms in the hotel, even though we didn't have the slightest hope of paying them."

A man in his early forties strode jauntily into the room, combing his damp hair straight back from his forehead. He checked when he saw Capucine and looked guiltily at Delphine.

"Prosper, this is a police officer who has come to tell me that it turns out that Jean-Louis was murdered."

Ouvrard pursed his lips slightly and lifted his eyebrows fractionally, but made no comment.

"So, Monsieur Ouvrard, you've taken charge of the kitchen."

"That's right, Madame. I'm the chef as long as they want to keep me."

"Who are the 'they'?"

"That's what I'd like to know. It's not clear to us who owns the restaurant. There are some investors, but they haven't said anything yet," he explained. "And I guess Chef Brault must have owned the majority, but we have no idea who'll inherit. So, for the time being, we're carrying on as usual. Delphine will pay the suppliers and meet the payroll, and I'll keep on cooking. We'll see what we'll see when we see it."

Delphine glanced at Capucine with a look of woman-to-woman conspiracy. "Voilà. The non-worrier." And then to

Ouvrard, "The restaurant will go on forever, and it will get even better with you in charge of the kitchen."

"Has business fallen off since the death of Chef Brault?"

"Just the opposite. We're taking reservations for three weeks from now. And when they learn that Chef was murdered, we'll be booked solid right through to Christmas. Nothing whets the appetite like scandal. Excuse me. I have to get down there and start the luncheon service." Without thinking, he started to bend down to kiss Delphine, but nipped the motion in the bud.

CHAPTER 7

The nineteen-century hulk of the Church of Saint François Xavier was far more colossal than Capucine remembered, larger even than most provincial cathedrals. Drab and grimy on the outside, the cavernous interior was bright with turn-of-the-century frescoes and dripping with gold trim.

Capucine sat next to Alexandre on a hard oak bench, her Sig Sauer biting into her lower back. She squirmed. Three hundred feet away, a huge gold tabernacle rose like a miniature vault over the gilt and marble altar. On a raised dais four black-clad priests droned out the mass.

Capucine nudged Alexandre. "I thought they were supposed to wear purple."

Alexandre groaned. "They're doing a full requiem mass. It's going to take forever. They wear black for that. That priest with the dried-prune face goes from one extreme to another. I hope you're comfortable. We'll be here for a while."

So far the high point of the ceremony had been Chef Labrousse's reading. Pale and drawn from his overnight flight from New York, he had moved many to tears with his delivery of Isaiah's "On this mountain the Lord of hosts will make for all peoples a feast of rich food, a feast of well-aged wine, of rich food full of marrow, of aged wine well refined." From his gilt throne, the pastor, whose face really did resemble a dried prune—resplendent in a ponderous black silk, gold threaded chasuble—had stared daggers at Labrousse, furious at having been upstaged.

Clearly delighted to be back at center stage, the pastor in his finery raised an enormous wafer on extended arms and pirouetted, almost on tiptoe, to display it to the entire congregation. He then repeated the dance step with a jewel-encrusted gold chalice. In both gestures, the priest's self-admiration drowned any notion of the worship of the Deity. Capucine felt the temperature of the congregation drop by a few degrees. No wonder the Church in France was losing its constituency so quickly.

When the interminable mass was finally over, Paul Bocuse slowly mounted the steps to the lectern and delivered a eulogy moving both in its content and brevity: the bright light of French haute cuisine had dimmed, darkening each of our lives. Next, Jean Troisgros ratcheted his arthritic bulk painfully up the steps. He spoke at greater length than Bocuse about an intense young man, a boy, really, who had promised greatness even as an intern. He told stories so dense with kitchen jargon, they must have been comprehensible only to the culinary professionals. At one point his eyes became liquid and his voice broke. He shook his head, explaining that he was unable to go on, and lumbered down the steps. There was a leaden silence in the church, largely at the sight of both of the two living grand masters of French cuisine so moved.

To the resonance of an enormous brass organ playing Fauré's Requiem, the congregation shuffled out of the church. The black-draped coffin was wheeled out and carried down the steps by uniformed pallbearers. Outside, two news vans disgorged camera crews. Capucine recognized Lucien Folon scuttling down the sidewalk. She wondered if he had been at the back of the church or if he had simply stood outside during the service.

The body was placed in a waiting mortuary van, and a hundred or so mourners squeezed into cars to follow it the short distance to the Montparnasse cemetery, where the same priest vaingloriously sprinkled holy water on the coffin with an elaborate silver ciborium. He grandiloquently proclaimed a few words, and what was left of Jean-Louis Brault was returned to the earth in the brilliant sunshine of a crisp autumn morning.

After, a group of fifteen, mainly critics and chefs, gathered in nearby Diapason, a restaurant that had been demoted to two stars after Jean-Basile Labrousse sold it to a consortium of investors and exiled himself to New York. The new chef, Bruno Gautier, greeted them nervously at the door. It was the first time Labrousse had been back to his old restaurant, and Gautier was visibly intimidated.

Even though Labrousse had never met Gautier, they hugged and patted backs as if they had been classmates at the *école hôtelière*. Labrousse smiled at the sight of the lustrous, undecorated African hardwood paneling, the chrome-legged tables and chairs, the gleaming white linen tablecloths, the enormously long-stemmed wine glasses.

"You haven't changed a thing," Labrousse said.

"The menu is completely different," Gautier said. "And I've added one or two touches to the dining room. I don't have your depth of understanding of vegetables, so meat is more important in my cuisine." With his head he indicated an almost black ham held by the bone in a silver clamp attached to a walnut base.

"Spanish *jamón Serrano?*" Capucine asked, proud of her knowledge.

Labrousse smiled at her and then at Gautier. "*Pas du tout,* ma chérie. This is *jamón ibérico de bellota,* the king of all hams. It comes from the Dehesa oak forests between Spain and Portugal. Cerdo pigs, a breed unique to the region, gorge themselves on the acorns. Then the ham is cured for three years. It's one of the things I miss most in America. The USDA has only allowed imports for a year or two, and the prices are beyond belief. Ham at three times the price of foie gras. Can you imagine!"

Capucine looked abashed. Alexandre rubbed her back and kissed her ear.

"Gautier," Labrousse said, "you don't know how lucky you are to have so much produce. I've had to add more meat to my menu, as well. The Americans are a nation of beef eaters." Both chefs laughed heartily. "But I've just bought a small farm in Pennsylvania and started plowing with a horse. Next year we'll see what we'll see."

As the maître d'hôtel showed the group to its table, Gautier whispered earnestly to Alexandre, "I was at the church, but I skipped out on the burial. I know it was a grave faux pas, but I just had to be in my kitchen. Was it a terrible gaffe?"

Alexandre shook his head. "Not at all. Brault would have done exactly the same thing. In fact, he wouldn't even have gone to the church. He's up there right now smiling at you."

Gautier wasn't sure he wasn't being kidded, and scuttled off to the kitchen where he would remain for the rest of the meal, with one eye on his ovens and the other at the judas in the kitchen door.

They sat; the inevitable flutes of champagne arrived. The mood was glum.

A fifty-year-old man announced to the table at large, "I lost my second star five years ago. If my wife hadn't been so supportive, I would have thrown myself into the Seine."

A sveltely elegant woman with patrician features nodded vigorously in agreement. "I lost my second star last year, too. That reptilian Folon gloated. He said that my restaurant had never been at the two-star level, and that with only one star, I would relax, fit better into my skin, and become a happy woman. *Quelle connerie!* If I don't get my second star back in a year or two, I really will throw myself in the Seine. Thank God I don't have a husband who'll try to stop me."

As the conversation progressed to the alternative response to a lost star of refusing to be listed in the Guide—something both Maxim's and the Tour d'Argent had done—Gautier's tasting menu was unfolded like a hand of gilt-edged tarot cards laid out to tell a fortune. They started with spoonfuls of beluga caviar on halves of baked potato and smoked eel surrounded by dots of creamy horseradish sauce. That was followed by creamy asparagus velouté with nuggets of sorrel sprouts. Next came medallions of warm duck foie gras decorated with a sauce of cherry and fresh almond. Then soft-boiled eggs served in their own shells with a creamy sauce of girolle mushrooms. Once the appetizers were over, the meal shifted up a gear with sliced fillets of sole served with a creamy violet sauce. The next gear shift brought two main dishes, sweetbreads studded with little nails of fresh bay on a bed of romaine lettuce, followed by a quail stuffed with foie gras and accompanied by a caramelized apple and summer truffle sauce.

The mood of the group remained somber even when the food arrived. Normally, the professionals of *haute gastronomie* felt it was as insulting to talk while eating as it was to check one's BlackBerry while kissing a beautiful girl. Even though a hint of cheer eventually bubbled up through the semi-silence, gloom had jelled over the meal. The few exchanges were sorrowful ones of the sort that reposing in noble dignity at the bottom of the Seine was infinitely preferable to drifting ghostlike in the limbo of unlisted restaurants, to be noticed only by tourists. Gautier fretted at his judas window, wringing his hands in his apron and upbraiding his line chefs mercilessly.

It wasn't until the dessert was reached—a small scoop

of cacao ice cream on a bed of creamy chocolate ganache made with Venezuelan Araguani chocolate—that the traditional ebullience of a pack of gastronomes at a renowned watering hole returned and the topics of abusive critics and suicides over lost stars were finally abandoned.

Capucine was amazed that the police's announcement that Brault had been murdered had had no effect whatsoever on the conventional wisdom that Brault had committed suicide as a result of Folon's insinuations that he was about to lose a star.

An anxious Gautier came out bearing a crystal decanter of *alcool de framboise*—raspberry liqueur. Four *aide-serveurs* followed him with tiny stemmed glasses and coffee, which they placed before each guest as Gautier searched their eyes, trolling for approval.

He asked Labrousse, "*C'était?* Was it?"

Labrousse rose, beamed at him, and said, "*Rien à dire.* Nothing to say." It was the highest possible praise in the restaurant code. It had been so good, no criticism of any kind was possible.

Labrousse gave Gautier a hug. "It fills me with pride to see cuisine of this excellence made in what used to be my restaurant. I used to feel in New York I had to live up to my Paris standards. Now I have even higher standards to live up to."

The entire table lit up with smiles. Still, as far as Capucine could tell, the group's conviction was that while the only true criticism came from a peer, the only significant criticism came in print from a professional critic.

Capucine and Alexandre did not get home until four in the afternoon. Alexandre closeted himself in his study to write a short piece on the funeral for the last edition of *Le Monde*, while Capucine sat in the living room, on the phone to her brigade, reviewing the incidents of the day.

When Alexandre appeared an hour later with two flutes of champagne, Capucine grimaced and said, "I can't face the thought of another meal. I'm stuffed with lunch and drained by the funeral. I feel like a sagging party balloon."

Alexandre smiled at her. "A little massage and you'll be as good as new."

As was the way with connubial massages, one thing led to another, and the living room sofa led to the bedroom four-poster.

Much later, Capucine shook Alexandre awake.

"You know, I believe I actually am becoming a little peckish."

"Good," Alexandre said into his pillow. And then, rising like a whale bursting through sea foam, he added, "I'm always hungry when it comes to you."

"No, no, I mean *really* hungry. Let's eat something."

Alexandre pouted. "I suppose I could make us a light *souper*."

He paused for a moment, deep in thought.

"Actually, there is a new recipe I'd like to try. I think it would be perfect."

He jumped up, shrugged into a red and gold kimono Capucine had given him for Christmas, and made off energetically for the kitchen as Capucine disappeared into the bathroom.

A few minutes later, Capucine found a flute of champagne waiting for her on the long table in the kitchen and Alexandre chopping furiously with a long kitchen knife. It looked like salmon.

"I'm making you a Japanese delicacy. Actually, it's not Japanese at all, just a clever recipe by a Japanese chef, Aiko Kikuchi. She's apprenticed in two three-star restaurants and is now looking for a place of her own." He paused. "There, that's the salmon," he said, scraping the pink cubes off the cutting board onto a dish. "Now for the onion," he said, attacking a large red onion. Next came a cucumber and finally an apple, all cubed identically.

He placed the cubes in a big glass bowl, poured in a

healthy dose of soy sauce, and topped it with sections of chives snipped with a pair of kitchen scissors. He cut a lime in half, squeezed the contents over the mixture, then mixed it all vigorously with a wooden spoon.

"Voilà," he said. "Salmon tartare à l'oriental."

"When do we get to eat it? I'm famished."

"It needs to chill for an hour, and I'm exhausted after all that chopping." He mimed a sad, drooping Pierrot. "Please, oh, please, help me to my bed before I collapse right here."

An hour later they were back in the kitchen. The tartare was delicious, cold, salmony, crunchy from the apples, onions, and cucumbers, tangy with chives and soy and lime. More than enough to fill the palate with taste, but not bulk.

When they finished the tartare, they took their thimble-sized glasses of Armagnac into the living room, collapsed onto the sofa, and turned on the eleven o'clock TV news, wondering if the funeral would be covered. Alexandre nibbled Capucine's ear. Capucine kissed Alexandre's nose. He kissed her neck at the sensitive spot where it joined her shoulder. Capucine reached for the remote to switch off the TV. As she looked up, she was astounded to see her face. She turned the volume up.

A very pretty young lady was reading from the next morning's press. The screen would flash the headline and then cut to the face of the young woman, who was smiling with provocative cynicism, making knowing comments.

"And so, the burning question earlier today at three-star Chef Jean-Louis Brault's funeral was . . ." The talking head paused to pout coquettishly at the camera. "Whether über–restaurant critic Lucien Folon really drove Brault to suicide with his merciless attacks in the press."

Alexandre sat on the edge of the sofa, elbows on knees, engrossed in the screen.

The program cut to a clip of Folon scuttling off, head

bowed, from the parvis of the church as the congregation began to emerge, and then flashed back to the pretty woman.

"It certainly *looks* like he's the guilty party. But the police tell us a different story. According to a press release issued early this morning, it seems Chef Brault didn't commit suicide at all. He was murdered."

The talking head smiled with dripping sarcasm. "And the Police Judiciaire have placed the case in the hands of our favorite flic, couture cop, socialite, and girl about town, Commissaire Capucine Le Tellier, who . . ." The woman paused again for maximum effect. "Just happens to be married to *Le Monde's* top restaurant critic, Alexandre de Huguelet."

The screen cut to a shot of Alexandre and Capucine leaving the church after the funeral. As they walked down the steps, Capucine gave Alexandre a look that seemed laden with complicity, as if she had just pulled off a fast one. Capucine moaned.

The talking head came on again and favored the audience with her three-quarter profile, as if she was lost in thought. Then she molded her mouth into a coy, first-date smile. "What's your guess? Is the much-mediatized commissaire just trying to cover up for the lethal consequences of her husband's profession? Or do you think it might *really* have been a murder? But why would anyone want to extinguish the rising star of French cuisine? Maybe we'll learn a little more tomorrow afternoon, when *Le Monde* appears on the stands."

CHAPTER 8

"The tragedy was that Jean-Louis Brault allowed himself to be sucked into an Icarus flight of fancy," David read mellifluously from the morning edition of *Le Figaro*. "Had this doggedly pedestrian cook accepted his terrestrial limits, we might still have a friendly little *bistrot* perfect for a Sunday family lunch prior to an afternoon's leisurely stroll through the Parc de Saint-Cloud—"

Capucine bustled into her office. Isabelle looked up with a girl-to-girl smile. "Voilà, our very own couture cop."

Capucine shot her a look so hostile, it was obvious she was restraining herself from administering a bitch slap. There were three long beats of shocked silence. Capucine attempted to unload the situation and dominate her anger.

"What were you reading?"

"Lucien Folon's so-called eulogy of Jean-Louis Brault in this morning's *Le Figaro*," David replied.

"You'd think he'd be the last person to hang on to the myth that Brault committed suicide," Capucine muttered through clenched teeth.

The meeting was off to a bad start. Normally her briefings with the three brigadiers were friendly and relaxed. They had been her constant companions ever since Capucine—then a rookie fiscal brigade lieutenant—had wormed herself into the Police Judiciaire's fabled La Crim', the section that dealt with serious felonies. The four saw themselves as close colleagues, accomplices who spoke to each other with the familiar *tu,* not the formal *vous.* But that clearly was not going to be the order of the day.

"All right," Capucine said with a sharp edge to her voice. "This one has to get solved fast. Very fast. Do what you have to. Don't worry about regulations. I want to tie this one up quickly with a nice red bow so we can shove the killer in the face of the press so hard, he sticks in their gullet."

It was the first time they had seen Capucine seriously angry. They sat up straight in their chairs, waiting for orders.

"The news of the day is that Brault's car was found at the *préfourrière* on the avenue Foche where they keep the vehicles the police have towed in the north of Paris. The car had been sitting unclaimed in an underground public parking lot on the boulevard Haussmann since the Friday of the murder. They don't allow long-term parking and called the police to tow it after twenty-four hours. At the préfourrière, they checked the registration, discovered it was Brault's, and called us. Forensics has already had a look at the car. The steering wheel and dashboard had been wiped clean. There was hunting stuff in the trunk . . . rubber boots, an olive-green coat, a cartridge bag, two boxes of twelve-gauge shells. No gun. The only prints on the objects in the trunk were Brault's.

"Isabelle, I need you to get on the computer and take Brault apart. I want to know everything we have on him for the past five years. Bank accounts. Credit card records. Travel out of the country. The works. And get it done today.

"David, I need you in front of a screen, too. Find out everything about Brault's family. They're from a place called La Cadière-d'Azur in the Var. It's near Bandol. Find out if the parents are still alive. If they are, get them on the phone. Press them a little. See if they know about any friends, enemies, financial problems, anything we should know about. In other words, the usual, but go deeper than normal.

"Momo, get down to the delivery company and interview the two guys who delivered the trunk. I need to know exactly what they saw when they picked it up. Spend time with them. Find out how they reacted to picking up a trunk that turned out to weigh a hundred and sixty pounds."

"What are you going to be doing, Commissaire?" Isabelle asked.

"I'm going down to the Puces to see the person who owns the stand where the trunk came from. I want to find out how he fits into this. After that, I'm going to see what I can discover at Brault's restaurant. . . . All right, let's get going. I want you all back in here this evening. We'll sit down and see what we have."

Paris' largest flea market, the Marché aux Puces at the Porte de Clignancourt, was actually a dozen separate markets, running the gamut from the Marché de la rue Jean-Henri Fabre, with its heaps of discarded, undoubtedly lice-ridden clothing, to the Marché Paul Bert, which offered antiques so precious, they rivaled those of the rarified shops on the Faubourg Saint-Honoré.

Cécile had bought her portmanteau at the Marché Cambo, which was a notch or two down from Paul Bert but still pricey enough to exude an odor of luxury. Cécile's explanation of the location of the stand had been vague. "I think it was one or two rows after a stand that sells an amazing selection of apothecary jars."

From the outside, the Cambo market looked like a nondescript, low-ceilinged warehouse, but the inside was a veritable Ali Baba's cavern. The rows of open stalls formed compact, dark little streets, an almost oriental bazaar of antiques and bibelots. Every château in France seemed to have been pillaged and the booty placed on display.

Capucine walked down the central alleyway and found the stand with the apothecary jars. She zigzagged up and down the rows, looking for Vuitton trunks. It was only at the sixth row that she found it, a brightly lit cubicle, open at one end, with steep piles of Vuitton trunks and suitcases and tall glass display cases filled with handbags and leather accessories. The stand was unattended. She took a quick look without going in and then continued on down the row. Twenty feet away, a dozen people lounged at a long, thin monastery table that had been set out in the middle of the alleyway. It was clearly the end of the stand holder's lunch break.

The group exuded intellectual shabby chic with the emphasis on shabby. The sole exception, a trim young woman with fire engine–red lipstick and nail polish, wearing a vintage, tight-waisted, bright red- and black-striped dress, was made even more conspicuous by the drabness of her colleagues. The table was littered with empty plastic and metal containers of food and nearly empty bottles of wine. The group chatted monosyllabically, smoking and sipping the last of the wine. As she passed the table, the woman in red scrutinized Capucine's Gaultier suit out of the corner of her eye.

Reluctant to intrude, Capucine sauntered back down the row, peering into stalls. The world of the Puces was a mystery. Endless hours waiting for a passerby to show a flicker of interest, spending the day reading paperbacks or pouring over catalogs, with only brief breaks for a chat with a neighbor over a cigarette. How could any intelligent person want a life that idled along so placidly at five miles an hour?

She entered the Vuitton stand and examined a stack of trunks piled ten feet high.

A man in an ill-fitting green tweed jacket and baggy corduroy trousers rushed up with a yellow-toothed smile, hastily swallowing a mouthful of food.

"I see you're fascinated by the striped ones," he said, indicating a pile of beige- and brown-striped trunks. "Louis Vuitton designed those stripes, which replaced the original Trianon design, for the eighteen seventy-six exhibition in Paris. They really belong in a museum."

He led Capucine to a stack of heavily distressed trunks and suitcases covered in the well-known brown cloth with the gold LV monogram. "These are from the very first run of the now famous Damier design, which was introduced in eighteen eighty-eight. They all date from the period between eighty-eight and ninety-two, when Louis Vuitton died and his son took over the business."

"You're the owner of this stand?"

"I am indeed, madame. Arnaud Boysson at your service."

Capucine produced her police wallet, badge on one flap and tricolored striped ID card on the other. Boysson's ebullient mood deflated like a collapsed soufflé. He looked at her guardedly.

"You sold a Vuitton trunk to Madame Cécile de Rougemont last week. When it was delivered, a dead body was found inside. I'm here to talk to you about that."

Boysson became ashen. "This isn't about Chef Brault, is it? The papers all said his body had been discovered in a Vuitton trunk, but I just didn't make the connection."

"Of course you did."

"Madame de Rougemont's name wasn't mentioned in the press. I had no way of knowing the body was found in the trunk I sold her, now did I?" he said with a sullen look. He went to a desk in the corner of the stand and produced a large ledger bound in green cloth so old, it must have come from one of his Puces colleagues.

On the defensive, Boysson pointed a grimy finger at an entry. The name had been misspelled. "C. De Rouge-Mont." Capucine had seen the amount on the receipt, but was again taken aback that Cécile had paid the price of a secondhand car for an old trunk.

"Monsieur, I congratulate you on keeping such thorough financial records. That's something one doesn't expect at the Puces."

Boysson sniffed a sniff of righteous indignation, but said nothing.

"Your trunks don't come cheap, do they?"

"The trunk Madame de Rougemont acquired is pre–World War I. It's a true collector's piece, complete with *all* fifteen of the original wood hangers. A very wise investment. I'm sure she's an important collector."

Even though Capucine found the little man profoundly irritating, she resisted the temptation to tell him what Cécile planned to do with the trunk.

"Did you notice anything unusual when you arrived here on Saturday?"

"Yes, both of my shutters were down, but the padlocks had disappeared."

"Show me."

Boysson found a long pole with a steel hook at the top, went to the front of the stand, and pulled two screens halfway down.

"All the stands are equipped the same way. The inside screen is mesh. You pull it down if you have to go out when the market is open. That way people can see the merchandise. The second screen is solid metal. We all lock both of them when the market closes. I thought it was the men from the delivery company who had forgotten to put the padlocks back. I called and scolded them, but the dispatcher didn't seem to know anything about it, so I just bought new locks and forgot about it."

"I'm amazed you leave such valuable objects with so little protection."

"It's more secure than you'd think. The doors to the building are locked at night, and there's a night watchman with one of those portable time-clock devices to keep him patrolling all night long."

"And who has the keys to the building?"

"All the stand holders do, of course, as well as the delivery companies. They usually make their pickups very early in the morning to beat the traffic."

"How does that work?"

"We all have our own systems. Personally, I put a bright red sticky note on the piece to be picked up and also tie the bill of lading to the handle. That way the delivery people know where it goes and I get a signed receipt. The delivery people have the keys to my padlocks and are normally very scrupulous in locking up after they leave."

"We're not sure where Chef Brault was killed. If it was here, do you think anyone might have heard the shot?"

"I have no idea. I've never been here much after closing time. But when you think about it, the watchman's circuit takes him to the far end of the building. You might not hear a shot that far away."

"Did you know Chef Brault? Had you ever been to his restaurant?"

"Good Lord, no. I couldn't begin to afford places like that. It's true my pieces are valuable, but this is not a very profitable business. The holding costs for the inventory are enormous. When you work at the Puces, you trade a life of luxury for the privilege of spending your day surrounded by the things you love."

CHAPTER 9

"Prosper!" the shirt-sleeved maître d' called out. "Someone to see you."

He used the familiar tu. Ouvrard was obviously still one of the boys, clearly not yet Chef Ouvrard to his staff.

Capucine had arrived at the restaurant just as the cleaning crew was getting to work after the luncheon service. Standing in the foyer, which was identical to the one in the hotel with its satin drapes and expensive-looking faïence on Greek pillars, she could hear the vacuum cleaners at work in the dining room. Ouvrard arrived with a blend of diffidence and truculence. Playing to his vanity, Capucine stuck her hand out to be shaken.

"Chef, it's good of you to find the time to see me. I know how busy you must be."

"No problem. Let's go to the office. It'll be quieter there." Capucine couldn't help but notice that it wasn't *his* office yet.

The small glass-walled room looked out onto the kitchen, which was being mopped down while the *plongeurs* attacked pots and pans in a deep, steamy stainless-steel sink. Capucine and Ouvrard sat on either side of a small marble-topped table strewn with papers. The only decoration in the tiny room was a tall cylindrical faïence vase containing a few tortured, twisting branches.

Ouvrard noticed Capucine examining it.

"Chef loved this thing. It's apparently a very valuable piece. I should probably move it into the dining room, but I don't like to tamper with his stuff." He seemed to realize the incongruity of what he had just said, and gave a short laugh. "I'm in a funny spot. I'm a sous-chef with no chef to report to."

"That can't be easy."

"For now it's not a problem. I just do what sous-chefs do—cook the boss's cuisine. Sous-chefs exist so the chef can take a day off without anyone noticing." He paused. "We keep our three stars until the new Guide is published on the last day of February next year. But they're not my stars. They're Chef's. Until February I have to carry on as if he was still here. So I'm trying to fit into his clogs and lead my life as if it was his." He looked at Capucine with a quizzical smile and snorted. "Right down to fulfilling his obligations to his girlfriend."

"And when you're free to do your own cooking, will it be very different from Chef Brault's?"

"Of course. Chef was famous for his passion for vegetables. He took Alain Passard's hyper-organic, neo-vegetarian school one step further. The blossoming of the philosophy of not putting anything on the table that doesn't come from a horse-plowed field."

Capucine told herself that she was going to have to ask Alexandre to explain these horse-plowed fields chefs never seemed to stop talking about.

"Actually, I think Chef was just neurotic. It wasn't so much that he loved vegetables. It was that he was afraid of meat. Protein was an alien substance to him. But the result was phenomenal. His cuisine was truly ephemeral. He managed to create intense flavor without the burden of substance—foams, purées whipped as light as air, magical things no one had ever eaten before. His dishes were like a chiffon veil wafting behind a dancing ballerina." He looked up at Capucine to see if she understood. "Me, I want to hold the ballerina in my arms and feel the warmth of her body."

"Does that mean you're going to do more meat?"

"Naturally. Spring lamb, sweetbreads, *poulet fermier* raised on the farm of a friend of mine in Brittany. But it will be done with a delicacy that Chef would have appreciated. Absolutely nothing heavy. No beef and, above all, no game."

"Chef Brault enjoyed hunting, didn't he?"

"I don't know if he enjoyed it, but he certainly went pheasant shooting every now and then during the season. It was odd. He never brought back any birds. He said he didn't want the reek of them even in the trunk of his car. If you ask me, it was another one of his neuroses. Did you know his father is a baron? I think he only went shooting because he thought it was a baronial sort of thing to do. It was his duty. A way of keeping a link to his family traditions."

"Did he have any enemies that you knew of?"

"Enemies? Chef didn't know enough people to have enemies. Other than the staff at the restaurant, he only talked to his producers, and he had a love relationship with every last one of them. And, of course, his financial backer, who was the closest thing he had to a best friend."

"No girlfriends other than Mademoiselle Duclos?"

"Not that I knew of, and Delphine tells me he wouldn't even turn his head to look at a pretty girl on the street. She kept hoping he'd have a little fling on the side and cut her some slack." Ouvrard laughed.

"Tell me about the financial backer, Monsieur Brissac-Vanté."

"A bigmouthed playboy. The front-of-the-house staff didn't like him all that much, because he'd come in and act like he owned the place. But I didn't mind him, because he was good for Chef."

"Did he come here often?"

"About once a month, sometimes more. Always a six- or eight-top, and he'd only call the day before. That would create real problems for the maître d', as you can imagine. Then he'd talk big at his table, order very expensive grand crue wines—all of which we'd comp, of course—and expect Chef to come out so he could make a big production and tell his guests he was the éminence grise of modern haute cuisine and Chef was his favorite protégé."

"Did this irritate Chef Brault?"

"Au contraire. He adored Brissac-Vanté. They'd spend hours on the phone. Brissac-Vanté was the only one who could get Chef out of the dumps. And thank God he could, because Chef could get very depressed when he set his mind to it."

"But Brissac-Vanté refused to invest more money in the hotel."

"Damn straight he did. That hotel was a complete waste of time. Brault probably picked up the idea from the Troisgros when he was an intern down there. It was right out of the Michelin Guide of the nineteen thirties. One-star restaurants were 'very good,' two-stars were 'worth a detour,' and three-stars 'merited a trip.' So naturally, the idea was that if you were taking a trip to a restaurant, you had to spend the night in the restaurant's hotel." He laughed. "Not only was that from another age, but it made no sense at all if you're twenty minutes from Paris. I think Brissac-Vanté only staked Brault because he wanted to keep him happy and motivated in his kitchen. The idea of doing up more than three or four rooms was insane, but it was Chef's biggest hobbyhorse."

"So who owns the restaurant now?"

"The court hasn't decided yet. Brissac-Vanté acts like he does. He came the other day with his wife and had a long lunch with some very heavy-duty wines. He stayed until the service was over and then gathered everyone in the kitchen for a pep talk. He was going to insure that no one had anything to worry about and the restaurant was going to go on forever and climb to new heights. He implied that I was in full charge, but didn't actually say it. That didn't make my job any easier, let me tell you."

"So Chef Brault had no enemies that you knew of?"

"The only person that came even close to being an enemy was that son of a bitch Lucien Folon. That guy couldn't stop hammering away at Chef. He'd write these reviews that you wouldn't believe. Always the same stuff. Chef's cuisine was limp-dicked, tasteless vegetarian crap, sexed up with bizarre, exotic spices. Everyone in the kitchen hates his guts. And he couldn't stop coming. He'd be here at least once a month for lunch or dinner. If Chef didn't insist on cooking everything that went on Folon's table himself, the guys would probably have pissed on it." Ouvrard chuckled.

"Why do you think Folon hated Chef Brault's cuisine so much?"

"That's the funny thing. I don't think he hated it at all. He'd clean off his plate. I'd watch him through the judas. You know when they love the meal. You can see it in their eyes. Folon absolutely relished what he ate. Every time, we were sure he was finally going to write a good review, but the more he seemed to like his meal, the more he trashed us in the press. Go figure."

CHAPTER 10

At seven thirty that evening Capucine sat in her office, reading the final edition of *Le Monde,* waiting for David to get off the phone so she could start a meeting with the three brigadiers.

Once a week Alexandre wrote a column called *"Celui Qui Ecrit la Bouche Pleine*—He Who Writes with His Mouth Full." It was about various food topics: a little restaurant gossip, his views on current food trends, comments about what he had been eating, maybe a dish he had invented and thought would be perfect for one chef or another. It was one of the more popular columns in the paper. That day's was a eulogy of Jean-Louis Brault. Under the column's logo and his picture, Alexandre had started with a quote from Destouches.

"La critique est aisée, mais l'art est difficile. Criticism is easy, but art is difficult."

Capucine had no idea who this Destouches was. The biographical Robert dictionary told her he was a composer famous for an opera she had never heard of, and had died in 1749. She went back to the article.

This has been a black week indeed in the annals of food criticism. One of my colleagues has completely lost sight of what the word criticism *means.*

Every lycéen *knows it comes from the Greek* kritikós, *"capable of discernment or judgment." That is—or should be—the goal of all food critics.*

Yet Lucien Folon published a piece in Le Figaro *declaring that Chef Jean-Louis Brault's fatal flaw was his hubris, which deluded a vegetable prep cook into believing he was a true chef, tempting him to fly so close to the sun of haute cuisine he singed his feathers and plunged to his nemesis.*

I'm dumbstruck. Chef Brault had been crowned with the highest accolade our country has to offer its most cherished culinary artisans: the third Michelin star. How dare anyone defame him? Folon dares, dear readers, because he has so lost sight of the meaning of kritikós, *he seeks to sell newpapers by spitting on angels.*

Do you know why we all persist in believing Chef Brault committed suicide, when there is such abundant evidence to the contrary? The answer is obvious: Folon had driven him to the brink. The assassin merely completed the task.

Capucine found the depth of Alexandre's anger almost erotic.

Isabelle clomped through the door, followed by David and Momo.

"It's nearly eight o'clock. I'm starving," Capucine said. "What if we have this session over at Benoît's?"

There were enthusiastic nods from all three brigadiers. Capucine folded the newspaper, tucked it under her arm, and walked out with her team.

Benoît's, on the corner twenty yards down from the

brigade, was one of a dying breed of *restos ouvrier*—workers' restaurants—and a jackstay for the flics of Capucine's brigade. It wasn't that worker's restaurants were closing; the problem was they were going upmarket. But at Benoît's you could still get lunch with an appetizer, a main dish, cheese, dessert, and a quarter bottle of red for only five euros on top of the *ticket restaurant*, the meal vouchers supplied by the Ministry of the Interior. Sadly, the working-class Twentieth was rapidly becoming a hip new frontier, complete with trendy restaurants. If Benoît's went that route and began charging thirty or forty euros for lunch, the brigadiers would find themselves eating at McDonald's. But that was—hopefully—unimaginable.

The four detectives trooped into the restaurant, retrieved their napkins from cubbyholes labeled with their handwritten names—complete with rank so punctiliously noted that many brigadiers had first learned of their promotions by the change in their cubbyhole labels—and moved to a corner table. Angélique, a woman of heroic rotundity, announced what they would be eating: boudin—blood sausage—with sautéed apples for the men, and a *pavé de saumon grillé*—a paving-stone–sized hunk of grilled salmon—on a bed of *lentilles du Puy* for the women. And, of course, they would be drinking the house Tavel, which was universally known to be the best that had ever come through the gates of Paris.

When the food arrived, the detectives waited for Angélique's back to be turned and rapidly exchanged plates. Capucine loved boudin; Isabelle hated fish, but David adored it; and—completely erroneously—none of them thought Momo cared what he ate.

Once the wine was poured and the mandatory thirty seconds of silence to concentrate on the food had been observed, Capucine put down her knife and fork.

"Let's start with you, Isabelle. Did the database have anything interesting to say about Brault?"

"Not really. His bio is pretty much what you'd expect. He graduated from the *maternelle* and *école élémentaire* in La Cadière-d'Azur and then matriculated in the town's lycée. After a year in high school he transferred to the école hôtelière in Paris."

"He went to Paris all by himself?" Capucine asked. "He must have only been fourteen."

"He had his fifteenth birthday over the summer. The records show he lived on the seventh floor of a building on the boulevard Pereire owned by a certain Frédérique Brault. I'm guessing that Frédérique Brault is some sort of cousin who had an apartment that came with a *chambre de bonne* under the eaves with no heating, a cold-water tap, and a Turkish toilet at the end of the hall."

"Do you think the cousin supported him financially?" David asked.

Isabelle shook her head. "He worked at night doing the *plonge*—washing dishes—in a restaurant called the Repaire de Pereire, which was a few blocks away on the boulevard Pereire."

"Cheerful," David muttered.

Isabelle gave him a scornful look. "Don't feel too bad. He only did that for two years. The cycle at the école hôtelière is shorter than the other lycées. He got his BEP, his professional studies certificate, at the end of his first year, and then his BTS, his superior technician's certificate, the year after that. He was quite the star. He got the best grades in his class."

"Then what?" Capucine asked.

"He got an internship at the Troisgros restaurant in Roanne. That must have been the prize job. He stayed there four years and moved as sous-chef to a one-star restaurant in Le Perreux-sur-Marne called Les Pieds dans L'Eau. A year later the owner of the place fired the chef and put Brault in charge of the kitchen."

"How old was he at this point?" Capucine asked.

"Twenty-two. A real whiz kid. After four years he quit the place in Le Perreux and bought the restaurant in Sèvres. We have a lot of stuff on that transaction. He put twenty thousand euros down on the table, and a bank gave him a mortgage for the rest. Five years later, he bought the small building across the street and began converting it into a hotel. The purchase was done with a short-term loan by an operation called Athénée Investments. I looked them up. It's a financial holding company with only two share-holders, Monsieur and Madame Brissac-Vanté. Thierry Brissac-Vanté is listed as *gérant*—manager."

"Good work. According to the sous-chef, this Brissac-Vanté's acting like he's the new owner of both the hotel and the restaurant. He's going to be my next stop," Ca-pucine said. "David, what did you find out about Brault's family?"

"His father, the baron, has been broke as far back as our records go. His bank file goes on and on—heavy mort-gage on the château to pay for upkeep, mortgage payments frequently in arrears, multiple threats of foreclosure, de-clined requests for loans, a good number of fines for bounced checks. The story is obvious. He inherited a small château but didn't have the money to keep it up. If you read between the lines, he didn't have enough money to buy groceries, either.

"Then, one day, he got his big break. But that didn't pan out. A development company made an offer to buy his château. They wanted to build retirement homes on the land and use the château as the center of attraction with a restaurant and game rooms and stuff like that. Brault got a few thousand euros in cash, which the bank immediately snapped up to cover his delinquent loans. The contract gave the baron a share of the profits once the development company had sold enough houses to get past its break-even point."

David slowly cut a piece of salmon and chewed it carefully, letting the dramatic tension of his story build.

"*Allez, allez,*" Isabelle barked.

"The development company built the homes and then went bankrupt. They didn't come close to selling enough houses to cover their costs. The baron never got a sou."

"He was out on the street?" Capucine asked.

"No. The one smart thing he did was to hang on to the gatehouse and keep it out of the deal. But judging from the property taxes, it must be tiny."

"Siblings?" Capucine asked. She trusted police records more than the social register.

"A brother. Antonin. Five years older than Jean-Louis. A long arrest record for minor stuff—fights in cafés, disturbing the peace, things like that. The gendarmes would haul him in, give him a dressing-down, and release him without a booking. Then, four years ago, he went on the lam. His last job was in a garage near Bandol. He either quit or got fired—the job termination form was never filed—and disappeared. Not on La Cadière's or any other civil register, no bank accounts or Carte Bleue bank cards. Sounds like he's hiding out somewhere, living off odd jobs he does for cash. My guess is that he finally did something serious and figures the gendarmes are after him."

"Did you speak to the father on the phone?" Capucine asked.

"That's what I was just doing. Waste of time. He wasn't entirely lucid. Also, between the blaring TV and the loose false teeth, he was almost impossible to understand. He did say he had no idea where Antonin was. It didn't seem to bother him. I also got the impression he either hadn't heard that his other son died or he hadn't really taken it on board. He certainly doesn't know anything about his son's life after he left the village."

"Cheerful," Isabelle said. David smiled sweetly at her.

"What about you, Momo?" Capucine asked. "How'd you do? Find the guys who delivered the trunk?"

"Yup. They're good old boys. You know, guys who toss down a couple of Calvas first thing in the morning, before the coffee arrives on the zinc at the café. The trunk was one of three deliveries they made that day. There was also an armoire that was a breeze because it came apart and a dining table that was a bitch because it didn't.

"They were at the Puces at five thirty in the morning, picked up their stuff, and piled it into their truck. The trunk was their last delivery. The people that own the stands they deliver for gave their dispatcher the keys, and they picked them up before they went home the day before. When they arrived at the stand in the morning to load the trunk, the screens were down but the padlocks weren't on. They said that happens every now and then. The owners pull down the screens but forget to put on the locks.

"The trunk was in the front of the stand, lying on its side with a red tag on it. They noticed that the hasps hadn't been shut, so they snapped them and loaded the trunk. They didn't notice there was a hole, which makes sense since it was on the bottom. They said they didn't find it odd the trunk was so heavy, 'cause they're used to weird shit like that at the Puces."

The dearth of clues cast a pall over the table. Capucine stood up. "Why don't you stay and have cheese and dessert and talk it over? Maybe you can find an anomaly in this somewhere. I need to get home to Alexandre." She tossed the copy of *Le Monde* on the table. "This might be something else for you guys to think about."

CHAPTER 11

The office, with its look-at-me ostentation, could have been any one of the myriad boutique marketing and consulting firms on the Champs-Élysées. All the components were there: the minimalist Knoll furniture, the view of the hallowed avenue through plate-glass windows, the inch-thick glass desk populated with computer screens and expensive executive toys, the starlet-grade secretary in the ultra-miniskirt and the ultra-maxi heels.

The de rigueur secretary placed a de rigueur demitasse of office-made *express* on the desk in front of Capucine and then minced sensually to give Thierry Brissac-Vanté his cup. As convention required, he ran his eyes up and down her body, but it was from behind a curtain of reserve so opaque there was no doubt at all he had never had, nor would he ever have, the slightest lascivious interest in her.

"How much of La Mère Denis do you own, monsieur?" Capucine asked.

"Maybe the majority. Maybe nothing. A judge is deciding as we speak."

Brissac-Vanté opened the lid of a faïence apothecary jar, removed a pinch of paper clips, and began making little patterns with them on the glass desk. Capucine raised her eyebrows to encourage him to explain.

He thought for a few seconds, squeezed the paper clips together in a small mound, and said, "You see, my investment in La Mère Denis is in the form of an automatically renewing, convertible short-term loan. One of the conditions that would trigger the conversion was the last thing anyone expected, the death of the company's *président-directeur général,* Jean-Louis Brault." His head drooped fractionally for a few seconds in mourning, but he looked up quickly at Capucine with a boyish grin. It was obvious he expected to find that Capucine had been overwhelmed by the financial jargon.

He went on. "You see, the idea was that debt turned into equity if something happened that made it look like the company couldn't pay it off. It's pretty standard stuff."

"I gather from pictures and press clippings in the waiting room that your business here is promoting sports personalities."

"We don't promote them. We sign them up for our clients." With a toothy smile, he switched into sell mode and rolled his chair around the desk so it was next to Capucine's. "Let's say, to pick a crazy example, that the Police Judiciaire wanted to improve its image." He held up both hands as if in surrender. "Hey, I'm only using this as an example, but it really might not be a bad idea. We'd get, say, the soccer player Zinedine Zidane.... No, no, wait, he's no good for you, way too aggressive with that head-butting stuff at the World Cup.

"Let's make it Yannick Noah, our iconic black tennis player, who sings those great songs with an African rhythm for kids. So, we'd cut a bunch of upbeat TV spots with a voice-over while Noah's singing in the background to let the world of immigrants know how important the Police Judiciaire is in making their lives safe and comfortable. We'd map out the whole campaign for you and sign up Noah." He paused, looking at Capucine hopefully for a sign of enthusiasm. "It was only an idea, but something like that could really help you guys out."

"Are your investments part of your sponsoring business?"

"Not at all," Brissac-Vanté said with a laugh. "Completely separate. The investments are important, of course, but this is the real love of my life. It's where my entrepreneurial talent shines through."

"Do you invest primarily in restaurants?"

"I don't specialize in anything. I'm on the lookout for projects where I can really add value. Succeeding in the investment world takes a whole lot more than writing checks. Let me tell you. We're very diverse. We have three restaurants, an art gallery, an Armagnac producer, and the pride of our crown, the Tours soccer team. You probably know we won the league championship last year. I was hoarse for a week after." Brissac-Vanté laughed happily.

"And what sort of value did you add to La Mère Denis?"

"It was—is—a very complex situation. Chef Brault was one of the towering chefs in France. I supported him through a very difficult period in his life by tailor making financing that not only fit his financial needs but also his psychological ones. I may be bragging, but I think I'm one of the forces that enabled his fabulous genius to blossom."

"A difficult period in his life?"

"You have to understand the full complexity of Chef Brault. He was a true genius, with all the strengths and weaknesses of a genius. You need to grasp the fragility of his ego. He was one of the most gifted chefs France has ever produced, but he always doubted himself. When he came to me, his restaurant was producing food that easily merited three stars, but the Guide had only given him two. The third star was clearly coming, but Michelin likes to take it slow. Chef Brault got it in his head that they were holding back the third star because he didn't have a hotel attached to his restaurant. He was completely unglued. His bank wouldn't finance the hotel, because it was a bad idea commercially. Fortunately, he came to me. I saw that the hotel thing was seriously distracting him from his cooking—which was the only important thing, after all— and I made the hotel happen so he could concentrate in the kitchen."

"And did it work?"

"Absolutely. The minute we bought the building across the street and the renovation started, he was a changed man. And then, of course, he got his third star the next year." He laughed. "Which just happened to be the year the hotel opened. Pure coincidence, but Jean-Louis couldn't be shaken in his belief that it was all due to the hotel." He smiled warmly at the memory.

"Do you usually do your deals for convertible debt?" Capucine asked.

Brissac-Vanté looked at her sharply. The question wasn't in keeping with the altruistic spirit of his message.

"The raison d'être of my investments is philanthropic, but I'm also a professional financier. Our investment firm is owned jointly by me and my wife, and she's a very prudent woman. Brault was in a tough spot. His bank categorically refused to lend him money for the hotel. Of course, he could have sold off a part of the ownership in the restaurant, but it was critical to his psyche to be sole owner. I understood and respected that. So I let him have his cake and eat it. In fact, as we say in French, I gave him *le beurre, l'argent du beurre, et le sourire de la crémière*— the butter, the money for the butter, *and* the smile of the girl behind the counter. My convertible loan structure gave him everything he wanted and let him retain full control of everything."

"So Brault's death is a windfall for you."

Brissac-Vanté seemed sincerely offended. "Just the opposite, Commissaire. Just the opposite. It's a catastrophe. Even if the court awards me ownership of the restaurant— and that's a very big if—all I'll get is a restaurant site in Sèvres. Without Brault, the place has no more value than the premises and the pots and pans in the kitchen. Even if Ouvrard keeps it limping along, I'm still going to have to post a very big write-down." He paused and drummed his fingers on the glass desktop. "I really don't think you appreciate the magnitude of the loss of Chef Brault. His death wasn't just a catastrophe for me. It's a catastrophe for the nation."

"So what happens next?"

"If the court awards me control, nothing. Ouvrard seems to be holding his own. We'll see how many stars the Guide will take away from us next February. When the Guide decides, then I'll decide."

The long-legged secretary came in with a bright blue file folder. She bent over to hand it to Brissac-Vanté, revealing a maximum of décolleté.

"Can I ask you to sign these, monsieur? I need to get them in before the accountant leaves for the day."

Brissac-Vanté extracted a sheet of paper from the folder. "Excuse me," he said, beaming his best smile. "These are my expenses for a trip I took to London the weekend Chef Brault died. I'm working on a very big promotional deal over there." The smile faded in homage to the tragedy. "I somehow feel that if I'd been here, if he'd had someone to talk to, this might not have happened."

It was amazing, Capucine reflected, how everyone— even she on occasion—persisted in the belief that Jean-Louis Brault had committed suicide.

CHAPTER 12

———

Capucine had never understood Alexandre's abiding love of restaurant openings. They struck her as being as pointless as office Christmas parties. If it was a restaurant of stature, the gratin of the culinary world would be invited. Naturally, none of the critics would even think of writing a critique of a meal consumed in a nimbus of alcohol-fueled jollity, and the best the restaurant's owners could hope for was one or two column inches announcing they had opened for business. Still, Capucine felt the occasional appearance at an opening luncheon was a wifely obligation. After all, Alexandre put up with the impositions of her police career.

This particular opening was the renaissance of the venerable Brasserie Brech—long renowned for the perfection of its seafood—the third historic bistrot taken over by France's most starred chef, who had developed a lucrative side business of revamping classic eateries and coating them in a shining luster of dernier-cri chic.

Capucine exceeded her usual fifteen-minute lateness and arrived a good half an hour after the affair was to have started. Alexandre waved at her cheerfully from the middle of what was clearly the table of honor, a vacant chair by his side reserved for her.

Capucine had been to Brech many times over the years. Even though nothing seemed to have been changed, the décor had an entirely unfamiliar feel, almost as if she was entering the restaurant for the first time. She wondered how the effect was achieved. The bar now seemed to be partitioned off from the twenty or so tables behind a gleaming, head-high, varnished wooden partition, topped by opaque, turn-of-the-century cut-glass panels. Capucine asked herself if it had been recently added or if it had always been there and she had just never noticed it.

As she sat down, the hilarity at the table was just shifting up a gear.

"*Mon chou*—my cabbage," Alexandre said, loading her plate with oysters from a platter of crustaceans on crushed ice raised high by a wire frame, "you have to try these. They're fabulous."

For the thousandth time Capucine wondered why being called a cabbage was the universal French form of endearment for women and children.

"The big ones are Gillardeaus, these smaller ones are fines de Prat-Ar-Coum, and of course, these are fines de Claire, but they're the largest ones I've ever seen."

The oysters were delicious. Even after an overnight ride in a refrigerated truck from Brittany, they still brought the full delight of the briny tang of the sea to her mouth. A woman at her right—well into her late seventies, her skin leathery and nut-colored from endless summers in the Midi, the red ribbon of the Légion d'honneur winking out between the tweedy pastel threads of a Chanel suit—smiled at her. "Pure bliss, n'est-ce pas?"

Just as Capucine eyed the depleted plateau, about to grab the last remaining *tourteau*—a tiny pink Mediterranean crab—a waiter snatched away the platter and its supporting stand. Another waiter emerged from behind him and placed a large, shallow soup bowl in front of her.

"That's going to be far better than that crab," Alexandre said. "I ordered for you. Lobster *ravioles* in a sauce of crustacean butter."

A waiter placed a dish in front of Alexandre, intoning, "*Aiguillettes de saint-pierre vapeur aux poireaux et truffe.*"

"I love John Dory, and this one has been steamed and truffled and is served with leeks." He took a bite. "Absolutely perfect."

A man across from him, who had been given the same dish, said, "Absolutely. It would have been delicate enough even for Jean-Louis Brault."

At the table there was a silence as shocked as if someone had passed wind loudly. Brault's suicide-murder had unquestionably been placed on the *index* of the culinary world.

Mercifully, there was a buzz when the multi-starred restaurateur appeared to make his lap around the tables, accompanied by the executive chef of the restaurant, a fresh-faced young man still in his twenties, wearing a highly starched chef's outfit with an immaculate white kerchief knotted around his neck. Significantly, the restaurateur wore a business suit, making it clear that, while the cooking was the domain of the executive chef, his was the genius of creation.

As hands were shaken and backs patted, the elderly woman next to Capucine leaned over and said in a loud aside, "How young they are nowadays. I can remember when chefs had to be in their sixties and have enormous bellies."

Another unfortunate comment. The table was cued to recall that Jean-Louis Brault had been the second youngest chef in France to receive a third star.

With intense fervor the diners at the table applied themselves to their dishes.

A man lurched out from behind the bar screen, squinting angrily into the room with deep-sunk, cadaverous eyes over frameless half-glasses. Visibly drunk, he careened into a table, coming to rest by supporting himself with both hands on the back of a diner's chair. The room iced in embarrassed silence.

"*Mille fois pardon, Monsieur Ducon.* A thousand apologies, Mister Asshole," the drunk sneered when the man turned angrily.

"Lucien Folon," Alexandre whispered to Capucine, who had never met him and had only had a glimpse of his profile as he scuttled away from Brault's funeral mass.

Hands still on the back of the chair, head jerking, Folon laboriously examined the room until he singled out Alexandre.

"*Ah, voilà le petit bougre.* There's the little bugger," Folon said in a loud voice and zigzagged over to Alexandre's table.

"Listen up, *connard*—you complete asshole," he said, latching on to the back of Alexandre's chair like an exhausted swimmer grabbing the edge of the pool. "*Kritikós,* my fucking ass. Not only are you a goddamn snob who doesn't know the first thing about cuisine, but you're also illiterate."

He rattled Alexandre's chair violently.

"You write another word about me or that no-talent, limp-dicked Brault and you're going to see what you're going to see!" Folon shouted, reeling and waving his fist in the air.

A Junoesque redhead across the table, the wife of the food critic of *Le Parisien,* said, "That's quite enough, Lucien. High time for you to go home and sleep it off. I won't have you say another word about poor Jean-Louis. And for what it's worth, if Jean-Louis Brault had ever looked my way, I would have jumped right into his bed. But, sadly, he never did." Her husband rubbed her back affectionately.

The little color left drained from Folon's face. Ashen, he renewed his grip on the back of Alexandre's chair with both hands, breathing shallowly, spitting in the effort to make a spiteful retort.

"The elderly woman next to Capucine said, "Yes, little man, Agnès is perfectly right. If I were ten year younger—goodness, forget about that—if he were still alive, I'd be delighted to slip under the eiderdown with him anytime he wanted. Now, go crawl back under your rock, you repulsive little insect."

Fanned by rage, the dim coals in the recesses of Folon's eyes glowed dark red in their orbits. His prissy dark lips opened and twisted downward into a scowl, revealing sharp, rodent-like incisors. He lifted his arm high and open-handed, intending to slap the elderly woman.

Capucine rose and, with a fluid motion, twisted Folon's arm behind him in a policeman's lock. While he snarled and growled, another diner grabbed Folon's other arm, and the two of them marched him to the door. Capucine let the man put the sole of his shoe to Folon's posterior and propel him violently into the street. Folon bounced off a parked car, regained his balance, and shambled off.

When she returned to the table, the elderly woman said to Capucine, "Goodness, my dear, you didn't need to do that. I was all set to knee him in the balls."

The table dissolved in laughter.

CHAPTER 13

It had been a disappointing meeting. None of the three brigadiers had anything that even looked like an idea. The case seemed completely stalled. Capucine got up from her desk and paced the room. After a lap she stopped in the far corner.

"We need to focus on Lucien Folon," she said.

"The critic guy?" Isabelle asked.

"You think he might have rubbed Brault out because he didn't like his cooking?" David asked. "Now, that really would have been a scathing review." He twirled a silky ginger lock around his finger. Isabelle shot him a dark look. Momo uncoiled his frown a notch, his version of a smile.

"I met him for the first time yesterday. It was an impressive display. He's definitely strung out about something. I want to find out what. He also has quite a violent streak. Isabelle, can you run him down on the screen for me?"

Two hours later, a very upbeat Isabelle returned, trailing the other two brigadiers.

"Commissaire," Isabelle said, "you're a genius. Get this. Folon and Brault come from the same town, and they were born in the same year. They must go way back together."

Capucine waved the brigadiers into chairs.

"Start at the beginning," Capucine said to Isabelle.

"Like I said, Folon's thirty-three, same age as Brault. Both were born and grew up in La Cadière-d'Azur, in the *département* of the Var. Folon's story is straight out of the good old South. His parents ran the village bakery. They still do." Isabelle paused to give the next section its proper emphasis.

"His mother got married when she was sixteen. On her birthday. She had a child four months after the wedding. Nice, huh? She married the baker's son. Our records show she drew a salary at the bakery from her fifteenth birthday, the earliest she could legally go on the payroll. My guess is that she worked there for years, the baker's boy knocked her up, and her family made her marry him as soon as she could, which was on her sixteenth birthday. Nice birthday present." Isabelle glowered.

"Was that child our man Folon?" Capucine asked.

"No. That was a daughter, Françoise. Lucien was born four years later. He graduated from the village's primary school and the lycée and was one of the only two students in his class to pass the *bac*." Isabelle snorted at the primitiveness of a small southern village where virtually no one bothered with the baccalaureate certificate, because they had no interest in going to university.

Momo's frown deepened three notches. He didn't have his bac, either.

"Folon shows up next in Marseilles, where he spends six years getting a *license* and a masters in journalism. Then he goes to work in the Marseilles office of the Agence France-Presse. After a few months they send him to the U.S. to work in their office in New York as a junior photo editor. He quits the AFP after six months but doesn't set foot in France for a year and a half. We don't know what he was doing, because he didn't file a French tax return, legal enough if he wasn't earning money in France. Next, he comes back to Marseilles and gets a job as a fashion reporter for *Le Dauphiné Libéré*—"

"Fashion reporter?" David asked. "How did he get into food criticism?"

"I'm getting to that, asshole. If you just sat there with your trap shut, like you're supposed to, you'd find out." Isabelle raised her eyebrows and shook her head in exasperation. "Next, he moves to Paris and gets a job with *Le Parisien,* writing for the women's page. I guess that would have been recipes, fashion, and all that crap, right? He does that for two years."

Isabelle made a sarcastic moue at David. "Here you go, num nuts. He joins *Le Figaro* on the staff of the restaurant page. He must have started at the bottom of the heap, because from his tax returns he was making peanuts. Nowadays he's raking it in, though. He gets a good salary from the paper, has royalties coming in from three books, and does stuff on TV two or three times a month. That's it."

"Good work," Capucine said.

"No. It's thin. I don't know anything about his life. We'd know if he'd ever been married, which he hasn't. I had a quick look at his credit card records, and you don't see him eating out all that much, but I'm guessing he gets comped wherever he goes."

Capucine laughed. "He definitely eats for free in the upmarket places, and I doubt he often gets a yen for a Royal Cheese at McDonald's."

"So what do we do now, Commissaire? I can go out with the guys and start doing interviews and take his life apart."

Capucine stared at Isabelle, unseeing, for a few beats.

"No," she said finally. "We need to start at the beginning, in La Cadière. That's where he knew Brault. Were they classmates?"

"Bound to have been," Isabelle said. "They're the same age, and the village only has one primary school and one lycée."

"We need to dig deep into La Cadière. There may be something to find, but it's not going to be easy. They're notoriously closemouthed about their private lives in the Midi." Capucine resumed her pacing, thinking.

She stopped behind David's chair and put her hands on his shoulders. "You're from down there, aren't you?"

"Not as far as those guys are concerned, I'm not. I'm from Provence, almost on the Italian border. I grew up in a village east of Cannes, high up in the hills. In the Var they think that's a different country."

"But you know how to play *boules* and drink pastis, right?" Momo asked.

"Wait just a minute!" Isabelle said. "David's not going anywhere. He's an inch away from making an arrest on that child pornography case. He's got the perp tagged and is just putting the finishing touches on the magistrate's file. But the magistrate's being a real pain and keeps wanting more stuff."

Capucine ignored her. "Here's what we're going to do. We're going to send David down to La Cadière under cover so he can soak the place up. We'll have to cook up a good story for him." She paused, contemplating David.

"David, do you think you can pull off being a journalist? No, even better . . . how about a writer doing a biography of Chef Brault? That would be perfect. It would be entirely natural for you to be finding out about Brault's childhood pals."

David's eyes began to light up.

"Hang on just a minute, Commissaire. David can't go anywhere until he wraps up his case. Let's be clear about that," Isabelle said.

"How long is that going to take, David?" Capucine asked.

"I don't know. End of the week, maybe." David said absently, lost in thought. "See, the way I'll do it is lug a laptop everywhere and take real notes for the book. People will read over my shoulder and see that I'm actually working on something. This is going to be great. I'd get to run expenses and ply people with pastis, right?"

"Everybody's best friend, the boozy writer," Momo said.

Isabelle sat rigidly in her chair, livid.

"The tricky question is what to wear. I wouldn't want to be the scruffy author with a five-day stubble. That just isn't me. What I might do is a sort of Gallic Tom Wolfe look. White is particularly suited to the Midi and—"

"Let's get serious, Commissaire," Isabelle interrupted. "I really need David here until he buttons up his arrest. We just can't let him drop that."

"Isabelle, calm down. He'll make his arrest."

David paid no attention to this exchange. "Commissaire," he said. "This is going to be great. I'm going to take myself to one of those old Pagnol movies tonight to start getting into the role. Maybe I should get a new laptop. That could really set off my imag—"

"All right, David, plan on taking the TGV to Marseilles Saturday morning and renting a car at the station. But that's on the assumption that the magistrate is happy and he lets you make an arrest before the end of the week."

David nodded, only half listening. "No prob. I can do that avec *les doigts dans le nez*—with my fingers up my nose," he said in the broad, rolling accent of the Midi.

CHAPTER 14

Capucine picked up the ringing phone. "*Pardon,* Commissaire," the brigadier at the front desk said abruptly and then paused awkwardly.

"What is it?"

"There's a person on the line for you who claims to be an officer of police, but I'm not sure if he is. He doesn't sound like one."

"What do you mean?"

"He says he's a *commissaire-priseur.* Do we have those on the force?"

Capucine laughed. "He's not a flic. He's a licensed auctioneer. Put him on."

"Commissaire, this is Bertrand de Bertignac. I'm a commissaire-priseur at the Hôtel Drouot. I think I have some information that might have something to do with one of your cases."

"Which case?"

"Chef Brault's murder. I could tell you about it over the phone, but since it involves a physical object, it might make more sense for you to come down here and let me show you what I've come across."

*   *   *

Two hours later a frustrated Capucine wandered up and down the threadbare carpeting of the halls of the Hôtel Drouot, looking in vain for a receptionist or wall panel that might indicate the location of Bertignac's office. Rounding a corner, she came across Théophile, Cécile's husband, avidly making notes in an auction catalog, brows knit in concentration. With a start, he jerked up at Capucine's approach.

"Capucine! What a surprise. You're the last person I'd expect to see at a wine auction." They exchanged air kisses.

"I'm looking for a commissaire-priseur by the name of Bertignac. Is there a list somewhere that tells you which office he's in?"

"Bertignac? He's holding the auction I'm bidding on. Right in there." Théophile pointed at a set of oversized double doors across the hall. "Actually, I should be getting back in. I bought two lots early on, but the one I really want will be coming up in ten minutes or so. The auction's nearly over. Bertignac will be out in about twenty minutes."

"Take me with you. I want to see this Bertignac à l'œuvre."

"Absolutely. But we need to get a move on." Hard in the grips of acquisition lust, he almost pushed Capucine toward the door.

"Let me tell you what we're after." He squeezed Capucine's upper arm excitedly. "Of course, you know that nineteen eighty-four was the worst *millésime* of the century, even worse than nineteen forty-four. Almost none of the Bordeaux châteaux bottled that year. One of the few exceptions was Pétrus. A whole case of it's for sale. I'm betting that even in an execrable year, France's best wine is still going to be remarkable. And with any luck, it will go for a song." He beamed and quickened his pace.

The auction room was long, narrow, low-ceilinged; the

walls were covered with panels of crimson cloth. Théophile, normally diffident to the point of shyness, marched purposefully up to the front, with Capucine in his wake. In the third row, two seats in from the aisle, a vacant seat had been reserved with a sale catalog. The man sitting next to it stood up and eased his way out.

"I see you've found a friend," he whispered to Théophile. "She can have my seat. I'm quitting for the day. I lost the Yquem. There are some lunatics in the back who are offering absurd prices, and there is a phone bidder who is a complete loose cannon. I'm wasting my time. I just stayed to hold your seat. I'm going to spend the rest of the afternoon in a café, in the company of sane people. Good luck."

Théophile and Capucine dropped into the two seats. From behind a podium a tall, spare man with thin hair and aristocratic features peered out intently into the room over tortoiseshell half-glasses, pointing at people with a gold pen, reiterating their bids in a loud voice. At a low table next to him two dark-suited young men and a pretty girl in a blue dress sat with telephones to their ears, raising their hands every now and then to place a bid. On the far side of the podium a man in a black jacket with shiny metal buttons and a crimson collar held the corners of a wooden case of wine, his hands in immaculate white gloves.

"The Savoyards," Théophile murmured. "They have a monopoly on moving and showing the pieces at Drouot."

At the podium the pace intensified. All the bidders seemed to have dropped out except a single individual in the back of the room and another on the telephone. Bertignac's head swiveled back and forth as if he were at a tennis match.

"*Neuf,*" Bertignac said, pointing his pen at the back of the room.

"Nine thousand euros for a single case of wine!" Capucine exclaimed.

"*Chut*," Théophile hissed, rapt. He dropped his catalog on the floor, bent down, and used the gesture to attempt to see the bidder in the back. The young woman at the telephone table raised a well-manicured index finger.

"Nine and a half," Bertignac announced, then, without pause, pointed his pen at the rear of the room. "Ten!"

"It's an American," Théophile snorted, sitting back in his chair. "I've seen him at work. He's dangerous. He must be made of money." Théophile was pink with excitement.

Bertignac scanned the room over his glasses as avidly as a cormorant seeking out a fish. There was a long moment of silence.

He tapped the podium three times with his pen and stabbed it at the back of the room. "*Adjugé*. Sold."

The room deflated with a collective sigh, and broke out in muted conversations.

Three more lots went by. After each one Théophile's pinkness intensified. The white-gloved Savoyard placed a new case on the table as gently as if it were a newborn baby.

"*Doucement*. Carefully," Théophile muttered.

"Mesdames et messieurs, this is an exceptional lot," Bertignac announced. "The only nineteen eighty-four Bordeaux cru worth drinking. I've never tasted it myself, but since it's from the glorious Château Pétrus, it's bound to be highly interesting. Can I hear two and a half?"

"Over two hundred euros a bottle for a bad wine!" Capucine whispered.

"Nuance, a bad *great* wine." Théophile gripped his thighs so tightly, the tips of his fingers disappeared into the folds of his trousers. He was having a hard time restraining himself from making the first bid.

The room was heavy with the leaden silence of a church. A man cleared his throat in the back.

Bertignac pointed his pen. "One and a half." He shook

his head with a tolerant smile. "Mesdames et messieurs, this is Pétrus, not Beaujolais Nouveau." The room laughed politely.

A man at the phone table raised his hand, thumb and index outstretched.

"Voilà, two!" Bertignac said. "Greatness is finally given its due."

Théophile raised his finger so slightly, Capucine almost didn't see the gesture. But Bertignac thrust his pen at him.

"Two and a half."

Almost immediately his pen was jabbed at the back of the room.

"Three."

There were two beats of silence. Bertignac shot an inquiring glance at the telephone table. The young man shook his head. His bidder had dropped out.

Tiny beads of sweat appeared on Théophile's brow. He squeezed his thighs in a death grip. Bertignac invited him to bid with a cocked eyebrow.

Théophile stared straight ahead.

Bertignac shrugged his shoulders microscopically and tapped his pen loudly on the rostrum. "Going once!" He looked around the room. "Going tw—"

Théophile's hand rose to the level of his chin.

"Three!" Bertignac said with a defiant look at the back of the room. "And three and a half," he added, darting his pen at the back wall.

In a low voice Théophile said, "*Cinque.* Five."

There was no answering bid. Bertignac waited barely a second, not even looking at the back of the room, then tapped his pen three times. "Once. Twice. Sold," he said with the pen thrust at Théophile.

Théophile was in heaven. A woman walked over and handed him a slip of paper. A man in the row in front of them turned and shook his hand. Théophile got up to leave and bent over to whisper in Capucine's ear.

"If you breathe a word about this to Cécile, I'll . . . I'll . . . I don't know what I'll do . . . but just don't." Inflated with the pride of victory, he floated down the aisle toward the cashier's table.

Two more lots and it was over. People started to amble out. A line formed at the cashier's table. Capucine went over to the rostrum. Bertignac bent down, chatting in a low voice with one of the men at the telephone table. Capucine stood patiently until he had finished. He straightened and looked at Capucine over his glasses with eyebrows raised inquiringly.

"Commissaire Le Tellier."

"My apologies. I saw you with Monsieur de Rougemont and thought you might be here to bid. Let's go up to my office." He gave one more instruction to the man at the telephone table and began to make his way down the aisle, nodding, smiling, shaking the occasional hand.

The office was a treasure trove. Paintings filled every available inch of wall space. Silver and porcelain and faïence jostled each other for room on every flat surface.

"If I had an office like this, I'd never get any work done."

"It's one of the perks of the métier. All of this stuff will be gone in a month, so I don't get attached to it. My clients have enduring relationships. My lot is to have one-night stands. But at least I have a lot of them. And they're often of very high quality."

"On the phone you said you had some information on the Brault case."

Bertignac led Capucine to a long sixteenth-century mahogany *table de travail,* littered with morocco-bound books and bibelots.

He picked up what looked like a large, green faïence cachepot decorated with delicate long legged darker green herons and handed it to Capucine. "A sixteenth-century Menton *rafraîchissoir.*"

"Rafraîchissoir? It's not a cachepot? My mother has two that look almost like that. She puts plants in them."

Bertignac laughed. "That's why they sell so well. It's very refined to have an antique cachepot. A form of philistinism I encourage. But they were made to cool wine. Until the beginning of the nineteenth century people drank mostly rosé, and the upper classes, who had access to ice, preferred it slightly chilled. Normally, I'd start this one out at three thousand euros and expect the bidding to climb to five, maybe six, or seven at the most." He paused. "But this is a fake. I had to pull it from the sale at the last moment."

Capucine said nothing.

Bertignac put the rafraîchissoir back on the table.

"Monsieur Brault sent it to me the week before he died."

"Why did you wait until the last moment to remove it from the sale?"

"That's a bit embarrassing. You see, this is really an extraordinarily good forgery. The decorations are perfect, and the cracking of the glaze is very realistic, but it just didn't feel right. Maybe because the green background is just a bit too. And, of course, there's a dead giveaway." He turned the rafraîchissoir upside down on the table and pointed to a tiny black coat of arms on the base. "This is the Menton manufacturer's mark. If you look carefully . . . Wait. Let me get you a magnifying glass."

He handed Capucine an oversized well-worn wooden-handled magnifying glass. "Look at the mark diagonally against the light. See, it's slightly raised. That's because under the glaze there's a transfer *décalcomanie,* what children call a decal. Menton did use those for the decorations but never for the manufacturer's marks. Those were inked through a cutout template. There's no doubt this is a fake, but it's still an extraordinarily good one.

"Unfortunately, this sale was assembled by one of my

assistants while I was in the States. She's highly competent but still a bit new to the profession. And since it came from Brault, who was well known here, she, quite naturally, didn't think to give it a good going-over. Of course, the minute I laid eyes on it, I saw it was a fake."

"Was Brault a good customer?"

"He bought a few pieces from me over the years. He had a good eye and was very knowledgeable. Recently he had been selling far more than buying."

"And why would you guess Chef Brault tried to sell a forgery?"

"It's puzzling. It's hard to believe Brault ever bought a fake, even though this one looks almost authentic. So good that once it was on a shelf or in a display cabinet, even an experienced collector wouldn't have noticed something was wrong. Still, I just can't imagine how he acquired it in the first place."

Bertignac hesitated. There was something else he was wrestling with. "And I'll tell you another strange thing."

Capucine relaxed her face to encourage him.

"This is probably a violation of confidentiality, but under the circumstances it seems warranted. The catalog for this sale has been out for a week. One of the ways you can bid is with a pre-auction preemption. You bid a price, which the auctioneer keeps secret. If the bidding on the floor doesn't reach your price, you get the item. Do you understand how that works?"

Capucine nodded.

"Well, we received a pre-auction bid for ten thousand euros for this particular piece. I was very surprised, believe me."

"Now that *is* interesting. And who placed this bid?"

Bertignac furrowed his brow. "That's confidential." But as he said it, he was already pecking at the keyboard of his computer. He tilted his head back and made an exaggerated frown, peering at the screen though his half-glasses, moving his head back and forth, searching for the right focal distance. "Here are the personal details."

Capucine walked over to the computer and took out her notebook.

"Madame Chéri Lecomte. I know her. She has a stand at the Puces. Obviously, she doesn't buy pieces at Drouot to sell at the Puces, but she does acquire the odd item every now and then for her own collection. But never anything even as remotely expensive as what she bid."

CHAPTER 15

According to the police database, Chéri Lecomte owned and operated stand D-44 at the Marché Cambo. Capucine decided to pay an unannounced visit.

This time around Capucine noticed that the rows and stands were labeled with little white enamel plaques high up on the walls. Row D turned out to be the location of the Vuitton stand she had visited. A sixth sense told her Chéri Lecomte would turn out to be the woman in the red dress at the communal lunch.

Her sixth sense was absolutely right, but what it didn't prepare her for was being recognized.

"Commissaire Le Tellier, what brings you to my stand?"

Like starlets running into each other at a cocktail party, there was a three-beat pause as the two women examined each other's outfits. Today Lecomte wore a white ruffled-front silk blouse and a pearl-gray pencil skirt that Capucine suspected was Givenchy from an antique clothing boutique. The bright red soles throbbing from the front of the heels of her black pumps shouted they were Louboutins. With ruthlessly plucked eyebrows and pearly white teeth beaconing from behind plump carmine-red lips, she had the radiantly healthy bloom of a sixties pinup. Capucine felt invulnerable in the elegance of her new pale blue silk suit by Rochas. And her dark blue Sergio Rossi slingbacks were way more attractive than those tacky Louboutins.

Capucine smiled sweetly. "How is it you know who I am?"

"The Marché Biron is a tiny village. It's news if anyone sneezes. And when a commissaire of the Police Judiciaire turns up, well . . ."

"Then you must be aware I'm investigating the death of Jean-Louis Brault."

"Of course. How could we not spend all day gossiping about a celebrity who turns up dead in a trunk from our neck of the Puces?" Lecomte said with a laugh.

Capucine was again struck with the difficulty of pigeon-holing Lecomte. It wasn't just the retro look. Even though her French was faultless and perfectly idiomatic, there was something unmistakably foreign about her. Maybe it was just that she seemed so out of place at her stand. In any event, Capucine was forced to concede she was a strikingly attractive woman.

"I hope I'm not going to disappoint you, but other than gossip, I don't know anything at all about that trunk or how Chef Brault happened to be in it."

"Actually, I'm here about something else. I understand you placed a pre-auction bid on a Menton rafraîchissoir at Drouot. Can we talk about that?"

Lecomte was momentarily taken aback. "How did you hear about that?"

"I was alerted that the piece had been sent to Drouot by Chef Brault just before he died."

"Oh my God!" She seemed genuinely surprised. "I had no idea. It says 'private collection' in the catalog."

"So it does. The interesting thing is that it turns out that the piece is a fake."

Lecomte's pencil-thin eyebrows rose almost to her hair-line.

"It's been removed from the auction," Capucine added.

"How odd. I didn't know that. I never met Brault, but I knew of his reputation as a collector. I wouldn't have thought he'd be easy to fool." She paused, thinking. "When I saw the piece on display at Drouot, it was in a glass-covered case behind several other pieces, but it shouted out to me. Love at first sight. I just had to have it."

"Wouldn't it have made more sense to go to the auction instead of making an exorbitant preemptive bid?"

"Of course it would have, but the auction is next Monday and the Puces is open then, so I had to be here. Sadly, only bigwigs get to bid by phone. You know the song, sometimes you just have to follow your heart no matter where it takes you. Anyway, money certainly isn't every-thing, and I really, really wanted that rafraîchissoir."

"I understand your bid was for over twice the estimate of the piece."

"I thought the estimate was way low. The decoration was very delicate. Did you see it? Delicate, long-legged herons with long, sensuously curved beaks. And the glaze was green, which is extremely rare for Menton. It's a fab—" She realized she was babbling and cut herself off.

"We were talking about your bid on that Menton rafraîchissoir. Why did you want it so much?"

"I told you. I fell in love with it. With that green deco-ration, the delicacy of the brushwork, it was almost unique. We women are entitled to be a little foolish about love every once in a while. Women's prerogative and all."

Lecomte beamed a toothy smile that shone out like a lighthouse on a stormy night through her dark lips. She raised her arms and pivoted, indicating her wares. "And faïence is my love. I live and breathe it."

A couple walked in, obviously American in their puffy down jackets, and smiled at Lecomte's gesture. They looked around the stand, respectfully taking great care not to touch anything. The woman stopped, riveted in front of a large four-footed terrine decorated with very detailed flowers: pastel pink roses and bright yellow buttercups.

"Look at this, honey," the woman said in English.

The husband went up to her, clearly already bored by the stand.

"See, the handles on the sides are leopards, and the handle on the lid is a cute little fish. And look how real the roses look."

The man gave a cursory look.

"Oh, honey, this would be perfect as a centerpiece for our dining room table."

Her husband did not reply.

Lecomte sidled up and said heartily in perfect, unaccented English, "It would make *anyone's* dining room." As if she thought she had gone overboard, she continued on more quietly. "It comes from the Fabrique de la Veuve Perrin," she continued, rolling the *r*'s of "Perrin" with an almost caricatural French accent. It dates from seventeen sixty and is one of the earliest examples of the *petit feu* technique."

The man looked at her with interest.

"You see, prior to the mid-eighteenth century the decoration was applied to porous clay, which soaked it right in. So it had to be simple, and the only really good color they had was blue, which is why so much older faïence is blue on white. And they needed a really hot kiln, the *grand feu*."

The woman continued to devour the terrine with her eyes. The husband seemed fascinated by the technology.

"So what happened then?" he asked.

"They developed new glazes. A first coat was baked on so the decoration could be painted onto a nonporous surface. That's how they got all the wonderful detail in the roses on this piece. And the glaze that went on top of that would harden at a lower heat—what they called a *petit feu*—so they could use more glazes and get a full range of colors. Look at the color nuances in the flowers."

"Oh, honey, the seventeen hundreds!" the woman said.

"It's an awesome piece," Lecomte said with her broad American accent. "And I'll give you a hella good deal."

"Are you from California?" the man asked.

Lecomte blushed. "No, I'm French, but I went to California a lot when I was a kid."

"It shows in some of the words you use. But your English is just about perfect. I like it when foreigners know how to speak English. Say, how much are you asking for this?"

"Oh, honey, I can so absolutely see this in our dining room."

The man gave her a stern look. He was getting down to business.

"Because I like you guys so much and you clearly love the piece, I'll give you my rock-bottom price, five thousand euros."

The man's face was so immobile, it was clear he was taken aback. Capucine, once again attentively examining a display case, guessed he would get it for thirty-five hundred.

The man said nothing for several long beats, while his wife looked at him with pleading sheep's eyes.

"Do you take American Express?"

"Of course, monsieur."

"Then you got yourself a deal, young lady," he said with a broad smile, sticking out his hand to shake Lecomte's.

This time the sale was wrapped lovingly in three layers of bubble wrap and then carefully swathed in brown paper, which was gently taped and tied with purple string.

The couple left, the woman with the beatific smile of a young girl who had received her first porcelain doll as a Christmas gift, and the husband with the tight-lipped, virtuous grin of a good soldier who has done right by his family. Capucine could easily imagine them that evening at the Tour d'Argent, eating the fabled pressed duck, watching the setting sun paint a rosy backdrop behind Notre Dame, rejoicing in the thought of finally getting back to Fort Wayne with their trophies.

CHAPTER 16

The brigadier at the front desk called, sounding very put out. "It's that commissaire whatever guy again. I called him Monsieur le Commissaire, and he laughed at me."

"*Allô*, Madame Le Tellier? I have another object I think is going to interest you," Bertignac said.

"And you're going to insist I come to Drouot to examine it."

"Pas du tout. One of our porters is already on his way up to you. It's not an antique, just an old leather jotting pad. But, given the monogram, it's not impossible that it belonged to Chef Brault."

"How did you come by it?"

"One of the stand holders in the Marché de la rue Jean-Henri Fabre down at the Puces—you know, where they sell the secondhand clothes and stolen car radios—found it in a Loden coat he bought with a bunch of other clothes. The pad had my card in it, so he called me. When he described the gold monogram on the back with a *B* surmounted by a crown, I was happy to give him twenty euros for it. I know I should have alerted you, but if a flic showed up, the pad would have disappeared."

"I'm very grateful, and of course, the police will reimburse your outlay."

"Why don't you come to one of my auctions and buy something pricey instead?" he said with a laugh.

When Bertignac hung up, Capucine buzzed the front desk and told the brigadier to get forensics to come and pick up something for examination.

"Yes, Commissaire. And there's a guy here in some sort of uniform with a package for you that he says he has to deliver to you in person."

A red-collared Savoyard from Drouot handed her a thick manila envelope, bowed smartly, and left.

Inside the envelope she found an ordinary self-sealing kitchen bag with Bertignac's elegantly engraved business card paper-clipped to the top. There was a note in green fountain-pen ink on the front of the card.

Commissaire,
   The provenance of this piece is Amid Al-Risha, Marché de la rue Jean-Henri Fabre, Stand BB-34. Cell phone: 06 72 31 29. Hope it's of some use.
   Cordially,
   B. de Bertignac

The plastic bag contained a very old, scuffed and scarred black-leather jotting pad that had long lost its original sheen. The corners were trimmed in what looked like solid gold. There was no paper on the front of the pad, but the slot on the back was overly full enough to make it look potbellied. In the exact center of the paunch was a large gold-leaf monogram that had almost worn away. The design was so convoluted, Capucine would never have recognized it as a capital *B* unless Bertignac had alerted her. A gold crown in the shape of an unadorned band with a string of pearls wrapped around it surmounted the monogram.

Capucine opened the center drawer of her desk, dug through the disorder until she found a Swiss Army knife, rooted some more, and snapped on a pair of latex gloves she drew out of a pop-up box.

She zipped open the plastic bag, dumped out the pad, and gently squeezed the ends with the middle finger and thumb of her left hand. Ten or so pieces of paper of various sizes and colors fell out on the desk. With the large blade of the pocket knife she arranged them in two neat rows. There were five business cards: Bertignac's, that of an antique dealer who specialized in faïence in the Sixth Arrondissement, and those of three suppliers of kitchen equipment. There was no doubt in Capucine's mind that this had belonged to Brault.

There were also six scraps of paper, some folded in half, some in four. Capucine dug through the contents of the drawer and found a letter opener. She carefully unfolded the bits of paper with her two tools. Four were ragged-edged, square-ruled pages torn from ring-bound notebooks, and the other two were scraps of what could have been copier or printer paper. All were covered with the author's personal shorthand, written in an introvert's left-sloping cursive. The shorthand was easy enough to decipher once one knew food would be the central topic: there were rough ideas for recipes and lists of produce that needed to be ordered. Only one defied comprehension. *Vieillard, Bordeaux, BV rafr. V 8—*. Capucine guessed it was some wine or other Brault wanted the sommelier to obtain.

Capucine picked up her phone and pressed the speed dial for Momo.

"Momo, I need you to go back to the Puces. Go see someone called Amid Al-Risha, in Marché de la rue Jean-Henri Fabre. He's at stand BB-thirty-four. He found a jotting pad in some clothes he bought. The pad is probably Brault's. First prize would be getting those clothes. Second prize would be finding out who sold them to Al-Risha. Oh, and don't forget to print him."

There was a polite knock on her office door.

"*Entrez,*" Capucine said loudly.

A very young, clean-cut man stuck his head around the partially opened door and then slipped in diffidently, carrying a large square aluminum case by its handle, obviously the forensics technician. When he saw the pile on Capucine's desk, his eyes opened wide in horror. His thought was as clear as if he had yelled it: *A crass police officer has been pawing through evidence.* A solecism so grave, it was beyond comprehension.

Capucine smiled at him sweetly. "Please bundle all this up and take it down to your lab. Print it very carefully."

The technician choked back a retort and extracted rubber gloves and two pairs of tweezers, flat ended as platypus bills, from his case. With great care he placed the scraps of paper and the jotting pad in separate plastic bags. With a reproachful look at Capucine, he made for the door.

"Ajudant. I need you to e-mail me photos of the pad and its contents this afternoon."

"I doubt very much, Commissaire, we'll be able to get to it 'til tomorrow. Maybe not even 'til Monday."

"Five today, at the latest," Capucine barked.

The technician recoiled, set his face, and marched out of the office.

Capucine sat for a long moment, staring out the window, unseeing. Snapping herself out of her reverie, she dialed her mother's number.

"Allô, Maman? Do you have a minute?"

"A minute, ma chérie? I have a whole life for you. Is this more about heraldry?"

"Someone turned in one of those leather jotting pads, which I think might have belonged to Jean-Louis Brault. It has a heraldic monogram on the back, but it's very different from the crest on the chevalière."

"What does it look like?"

"There's a very elaborate initial that's hard to make out. It could be a *B*, but I'm not a hundred percent sure. And there's a coronet on top. But this one is not at all like the one on the chevalière. Instead of having pearls stuck on top, there's a string of pearls that has been wrapped around and around the coronet."

"It might or might not be Brault's. I'd have to see it."

"I can stop by after work and show you a picture, if that's good for you."

The next morning Capucine arrived at the brigade an hour later than usual, wearing a long-sleeved silk blouse under her coat. The blouse served to cover a large, multi-hued hematoma on the underside of her left forearm.

The evening before, she had supervised the arrest of a serial rapist who had abused three women he had apparently followed from different stops on the Number 3 metro line as it passed through the Twentieth Arrondissement. The lieutenant in charge of the case was positive the perp, particularly punctilious in his tastes, rode the line each evening between nine thirty and ten thirty in search of tall, small-breasted, svelte, short-haired brunettes in their early twenties. He would follow his victims out of the station and attack as soon as they reached a dimly lit street.

The arrest plan involved over half of the brigade's roster, with officers posted at all seven of the Line 3 stops in the Twentieth, lieutenants at the République and Gallieni stops at either end of the arrondissement, and Capucine in the exact middle, at the Père Lachaise station. As it happened, that night's intended victim had emerged from the Père Lachaise station.

The suspect had been arrested smoothly as he closed in

on the girl in a badly lit passageway between two buildings. Hands cuffed behind his back, resignedly passive, the man was held by the arms as the officers waited for the van to arrive. Slight framed and stoop shouldered, he looked for all the world like a meek low-level accountant. Capucine, who was enraged by rape far more than any other crime, had stepped up to peer into his face to see if there was any reflection of degeneracy in his eyes. With blinding speed he had aimed a savate kick at her head. Capucine's parrying forearm had received the full force of the blow.

Her officers had insisted on taking her to an emergency room, where she had been x-rayed, given an envelope of meticulously counted-out high-powered painkillers, and sent home.

The morning drive to the brigade had started her arm throbbing, so she had taken two of the pills before walking in. She was decidedly lightheaded by the time she sat down at her desk.

The evening before, the forensics technician had sent an e-mail with two attachments. The first was a preliminary report on the jotting pad. They had found multiple prints from Jean-Louis Brault, Amid Al-Risha, and Bertrand de Bertignac, but no others. Capucine assumed that Bertignac's prints were in the police system because they had been taken when he had applied for his commissaire-priseur license. Forensics had also concluded that the handwriting was Brault's. The second attachment was a series of five extremely detailed pictures of the jotting pad.

That was that. The jotting pad was Brault's, but it didn't tell her anything. The only possible lead could come from what Momo had discovered. And that was—

The phone rang. Capucine's mother was on the line. The receptionist had put her straight through.

"*Alors,*" said Capucine's mother, "has my daughter become too busy or too forgetful to remember her promises to her mother?"

"Oh, pardon, Maman. It got so hectic last evening, I completely forgot. Anyway, forensics has identified the jotting pad as definitely having been Brault's." As Capucine spoke, she had the delicious sensation of floating out of her body and looking down at herself.

"I could have spared them the effort. I did some research last night and—"

"Maman, if it would interest you, I could send you some pictures."

Capucine was vaguely aware she had made a tactical error.

"Send them to me? You know La Poste isn't as reliable as it used to be. I wouldn't get them until tomorrow at the earliest, maybe not even until next week. You need to be more diligent in your work. You have a position of responsibility now—"

Capucine felt delightfully pleased with herself. No wonder people became addicted to painkillers. Oblivious to her own wants, she blundered on. "Maman, what if you came down here for lunch? I could show you around the brigade, you could have a look at the pictures, and then we could have a quick bite." The altruistic words were delectable in Capucine's mouth. Anyway, she was certain her mother would refuse.

"*Parfait.* I'll be there at twelve."

Momo was halfway through his report; Isabelle made notes in a spiral notebook; David played with his hair; Capucine sat back in her chair with her legs on the table, nodding at Momo's points. The painkillers had metabolized, her arm was throbbing, and she was developing a ferocious headache.

"Those guys don't have stands. They just have a folding

table and a wire cage behind. They buy junk. Old radios and TVs. Rags that used to be clothes. The gelt comes from the hot stuff, boosted car radios and crap that 'fell off a truck.' Our boy Amid tried to get me to believe an old woman whose husband had just died brought in a pile of old clothes, and when he went through the pockets—"

"Brave man," interjected David.

"He found the notepad. Since a jotting pad with gold corners is not what you usually find in a bunch of rags, I had to, uh, challenge him a little."

"Was he cooperative?" Capucine asked.

"Commissaire, if you mean did I have to rough him up, the answer is no. But I did tell him that I was very busy, and if he didn't tell me something useful pretty quick, I was going to stick him in the brigade lockup, and it might take me a day or two to find the time to listen to what he had to say. He got the message. Some homeless guy came up to him with a whole outfit, shoes and all. Says the bum found them in a dumpster out behind the Marché Biron. That sounds reasonable enough to me. He said there was no wallet, just the notepad, a few coins, and two plastic ballpoint pens. He put the clothes on his table, and they were sold five minutes after he opened up. I believe that, too. And, of course, he has no idea who this bum is. I also believe that."

"What happened to the pens?" Isabelle asked.

Before Momo could answer, the office door opened and a uniformed officer stuck his head in.

"Madame Le Tellier is here to see you, Commissaire. She says she has an appointment."

Before Capucine could take her legs off the table and sit up, her mother pushed past the officer into the room. The four detectives stood up. For a split second the three brigadiers—who had never met Capucine's mother—thought that some terrible tragedy must have occurred. They eased toward the door.

Capucine stopped them and introduced her mother ceremoniously. David—with his love of histrionics—played a role that more than made up for Isabelle's and Momo's reticence. He executed a perfect *baisemain*—a hand kiss performed with bent waist, lips stopping an inch before contact with skin was made. Capucine's mother was charmed.

"I had no idea such elegant people were in the police. Let's bring them along to lunch. I'd love to get to know your coworkers."

"Madame," David said, "I would be enchanted."

Capucine glared at him. Amazingly, both Isabelle and Momo seemed to like the idea. Isabelle's face relaxed, and Momo's frown became less severe.

Capucine, however, was close to panic. Keeping a *cordon sanitaire* between her private and professional lives was of the utmost importance. Her worst nightmare was having it known in the force that, by virtue of her marriage to Alexandre, she was a countess. If her brigadiers started calling her Madame la Comtesse behind her back, she'd quit the police. And, snob that her mother was, there was a real risk she would spill the beans.

Capucine made another miscalculation. Convinced a proletarian atmosphere would intimidate her mother into silence, she took them to Benoît's, around the corner.

To Capucine's chagrin, her mother adored the restaurant. Angélique, resplendent in her corpulence, greeted them warmly at the door, made much of Madame Le Tellier, herded them to a table in the middle of the room, scolded Capucine for not having brought her mother sooner, and itemized a long list of physiognomic similarities between the two women. Only when Capucine's ears were quite red did Angélique dictate what they would be having for lunch: *tripes à la mode de Caen* for the men and *médaillons de veau* for the women. Naturally, they would be drinking the house Tavel.

"Such fun!" said Capucine's mother, genuinely delighted. "It takes me back to my student days. I used to eat in a restaurant just like this one, right down to the napkins in cubbyholes."

Lunch started out with a large dented metal serving dish on which were laid out rolled slices of *jambon de Paris,* tranches of three kinds of pâté, and a heap of tiny cornichons. An equally dented wire basket, filled to overflowing with slices of baguette, was placed beside it. Capucine was sure her mother would be horrified by the plebian nature of the appetizer, but, no, she loved it all and even took seconds of the cornichons.

"I just adore these. We never have them at home. I'm going to make sure Yvonne starts buying them." Capucine offered a prayer to her guardian angel that her mother would not find it necessary to explain that Yvonne was the cook and that there was also a majordomo, a full-time maid, and a part-time laundress.

Over-brightly, Capucine said, "Maman, it's wonderful you could come today. Otherwise you wouldn't have met Brigadier Martineau. He's leaving for the Midi on Saturday to start an investigation down there."

"That is, if my boss, Brigadier-Chef Lemercier, lets me go. She's a very hard taskmaster," David said with a charming smile.

Isabelle gave him a black look.

"Oh, you must let him go, Brigadier-Chef. This is the perfect season for the Midi. The tourists have all gone, and it's still warm enough for the beach in the middle of the day."

"Madame, he's not going to be on any beach. I can guarantee you that," Isabelle said sourly.

"And are you my daughter's boss, as well, my dear?"

Isabelle was at a complete loss for a reply.

David gently placed his hand on top of Madame Le Tellier's. Capucine was sure she would leap like a gaffed salmon, but she smiled as warmly at David, as if he were a young nephew.

"We all report to your daughter, madame. She's *our* boss," David said.

"Maybe next time we could bring Capucine's superior, as well. I'd very much like to meet him."

"Madame," Momo said in his growling bass, "I don't think you get it. Your daughter is a commissaire. *She's* the big boss. All fifty-seven of us in the brigade are under her orders. And I'll tell you another thing." He leaned over the table to lend weight to his words. Taken aback by Momo's sheer mass, Capucine's mother recoiled slightly. "She's the best goddamn flic any of us have ever seen. And I'll tell you one more thing. She's going to be running the whole goddamn force before she's done."

Momo downed his half glass of Tavel in one go and thumped it down on the table to emphasize his point.

Capucine's mother inflated with pride.

CHAPTER 17

La Cadière-d'Azur turned out to be not too different from the village he had grown up in. Both were in the hills, a few miles from the coast, dotted with Parisians' fancy summer homes.

The village hotel was exactly what he expected: five rooms over a café, a single shower, and two Turkish toilets at the end of the hall. There were no pillows on the bed, only a hard upholstered roll with the bottom sheet wrapped around it. He hated those things. They gave him a crick in the neck.

The café, Le Marius, was like every other small village café in the Midi: ten or so tables, big glass windows looking out over the town square, long dark-wood bar in front of a thin row of bottles up against a fly-specked gray mirror.

David propped himself up on the bar and replied "Pastis" to the barman's querying eyebrow. *Merde*, the first time he opened his mouth, it had to be a big mistake. No one in the Midi called it pastis. That was Paris talk. Down here the closest you ever came was to call it *pastaga*. Usually you said something like "Fifty-one," one of the better known brands.

Hoping to recover from his gaffe, David took a small, square-ruled, spiral-bound Clairefontaine notebook out of his pocket, snapped off the rubber band that held it shut, and began to scribble. He was proud of the prop, which he felt sure was exactly the sort of thing a writer would have.

The only other patron was a thickset man, with a sun-baked face and work-stiffened hands, sitting at a table, his arms wrapped defensively around a glass of rosé, chin jutting out in an aggressive angle at the square. David picked up the square water pitcher that had been delivered with his drink and poured a thin stream into the glass. For the millionth time he admired the miracle of the clear golden pastis turning opaque and milky white.

Gradually the bar filled up and became thick with singsong meridional patois and tobacco fug. David continued to scribble nonsense in his notebook. In the mirror he could see the men casting glances at him out of the corners of their eyes: two parts hostility to one part curiosity.

Just as David was thinking about ordering his second apéro, an older man, who looked like he might be the elder of the village, walked up to the bar, his distance from David nicely calculated: not close enough to be an invasion of David's territory but close enough to indicate a desire to talk. David closed his notebook and snapped on the rubber band with a loud snick.

The man looked at him over droopy haws as mournful as a basset hound's. "*Hè bè, l'été n'est bien pas fini. Ça va cogner aujourd'hui.* Well, summer sure isn't over yet. It's going to be hot as hell today." The *hè bè* was a locution of emphasis so Provençal, it made David long for his village. Even though the conversation in the café continued loudly, David was well aware that everyone in the room had an ear cocked at them.

"*Hè bè, oui. C'est pour ça qu'on aime le pays, non?* Of course. That's why we love it here, isn't it?" David replied, unleashing the Provençal accent he tried so hard to repress in Paris.

"So you're from around here, *estranger?*" the man asked, using the Provençal word for *stranger.*

"Not at all. I'm from St. Jean de l'Esterel."

The man looked at him blankly.

"It's behind Cannes, up in the hills."

"A *Cannois,* eh?" He gave David a long searching look. David held his gaze without wavering. "You look like a *Parigot,* a Parisian. And the Var is a long way from the Alpes Maritimes. What good wind blew you to La Cadière?"

The conversation at the tables had become murmurs. A stranger outside of the tourist season who didn't look like he was selling farm machinery was almost unheard of.

"I'm an author. I write biographies. And I'm writing one about Chef Jean-Louis Brault." David let this sink in and stuck out his hand. "David Martineau," he said with a politician's smile.

The old man looked at him levelly and did not extend his hand. The abruptness of the proposed handshake was an imposition, but, then, so was asking an estranger what his business was. If the old man refused to take the hand, he would give offense and he might come to regret that later. But if he didn't refuse, he would lose face. He thought it over for a few beats and then grasped David's hand in a grip like a hare trap. He looked at the barman.

"A *cent deux,* Félix."

"A cent deux"—a hundred and two—was patois for "two glasses of Pastis Fifty-one."

David nodded his thanks.

"Come drink this with us," the old man said, using the familiar *tu* and indicating his table with a tilt of his head.

At the table, the old man introduced his three companions with juts of his chin, Félix, Piquoiseau, and Le Bosco. "And they call me Césariot," the man said.

"So, Le Cannois," Piquoiseau said, "you think you're

going to find out all about Jean-Louis Brault's life down here, do you?"

"Cannois," Le Bosco said, "no one down here has seen the Brault boy since he left when he was . . . what? Sixteen?"

"Fifteen," Félix corrected.

"I know that. My book is going to start with his childhood. It's going to explain how Brault's genius germinated in the smells of the wild herbs in the hills of La Cadière-d'Azur."

The men at the table glanced at each other out of the corners of their eyes and repressed grins.

"I want to find out all about his childhood. Was he a gifted cook even as a small boy? What did he like to eat at home? Who were his friends? Did he have a girlfriend? You know, stuff like that."

At the word *girlfriend* the four men at the table exchanged sharper glances. Césariot drew his lips into a frowning moue.

Changing the subject, Le Bosco turned to the elder and said, "*Hè bè,* Césariot, I hear tell these Cannois are not completely useless when it comes to boules."

"Do you play?" Césariot asked David.

"Do I breathe?" The question had been rhetorical. What man in the Midi didn't live to toss steel balls into the dust in the cool of the evening? The mood softened a tiny notch.

"What you want to do is go see the baron," Césariot said. "If you can understand him, you might just learn something about his son. When you've done that, come back so we can see if the Cannois live up to their reputation. But don't get your hopes up. You might wind up buying the pastaga tonight."

The noon Angelus rang slowly from the single bell in the church belfry. Three strokes. A pause. Three more strokes. And three more again, until the count of nine was reached. The men fell silent, counting, and then rose almost as a single person to go home and eat the meal their women had prepared for them. David sat alone in the café.

Three hours later, after a solitary meal—a *daube de canard,* a stew of wild duck marinated in white wine and then simmered for hours in a bath of broth, brown Niçoise olives, and orange zest—David walked up the hard-earth road to the town's château.

It wasn't much of a place. The iron gate was long gone from the crumbling stone archway. In the distance he could see the château, a small abandoned building pretentiously decorated with pseudo-Gothic crenellations, now gap-toothed, the façade ruined by blind eye sockets of frameless windows. The weed-choked land between the gate and the château was dotted with small, cheap, disintegrating prefab bungalows.

David banged on the cracked oak door of the gatehouse. Even through the thick door the television was painfully loud. There was no answer. He shouted. Still no answer. He pounded continually on the door with the heel of his fist. After a very long wait, the door opened. The din from the TV hit him like a falling wall.

An emaciated man in shapeless olive corduroy trousers bald at the knees blinked at him, working his jaws as if he was trying to chew gum on the sly. David knew he was fretting badly fitting false teeth.

"Monsieur le Baron?" David asked.

There was no reply.

David yelled his question. "I called from the village an hour ago, remember? I'm the author writing a biography of your son."

The baron looked confused. "Jean-Louis? Is he all right?" A tear rolled down his cheek. He took a none-too-clean, balled-up handkerchief from his side pocket and blotted the tear. Without a word he turned and walked into the house. David followed him.

There was a single room on the main floor. A threadbare Persian rug with a hole worn in the middle lay on a grimy floor of cracked black-and-white tiles. The few pieces of furniture all dated from the early nineteenth century but were broken and crudely repaired. On a dining table with buckled veneer and a fractured leg nailed back together sat three large faïence vases. All three had been broken, and the pieces glued by an unskilled hand. The noise from the television was far louder than a discothèque. David switched the set off. The sudden silence rang in the room.

The baron collapsed into a dusty Louis XVI *fauteuil* and waved David toward a rattan settee. Most of the rattan was missing. David sat on the edge of the frame.

"I've come to talk to you about your son," David yelled.

"There's no need to shout, my good man. I can hear you perfectly. I'm assuming you mean poor Jean-Louis. I haven't seen his brother, Antonin, in years and can't imagine why an author would have any interest in him. But Jean-Louis, now there's an exceptional son."

Over the next few hours the ball of handkerchief was in constant use as the baron rambled on about his son. Like a pointillist painter the baron flitted from one topic to another, from one era to another, but, in the end, the picture that emerged made up in depth what it lacked in clarity.

The baron's wife had died of cervical cancer when Jean-Louis was five. Shortly after her death the baron had been cheated out of his house and lands by an unscrupulous developer in a failed deal. He had managed to hang on to the gatehouse. He had gradually sold off his father's collection of faïence. All that was left were the three pieces on the table, which no one wanted to buy since Antonin had broken them in a fit of rage and Jean-Louis, then age six, had glued them back together, hoping his father would not notice. At this point the story paused for a full minute as the handkerchief was put to use.

The baron had always been a keen gardener and had been able to feed his boys on his produce. Without Jean-Louis, who had been a gifted cook even as a child, it might have been monotonous. But Jean-Louis made every meal a feast. More handkerchief. The harvest of his sweet red Midi asparagus, for example, lasted over two months, and they were on the table every night. But Jean-Louis made a different dish every meal. The handkerchief came out again. There was a summer salad Jean-Louis would make from fresh asparagus, summer squash, new potatoes, and one or two pinches of duck gizzard confit, the whole sprinkled with a few drops of olive oil.

"And this, monsieur, from the hands of an eight-year-old boy!" The handkerchief stayed in use for a full two minutes. "Even though we had no money, we had our family honor and our pride, and we were very happy. Very."

The baron proved as persistent as a leaky but valiant steam engine. At six, the evening Angelus rang out its stately nine strokes, reminding David of his promise to show off his prowess at boules. He rose to leave. The baron blinked in alarm. David turned on the television and rotated the dial to maximum volume. The thundering sound and flickering image mesmerized the baron so completely, David doubted his departure was noticed.

Two tables in front of the café had been pushed together. Five men sipped pastis and watched David cross the dusty square with his fluid gait. The sun was low in the sky, and the temperature had begun to drop, drawing in the odors of grasses and wild herbs from the hills. The cymbal rasping of cicadas had quieted, leaving the square in silence.

"Alors, Le Cannois," Césariot threw out, "you managed to escape from Monsieur le Baron?"

There was a peal of raucous laughter. It was obvious they had started on the apéros sometime before. In addition to Césariot, Le Bosco, and Piquoiseau, there were two men David didn't know. Césariot introduced them: Ungolin and Le Papet.

"Did he make you take a flat of his famous Thermidrome onions, the pride of the Midi?" Le Papet asked. There was another shout of laughter.

"Enough of that," Césariot said. "We're wasting daylight. I propose Piquoiseau and Le Bosco team up with me, and Le Cannois can play with Ungolin and Le Papet." There were grunts of assent as the men downed their drinks and moved out onto the powdery, cement-hard earth of the square.

Ungolin presented David with a much-dented set of three boules, which must have sat under the counter of the bar for the use of estrangers since well before the Second World War.

"They've never liked Le Baron here. They didn't like his father either. The old baron pissed his fortune away on the French attempt at the Panama Canal. His son was even stupider and lost the little that was left," Ungolin said confidentially to David.

"Alors, Ungolin, are we here to play *pétanque* or to gossip like old women?" Césariot said. He flipped a ten-euro coin high in the air with his thumb, caught it, and slapped it on the back of his wrist. "Heads or tails?"

Ungolin picked tails and won the toss. He drew a three-foot circle in the dust with a stick, stood in the middle, ankles together, and tossed the *cochonnet*—a small wooden ball—out into the dust.

"You go first," Ungolin said to David.

David stepped into the circle, sank down on bended knees until his buttocks almost touched his heels, holding the boule loosely, arm straight down, the back of his hand facing the cochonnet. In a single fluid motion he rose, hoisting his arm forward for the throw, at the last second imparting a hint of forward spin on the boule with his thumb. The boule rose high in the air, landed an inch in front of the cochonnet, and rolled gently until it just kissed the little ball. A perfect shot.

The five men exchanged covert glances. With a smirk, Piquoiseau muttered, "Beginner's luck."

Césariot's team retreated a few feet away to discuss their strategy.

"But don't get me wrong," Ungolin said. "The Baron had a hard row to hoe with his wife gone and no money. He did his best to bring his boys up. And he had his work cut out for him. That Antonin was a bad egg from the beginning. A born *voyou*—a delinquent—he hot-wired cars so many times for joyrides, the gendarmes would go straight to him every time a car was missing. They'd keep him a night in the *cabane* and then let him go without booking him."

"Anou did it only because the food in the gendarmerie detention cell was better than what he got at home. At least it had some meat in it," Le Papet said with a smoker's gurgling laugh.

Ungolin stepped into the circle and attempted to duplicate David's shot. His boule landed a foot away from the cochonnet.

"What happened to Antonin?" David asked.

"One day he disappeared," Ungolin said, flicking his fingers open into the sky. "No one knows why, but good riddance. Probably finally did something bad enough he knew the gendarmes wouldn't be letting him go in the morning. Bound to be a mechanic somewhere. He knew cars. Or at least he knew how to start them without a key."

The group chortled.

"Funny how the two boys were so different," David said.

"That they were," Césariot said.

"Little Jean-Louis was as shy as a goat kid, always hugging the walls when he walked through the village," Le Bosco said.

"That was because he didn't have a woman to bring him up when he was little. No man can grow up normal without a woman's tender hand to help him," Le Papet said. The men all nodded in reverence at this truism, despite the fact that the presence of the fair sex in the café and its environs was unthinkable.

The play continued for another two hours. The last shot was David's. As he rocked back and forth, pivoting on his ankles, his arm swinging like the pendulum of a grandfather clock, he felt a wave of perfect contentment wash over him like the warm surf of a Provençal beach. He rose in the liquid release of a loosely coiled spring and launched the boule, sending it off with backspin from his fingertips. It landed seven inches behind the cochonnet and rolled gently backward. From where David stood, it was the same distance from the cochonnet as Césariot's boule.

The men bent over the cochonnet in a huddle. Ungolin produced a twig and measured the distances with the care of a surgeon performing a brain operation. David's boule was microscopically closer, but still unquestionably the winning boule. It was a shutout: Ungolin's team had beaten Césariot's thirteen to nothing.

"We're going to make them kiss Fanny's ass!" Ungolin shouted, giving David a warm hug. "And they're going to buy us so much pastaga, they'll have to take us home in wheelbarrows." He was overjoyed. A shutout was something that almost never happened in pétanque.

Inside the bar Ungolin, as excited as a small child on a sugar high, rushed up to a well-patinated wooden box hanging on the wall and hysterically rang a small brass bell attached to the side, yelling, "They're going to kiss Fanny's ass. How sweet it is. They're going to kiss the relic!"

To loud shouts and much laughter, the two portals of the box were opened to reveal a woman painted in a crude naïve style bending forward, lifting her skirt and frilly petticoat to expose ample and shapely buttocks of plaster bas-relief. One by one the three men from the losing team went up and ceremoniously kissed the painting to choruses of loud ribald cheering. Drinks were at the expense of the losers.

Césariot brought David his pastis. "I guess it must be true. You Cannois do have a bit of talent at boules. I guess some of our Provençal blood must have flowed your way. Do you also have the tradition?"

"Absolutely. In my village we have an almost identical box on the wall, but I've never seen it used."

"Of course you haven't. You're all too good at the game. Or maybe the sun is too hot out there for you to have a taste for Fanny's ass," Ungolin said.

There was a soft rumble of sly laughter. David had been excluded from an inside joke. In a gesture of apology to the estranger, Césariot patted him on the back but didn't explain the joke.

CHAPTER 18

The banner headline of *Le Figaro* read FIRMIN ROQUE—HERO OF THE FRENCH COMMUNIST PARTY—DIES TRAGICALLY. It was not surprising the headline went across all eight columns. Roque had been an icon of the Party, an institution that, even though now toothless and backward looking, had once been a vibrant force on the French political scene.

It was the large box that took up most of page one above the fold that caught Capucine's eye: portraits of the five key individuals in Roque's worker-run and worker-owned company, with brief bios underneath. The face in the middle was Thierry Brissac-Vanté's, considerably younger, his hair curlier, his smile pearlier, looking even more like an empty-headed playboy.

The uniformed receptionist, who also served as her secretary, knocked on the door. "Commissaire, don't forget you have your weekly review with the lieutenants in five minutes."

"Push it back half an hour. Something's come up."

"Oui, Commissaire."

The reason for the big box filled with pictures was that there was no real information on Roque's death. All that was known was that he and his wife had gone out to a local bistro for dinner. When they came home, the lights wouldn't turn on, so Roque had gone down to the basement with a flashlight and was electrocuted as he inserted a new fuse. That was it. No commentary from the local gendarmes. Nothing other than a tearful quote from the wife, who, the reporter assured the reader, was "hysterical with grief."

Capucine sipped her coffee, now cold. Much had been made of Roque at Sciences Po. It had been quite a story, the archetypal liberation and revival of a dying business by its workers.

The Faïence de Châteauneuf-sur-Loire, an ancient concern that had been started just after the Revolution, had filed for bankruptcy. The chairman made speech after speech promising the workers that not a single employee would be fired after the debt had been restructured. The workers were convinced that the problem was mismanagement and that the business was fundamentally sound. A charismatic young foreman, Roque, became their spokesman. There were daily demonstrations of increasing violence.

One day, the chairman's driver attempted to force his limo through a crowd of demonstrators in front of the factory gates. A worker was knocked down. The crowd went wild. The chairman was pulled out of his car. Roque grabbed the chairman's briefcase and later found a list of two hundred workers who were to be dismissed as soon as the banks agreed to the board's terms.

The gates were chained shut, and Roque announced the factory had been lawfully taken over by the workers. Roque then moved the inventories to a warehouse at the edge of the factory compound and laid a bonfire over twenty butane tanks, announcing he would blow everything up if the police attempted to breach the fence.

Roque spent the night going through the files in the executive offices and discovered the details of the restructuring plan. In addition to the two hundred workers who were to be let go without indemnities, the factory was to be retooled to make cheap, mass-produced products. The faïence's artisanal skills, honed over the centuries, would be irrevocably lost. On top of it all, other documents revealed that management had received massive bonuses, while worker pay was frozen due to the crisis. The press lapped it all up.

In the end, the government capitulated and created a special form of bankruptcy that handed the ownership to the workers. The bank debt was rescheduled, and a pool of new investors was found to create a capital base. Much was made of the fact that the ancient production techniques, an important part of French heritage, would be preserved. Roque would act as "leader," since capitalist titles had been abolished.

The saga had held the nation enthralled for months. Roque became immensely popular, and it was even rumored that he would run for public office, but he never did.

The caption under Brissac-Vanté's photo explained he was pro tem head of the investors' pool, which held 25 percent of the faïence's shares.

Capucine asked the receptionist to find the number for the gendarme *capitainerie* that was responsible for Châteauneuf-sur-Loire and the name of the *capitaine*.

When she dialed the capitainerie, a crisp military voice answered, "Gendarmerie National, brigade de Gien."

Capucine announced her brigade and rank and asked if Capitaine de Crébillon was available.

"*Affirmatif,* Commissaire," the young voice barked, keen on leaving no doubt whatsoever that the gendarmerie was part of the military. Capucine's heart sank. She had a very bad track record with the gendarmerie.

In less than five seconds a suave voice came on the line.

"Bonjour, madame. What a pleasure to hear your voice again." Capucine was at a complete loss. The upper-class accent could easily have been that of any one of the denizens of her family's dinner table, but no memory popped into her head.

"Capitaine, a thousand pardons for intruding into your busy morning, but—"

"Chère madame, my mornings exist but to be of service to you."

There was nothing Capucine loathed more than these flowers of aristocratic politeness, but she had to admit it was a pleasure to deal with a gendarme cut from a different cloth.

"Capitaine, you're too kind. As it happens, there's some possibility—a minor one, really—that the death of Monsieur Roque might have something to do with one of my cases in Paris. Would it inconvenience you greatly if I came down to discuss his death with you?"

There was a pause. The *fleur de politesse* seemed to have wilted. But it quickly revived. "Commissaire, who could refuse an offer so politely put? When would it be convenient for you to come?"

"Would this afternoon be too soon? With the new autoroute I could be there in an hour and a half."

"Let's have lunch then. There's an army of journalists camped outside of my office. The last thing I want is for the press to think that the Police Judiciaire is investigating the case. There's a reasonable enough restaurant in Gien called the Auberge des Moines. I'll meet you there at one. How's that?"

Lunch was surprisingly good. They started with *friture de Loire,* little two-inch river fish that were deep-fried straight from the Loire and were eaten whole—heads, bones, and all. The uniformed captain turned out to be a rubicund, short man in his middle thirties with a perfect half hemisphere of hard, round belly. Capucine was sure she had run into him at some social engagement or other. The fact that he took some time over the wine list was no surprise given the complexion of his cheeks, prematurely rosy from ruptured capillaries. When the fritures arrived, they were deliciously crunchy and perfectly set off by the icy Domaine de la Garenne Sancerre the capitaine had chosen.

"They come from right out there," the capitaine explained, waiving his glass at the broad, listless, almost stagnant Loire outside the window of the restaurant. He raised his glass at Capucine. "Sancerre is the great asset of this posting." He aimed his glass at the region, a few leagues on the other side of the river. "I'm up for rotation next year and shudder at the thought of where they'll send me."

"Who knows? With a little luck you may wind up assigned to Bordeaux," Capucine said with her best smile. "Tell me about Roque's death."

"There's really nothing to tell. According to his wife, they went out to dinner, came home, the light switch didn't work, Roque went down to the basement, and didn't come back. She didn't know what to do. She's a fidgety kind of woman. Not what you'd expect with a husband like that. Anyhow, it took her ten minutes to find the courage to go down the stairs in the dark. She found her husband collapsed on the floor, his flashlight still shining at the wall. She ran back up and dialed sixteen. The SAMU people pronounced him dead. We weren't called."

"So how do you know the details?"

"How do I know? I know because I got a call from the lieutenant-colonel, my big boss, less than an hour after the SAMU picked up the body. He told me that Roque had died and they didn't want the press to run away with the story. Madame Roque was not to be interviewed, and I was to leave three brigadiers in front of her house until further notice to make sure the press left her alone."

As if he had uttered a dinner-party banality, he lifted the glass of Sancerre to his nose and inhaled the bouquet without drinking. He looked over the top of the glass at Capucine to make sure she had understood the nuance of what he had just said.

"Naturally, as common courtesy required, I offered my condolences to Madame Roque when I placed my men, and also had a quick look around the basement." He lowered his head confidentially, shook it, and whispered, "This current government is so unsubtle."

This gendarme really was cut from another bolt of cloth, Capucine told herself. "Would it be possible for me to see the scene?"

"I don't see why not. You're not the press, are you?" He gave a great rumbling laugh that made his rock-hard stomach jump up and down like a leather-covered exercise ball. "Ah, voilà," he said as the main courses arrived.

They both had *quenelles de brochet,* made from pike poached in court bouillon, crushed in a mortar, mixed into a creamy paste with eggs and flour, baked into quenelles, and served with a creamy, bright ocher Nantua sauce.

"The pike comes from right out there," he said, pointing at the river again with a stubby finger. "Doesn't it, Jean?" he asked the waiter.

"Oui, Capitaine. I caught it myself just this morning." They both laughed heartily, as if it was the funniest joke in the world.

Madame Roque turned out to be as skittish as promised. She greeted them at the door, wringing her hands in her apron, blinking like a startled fawn in a Disney cartoon.

"Madame," said the capitaine, "this is one of my colleagues. She needs to make a report, and I wonder if you would be kind enough to let her look at your basement."

Rather than reply, Madame Roque looked at the floor and shuffled over to a low door under the stairway of the modest cement house. The capitaine held his flashlight as they inched their way down the steep stairs. At the bottom, he flicked on the lights, and two naked bulbs revealed a damp cement cellar with an ancient washing machine and dryer, a metal wine rack a third full of wine bottles, and numerous baskets and plastic cases filled with the detritus of a modest life.

The capitaine walked over to the wine rack and picked out a bottle. Obviously, fingerprints were not top of mind at the gendarmerie.

"Wouldn't keep my wine in a cellar as humid as this." He held the bottle up, wrinkled his nose, and then sniffed the cork end. "It's cheap enough stuff, and the rotting cork isn't going to help it any. Good thing the Communists didn't win out, or we'd all be drinking this swill." He shuddered and made a histrionic grimace.

While he spoke, Capucine examined the fuse box. It was the old type that took screw-in fuses. Two or three spares were stored on top of a rag on the bottom of the box. On the floor underneath, a small puddle—no more than a foot in diameter—was surrounded by a large damp stain.

"The SAMU said they found Roque lying dead right there, still holding the replacement fuse. They put it back on the sill and screwed in another so the lights would go on."

"Which one did they take out of his hand?"

"This one here." The capitaine made to pick it up.

"Let's let it sit for a moment. When you were down here yesterday, was the puddle larger?"

"I'm not sure. Possibly. Why? Is it important?"

"Do you think I could take the fuse found in Roque's hand back to Paris? I'm curious how he was electrocuted."

The capitaine gave her a shrewd look. "You know you're playing with fire. It was made very clear to me that this entire incident was to go away very, very quietly. I'm sure you understand that."

"It's just that it may have a bearing on another case I'm working on. If it does turn out that there's a connection, I'll make sure you get full credit. If not, I'll forget all about it. Does that work for you?"

"As long as you leave me out of it altogether no matter what happens, feel free to take anything you want. If it turns out I've been useful to you and you insist on expressing your gratitude, you might ask Monsieur de Huguelet to suggest a bottle or two of wine you could send me." He winked broadly at Capucine.

Back in Paris Capucine called Pascal Challoneau in forensics.

"One of my brigadiers is bringing you something I picked up this afternoon. It's the fuse that electrocuted Firmin Roque. Can you work your magic on it for me?"

"If you suspect foul play, we should check the whole scene out."

"Too late for that. And the gendarmes have been ordered to downplay it."

There was an uncomfortable silence.

"Got it. Don't like it, but I've got it."

That evening, as she walked down the hall to the kitchen of her apartment to look in on Alexandre's dinner preparations, her cell phone rang.

"Tell me, Commissaire, was there a puddle under that fuse box?"

"A small one. But it looked like it had mostly dried up. My guess was that it was a lot larger yesterday."

"That figures. The fuse you sent me is coated with a highly conductive gel. It's probably the stuff that's sold with those electronic muscle-contracting exercise machines you see in the ads. We're doing tests right now to identify the proprietary formula, but there's no doubt it was highly conductive."

"So what does that mean?"

"It means, Commissaire, that it was murder. That's what it means."

CHAPTER 19

Even though she had more than half expected something of the kind, the directness of Challoneau's announcement had been a bolt. Without thinking, she dialed Capitaine de Crébillon's cell phone. He didn't pick up until nearly the end of the fifth ring. In the background Capucine could hear people laughing and the chiming of silverware on plates. Too late, she realized that she must be pulling Crébillon away from a dinner party, no doubt an egregious offense in his universe.

"What a joy to hear your voice, Madame le Commissaire."

"Capitaine, can I abuse your indulgence once again and request yet another favor? I'm afraid it's rather an important one." It had become obvious that the courtly approach was the one that worked best with Crébillon.

"Madame, what man could have any aspiration in life other than enhancing your happiness? How may I be of service?"

"I wonder if you could call Madame Roque and ask her one or two questions for me."

Even through the insubstantial cell phone Capucine could feel the chill. There was a long pause. Finally Crébillon said, "Of course, madame. I suppose it's not too late in the evening to make a call. What would you like me to ask her?" A flat tone had replaced the courtly melody in his voice. Capucine explained what she wanted.

As she waited for Crébillon to call her back, she became increasingly aware of the enormity of her imposition on him. She was amazed that he had even taken the call. The news that Roque's death was murder was going to be an embarrassment to the conservative administration. The press would jump at the chance of insinuating that the murder was a political act guided by the spectral hand of the government. It was precisely the sort of case where the police would be damned if they did and damned if they didn't. Careers had been blighted by far less.

Her phone rang. In a dry tone Crébillon told Capucine that Madame Roque had been at home and had been quite happy to answer his questions. She had never seen a puddle on the basement floor before. It was definitely odd, because there were no pipes anywhere near the fuse box. Also, she had noticed that there was a big plastic pitcher on the counter of the basement sink that had beads of water in the bottom. She found this particularly odd since the pitcher was kept under the sink and she never used it.

"Voilà, Commissaire, I trust your curiosity is satisfied. Now, I really must say I think we would both be well advised to drop this matter. Don't you agr—"

Capucine hardly listened. The only thing that now mattered was to get forensics into that basement and fingerprint everything as fast as possible.

Capucine stared at the dead phone in her hand with no recollection of having made her adieus to Crébillon. She hoped she had been as grateful as *politesse* required. But even if she hadn't, her short reverie had been worth it. She had defined her course of action.

*   *   *

"So you're absolutely convinced it was murder?" *Contrôleur Général* Tallon said with a slightly sardonic grin the next morning. Even though he was now in the stratosphere of the Police Judiciaire hierarchy, Tallon, who had been in charge of Capucine's first homicide case, continued to act as her mentor.

"Of course it is, sir. The evidence is conclusive. We need to get the INPS out there right away, while there's still something to be found."

"*N'ayez pas de zèle*, Commissaire, as Talleyrand liked to say. Don't be zealous. You've opened up a very nasty can of worms here. Far more nasty than I suspect you realize. Let me deal with it. I'll call you this evening."

When the call came, Tallon said nothing other than to invite her to lunch the next day.

They sat side by side on the cracked leather banquette facing the door at the end of the front room of Le Vieux Bistrot. Tucked under the shadow of Notre Dame Cathedral, over the years the restaurant had been carefully maintained to retain its dusty, between-the-wars feel. Capucine nibbled at a dish of a dozen quail eggs fried sunny-side up in country butter, tiny clumps of bright red smoked paprika and specks of brilliant green chives making pointillist dots on the white, tan, and dark yellow background of the eggs. Tallon dug large hunks out of an enormous *pavé de bœuf,* a two-inch-thick fillet steak covered in bone marrow, which had been brought to the table in an aluminum-foil papillote. Neither of them spoke.

Halfway through his steak Tallon put his fork down. "The worms in the can were a good deal nastier than I suspected. There was a meeting this morning at the Ministry of the Interior. Suffice it to say, it was held at the Hôtel de Beauvau so it would be more convenient for the minister to pop in." With a frown, he picked up his fork and cut a piece of pavé.

Several bites later he resumed his narrative. "As you can

imagine, there was no joy in the room. In the end it was decided that the PJ was to investigate the, ah, situation. Under my direct supervision. Of course, I'll appoint you to take charge of the day-to-day work."

A Château Beychevelle had been served in almost comically oversized stemmed glasses. Tallon rotated the base of his glass on the table with two fingers of his hand, making the liquid spiral up higher and higher in the glass. He was very angry about something.

"There is to be a press conference. Facts and photos will be put on display, but the intended message will only be hinted at. No more than the slight murmur whispering through the long grass of evidence. A suggestion will be planted that there is a possibility the murder was a domestic incident revolving around a mistress."

Tallon's frown intensified, and he puckered his lips. It looked like he wanted to spit in his glass. The plan was beyond Machiavellian, a perfect win-win for the government. Roche would be discredited by the breath of scandal, and the right wing would be absolved of any suspicion of harboring a lunatic fringe capable of a political murder. That Madame Roque would be devastated and might even be stigmatized as a suspect was of no concern.

Capucine gripped the long, thin stem of her glass so hard, it snapped. A waiter rushed up to give her a new one and pour more wine.

"I sent the INPS out there this morning. No useful prints were found, but the back door had been jimmied open, probably with a credit card. The marks in the wood were fresh. They have also identified the conductive substance on the fuse—a gel made by a company called Slendertone for some sort of machine that uses an electronic current to contract muscles to make women thinner." Tallon shook his head in disbelief. "Not surprisingly, Madame Roque doesn't possess such a machine. And they're American, relatively rare in France."

"So what do we do?"

"We follow orders. We hold their goddamn press conference. We supply what's wanted—a very high-level conversation with the press where the message is delivered in subtext," Tallon said sarcastically, looking at Capucine with hard eyes. "Oh, yes, one other thing," he said from the depths of his enormous wineglass as he took a deep sip. "Your name did not come up at this meeting."

That meant that Tallon had covered for her, absolving her of the unauthorized involvement of the gendarmerie and the INPS. Capucine's cheeks burned.

When it was all over, Capucine was gratified that it had been Isabelle who had saved the day. Isabelle's track record at press conferences was so dismal, Capucine had been half tempted to bring David back for the event. After all, he was the past master at dealing with the press, and he was only a few hours away on the high-speed TGV. But in the end she had decided against it.

The press conference was held in a large salon in the Hôtel de Beauvau, soothing with its delicately carved paneling gleaming with gold leaf and its French windows overlooking an autumn-tinted five-acre formal garden. One of the minister's cabinet members kicked off the conference and quickly handed it over to Tallon, who came across as the perfectly gruff, ruthlessly efficient senior police officer, which was exactly what he was. The bulk of the presentation was made by Capucine, who, after she introduced her as leader of the investigative team, had relegated Isabelle to the task of hitting the ENTER key on the laptop to advance the PowerPoint screens.

Isabelle, even though her back was to the audience, was nonetheless cataleptic with stage fright. In the past she had systematically frozen up during press conferences, taken it out in anger at the journalists, and invariably had to be bailed out by David's charm.

The public relations department of the Police Judiciaire
had also outdone themselves. Normally incapable of nuance, they had elected to convey their poisonous message
through innuendo. Three screens from the end, a police
psychologist was quoted as stating that as a true hero of
French history, Roque was a man of heroic appetites, a
fact that might have some bearing on the case. The allu-
sion was plain enough, but not so plain it could be used as
fuel for a newspaper story. It was obvious the PR department intended the inference to be given arms and legs during the question-and-answer period after the presentation.

Capucine had rushed through the offensive page as
quickly as possible and had lingered over the subsequent
one, a list of next steps so inflated, it bordered on complete
fiction.

A door in the back of the room opened, and the minister slipped in, made for the raised dais, and sat next to his
cabinet member and Tallon. The press reacted as if an electric current had been applied. A minister was real news.

Sensing the change in mood of the audience, Isabelle
quivered, sure she should do something but with no idea
what it might be. In order to prevent her from making one
of her press-conference gaffs, Capucine made an impatient
gesture at the laptop, indicating Isabelle should keep going
with the presentation. Confused, Isabelle grabbed the pile
of press kits next to the computer and stood up. Everyone
in the room assumed the conference had come to an end.
One of the reporters raised his hand to ask a question.

With as much deference as she could muster, Capucine
walked over to the minister and suggested he say a few
closing words.

The minister perked up like a trained bird dog, strode to
the podium, and, in a resonating, authoritative voice, proclaimed thirty seconds of substanceless platitudes to the
effect that the police, as agents of his ministry, would leave
no stone—absolutely no stone at all—unturned to appre-

hend the vile miscreant, ensure that justice was served, and continue to keep France the safest country in the world.

Fully aware that he was about to be barraged with questions, the minister made an imperious gesture with his hand, indicating that the press kits were to be handed out. Capucine snatched the pile from Isabelle and walked out into the middle of the floor. The journalists clustered tightly around her like chickens clucking for their feed, anxious not to be left out of the distribution.

While the press was distracted, the minister disappeared through a small door in the paneling. A few seconds later, the cabinet advisor followed and held the door open for Tallon, who squinched his eyebrows together, pursed his lips in a moue, nodded at Capucine, and joined the other two, no doubt for another high-level meeting. Capucine assumed Tallon's equivocal expression was some form of approval, but it brought her no joy. She felt sweaty, debased, and demoralized.

She decided to take the afternoon off and soak in a tub full of Guerlain's Shalimar Bain Moussant. That might get rid of the slimy feeling, but she also needed something to take away the bad taste in her mouth. A large glass of vodka with a big handful of ice cubes might just do the trick. Yes, a quarter bottle of tooth-cracking cold vodka and an afternoon-long soak just might tide her over until Alexandre came home to provide his solace.

CHAPTER 20

"Madame," David said, "your *fougasse* is a work of art. I used to think the fougasse of my village's *boulangerie* was the best in the world, but compared to yours, it's no better than fast-food pizza." David thought he might have gone too far, but Angèle Folon swelled visibly at the flattery. She smiled at him, propped her head up on her hand, and inserted the tip of her pinkie between her full lips. Encouraged, he continued. "Seriously, your fougasse is a poem written in dough. The slashes sculpt the windswept branches of a maritime pine, the virgin olive oil gives it the luster of a monkfish fresh from the sea, and it's punctuated with commas of black olive slivers and periods of wild herbs collected in the hills. In a word, your fougasse is as delectable as you are."

Angèle thrummed and ran her tongue over her lips. Even though David had no doubt she had put on more than a pound or two since the birth of her children, her sexual magnetism remained vibrant.

"Are all the Cannois as gallant as you are?" she asked coquettishly, pivoting her body into a three-quarter profile, putting her ample bosom to its best advantage.

"Madame, I'm sure your charms make all men gallant."

She rewarded David with a broad smile. "In the village they say you're an author writing a biography about poor Jean-Lu. I knew him very well when he was a boy. He was my son's best friend. He was very close to our whole family. My husband adored him."

"Really, madame? I had no idea. If you could find the time, any stories you could tell me about Chef Brault when he was a child would be invaluable. That's exactly the sort of thing I need to give my book color and depth."

"I can tell you plenty," she said from behind slightly lowered eyelids.

The noon Angelus slowly clanged out its hollow notes.

"I'm going to close the boulangerie for lunch. Why don't you stay and have a bite with me? I can promise you a *fougasse aux lardons et au vieux Comté*—you know, stuffed with bacon and aged Comté cheese—that's *really* going to get you going." As an afterthought she made a moue, forcing her lips into a perfect circle. "My husband will be sound asleep. Bakers never get up before five in the afternoon."

Angèle shot the bolt in the door, turned the little sign hanging from a suction cup in the glass panel so it read *Fermé* in an elaborate calligraphic script, and pulled down a green shade decisively. David felt slightly trapped.

"Voilà. We're on our own. No interruptions for two hours."

She led David into the kitchen, put two glasses on the table, and produced a bottle of almost pink wine from the refrigerator. *Château Pradeaux, one of the cheaper rosés of Bandol, but pleasant enough when sipped in the baking sun on a café terrace,* David told himself.

The cheese and bacon fougasse more than lived up to its promise. Between the wine and the olivy, spicy pastry David floated on a cloud of home love. With an effort he hauled himself back. He had a job to do, after all. He needed to retain control of the conversation.

Scrabbling for a topic, he said, "Your husband has no trouble sleeping all day?"

Angèle misunderstood. She stared at him with an enigmatic smile and put a shapely finger across her lips.

"We have nothing at all to worry about. You could shoot off a cannon down here, and he wouldn't notice." Her smile morphed into the merest hint of a leer to make sure the double entendre was not lost on him.

Angèle cut David a second piece of fougasse. As she put it on his plate, her arm brushed his. David pretended not to notice. She sipped her rosé and watched him eat, her eyes not leaving his face.

"You said your husband was close to Jean-Louis Brault when he was a child."

"That he was. I always thought it was because both of them were estrangers in the village they lived in. My husband was a creature of the night, and the Brault family members were the village freaks." She paused, brought to earth by her memories. "But actually, in a way, it was that Jean-Lu was the son my husband always wanted to have."

"But you have a son, don't you?"

"Lucien. He was a difficult child. Moody and unhappy. Very mocking and sarcastic with everybody. The other children in the village didn't like him. Jean-Lu was his only friend." Her eyes lost their focus as she stared down the road into the past. "It's funny. My husband was convinced Lucien didn't like food. He hated everything we made in the bakery. But you never know what your children will become, do you? Lucien wound up as a food critic for a newspaper in Paris. Can you imagine that?

"Jean-Lu was just the opposite. He loved everything that had to do with cooking. He'd stay late after dinner so he could see my husband make the dough and shape his loaves. Sometimes he came back in the morning, before school, and watched us make the fougasse. He was the perfect little boy. Often he would bring a crate of his father's vegetables and make dishes with them for our dinner. Even when he was ten, he made the best *tian* I've ever eaten before or since—sliced zucchini, eggplant, and tomatoes on a bed of onion and garlic, topped with wild herbs and chopped olives, sprinkled with a trickle of olive oil, and baked in the oven for half an hour." She smiled at the wall. "Even at that age he had a feeling for herbs I'll never have.

"Of course Jean-Lu got his love for vegetables from his father. The baron was just as cracked about his vegetables as he was about everything else," she said, returning her gaze to David. "He had these crazy theories. He wouldn't let his boys pee outside so he could treat his vegetables with what they left in their chamber pots. It worked, though. His zucchinis were by far the largest in the village. My daughter Fanny wouldn't touch them until they were washed and cooked, and she was a girl that size never frightened." She chuckled and gave David a sideways glance. David smiled back with wide-eyed innocence, ostensibly oblivious to the decidedly un-motherly double entendre.

"Fanny was Jean-Lu's favorite in our family. He loved to follow her around the house when he came over. Girls that age usually have no patience for twelve-year-old boys, but she was very fond of Jean-Lu. Fanny had no time for Lucien. They were always fighting, but she always had a little kiss for Jean-Lu. I think it was because she felt sorry for him with no mother and being brought up by that cracked father and juvenile-delinquent brother. Every time Fanny said something nice to Jean-Lu, Lucien would pout. It was adorable."

"Fanny left the village?"

"Oh, yes. She really had to." Angèle stopped awkwardly. Before David could ask the obvious question, she continued on in a rush. "She has her own boulangerie now in Cassis. I got her a job working with a boulanger there, and his son had muscles that still keep me awake at night thinking about them, so one thing led to another, as you can imagine, and they got married." She paused to catch her breath. "They have seven children and four grandchildren. Fanny runs the boulangerie now. Her fougasse is not as good as mine, but almost. So you see, everything worked out for the best," she said with an air of finality.

The sparkle had gone out of the mood. Angèle got up and put their dishes loudly in the sink. She smiled politely at David.

"I have to open up again in twenty minutes. But please come back. I'd love to . . . well, you know, talk some more." This was said with a suggestive smile that seemed to require a bit of an effort. David suspected the innuendo was intended to take his mind off the dialogue.

CHAPTER 21

Capucine's first stop in Châteauneuf was Madame Roque, who had become garrulous once in the press's limelight. Flanked in protective custody by her two daughters, sharp-eyed recent university graduates, she embellished what she had already told Capucine with a wealth of detail, none of it useful.

She and her husband had gone out to dinner at a workers' café. That was where they always went. Of course, there were real restaurants in the village, but her husband refused to go where workers didn't eat. Even though he was now "leader" of the company, he would not spend "one single sou" more than the foreman's salary, which was all he would accept. That suited Madame Roque just fine. The description of their meal of *steak frites* and of the conversations with the friends they ran into was interminable.

When they had come home, the lights wouldn't go on, and so her husband had gone down to the basement to see what was the matter. She was terrified when he did not come up or answer her shouts. At this point the two daughters put their hands around her waist and hugged her. She then explained that she eventually found the courage to look for a flashlight in the kitchen drawers and creep down into the dark basement. When she got to the part about what she had discovered, she dissolved into damp tears but recovered enough to provide a long, humid dithyramb about the agony of the wait for the SAMU.

The daughters, cooingly overprotective, made her sit down at the kitchen table. Capucine took English leave, as the French insisted on calling it. None of the three noticed.

Capucine's next stop was the office of Alfred Durand, the faïence's *directeur des opérations,* the chief of operations, who was now also in charge of the company until a decision on Roque's successor could be reached. Durand projected such a perfect ouvrier image that Capucine almost suspected it had been partially assumed. He wore the caricature of a blue-collar worker's Sunday best: baggy gray suit, shiny from use, over an ancient, thick, gray, coarse-wool cardigan zipped up to the neck. The knot of a frayed dark crimson tie peeped out over the top of the sweater.

Wardrobe aside, there was no doubt at all about either Durand's competence as a senior executive of a good-sized corporation or his intellectual baggage.

"Firmin—Monsieur Roque—was far more than a friend. We were *comadres de barricades.*"

"Barricade comrades?"

"I was at his right hand when we liberated the company."

There was a slight pause as Durand waited for Capucine to rise to the bait of the notion of "liberating the company." In his world the police were arch-villains.

"Politics have become trivialized in our country," he continued. "Political demonstrations are now a rite of passage in France. American students go to Fort Lauderdale and get drunk during spring break. French students go out on the street and amuse themselves by kicking tear-gas grenades back at the police. It's a game for them. It has no meaning. That's why the sustained political manifestation that resulted in the liberation of the Faïence de Châteauneuf-sur-Loire is such an important milestone of our era."

"Of course it is. We even studied it in depth at Sciences Po. You and Monsieur Roque were cast as true heroes."

"You went to Sciences Po?" he said with the hint of a sneer. Intellectuals had their place in the Communist world. But university students who turned into flics very definitely did not.

"Did Monsieur Roque have any enemies that you knew of?"

"Only the entire right-wing population of France, and that would include the government. That would make it about thirty-five million people. And their animosity increased every day the Faïence thrived under our management. What they hate most about us is that we succeeded where the capitalists failed, and we are empirical proof that the capitalist model is not the only viable game in town."

Capucine smiled.

"I'm not joking. The success of the Faïence is a thorn in the side of the right. The cornerstone of the capitalist industrial paradigm is the mindless quest for lebensraum—endless growth, ever-increasing market share, squeezing your competitors to death so you can capture their markets. Do you remember the strategy of the capitalists we threw out of here on their ear?"

"Only vaguely."

"They wanted to trash our artisanal skills that had been honed over centuries and make cheap, ugly products that would be sold in large volumes in supermarkets. They were going to gut our plant of its ancient kiln and replace it with automated, high-flow-through machines. And they

were going to fire close to fifty percent of the workforce—
with no compensation, I might add—and destroy the lives
of those who remained, because they would have lost the
joy of expressing themselves with their artistic talent."

Despite herself, Capucine was captivated. "So how did
you succeed where they failed?"

"Simple. We're not motivated by greed. We don't need
to compensate capital. We just need to pay ourselves an
honest wage for an honest day's work. Our shareholders,
who happen to be our workers, don't expect dividends.
Their fulfillment is what they can achieve with their
hands." To illustrate, Durand raised his thickened, cal-
loused hands in an almost papal gesture of benediction.

"Your success is very impressive. Can we talk more
about Monsieur Roque? Of his long list of enemies, did
any of them manifest themselves recently? Were there office animosities or anything like that?"

Durand shook his head slowly. "Roque was the most
honest and humble man I've ever met. When he became
president of the company, he continued to receive his foreman's salary. He remained in his old house. He wore his
old clothes. He drove his old car." Durand paused to make
sure Capucine was getting the point. "Once a week, if his
schedule permitted, he would go down and work half a
shift on one of the production lines. Not only because he
needed to take the temperature of the plant. Not only because of the profound solidarity he felt toward the plant's
workers. But also because he loved working with his
hands. He was a very skilled craftsman, and he didn't
want to lose that. I don't think there's a single employee
here who wouldn't have given his right hand—hell, his
life—for Roque. Does that answer your question?"

Capucine knew that extracting anything more from Durand would be as difficult as getting one of the apostles to
gossip about Jesus.

"Who was he close to at the plant?"

"Me, Mouton, and Tissot. If this was a capitalist company, we'd be the executive committee. But since it's not, we're just three guys. You know what I do. Mouton handles the finances, and Tissot is the product guy. You're seeing Mouton next, right?"

Jean Mouton was a trim fifty with a military haircut and military wire-rim glasses. He pumped Capucine's hand vigorously and led her to a plain pine table that served as a desk.

"I'm the only one on the management team who came after what's known around here as the Glorious Takeover. Roque realized he couldn't do without the banks. Someone has to finance inventories and deal with the suppliers."

"That must have been a tough job to fill. There can't be all that many qualified financial managers who are members of the Communist Party."

"More than you'd think. I was working for a group that published four Communist magazines. I jumped at the chance to come here because I wanted to be close to physical production—you know, something being made, not just words—and I wanted to be in a building filled with good, honest people I'd enjoy having a beer with, not guys with complicated, over-intelligent ideas, even if their hearts were in the right place. I'm sure that makes no sense to you."

"Actually, it does. That's more or less why I joined the police."

"The police!"

Mouton was genuinely shocked. Capucine told herself that you never really knew how deep the gulf was until you walked right up to the edge of the precipice and looked down.

"Is the company as solvent as the press tells us?"

"It's in no danger whatsoever of collapse, if that's what you're trying to discover. We make a profit, but not enough if we had shareholders who expected a return. But we don't, so that's not a problem."

"So you have no capital cushion? That must make you a poor sleeper."

"We do have a cushion. The way the restructuring worked is that the banks and the shareholders waived all claims. A new company was formed, and the shares were divided among the workers. Also a consortium of three private investors offered a pool of debt funds that was the cash nut that allowed the company to go forward. Those loans are technically interest bearing, but they are so subordinated that the interest is only due if there is the ability to pay it."

"And how did you find such a benevolent group of investors?"

"That was before my time. The consortium was already in place when I got here." He gave Capucine a hard look that did not completely mask his defensiveness. "And there's nothing benevolent about them. They're capitalists who extended us a perfectly straightforward financial product."

Guillaume Tissot could easily have passed for a poet. In his checked shirt and tight jeans, it became quickly obvious that he was continually half focused on some distant horizon that only he saw.

He explained his job dreamily. "I'm the guy that figures out what we make. I used to make suggestions to Roque and we'd decide together, but now I guess I'll have to do it all by myself."

"How does that work? Do you go and interview clients and do market research?"

"Oh no, that would be too much like capitalist market-ing. We just make things we like. Every now and then I walk through the warehouse, and if there are too many of any given product, we just stop making it for a while." He paused, lost in thought, got to where he wanted to go, and floated back to the conversation. He looked at Capucine as if he was surprised to see her still there. "You know, it's easier if I just show you instead of trying to explain it. Anyway, I need to check something in the warehouse. Why don't you come with me and I'll show you how the shop floor works?"

To Capucine's untutored eye, the factory couldn't have changed an iota from the eighteenth century. Long tables were stacked with powdery white "blanks" of dishes. Women in late middle age, interspersed with the occa-sional senior man, sat gossiping cheerfully, decorating the blanks with paintbrushes. The atmosphere was that of a ladies' bridge party.

Tissot stopped beside a woman in a florid housedress.

"*Ça va, Huguette?*"

"*Pas trop mal, Guillaume. Et toi?*"

The use of first names and the familiar *tu* to a senior ex-ecutive was not lost on Capucine.

Tissot explained that Capucine was a "visitor" from Paris, avoiding all mention of the police, which would have cre-ated a snap frost in this world, and asked Huguette to ex-plain what she was doing. Proudly, Huguette showed Capucine her brush, which consisted of a single partridge feather tied to a stick with thread. The feather was dipped in a little pot of light red glaze and gently laid at the end of a stalk that had been painted by Eugénie, who was sitting next to her, using a sable brush.

Laughing and bouncing with schoolgirl liveliness, Hu-guette pushed Eugénie aside to make room for Capucine on the bench. She handed Capucine her brush.

"I can't do this!" Capucine said with a shriek. "I couldn't even draw in the *maternelle*."

Huguette ignored her. "It's not drawing. You just lay the feather down, and it makes a petal."

Tissot smiled at her. "I have to check on something. I'll be back in a little while. If you're any good at this, I might be making you an offer." There was polite laughter from those at the table within earshot.

Huguette guided Capucine's hand, and a perfect petal was formed, but as Capucine lifted the brush, a small streak of glaze leached out, spoiling the flower.

"Tant pis," said Huguette. With indifference, she threw the ruined blank into a plastic bin behind them. She reached for another half-finished blank in the pile on the middle of the table, and they began again.

On the third attempt Capucine actually managed to finish a flower. During the twenty minutes it took, her ear had become attuned to the pattern of *Berrichon* patois, and she understood almost three quarters of the exchange at the table. It struck her that this was far from being an unpleasant way to spend one's day.

Tissot appeared at her shoulder.

"Your first plate. That's quite an achievement. Now you have to sign it, *n'est-ce pas*, Huguette?"

Huguette produced an extremely fine-pointed brush and a miniscule pot of black glaze, turned the blank over, and handed the brush to Capucine.

"You just put your initials or mark or whatever you want on the back."

Tissot added, "All our work is signed. Every piece produced at the Faïence carries the mark of the decorator."

Their next stop was another long table with a shallow water basin recessed into the middle.

"This process," said Tissot, "oddly enough, requires more skill than hand painting. They apply a décalcomanie to the blank. It's a technique that's been used since the sixteen hundreds. Now we use a photoreproduction process, and the décalcomanies are actually extremely thin plastic, but the process is essentially the same."

They watched as a man in his fifties slid a convoluted blue design onto a blank and positioned it with great care.

"It requires a special touch to do that without tearing the décalcomanie. After it's dried, the blank is coated with clear glaze, just as we do with the hand-painted ones, and given its final bake in the kiln."

The kiln looked like a museum piece. The well-patinated heap of white thermal brick bore a large bronze plaque announcing that it had been inaugurated by one of Louis-Philippe's ministers in 1836.

"This is the new kiln, apparently much larger than the one it replaced. It was originally wood fired, but that was changed to gas well before World War II."

Six stocky men with bright red faces and thick leather aprons loaded six-foot-high wire racks of dishes into the cavernous kiln.

"We operate the kiln sixteen hours a day, two shifts, from six in the morning to ten at night. The kiln operators are on a different shift schedule from the other workers," Tissot explained. "In the last one hundred and seventy-two years the poor old thing has only been shut down twice. Once when it was converted to gas and once when we liberated the plant. When we were squatting in here, the saddest thing was that the kiln was stone cold."

"Does it run all night even when there's nothing in it?" Capucine asked.

"No. At the end of the second shift the workers turn the gas off, and a timer turns it back on at four in the morning to get it hot for the first shift. But the brick walls are so thick, the temperature barely goes down at night. Actually, I was worried that when we shut down the kiln during the liberation, the bricks might crack when they cooled. The notion of the destruction of our beloved plant kept me from sleeping."

"But not the idea of blowing the place up?"

"Of course not. That would have been for a good cause."

CHAPTER 22

"What are you up to this time, Jacques?" Capucine asked into the telephone, tapping the black-bordered hand-engraved card on her desk at the brigade.

> *Monsieur Comte Jacques de la Fournière*
> *has the immense pain of announcing the demise,*
> *after a protracted and virulent onslaught of tædium*
> *vitae, on the 10th of October, Anno Domini MMVII,*
> *of his most cherished and revered ebullience.*
> *The wake will be held at 29, quai Anatole France*
> *on the 18th of October at 8:30 in the evening.*
> *No flowers*
> *Evening dress*

It was no secret in the family that Jacques was bored by his money. There was a great deal of it, and it bored him a great deal. He had been an heir to all four of his grandparents' families, and from the age of majority onward a stream of inheritances had flowed inexorably into the tutelage of his asset manager at Lazard Frères, a kindly and patient gentleman whose calls Jacques systematically refused to take.

One of the manifestations of his disdain was his apartment, the top floor of a building with a spectacular view of the place de la Concorde. Obeying a psychological dictate—which was far from fully understood by Capucine—Jacques redecorated his cavernous flat at least twice a year, each décor more extravagant than the last, and each presented to a close circle of family and friends at an elaborate dinner.

"I think I'm missing the point," Capucine said, rubbing her thumb over the raised printing on the card. "Taedium vitae? Weariness of Life? You?"

"We are each entitled to our own particular ennui, *ma cousine*. I've been rereading my Huysmans: des Esseintes mourned the temporary loss of his virility at a black dinner, and I'm merely following suit in my own little way."

"Ahh," Capucine sighed. She had written a paper at the lycée on *A Rebours—Against the Grain*.

"You see, you're not missing the point at all. I'm looking forward to seeing you in a disturbingly short black frock with the snaps of your garter belt peeping out from under the hem. And if you want to respect the author, black silk stockings woven with tears would be de rigueur. Why don't you get here early and we can have a quiet"—Jacques paused for half a beat, and Capucine could imagine his salacious smirk—"tête-à-tête before the festivities get going."

Capucine was greeted at the door by Madame de Sansavour, a caterer who was the rage of Paris's beau monde and who even Alexandre admitted was a highly talented chef. Jacques hired her frequently for his dinners, and she was normally charmed by his eccentricities. But her creased brows glimmered with perspiration, and the corners of her mouth were turned down in an exasperated frown.

"Monsieur is waiting for you in his room, madame. If

you could keep him out of the kitchen for a while, I would be deeply in your debt."

Capucine crossed the living room to get to the back of the apartment. The walls had been upholstered in black felt, the armchairs and the sofa were of creamy black leather, the black wall-to-wall carpeting was punctuated with somber Persian rugs, and a black marble fireplace with almost invisible gold veining had been installed, housing a flame made dark purple with some chemical. The room was so overdone, it dripped almost comically with fin de siècle angst.

As promised, Jacques was in his bedroom, the only room in the flat that was inviolate. As ever, it looked like it might belong to an unwashed student of poetry at the Sorbonne. Jacques sat on his unmade single bed, a dented tin wine cooler containing a single bottle of champagne on a wooden wine crate in front of him. He wore a black ruffled evening shirt and a floppy black velvet bow tie. He stood up when Capucine walked in.

"Isn't the living room delightfully horrible? It cost an arm and a leg, particularly the fireplace. But it was worth it."

He sat down, patted the bed next to him, and poured Capucine a flute of champagne. He put his hand on her thigh, stockinged in sheer black silk interwoven with little luminescent beads, and stroked appreciatively.

"You've got the stockings right," he said, squeezing her thigh.

Jacques refilled his own champagne glass and let his limpid eyes lap over Capucine's silhouette.

"So tell me quick before the madding horde arrives, have you made enough of a hash of your current case to get on bended knee and beg for my help?"

"Not at all. Maman's joined the team. Her latest craze is having lunches with my brigadiers in proletarian restaurants in the Twentieth. It's a whole new her." Capucine laughed happily.

"And you're really quite sure you haven't made your usual balls-up?" Jacques asked, a little more seriously than Capucine would have liked.

"Au contraire, we're almost drowning in clues."

"Voilà," said Jacques with his all-knowing Cheshire cat grin. "That's the difference between the police in fiction and in real life. Fictional detectives always have too many clues. Real live ones never have enough."

Madame de Sansavour tapped discreetly on the door.

"Monsieur de Huguelet has arrived."

"No point in pushing Tubby Hubby's blood pressure into the red zone by letting him catch us in bed together, ma chérie. Let's greet him in the salon."

They followed Madame de Sansavour into the living room, her stiff gait eloquent testimony to her displeasure. Alexandre, a glass of whiskey in hand, studied a jumble of dark etchings over the mantelpiece. Jacques slipped on his evening jacket, smoothed his hair with his hands, and tugged on Capucine's sleeve to straighten her frock, as if they had both dressed hurriedly at the announcement of Alexandre's arrival.

For once Alexandre did not rise to the bait.

"Your Madame de Sansavour is seriously displeased, Jacques. She is now an official *vedette*—a star—in the culinary world. I would suggest you not trifle with her."

"Asking her to honor one of the great classics of French literature hardly constitutes trifling. I merely suggested she follow Huysmans's black dinner to the letter and have it served by naked Nubians clad only in black silk stockings—"

"Woven with tears," Capucine interjected, showing off her leg with an elegant turn of her ankle.

"Exactly. Woven with tears and worn with black satin mules. Was that too much to ask?"

Alexandre smiled. "I see your point. There would have been an undeniable charm to that. However, apparently it was the bats that exercised her."

"Bats?" Capucine asked.

"Of course," Jacques said. "The food is supposed to be all black. So I had a few Seychelles *roussettes*—you know, those gigantic bats they have—flown out in the diplomatic pouch. And I asked her to make a *civet* with them. But the silly woman refused. Now I can't even make ice cubes, because my freezer is packed with bats." Jacques pouted at the injustice of the world.

Madame de Sansavour rushed into the room, her brow wrinkled in recrimination and concern. "Monsieur, when I make the risotto with the 'forbidden rice' you gave me, it comes out violet, not black. I've added squid ink. Now it's jet-black. Is that all right?"

"Madame, you are a paragon among chefs. You always know exactly what to do," Jacques said. "Without you, my life would be no more than a heap of dry ashes."

Only partially mollified, Madame de Sansavour retreated to the kitchen.

"I'm definitely looking forward to this dinner," Alexandre said. "Who have you invited to your funereal bacchanal?"

"Familiar faces and some new ones to give the soirée *piquant*. Of course, Cécile, our nubile childhood playmate, and her enologically inclined consort. There will be a rotund éminence grise from the Ministry of the Interior, so Capucine will have her very own string to pull when she's thrashing about in the choucroute."

Capucine scowled at him.

"There will be a publishing luminary, scion of a great family, who owns any number of magazines and publishing houses. He's recently become a widower and is making his first timid steps into *le beau monde* to mend his heart. And, of course, a femme fatale, an unknowable woman of great allure and infinite layers, which, when peeled away one by one, eventually reveal a gossamer veneer of La Perla lace, complete with straps and stockings. But once that's removed, poof, there's nothing left."

"Do you speak from experience?" Alexandre asked.

"Hardly. She's here merely to illustrate the virtue of knowing when to stop. The domain of unrequited experience is embodied by another guest. A Greek goddess with the body of a nymph. Sadly, a mere acquaintance. It was a coup to get her to come to dinner. Careful, cousine. Portly Partner may well lose his head tonight."

"Lose my head, indeed!" Alexandre said. "I'm sure this woman will be one of the androgynously muscular creatures you dig out of the DGSE operative pool. She'll be decked out in the standard ministry-issue little black dress, with the silencer of her long phallic pistol tucked in between the cheeks of her over-muscular *fesses*. Another harried junior civil servant pressed into dinner service."

"Cousin, you're making progress. The concept of the silenced pistol as a sex toy is fraught with potential."

The guests were ushered into the darkened living room by a black-clad valet, one of Madame de Sansavour's extras. Each was handed a jet-black Blavod vodka martini with a black kalamata olive sunk into the turgid depths, and then plied with canapés of beluga caviar on black Russian bread.

The first to arrive was the ministerial éminence grise, who proved to be toad-like in appearance and utterance. Then came a young woman in her early twenties who looked like she rose every morning at four thirty to swim fifty laps in a pool. Her knee-length, tightly clinging silk shift made it abundantly clear there was no holster at her back.

Capucine's eyes widened perceptibly at the next arrival: Chéri Lecomte. She wore Yves Saint Laurent's famous Le

Smoking from the sixties: a man's tuxedo cut high-waisted with trousers outrageously flared. As she made her entrance, the bloodred soles of Louboutins pumped arterial jets from under the flapping pant legs. She had completed her look with jet-black lipstick and nail polish and an unlit cigarette in a two-foot black holder. Even though the ensemble smacked of mothballs from various eras, there was a perceptible hush in the room as she entered.

The publishing magnate arrived, surfing into the room on a breaker of epigrams and bons mots. Introductions completed, he made a beeline for Capucine and Chéri's settee.

"Madame," he said to Capucine, executing an elegant *baisemain*, "I am a great admirer of your husband's." He wagged his finger at her. "Warn him that I intend to steal him away from *Le Monde* and get him for one of my magazines." Duty done, he turned to Chéri and took possession.

"Gérald de Boysson," he announced.

"Chéri Lecomte," Chéri said. The brilliance of her toothy smile in the frame of her black lipstick created a pool of light between them in the somber room.

"What a charming name."

"My mother was very fond of Colette."

"But wasn't Chéri a beautiful young man?"

"Was he? My mother was American, and I'm sure she never actually read Colette. And you have to admit it really *does* sound like a girl's name."

Boysson bent over Chéri, entranced.

Manifestly excluded from the conversation, Capucine rose to wander around the room. Chéri's recitative of her biography pealed on loudly behind her.

"But I *am* French. Entirely French in spirit. I love it so much here, I never went back from my junior year abroad, when I was at Vassar. . . ."

Capucine turned to look.

"*Of course,* there was a man involved, Géri. Can I call you that?" Chéri gave Boysson a playful punch on the shoulder. "But the silly boy left to make movies in Rome, and Mama bought me his stand at the Puces. And then . . ."

Alexandre sat next to the nymphet at one end of the long black sofa. Every time she turned to glance anxiously at Jacques, Alexandre scoured her lower body with his eyes. Capucine beckoned him with a crooked index.

"Got it figured out yet?" she asked.

"No, but she's clearly nervous about something."

"She's got a small holster taped to her inner thigh. You can see the outline through the dress when she stands in front of the light. She's probably worried the gun will fall on the floor. Or she might just be put out that Jacques is ignoring her."

"Don't be silly. Who on earth would care if Jacques wasn't paying attention to them?"

Madame de Sansavour opened the door to the dining room and announced dinner in a loud voice.

The once-large dining room had been transformed into a theatrical version of a dessert tent with hangings of shimmering black satin. The oppressively claustrophobic gloom was relieved only by the purple flames of black candles set in ornate silver candelabra placed among black-rimmed plates and black napkins on a black linen tablecloth. The tent blocked out all street sounds, leaving a humid, unnatural silence.

Black cards inscribed with silver flourishes placed the guests. Capucine found herself between Jacques and the toad-like ministerial official, catty-corner from Alexandre, who sat next to the putative DGSE operative. At least he would be amused. Directly opposite, Chéri had been placed between Théo and Boysson. Théo peered around the table, blinking, apparently wondering what he was doing there. Boysson concentrated on Chéri, his eyes saccading rapidly back and forth between her face and her ruffled silk bosom.

Chéri's voice was a quantum louder than the other guests'.

"You're *so* right, Géri. It *was* a challenge to become an expert in faïence. But I had a head start. I had studied a *lot* of art history at Vassar."

At each emphasized word, the magnate's eyes shot up to meet Chéri's and then sunk south slowly, only to rise again in a few seconds.

Madame de Sansavour opened the door to admit two of her staff, bearing large oval serving dishes. Capucine caught Alexandre eying the girls, his thought process ridiculously transparent: he was imagining them naked in the much-touted stockings and backless stiletto heels. Capucine winked at him. Alexandre scowled and picked up one of the two black menu cards that had been placed in the middle of the table. The silver calligraphy announced the first dish would be a *feuilleté de truffe noire*—slices of truffle between thin layers of puff pastry. The dish arrived completely enrobed in a thick black truffle sauce. As the serving girls placed the dishes, a third girl poured ink-black wine from a crystal decanter.

Théo and Alexandre inhaled and sipped the wine critically.

"Cahors," Alexandre said.

Théo swirled the wine in his glass and sniffed loudly. Heads turned. Cécile pursed her lips in disapproval. He took a deep drought and swished it in his mouth as if rinsing after brushing his teeth. Cécile's pursed lips became an exaggerated moue.

"Château Lagrézette Malbec Le Pigeonnier. No doubt about it," Théo said. Alexandre nodded in agreement.

The next dish was to be the *risotto interdit*—the forbidden risotto. The serving girls, their uniforms no longer crisp and their hair wilting, returned with the risotto, mounds of jet-black creamy rice, the grains half the size of normal risotto.

"Jacques, why is the risotto forbidden?" Chéri asked in her ringing voice.

It was Alexandre who answered. "Centuries ago, the Chinese developed an heirloom cultivar for black rice. But it was reserved exclusively for the emperor and forbidden to everyone else. It's still very hard to obtain."

Ignoring Alexandre, Chéri continued to look at Jacques. "Someone told me that you just redecorated your fabulous apartment."

Cécile said, "Jacques's always doing it. It's his hobby. He does it twice a year."

"Twice a year? That must cost a fortune."

"It's not the fortune that's the problem," Cécile said. "It's getting it done. My own redecoration has stalled. It's exasperating. Particularly since my best friend won't return my pièce de résistance." She darted a half-friendly dagger at Capucine.

Jacques looked back and forth between the two women, smiling his Cheshire cat grin as if savoring a secret memory. The expression was lost neither on Alexandre nor the DGSE nymphet. Unheeding, Théo sipped his wine with great attention.

A little later the serving girls returned with the next dish, roasted black Chinese chicken and Brazilian black beans. The girls seemed even more limp. Their hair straggled in damp ribbons, and large sweat stains darkened the black silk of their uniforms.

The dish was one of Madame de Sansavour's triumphs. The pieces of black-meated chicken lay on beds of creamy black beans. They had been cooked with a miraculous pepper that started out sweet in the mouth and rose to a crescendo of almost painful pungency. The joyous discovery was that the invasive blandness of the beans immediately quenched the conflagration. The creation had an interchange of passion and comedy as delicate and subtle as an Italian opera.

Alexandre decided to explain the ins and outs of the Silkie breed of chickens to an obviously bored Chéri.

"They're not really Chinese. They're called Chinese because only the Chinese eat them. The black meat seems to put everyone else off."

"A chicken is just a chicken, right, Aléx? And this stuff would be a whole lot better if it didn't have all this pepper in it."

"So tell me, Monsieur le Conseiller, what was the government's view on the death of Firmin Roque? Is this the demise of the nation's last surviving Communist experiment?" Capucine asked the ministerial toad.

"Of course, operating a stand at the Puces is nowhere near as complicated as running a huge publishing business. But I *do* have to spend a lot of time on buying trips. That's the best part. Last summer I went down to the Midi and came back with some fabulous pieces. You have to know *exactly* where to go."

"I hardly think Faïence de Châteauneuf-sur-Loire really counts as a Communist experiment. If it were, the government wouldn't be supporting it. It obviously has always been a perfectly viable business that would thrive under any competent management in a free-market economy."

"The Midi. The cradle of France's passion. I have a house in the hills behind Villefranche. Are you going back there this summer? Would you like to come and have a meal and perhaps a splash in my pool? Would that tempt you?"

"My dear, it's not any old pepper. It's made with malagueta chilies soaked in *cachaça*, Brazilian rum."

"Of course it would tempt me, Géri. But the summer is so far away. Maybe we could do something sooner."

"Don't be too sure, Monsieur le Conseiller. Remember,

'*Sous les pavés, la plage.* Under the paving stones, the beach.' "

Everyone laughed. The phrase was one of the clichés of the May 1968 revolt. When students prized up the paving stones of the Latin Quarter to throw them at the police, they had found the sand used as bedding underneath.

Perplexed, Chéri looked back and forth between Boysson and Alexandre for an explanation, but none was forthcoming. She flushed with embarrassment.

Dessert—a licorice sorbet—arrived, borne by the three girls, who were now limp, slack-jawed, and bathed in sweat, followed by an obviously mortified Madame de Sansavour.

Capucine leaned over and put her lips close to Jacques's ear. "What have you done to those poor girls?"

"Not me, petite cousine, Madame de Sansavour. That stuffy bourgeois woman deprived me of my naked Nubians. But, humanitarian that I am, I had installed a special heater in the kitchen so that my Nubians wouldn't catch a chill. I merely turned the apparatus up a bit in the hopes that Madame de Sansavour would let her girls serve in a more comfortable attire. Ivory is hardly as attractive as ebony, but it would have done in a pinch." His high-pitched, braying laugh stopped all conversation at the table.

After dinner, coffee was served in the living room, accompanied by a perfectly black liqueur served in small stemmed glasses of cut crystal. It was as alcoholic as it was bitter.

Alexandre and Théo sniffed their glasses and conferred in front of the fireplace with its bizarre purple flame.

"One of these horrible Italian walnut-based liqueurs," Alexandre said.

"No. Nocino della Christina. Not Italian at all. California. They seep Napa Valley walnuts in raw local brandy."

Théo drained half his glass, shook his head in disapproval, and spat into the fireplace, creating a satisfying burst of bright orange flame that lit up the room.

The flash of light triggered the departure of the guests. Cécile and Capucine came up to their husbands.

"What have you two been plotting?" Cécile asked.

Chéri had gone up to Jacques to thank him for the evening. As they spoke, the ministerial toad joined them. Chéri threaded her arm through his and allowed herself to be swept out the door. Alexandre and Théo raised their eyebrows.

"She has a better eye for men than for clothes," Cécile said.

CHAPTER 23

Even though that was exactly what he was, the last thing Firmin Bouchard looked like was a flic. He came across as a dogged, hardworking middle manager in one of the four French mega banks.

He had sat in the cubicle next to Capucine's when she was in the financial brigade. She knew for a fact that his Sig Sauer was still in its original box, wrapped in chemically treated paper, at the very back of the center drawer of his desk, from whence it emerged once a year, when, eyes squinted almost shut, Bouchard fired the required fifteen rounds into a paper target. Firearms frightened him. His weapon was the computer.

"Capucine, I don't understand you. You were doing extremely well in the serious-fraud section of the financial brigade, which is, after all, the cutting edge of the cutting edge of the police. And you gave it up to join the hoi polloi and chase wife beaters and child molesters. It doesn't make sense."

They walked down rows of cubicles where well-scrubbed young people speed typed on keyboards. Three years before it had been Capucine's home. She had hated every second of it.

The previous day, Capucine had called Bouchard and told him she wanted his advice on a case. He had invited her to lunch. For a split second she had imagined a fuggy bistrot on the rue de Tolbiac and a stew made with love and produce from the local market, but, silly her, that wasn't at all the way it was done in the fiscal brigade.

At the end of the hall they reached the interrogation room, a conference room, really, where suspects in elegant suiting usually sat, flanked by prosperous lawyers, confronted by necktied and beskirted police officers.

Lunch had been laid out by the catering service: crinkly cellophane-wrapped sandwiches of factory Gruyère and industrial ham with a selection of Fanta Citron, fizzy Orangina, and small, squat bottles of Perrier. *The cutting edge of the cutting edge,* Capucine reminded herself. Still, insipid as they were, these people really did know all there was to know about the world of finance and had an uncanny ability to winkle secrets out of the ether of the cyber world.

"I need to know about someone called Thierry Brissac-Vanté. He's popped up as an extra in two of my cases, and there may be a financial angle."

"I'm all ears."

"Brissac-Vanté's day job is a small-time celebrity promotion marketing boutique. As a hobby he makes investments in companies. Needless to say, he and his wife are very well heeled. He happens to have investments in two of my murder cases, Chef Jean-Louis Brault and Firmin Roque."

"Firmin Roque was murdered? I thought the death was accidental."

"It was made to look like an accident, but it was deliberate. We're not releasing that information."

Bouchard looked at Capucine levelly. "What do you want me to do?"

"Nothing much. Run Brissac-Vanté and his wife through

the labyrinths of your computer and tell me what comes out." She stood up. "If you find something interesting, we'll have lunch in my neck of the woods. That way you can see how the other half lives."

Two days later Firmin Bouchard was given the grand tour of Capucine's brigade. He was uncharacteristically ill at ease. As they wandered through the large staff room, shaking hands with scruffy, bestubbled detectives, Capucine realized there were two reasons for his discomfort. The first was obvious: the miasma of physical violence in the room. The second was more subtle. On her own turf, the fact that Capucine was now a commissaire was manifest. Even though she might be only one notch above Bouchard in the police hierarchy, Capucine had passed the impossible exam, had spent nearly a year in training, and had crossed the watershed into the world of senior officialdom. The crackle of her authority in the squad room was almost audible.

The situation was exacerbated at Benoît's, where Capucine was treated with a respect that bordered on veneration. Unconsciously, Capucine had shrugged into the mantle of her rank.

"So, Firmin, do Brissac-Vanté's financial secrets lie naked and gasping on your desk?"

Bouchard looked a little bewildered. "I did get a fairly decent rundown. Brissac-Vanté's story is pretty simple. His wife has all the money. She's the granddaughter of the owner of a large edible oil company that was bought out by Lessieur in the sixties. Her father invested well—very well, actually—and she inherited a substantial fortune. She grew up as part of the gratin of the gratin of the Sixteenth Arrondissement. Her husband comes from the same milieu, but his parents don't have a bean. After the lycée he took a yearlong prep course for the elite business school exam. I made some calls, and it seems he worked hard, but he couldn't get in anywhere and so wound up taking a two-year course in public relations at one of those schools for dumb rich kids. The parents had to take out a big loan to pay for it. He got married the month he graduated."

"And the wife paid for setting up his marketing boutique."

"Just the initial start-up money for the office and furnishings. He's keeping his head above water. He's not supplying the family with caviar, but he's not losing money, either."

"And what about the investments?"

"Ah, that's more interesting. The bulk of them are what I call vanity investments. The sort of things rich people buy to make them feel good. There are minority investments in two restaurants in addition to Brault's, an art gallery in Saint-Germain, and a tiny Armagnac producer. Standard stuff. The idea is you take your friends to your restaurants, openings at your art gallery, and send them a bottle of your Armagnac at Christmas. To his credit, Brissac-Vanté must have something of an eye, because none of them are losing money."

"What about Firmin Roque's Faïence?"

Bouchard smiled. "That's the reverse of the medal. The value of the loans they made to the Faïence was considerably larger than all their other investments put together. And it's a shitty deal for them. They get almost nothing back, and that would have been obvious even as the deal was structured."

"Why would they have been takers? You seem to think Brissac-Vanté has a good nose for investments."

"I have a little theory. So I did some digging. It turns out that Yolande Brissac-Vanté is best friends with Sidonie Le Dréau."

Capucine looked blank.

"Who used to be Sidonie Dabrowski."

"The president's wife? And you think this had something to do with the Élysée?"

"Let me tell you this. The year after the investment in the Faïence, the Brissac-Vantés managed to buy a significant holding in the Tours football team. It's an absolutely plum deal. The soccer club had gone bankrupt, and a few investors were invited to buy equity in a squeaky-clean new corporation that was almost guaranteed to be a gold mine. The local municipality decided who the new shareholders were going to be. And here's the punch line: the tranche the Brissac-Vantés were given was almost exactly the same amount they had put into the Faïence."

"A payback?"

Bouchard shrugged his shoulders.

CHAPTER 24

The Brissac-Vantés lived on the avenue Henri-Martin—the epicenter of the moneyed citadel of the Sixteenth Arrondissement—in an apartment that took up the top floor of a Haussmann-era building. When Capucine introduced herself, Yolande extended her hand as if they were at a cocktail party. She had a pleasant, horsey face with a mouth that seemed to contain too many teeth.

"I'm Yolande Brissac-Vanté," she said, eyeing Capucine's light tan Sonia Rykiel blazer. "You look so familiar. I'm sure we've met before. But your name doesn't ring a bell."

"Maybe because I use my maiden name at the police and my husband's name, Huguelet, when I'm off duty."

"Capucine de Huguelet, of course. How silly of me! We met at a show-jumping event last summer. I remember you perfectly. Your husband was at home, writing a restaurant review, and mine was off doing Lord knows what."

Capucine had completely forgotten the June afternoon at l'Etrier, Paris's riding club. Show jumping had been one of Jacques's momentary whims, and he had dragged her off one Saturday afternoon when Alexandre had been agonizing over a lengthy piece for his paper.

It was a turning point in the interview. If Capucine allowed Yolande to meander through their common acquaintances, they would bond as social equals, and Capucine needed to talk about money, an impossible barbarism among friends in Yolande's circle.

"I'm sorry to intrude on your time," Capucine said. "I'll be brief. There are only a few questions I need to ask."

Yolande did not miss the rebuff, mild as it was. Wordlessly, she led the way down an endless hallway covered in flowered silk into a darkly paneled living room, easily large enough for indoor polo.

"I'm investigating the deaths of Jean-Louis Brault and Firmin Roque. Your company has investments in both of their businesses."

Yolande showed her many teeth in a broad smile that stopped just below her nose.

"I don't deal with any of that. Thierry's in charge of the investments." She looked defensively at Capucine, as if admitting a serious fault. "You see, I don't know anything about money. I see to the children and the houses. Thierry has been an excellent custodian of my father's inheritance. Part of it's still in trust, and the trust officer told me I should be very pleased with the way Thierry's handling things." She smiled virtuously, as if she had scored a telling point.

Capucine said nothing. A clock ticked loudly somewhere in the room.

At length Capucine said, "I understand that you're very close friends with Sidonie Le Dréau."

Yolande colored. "Sidonie Dabrowski. The president doesn't like it, but she's keeping her married name. The church is right; marriage is forever. Sidonie has been my closest friend ever since we were at boarding school together."

Yolande paused and stared at her feet, flat on the floor, awkwardly pigeon-toed.

"She's much happier now that she's . . . estranged . . . from her husband. She's a little like me. A bit . . . well . . . shy. She loathed all those receptions and dinners. Of course, Thierry and I helped out all we could and went to as many of them as possible to support her, but there were a great number we couldn't attend. And . . . well . . . it was all a great strain on her. Now she lives in the country with the children. It's a much more normal, more balanced life, filled with horses and dogs and green things that grow." Yolande shored herself up with the reassuring image.

"There are rumors that some of the investments you've made might have a connection to Madame Le Dréau or her ex-husband."

Behind the rigid rictus of her smile, Yolande was outraged.

"*Quelle idée!* Sidonie is just like me. She has no interest whatsoever in things that involve money. And as to her husband, you can't think I'd have anything to do with a man who has taken up with a foreign woman a third his age with the morals of a prostitute."

A radiant Thierry Brissac-Vanté burst into the room, dispelling the storm clouds like an emerging sun. He hugged his wife affectionately, turned to Capucine and started to kiss her on the cheek, caught himself, and said, "Commissaire, what a pleasant surprise to find you here. I've just got off the Eurostar from London and had no idea we had guests." Not giving Capucine a chance to reply, he turned to his wife. "Darling, let's drink some champagne. We need to celebrate."

"Oh, darling, you completed your deal with Samantha Chilcott. How perfectly wonderful!"

Smiling at him with adoring eyes, Yolande left the room to get the champagne.

"Samantha Chilcott?" Capucine asked.

"Don't pretend you don't know who she is. The rock singer who married a famous soccer player and then started her own line of clothing? I signed her as the spokesperson for a new line of French lingerie."

Yolande returned, followed by a male servant in a short striped jacket who was carrying a tray with three flutes and a bottle of Cordon Rouge tinkling in an ice-filled silver cooler.

Once the three glasses were filled, Brissac-Vanté raised his. "Let's drink to Samantha Chilcott and the brand-new French chapter of her fabulous career."

"Oh, darling! I'm so proud of you." Yolande looked at Capucine, beaming. "Isn't he wonderful?"

Brissac-Vanté assumed the expression of a humbly victorious warrior. "It wasn't easy. I had the decisive dinner with her at the Connaught Hotel restaurant right after I arrived. That's the one that's been taken over by that young French chef. I thought adding a French touch to the occasion would be a good idea. Samantha had her agent with her. It was tough going, but I laid a pretty damn good deal on the table. They said they would think about it and get back to me the next day." Brissac-Vanté paused to give his story dramatic effect. Yolande stared at him, unblinking, breathing through parted lips.

"And then the catastrophe. The press got ahold of my cell phone number and started calling me nonstop first thing the next morning about Firmin Roque's death. My cell phone became useless. It wouldn't stop ringing. An impossible situation. I had no idea the poor man had died the night before, and I had absolutely nothing to say to the press. Anyway, all I cared about was getting the call from Samantha's agent. And I had to turn my damn phone off because of all these stupid calls from reporters. I tell you, it was a real dilemma."

"You poor dear. What did you do?"

"Well, I thought about it very hard all though my breakfast and then bit the bullet and called the agent at exactly ten o'clock. I was going to tell him that my cell phone had broken, but before I could, he said he had been trying to reach me all morning because they *loved* the deal I had proposed and wanted to draft a contract so we could sign it."

"Oh, darling, that must have been ever so exciting."

"Of course, it took days and days to hammer out the wording of the contract, but now it's all signed, sealed, and delivered." He raised his glass in an exaggerated gesture and then drained it.

"Thierry is a real genius," Yolande said to Capucine. "His firm is really getting going. You'll see. In a few years he's going to be a key figure in the French business world." She twinkled lovingly at her husband.

"Just before you arrived, your wife and I were talking about your investments."

The statement dampened the mood as if a heavy sea fog had descended. Yolande's lips compressed in distaste at the breach of manners, but Brissac-Vanté smiled on resolutely at Capucine.

"Yes, we're very proud of those projects. We add real value. It's not about money. We give of ourselves, holding the hands of our managers and counseling them, fueling their growth."

"Even the Faïence de Châteauneuf-sur-Loire?"

"Oh, yes," Yolande said. "Thierry has been very supportive of the new management. And he's going to be so needed now. It's been a great strain on him going to all those board meetings. The Loiret is so dismal, and those awful Communists never even offer the board members a decent meal. Can you imagine?"

Capucine got up to leave. Brissac-Vanté accompanied her down the long hallway to the door.

"You know, Commissaire, that train going through that endless tunnel always frightens me. It's the pressure of all that water. I always think if someone sneezes, the whole thing will come crashing down and I'll be crushed to death by the weight of an entire sea." He stopped short. "In the tunnel I couldn't shake the thought that someone's after me."

"After you?"

"The standard-bearers of two of my investments have died violently. My assets are people, not companies. Do you think there's any chance *I* might be the real target here?"

At eleven that night Capucine was stretched out on the crimson leather chesterfield in Alexandre's study, her head on his lap, draining the last drops of a clear liquid from a tiny stemmed glass. After a Gorgonzola and red pear risotto and an arugula and radicchio salad with vinaigrette and walnuts, they had moved to the study to finish the evening with glasses of Poire William, an *alcool* that boasted it took seventeen pounds of Bartlett pears to make a three-quarter-liter bottle.

"Let me get you another," Alexandre said, gently extracting himself from under Capucine's head to go to the kitchen. In a moment he returned with a bottle and refilled her glass with the Poire, oily thick from the freezer.

"Isn't Poire William supposed to have a pear inside, like those little ships in bottles?"

"Usually. But this is Swiss, and they probably haven't figured out how to make a pear that will puff up when you pull a string." Capucine slapped him playfully. "Also, it would be very un-Swiss to inflate their margins by filling a quarter of the bottle with a fruit." Alexandre ticked Capucine's ear and slipped back onto his spot on the couch. "How's your case going?"

"I ran into another brick wall this morning."

"Poor baby."

"It's very frustrating. Not only did I waste my morning, but now I have to fill out a lot of useless paperwork."

"What happened?"

"I was being zealous. Brissac-Vanté is on the persons-of-interest list, so I dropped in on him. His wife was there, too. As it happens, he has an ironclad alibi for Firmin Roque's murder. He was in London, having dinner with Samantha Chilcott, trying to get her to agree to some tacky deal with a sexy lingerie company."

"Some people have all the luck," Alexandre murmured.

"But the alibi still has to be confirmed. In the police anything international has a Kafkaesque bureaucracy all its own. Forms in triplicate with long explanations just so some designated official can e-mail Scotland Yard in order to get us a statement steeped in mealymouthed officialese with three drops of content per gallon of text."

"Hang on."

Alexandre gently lifted Capucine's head, stood up, and extracted a well-worn leather address book from the inside pocket of his tweed jacket hanging on the back of a chair. He picked up the cordless phone receiver and, lifting Capucine's head, resumed his position.

He dialed a number.

"Phoebe, *ma belle*," Alexandre cooed into the phone. There was a momentary pause and then a girlish shriek, followed by an excited exclamation of "Alexandre!" more than loud enough for Capucine to hear. A minute of flirtatious patter in Alexandre's accented English ensued. Halfway through, he cupped the receiver and said, "It's Phoebe, the hostess at the Connaught restaurant."

Capucine sat up. "I'm going to watch television," she said frostily.

Alexandre raised a hand, wrinkled his forehead, and pursed his lips in admonition.

"Listen, Phoebe. Can you have a peek into your reservation book for me? I need to know if Samantha Chilcott—" He was cut short; loud exclamations leaked through the receiver.

"When did you say she was there? Last Friday? That

was the twenty-second, right? And who was she with?"
Long pause. Alexandre cupped his hand over the receiver.
"She remembers Chilcott, and now she's checking the reser-
vation book."

"So the table was booked in the name of Brissac-Vanté,
I see. And who paid? Can you find that out for me? Be a
dear. I'll make it up to you." There was a pause. Rapid
chatter at the other end came out as unintelligible babble.

"That's a very stiff price," Alexandre said with a laugh.
"But with you it would definitely be fun."

Capucine frowned.

"She's checking the credit card registry."

"I'll bet," Capucine said, sitting on the edge of the sofa.

"American Express. Thierry Brissac-Vanté. No, I don't
need the card number," Alexandre said with a chuckle and
began cooing into the phone again.

"I won't be back in London for a couple of weeks. . . .
Of course we will. . . . You know you're the only reason I
go to London, ma chérie. . . . Bisou, bisou . . . Can't wait."
He hung up.

"Voilà. Alibi confirmed beyond a shadow of a doubt
and with no bureaucracy at all."

"I'm not impressed. And I'll tell you something else.
You're never going to London again without me."

CHAPTER 25

Capucine could never make her mind up about Dong. The last time she had been there was to examine a dead body in the men's room, famous for its urinals painted to resemble openmouthed women in garish make-up. That had revolted the feminist in her far more than she had found the murder odious.

Since then, the restaurant had been entirely revamped. A famous designer had transformed the décor into a fantasy world of bottom-lit Lucite, setting off the tracery of nighttime Paris seen through the glass dome of the rooftop greenhouse of what had been Paris's largest department store. The cuisine was no longer an afterthought; it was now intended to be the showstopper. Aiko Kikuchi, a willowy young Japanese chef who had trained in the kitchens of the most august of three-star establishments, had taken over with éclat. As a result, the ever-bored *jeunesse dorée* had trooped back en masse.

Aiko seemed to have a genuine flair for Japanese dishes with a French twist. Belle and Zen duo of foie gras, yellowtail carpaccio, and glam-chic tomatoes all sounded undeniably inviting.

As Jacques studied the menu, Capucine examined a

young thing two tables away, wearing a skirt that barely covered her crotch and, except for the three-inch heels, what looked like normal L.L. Bean rubber-soled, leather-topped boots.

"You should have invited Alexandre, too. He loves this place in its new incarnation. Well, he loves the food. The fauna, not so much."

Jacques brayed his impossibly loud donkey laugh. The girl in the high-heeled Bean boots turned toward them with a disdainful sneer, caught sight of the source of the bray, and the sneer evolved into something decidedly more coquettish.

The meal was a success. Capucine opted for the Délice de Dong, a tasting dish of lobster spring rolls, yellowtail sashimi, tuna tartare, shrimp satay, and shiitake macaroni. Jacques ordered yellowtail carpaccio with yuzu sauce and coriander, followed by udon noodles with lobster.

They chatted away happily with their usual insouciance, each finishing the sentences of the other, as they had done virtually since they were old enough to speak. Still, the mood was not quite right. Capucine and Jacques met frequently for lunch to gossip and exchange mock flirtation, but the handful of tête-à-tête dinners they had shared had all revolved around some professional problem. Truth be told, there had only been three of them since her marriage, all at Capucine's request when she needed her cousin to use his astonishingly broad political connections to extricate her from some quagmire or other. Jacques himself had never suggested a *dîner à deux*.

Yet nothing was forthcoming. Capucine poked at her food and listened to Jacques prattle. Champagne flutes arrived inexorably. Within an hour Capucine's shoulders had dropped a good two inches in relaxation. Maybe this was just luncheon transmogrified to a later hour. In any case it was doing her a world of good.

Plates removed, dessert refused, bubbling blue drinks

emitting puffs of vapor arrived in test tubes, tokens of appreciation from the management.

The bill paid, Jacques stifled a yawn. "Bed for me," he said.

As they left, out of the corner of her eye, Capucine caught the girl in the rubber boots following Jacques with her gaze. Capucine wondered if her own legs had looked that long when she had been that age—all of five years before.

When the valet-parking attendant drove up in the miniscule Smart Car, Jacques's latest toy, Capucine decided that moving the fraternal lunches to the dinner hour had not been a bad idea at all. She felt at one with herself, and the frustration of her unsolvable cases had retreated to a safe middle distance.

She was so relaxed, it took her a few seconds to realize that Jacques had taken a wrong turn. They had torn up the rue du Pont Neuf at a speed faster than she would have thought possible for the little car, but instead of continuing on down the street and turning left at the rue des Halles, Jacques had ducked into the subterranean labyrinth of roads that had been built when the infamous Trou des Halles had been transformed into an underground shopping mall.

"It would have been quicker if you'd stayed on the rue du Pont Neuf 'til the end," she said.

Jacques shined his Cheshire cat grin at her and put his index finger gently to his lips.

The drop into the underground roadway was so steep, Capucine's stomach lurched and she tasted a redux of yellowtail. Her cell phone chirped loudly, letting her know it had lost its signal. Jacques slowed the car to a crawl. The roadway was completely deserted.

"My little cousin made me very proud today. She was brought up at the meeting of the DGSE senior officers this morning all by herself, without any help from me."

Capucine sat up straight and stared at him intently. Jacques slowed the tiny car even further.

"Of course, I'm violating all my vows by even alluding to it." He put his hand on Capucine's thigh, and his fingers wandered under the hem of her skirt to the very edge of the no-man's-land he couldn't have breached legitimately without papal dispensation. "But our ties transcend the confines of mere words." He snapped her lace G-string panties. "Don't they?"

Capucine continued to stare at him wordlessly.

He put his hand back on the wheel.

"There is concern in high places about the possibility of a brouhaha surrounding the Firmin Roque case."

"Brouhaha?" Capucine asked with a little snort.

"As I believe you've been told, a message was passed to the highest echelon of the police hierarchy that the case was to disappear from the public view. There is concern that this"—Jacques paused and turned to smile his irritating grin at Capucine—"*directive* will not be entirely respected at the implementation level of the force. I had to give my most ringing assurance that it would."

Jacques slowed the car to the speed of a walking man and gave Capucine a long look, clearly searching to see if she had taken the message on board.

"You need to understand, cousine, that even if your inept efforts eventually identify a murderer, there won't be a trial."

"That's absurd. Of course there will. Otherwise, it would be a miscarriage of justice."

"It's you who's being absurd. Great pains were taken to achieve a successful denouement for the so-called liberation of the Faïence de Châteauneuf-sur-Loire. A catastrophic end to that episode could easily have polarized the nation's political factions." Jacques paused to let this sink in. "Obviously, no one wants that success to be reversed."

"So I'm supposed to drop the case, is that it?"

"*Pas du tout.* High places have an unquenchable thirst for information, even if no action is planned."

"And when I catch the murderer?"

"If that happens, a decision will be taken *en famille.*"

Capucine gave him a very black look.

As the car inched along, Jacques stared back at her. "Contacting a *juge d'instruction* or magistrate out of school would make things difficult for everyone, particularly you and your muscled mentor, in whom you seem to find such a satisfying outlet for your Electra complex." He whinnied an attenuated form of his braying laugh.

"Jacques, is your shabby outfit bugging my home?"

Jacques put his hand back on Capucine's thigh and accelerated the cramped car. They soared up the ramp of the rue de Turbigo exit.

"Spy on your domestic life? You can't possibly think we'd corrupt the morals of our pure young operatives by subjecting them to the caterwauling that emanates from your bedroom." His strident cackle was cut off by the happy chirp of Capucine's phone announcing it was back in service.

"And so this insufferable tailor," Jacques said loudly, "had the impertinence to attempt to convince me that Prince of Wales checks were démodé. He insisted on pinstripes. I look positively anorexic in pinstripes. I was so upset, I went right out and had three suits made at Lanvin, even though they just don't understand my leg. They really never have. . . ."

CHAPTER 26

Like every other small-village café in the Midi, Le Marius was deserted from the evening Angelus at six—when the men went home to their dinners—until around eight thirty, when they began to trickle back. These were solitary hours for David, the only resident of the hotel above the café. Still, between rumination and pecking at his laptop, he found them satisfying. At six fifteen, Casimir, the owner, would serve David a large pastis and retreat to his quarters. At around seven thirty, Casimir would return, serve David another drink, put a plate of whatever his wife had cooked in front of him on the bar, and set a half-bottle flask of wine next to it. It never even crossed David's mind to question why he was never invited to sit at Casimir's dinner table. This was the Midi.

That evening's dinner was particularly satisfying, a *bourride*—fish soup—this one made with clams and monkfish, the broth made rich with spoonfuls of aïoli, the seafood so fresh, it must have come up from Cassis that morning.

At eight thirty Casimir returned to clear David's plate and immerse himself in his manic polishing of glasses. David looked over his laptop screen, contemplating the closed box on the wall shielding Fanny's virtue. Césariot, the first of the evening throng to arrive, slid his elbows onto the bar next to David's.

"She intrigues you, our Fanny, doesn't she?"

"She's like an elephant in the room that everyone can see except me."

Casimir arrived with Césariot's pastis. "*Quelle idée.* An elephant is the very last thing she was."

When Casimir left to take a tray of glasses to a table, Césariot scratched the surface of the bar contemplatively with his thumbnail.

"*Tu veux que je te dise?* Do you want me to tell you? There are some things no one in a village ever talks about."

"Yes, at home it's the same thing."

Césariot went back to sketching on the bar with his thumbnail.

"You're a good sod, Le Cannois. If I were you, and I had nothing to do one afternoon, I might pay my respects to Pamphile Cadoret, our mayor for nearly forty years. He finally got too old to fend for himself and went to live in one of those homes they have for old people."

"Your old mayor's not going to tell me anything. He's a villager, too. Secrets are secrets."

"He's a villager for sure, but he's also a very thirsty one. They don't serve you the apéro in these nursing homes, and I hear tell he's gotten so parched, he can hardly swallow anymore."

Despite the fact that Monsieur le Maire, as he was still called by everyone, lived comfortably enough in a large room equipped with a hospital bed and rustic dark-wood furniture that must have come from his home, he seemed depressed and listless.

"You're an author and you're writing about Jean-Lu Brault?" he asked lethargically. "I don't think I can help you. I have no memory left."

"I've been staying in La Cadière for the past two weeks, and it's beginning to feel like my second home."

Monsieur le Maire paid no attention. "Tu veux que je te dise? Do you want me to tell you? I can't even eat. How good is a meal going to taste if you don't have an apéro first? Tell me that."

"I couldn't agree more, Monsieur le Maire. That's why I brought us a little pastaga."

The mayor sat bolt upright in his chair, his eyes as alert as those of an egret about to pluck a fish out of an estuary. David produced a mignonette of Pastis 51. The mayor's eyes became saucers.

"It's true I can't remember what I had for dinner last night. But I can sure as hell remember everything that happened ten years ago as clear as if it was happening all over again. And—do you want me to tell you?—not remembering about dinner is no problem. It was bound to have been pure merde. It always is here."

After three mignonettes of liquid gold turned milky white by cool tap water in a tooth glass, Monsieur le Maire was a man restored.

"*Ça fait du bien.* That does one good. So you're interested in our village, are you, young man? And why shouldn't you be? It's a square acre of heaven that fell to earth."

"As I told you, I'm writing a biography of Chef Brault, and I'm looking for background stories about his childhood. I learned that he was very close to the Folon household and had a particular fondness for Fanny."

"*Particular fondness,*" the *maire* said with a chuckle, which turned into a deep laugh, which turned into a desperate convulsive heaving so severe, David thought he might have to summon a nurse.

The fit calmed.

"*Close,* you say. I'll say he was *close* to Fanny." The fit of laughter began again. It wasn't until David produced another mignonette of pastis from his pocket and began to play with it absently that the fit calmed.

"So they told you about the incident, did they?"

David shook his head.

"Good for them. Do you want me to tell you? I'm amazed it didn't happen before. Butchers and bakers put their wares in the window to excite consumers, and that girl's *lolos* were always out there on display, so obviously the kids got excited. And what *lolos* they were, too! Round and firm, like grapefruits." He shook his head sadly. "They say that growing old is a virtue, like wine maturing in a cellar, but . . ." His voice faded off. David produced another mignonette to get the mayor back on track.

"What exactly happened?"

"It was that *voyou* Antonin, the baron's son. The way I heard it, Anou, as they used to call him, was out cruising one night with his little gang and came across la Belle Fanny having it on with her shriveled-up little boyfriend, the butcher's son, in a copse at the edge of the village. Anou decided that Olivier—that's the butcher's son—should share his bounty. And bounty it was, let me tell you!"

The mayor tapped David's side pocket, making the stock of mignonettes clink brightly. He waited for his first sip before resuming his story.

"The way I heard it told, Fanny was willing enough. She made some sort of sign to Anou, and he went *droit au beurre*—right for the butter. It seems Anou wasn't enough for her, so she amused herself with two or three of Anou's pals. Then she got sick of the game and shooed them off, and they scattered obligingly enough.

"If it had been up to me, I'd have let the incident drop, but we live in funny times, and I suppose in some highfalutin places that sort of thing might even be considered a crime. So I had the gendarmes investigate. Their report said there were five of them in all—Antonin Brault,

Galinette Brun, Jean Cadort, Philoxéne Cabanis, and Escartefigue Anglade. Well, six, really, because young Jean-
Louis Brault was also there. He was only twelve at the
time, and you wouldn't have thought he'd have enough of
a *gourdin* at that age to do anything, but you can never tell
with all the hormones they put in the beef nowadays, can
you? Anyway, the gendarmes didn't want to haul in a
child, so they left Jean-Louis out of the procès-verbal. The
other five denied everything, and of course, Fanny didn't
press charges, so that was that." He paused. "That girl
certainly had unbelievable *lolos*, though, that's for damn
sure." He shook his head in wonderment at the memory.

"And there was no question Jean-Louis Brault was
there?"

"He was present, all right. For sure. I interviewed the
boys myself. They were a lot more open with me than with
the gendarmes."

"And so it was the boyfriend, Olivier, who took Fanny
home?"

"No, it wasn't. The gendarmerie report said that Olivier
had run off in terror when he saw Anou's gang arrive. I
told you he was a limp dick. It seems that Angèle, Fanny's
mother, had sent her son, Lucien, out to get Fanny to bring
her back to dinner, and he arrived just as Anou and his
gang were running off. It must have been Lucien who took
her home. But that didn't come up in anybody's question-
ing. Don't get yourself in a state about this. But I'm sure it
was just business as usual for Fanny. All that girl ever
wanted to do was *faire la planche*."

David looked at the mayor blankly.

"You know, make like a plank and spend as much time
as she could flat on her back." The mayor laughed and
tapped David's pocket again, relishing in the cheerful
clinking sound.

As David poured out the final drink of the afternoon,
the mayor looked at him wistfully. "You know, young

man, you have a *bonne tête*—a good head. With your love of the village and your knack of making people talk, you'd be a natural for politics. Why don't you come back again and we can chat about that? And don't forget to bring your little friends." He tapped David's pocket and grinned at the jingle.

CHAPTER 27

The Travellers Club was quartered in the last remaining *hôtel particulier* on the Champs-Élysées, a memento of more opulent days, when the broad avenue served as a carriage promenade for *le tout Paris* to show off hats, spouses' coifs, and perfectly matched steeds.

Because women were only admitted on Thursday evenings, Capucine, indignant with self-righteous feminism, refused to set foot in the place. Alexandre himself—who had joined in his university days—had ambivalent feelings about the antifeminist implications of his membership, but they didn't prevent him from popping in for the occasional lunch. The appeal was the long members' table, where he could breeze in and natter with fellow members, an attractive alternative to a solitary lunch shared with a newspaper on a café terrace.

At twelve Alexandre had completed an interview of the chef of a new restaurant on the Champs and realized that he was a good number of notches beyond peckish and only three minutes away from the Travellers.

Expecting nothing more than an adequate tournedos and an unremarkable Bordeaux, he climbed the onyx staircase and made for the long table.

Only two adjoining seats were vacant. Alexandre slid into one of them, cast a quick look at the succinct menu, and gave his order to a waiter: pheasant pâté to begin with, followed by a beef fillet with boiled, buttered, and parsleyed potatoes, the lot to be washed down with a half-liter carafe of the club Bordeaux.

The slightly gelatinous pâté arrived in less than three minutes, accompanied by two slices of very toasted sliced bread. Alexandre poured himself a glass of the Bordeaux and reluctantly began on the pâté.

An exceptionally well-dressed young man slid into the seat next to him. Alexandre recognized London tailoring and amused himself by attempting to guess which of the Savile Row tailors had made the suit. It took his mind off the pâté.

The newcomer fidgeted, played with his silverware, fussed with his napkin. Thinking he was a new member, Alexandre took pity on him.

"It's not the done thing to shake hands in the club, but I can still introduce myself. Alexandre de Huguelet."

"Thierry Brissac-Vanté," the young man said, extending his hand and immediately pulling it back with an embarrassed grin. "I know you so well by reputation, you're almost an old friend."

The waiter approached to take his order.

"You can't drink that plonk," Brissac-Vanté said, indicating Alexandre's carafe with his chin. "Let me order a bottle of something halfway decent for the both of us." He flipped through the wine list with a clearly put-on air of knowledgeable insouciance and ordered a bottle of 2005 Belair-Monange.

Alexandre raised an internal eyebrow at the idea of a three-hundred-euro bottle of Saint-Emilion for a *déjeuner sur le pouce*—a snack lunch eaten on the run—but even though he found the ostentation offensive, he was the last person to look a gift horse in the mouth.

"The food's appalling here if you don't stick to steaks and chops, but the wine list's absolutely first rate, don't you think?" Brissac-Vanté said.

Alexandre didn't. A substantial fortune in grand crus tossed and turned fitfully in the cellar, kept awake by the rumbling of the Number 1 metro line, which ran feet away from the building. Even though the beleaguered wine committee had managed to agree on an acceptable house wine, it was well known in the club that between that and insomniac grands crus lay a deserted wasteland. The young man was definitely no oenologist.

With the fresh-faced enthusiasm of a Boy Scout, Brissac-Vanté continued on. "I commiserate with you on your battle with Lucien Folon. I've read all the articles in the press. I was honored to be a partner—purely financially, of course—of Chef Brault. It's offensive to me to see his memory tarnished by a hack like that Folon."

Alexandre was grateful that the Belair-Monange arrived and that Brissac-Vanté's insistence that he do the tasting spared him the necessity of commenting on his feud with Folon.

The food arrived, and they maintained desultorily club patter for a brief half an hour. As they put their knives and forks on their plates, Brissac-Vanté looked at Alexandre with wide-eyed keenness.

"It's absolutely fabulous that I ran into you," Brissac-Vanté said. "Can I ask you a professional question? How do you think Michelin is going to rate Chez La Mère Denis in their next Guide?"

Alexandre laughed. "Michelin is as inscrutable as the Oracle of Delphi. Like everyone else, you'll have to wait for the Guide to come out on February twenty-eighth to learn the answer to that one."

The tradition at the Travellers' was to take coffee in the downstairs bar. Alexandre and Brissac-Vanté beat the rush and found a table next to the window overlooking a pocket courtyard. On the other side were the curtained windows of the so-called card room, where members played backgammon for high stakes in flagrant violation of the law.

A waiter came and took their orders: a coffee for Alexandre and a coffee with a double cognac for Brissac-Vanté.

The room began to fill as members came down from the dining room. Brissac-Vanté became as skittish as a young mare who had heard thunder in the distance. Impatiently he signaled the waiter and ordered another double cognac.

A group of six men burst noisily into the bar, installed themselves on the upholstered rail in front of the enormous fireplace, and lit cigars. Brissac-Vanté ordered another double cognac. His nostrils flared.

The group at the fireplace rapidly downed their coffees and made for a door at the back of the bar. Two of them stopped and smiled at Brissac-Vanté.

"Are you joining us this afternoon?" one of them asked.

Automatically, Brissac-Vanté stood up and took a step toward the back door. Remembering his manners, he turned back, gave Alexandre a half bow, and left the room in a rush.

Alexandre went to the bar and ordered a Calvados and a second demitasse of coffee. The venerable barman was the only club servant who got away with open sarcasm about members.

"Your friend is a fool," the barman said to Alexandre as he brought his espress and Calvados. "You stand some chance of surviving drinking and driving, but drinking and backgammon is invariably fatal. Especially with those sharks."

CHAPTER 28

At ten the next morning, as one of Capucine's lieu-tenants walked through her office door for a meeting to review his open cases, Isabelle pushed through the doorway, elbowing him aside none too gently.

"Excuse me, sir," Isabelle said to the lieutenant, "but something urgent has just popped up that the commissaire needs to know about right away."

The lieutenant and Capucine exchanged sympathetic glances. They both had built up a level of tolerance for Isabelle.

The lieutenant gone, Isabelle kicked the door shut with her heel.

"Folon's our man. No doubt about it at all."

"What makes you say that?"

"It turns out that three of the other rapists have been killed in suspicious circumstances."

"Isabelle, you're getting ahead of yourself. What 'other' rapists? What are you talking about?"

"The ones who weren't the Brault brothers. Remember David's report? There were four of them. Well, three have been murdered."

"Murdered?"

"Well, it's not in the files, but that's obviously what happened. Get this. Galinette—whose legal given name is Hugolin, by the way—Brun died just outside of La Cadière, shot in the head with a shotgun while he was out hunting hare in the hills."

"There's a gendarmerie report?"

"For once, a thorough one. Brun was found on a deserted hillside that was covered with low scrub. He'd been shot in the back of the head at relatively close range. The report makes it clear Brun had been standing in the open when he was shot. It was obviously intentional."

"And the gendarmerie conclusion?"

"Accidental death, of course. But they always say that. Then, a year later, Escartefigue Anglade apparently 'fell' "—Isabelle made ironic quotes with her fingers—"off a rock into a gully while he was collecting wildflowers used to make herbal teas. It seems he supplemented his revenue as a pig farmers' hand by going into the hills to collect things that he would sell to a Lyon company that manufactures and distributes natural products for tree huggers."

"Escartefigue must be a nickname."

"No, that's what shows on the civil register."

"And he would go to Lyon to sell what he collected?"

"No. I called the company. They have an itinerant buyer who travels up and down Provence, buying this stuff from locals. It's all dried, anyway, so there's no rush. The man I spoke to said that Anglade was one of their best suppliers. Very experienced. See the pattern emerging?"

"And the third one?"

"Jean Cadort. He died the year after. Hit by a tractor while he was riding his Solex. Of course, those ridiculous bicycles with the little motor on top of the front wheel should be outlawed, but it would still be easy enough to get one out of the way of a tractor, wouldn't you think?"

"What did the gendarmerie report say?"

"Road accident. No comment."

"And you think it was intentional?"

"Of course it was. All three of them were. It's obvious. Look. Four out of the six rapists have died, and one is missing. Dead, too, for all we know. One of them was definitely murdered, and I'll bet a month's pay the others were murdered, too."

"And how do you explain that Philoxéne Cabanis was spared?"

"Spared so far, Commissaire. Only so far. He's got to be next on the list. Either him or Antonin Brault. That is, if Antonin isn't already dead."

"And the killer would be?"

"Lucien Folon. Who else? He has the motive, and he had the means. Of course he's our man. No doubt about it. Now all we need to do is to dig up some supporting evidence and let the juge d'instruction wrap it up for the prosecutor. A big red bow on a sweet little package for *Monsieur le Procureur de la Justice*."

"Isabelle, remember that phrase from Sherlock Holmes I always like to quote. Let the facts dictate your theory. Don't try to force them into your preconceived notion."

"Commissaire, this isn't some mystery novel. This is the real world, where there are no coincidences. Four out of six people who were perps in a rape have died violently. We can't walk away from that."

"All right. You win. This is something that needs to be investigated. Have David interview this Philoxéne Cabanis. Also, get him to see if he can find Antonin Brault. Why don't you put in a call to the gendarmerie headquarters of the department of the Var and see what they can dig up for him? You've piqued my curiosity. I'd like to know if brother Antonin is still alive and hear what he has to say about all this. And I want you to do some research on Folon and see if he could have been present during these deaths. If it turns out he was doing restaurant reviews in Tokyo, your theory goes out the window."

"Now you're talking, Commissaire. Don't you worry. I'm on it. We'll have this one wrapped up in a few days."

Isabelle was so happy, she almost skipped out of Capucine's office.

CHAPTER 29

"Allô, Capucine!" Chéri Lecomte said brightly over the brigade telephone. Capucine thought the use of her first name was a bit much.

"*Je te téléphone parce que . . .* I'm calling you because . . ." The first name might have passed, but the *tu* was definitely over the top for a mere acquaintance.

Capucine replied with a frosty "Oui." Apparently, her tone passed unnoticed.

"Listen, I know absolutely nothing about police procedure, and I thought you could help me out with a problem."

"What sort of problem?"

"It's . . . personal . . . sort of intimate . . . Would it be all right if I came to see you? It's not something I can really talk about on the telephone."

"I think I can give you an appointment next week. I'll have the brigade receptionist call you. He handles my schedule."

"Next week! This is really urgent. Can't I come by this morning? You can find a few minutes for a friend, can't you?"

Capucine was torn. The presumptuous tone irritated her, and she suspected that this probably had to do with a uniformed policeman banging on her door about a pile of unpaid parking tickets. On the other hand, there was a remote chance that it might have something to do with the case.

Capucine smiled down the line. "For you, I could prize open a slot tomorrow morning. Say at ten. Is that soon enough?"

"It'll have to do, won't it?"

At nine thirty the next morning the receptionist called to announce that a Madame Lecomte had arrived.

"Let her sit. It's going to be a while before I can get to her."

Capucine continued her discussion with one of her lieutenants about an arrest planned for later that morning and then listened to a report by her other lieutenant about his current case—a very tricky one—which he seemed to have satisfyingly in hand. The lieutenant left at ten twenty. Capucine picked up the duty roster and began making changes, assigning two more brigadiers to the lieutenant's case. At ten thirty the uniformed receptionist walked through the open doorway.

"This Madame Lecomte has been waiting for an hour. Do you want me to send her away?"

"Good Lord, no. I completely forgot about her. Show her in."

Despite her belted bright-print dress from another age and the inevitable red-soled Louboutins, Chéri was far less radiant than usual.

"It's so kind of you," she said, again using the offensive *tu*, "to see me on such short notice." Chéri moved in for an air kiss, which Capucine parried, retreating behind her desk and calling the receptionist to ask him to get the café on the corner to send around two expresses. An abiding French myth was that the slightly bitter café coffee was invariably better than anything that could be produced in house.

They exchanged banalities for a few minutes, until a waiter in an ankle-length white apron—still immaculate at that hour of the morning—appeared with a cork-lined tray containing two demitasses covered by their saucers to keep them hot. Once the mysterious bond that humans construct by jointly ingesting food substances was established, Capucine smiled encouragingly at Chéri.

"Why don't you tell me about the problem you want to discuss?"

Chéri fidgeted. In earlier eras she would have wrung a handkerchief or gone through the elaborate ritual of lighting a cigarette. But, deprived of these props, all she could do was dart her eyes from side to side, seeking escape in the corners of the room. Eventually, she cleared her throat and launched into her story.

"It's very embarrassing. The sort of thing only a woman would understand. That's why I'm turning to you." She stopped short.

Capucine said nothing. Silence was the most powerful goad the interviewer possessed.

"For a good number of years I ... well ... I have been deeply in love with a certain monsieur."

Capucine groaned inwardly. This was going to take over an hour, and it would have something to do with the unrequited love of a married man and some form of monetary compensation. She snuck a look at the appointment list that had been printed out for her. Her next appointment was at eleven: a case involving a father who disciplined his six-year-old boy so severely, he was frequently in the emergency room and missed so much school, he was in danger of repeating the year.

"The monsieur's name is Thierry Brissac-Vanté. I'm sure you know about him since he's one of the owners of Chez La Mère Denis."

Capucine looked at her levelly for several long beats, hoping the rest of it would come gushing out. Chéri said nothing but found enough self-confidence to meet Capucine's gaze.

Capucine broke the silence. "Why do you think the police should be involved?"

"I think harm has come to Thierry."

"Why?"

"Thierry and I would call each other at least once a day. Even if he couldn't get away from his wife, he always called me." There was a long pause. "But he hasn't called in a week. And every time I try his cell phone, it rings six times before it goes to voice mail. That means it's on. I just can't believe he's looking at my name popping up on his screen and refusing to take the call. Something's happened to him." There was another long pause.

"So I called his house on the landline. Something he told me never to do. I pretended I was a charitable organization he had pledged some money to. The person that answered, some sort of servant would be my guess, said that he was away for the day and that she would take a message. Of course, he never called back. I don't know what to do." Her eyes filled with liquid.

In the normal course of events this was the sort of incident that would not even be recorded on the police blotter. Since time immemorial men were notorious for jettisoning their rejected women over a wall of silence. But, of course, Brissac-Vanté was a central figure in Capucine's cases. Exactly when was the last time she had heard a real-time report about him? Come to think of it, it did seem a long while back.

"Was there any incident? A dispute? A misunderstanding?"

"No, nothing. That's just it. I spoke to him just last week. We made plans to have dinner." Chéri licked her lips. "He wanted to take me to a new restaurant that serves food from Réunion Island. He says they have a dish of very spicy baby goat that is just fabulous. He read about the place in *Elle* magazine and had a reservation for the next day—"

Capucine cut her off. "And he never called back to confirm your date? Is that it?"

Chéri nodded, almost gratefully. "I keep on calling and calling, and he never picks up."

Capucine stood up. "I'll look into it. Informally. There's not enough here to open a dossier, but I'll call you in a day or two and tell you what I come up with. Will that do?"

Chéri smiled weakly. She had expected something more. Capucine had no idea what. The only thing she was sure of was that a good part of the story had been a fib.

CHAPTER 30

"Bonjour, Monsieur le Maire. I stopped by because I need your help."

David had half expected the old man not to remember him. But the minute the mayor caught sight of David walking through the door, he peered intently at the side pockets of David's jacket. The mayor beamed when he saw the lumpy bulges.

"Le Cannois! I figured you'd be back."

Apparently, the tide of village gossip had floated David's local nickname as far away as a nursing home in the outskirts of Cassis.

"Just in time for the apéro before lunch." It was ten thirty in the morning.

David collected the glass and carafe from the night table, set them down on the stand next to the mayor's reclining armchair. The mayor pulled a lever, and the chair shot upright. David twisted open a mignonette of Pastis Ricard and poured it into the glass. The mayor added water and fell silent, transfixed at the transformation of liquid gold into mother's milk.

"You have good taste in pastaga, mon ami. But you're

not going to make me drink alone, a man of my age. There's another glass in the drawer of my night table. I filched it from my dinner tray last night."

David smiled at the thought of Isabelle's reaction to him drinking on duty in the middle of the morning. This was definitely better than Paris. Maybe there might even be something in the idea of local politics. The mayor picked up the trace of David's grin.

"Nothing better than a little apéro." He clinked his glass against David's and glanced at the door like a guilty schoolboy. In an effort to regain his gravitas, he tucked in his chin and looked sternly at David.

"You said you needed my help, Le Cannois."

"I'd like to interview Antonin Brault and get his input on Jean-Louis's childhood. You know, the point of view of the elder sibling. The gendarmes say they have no idea where he went."

The mayor looked at David shrewdly. "I'm amazed they made any comment at all. You authors must have quite some pull." He tapped David's pocket for another mignonette, which he emptied into his glass and topped up with water. He took a long appreciative sip. "But you're in luck. I know where he is."

"You do?" This bit of good news vastly exceeded David's expectations.

"Of course I do. Keep very close tabs on your constituency. That's the secret to success in politics. Keep that in mind when your time comes."

It would appear that Antonin was working as a temp mechanic for a Peugeot garage in a village a half an hour away. By a stroke of luck David's rental car happened to be a Peugeot. David planned on a trip to the garage first thing the next morning.

It took him a good two hours to extract himself from the mayor, who went on at length reaffirming his opinion that David was a natural for village politics. It was not clear to David if this was a ploy to keep the Ricard tap open or if the view was sincere. David was unable to pry himself loose until well after the Angelus would have sounded in La Cadière. He left with more insights into the subtleties of village mayoral politics than he had ever imagined existed.

By the time he drove the twenty minutes back to La Cadière, he was starving. Casimir, the owner of Le Marius, was back from his lunch, energetically polishing glasses behind the bar. The café was completely deserted, save for a lanky man in his middle thirties who David recognized by sight as Felix Olivier.

"I heated this up for you," Casimir said, serving David an enormous slice of fougasse packed with black olives, sun-dried tomatoes, and dark air-cured ham. He set a quarter-liter carafe of rosé next to it. Under the cover of the clank of dish, glass, and carafe, Casimir jutted his chin microscopically in the direction of Olivier and muttered, "He's been looking for you, Le Cannois. He's asked after you three times already."

David shrugged his shoulders in acceptance of the ways of the world.

When Casimir went back to his obsessive-compulsive glass polishing, Olivier came up to the bar, glass of chalky white liquid in hand. He was careful to station himself a good two feet beyond David's territorial perimeter. There was a long awkward moment.

"You're the writer," Olivier said, posing the question as a statement of fact, with no upward inflection on the last word.

"Guilty as charged," David said as he cut off another piece of fougasse.

"Let me introduce myself. I'm Felix Olivier." He turned toward David but did not presume to extend his hand.

"The butcher's son," David said, concentrating on chewing. He realized how much he missed real fougasse when he was in Paris.

"And you're writing a book about Jean-Louis Brault."

"Guilty again." David swallowed his last bite of fougasse, washed it down with the last swallow of the rosé, and edged into Olivier's space. "I was going to sit outside and have a pastaga. Care to join me?" Without waiting for a reply, David turned to Casimir and said, "We'll be on the terrace. Can you bring us One Hundred and Two?"

At the luncheon hour the village square was deserted. Not even a stray dog wandered by to lift his leg. The din of the cicadas was almost deafening. David savored the liquorish taste of the pastis, his third of the day.

Olivier took a quick deep draught, downing a quarter of his drink.

"You're going to write about that . . . incident . . . with Fanny?" This time it came out as a question.

David said nothing.

Olivier downed another quarter of his drink, choked, and coughed.

"Well, I don't want to look bad in your book. I want you to say what really happened."

David said nothing, egging Olivier on with his silence.

"The village will tell you that Fanny encouraged Anou. But that's not true at all. Not at all. It's important you know that."

David looked at him and slowly took a sip of pastis. "Let me try and visualize the scene," he said. "You were, if I understand the situation, on top of Fanny when Brault came up with his pals?"

"Of course I was on top of her. She was my girlfriend. And let me tell you, she was writhing and moaning and having a wonderful time. She really was. It's important you understand that."

David nodded dispassionately. "And so what happened?"

"I noticed Anou and a bunch of his pals hiding in the trees, sniggering at us. They all had cans of beer in their hands and were having a good time at my expense. Fanny saw them, too, and stopped moving around. It's true she looked at them. Who wouldn't?"

There was another long pause. Both men finished their drinks.

"Then Anou came over to us and hauled me up by my collar and made me stand. I told him to let go. That's when he hit me in the ear. It started bleeding."

"Did Fanny scream?"

"No. She was so shocked, she just lay there with a funny expression on her face. That was all that happened."

"So what did you do?"

"What did I *do?* Five of the biggest bullies in the village were about to beat me up. I got out of there as fast as I could. I was lucky to get home in one piece. Anybody would do that, right?"

"And was Jean-Louis Brault there?"

"I don't know. Probably. It happened very fast. Jean-Louis was always hanging around with his big brother. He might have been behind the other boys. Yes, now that I think about it, he *was* there. Definitely!"

A scrawny man in patched work clothes came up behind Olivier and called out, *"Salut, Le Cocu!* How's it going, Cuckold!" Judging from the slur in his voice, the newcomer was a fervent adept of the maire's school of mid-morning drinking.

Olivier turned as sharply as a skittish cow prodded with a sharp stick.

"Oh, salut, Philoxéne," Olivier said meekly, his glow of

self-righteousness evaporating like a wisp of mist in the morning sun.

Philoxéne Cabanis, the fourth victim. The very man he was going to spend the rest of the afternoon tracking down. The Midi was definitely the place to do police work. Here, all you had to do was sit at a café table, sipping pastaga in the warm sun, and everyone you wanted would eventually come and sit right down with you.

"Sounds like you were talking about my girlfriend, Fanny," Cabanis said, making a sign at Casimir through the window of the bar. Casimir ignored him, industrious with his glasses.

Olivier clenched his teeth and scowled at Cabanis.

"What's the matter, you wimp? Are you afraid I'm going to tell Le Cannois about how Fanny was so bored with your tiny little dick that she was begging Anou to come over and give her something man sized to moan about?" Cabanis grinned at David. "If this guy was an inch shorter, he'd be a girl!" He roared with laughter.

Olivier stood up, his face flushed bright carmine.

Cabanis stood up, too. "What are you going to do? Punch me, you little half-pint? Go on. Get out of here. Run back to your daddy and hide behind his apron, like you always do." He pushed Olivier violently in the chest. Olivier staggered and regained his balance. "Go on. Get. No room for a little boy at a table of men."

Olivier's eyes moistened. He pivoted and walked off almost at a trot.

"That's the same thing that happened the evening we had that laugh with Fanny. Daddy's boy there took one look at Anou and galloped off home. What he can't get over is that Fanny had smiled at Anou and had beckoned him to come over. Can't nobody say that's not true. I was there. That Fanny always knew a real man when she saw one. She sure had an eye for it."

Cabanis made another gesture at the barman, with as little success. David turned in his seat and motioned to Casimir with his fingertips.

"A Hundred and Two," he ordered, putting a little twist on his grin to take the sting out of the incident.

Cabanis nodded his thanks. "I guess it's true that you're becoming a *caïd* around here," he muttered almost inaudibly.

"I owe it all to clean living," David said, clinking his glass against Cabanis's. Both men chuckled.

"So what's your version of the story?" David asked.

"Same as everybody else's. We was just out having some beers and roaming around, seeing what was happening, and Anou gets an idea. 'Let's go over to that wood on the hill behind the village. That's where that pussy Felix Olivier takes his girl. Let's see if Fanny likes it or just lies there, wishing it was somebody else.' So we go up there, and sure enough, they're hard at it. Felix is trying to get her to take her dress off, but she wasn't having any of that. Finally, she gives a snort and lifts her skirt and lies back in the grass. Felix was in and out in about three heartbeats. Fanny was really pissed off. 'It happened again, you idiot. I told you, you have to learn to take it slow.' That's when Anou goes up to them.

"When Fanny sees Anou coming up, she gets all smiley at him. So what was Anou going to do? He lifts Felix up by the collar and goes, 'Let me show you what she means, wimp.' Felix says something, and Anou gives him a good one up the side of the head and he runs off. *Tu veux que je te dise?* Do you want me to tell you? It was a whole different story when Anou got going. Fanny started moaning loud enough to get the whole village up there."

"And then you all had a go at her."

"Nah, just two of us. And then Fanny says she's getting sore and it's time to go home to dinner, anyway. So we go back down the hill. On the way down we run into Lucien Folon coming up. I guess his mother had sent him looking for Fanny to get her home to dinner on time. Lucien gives us all a dirty look, but nothing happens."

"And Jean-Louis Brault was with you."

"Funny thing that. He was with us when we went up the hill. That's for sure. When we were up there, I sure didn't have my eyes on no little kid. You can bet on that. But when we went back down the hill, he wasn't with us. Maybe he'd run off scared. He didn't want to go in the first place, but Anou made him." He stopped short. "Think you can get your pal Casimir to bring us some more pastaga? He won't serve me."

When the next round had been brought and water added with care, Cabanis resumed his tale. "Thing is, if that Folon kid hadn't gone off the deep end, everybody in the village would have forgotten about it in three days. But no, Folon goes ballistic. First thing he does is beat the shit out of Jean-Lu every day at school. Got so bad, Anou had to show up and put a stop to it. That only made him wilder.

"Next thing he does is pinch a fifty-pound bag of sodium chlorate from the gardener's shed at the school— you know, the stuff they use to kill weeds in gravel drive-ways—and sprinkle it around the base of the baron's olive trees one night when it's beginning to get stormy. There was no trace of it after the rain, but the day after, the leaves start falling off. I tell you, those damn trees *still* don't give a decent crop of olives." Cabanis shook his head in amazement.

"But that wasn't enough for Lucien. So he goes out looking for stray cats and gets about six of them in a burlap bag. He goes over to the Brault place real quiet in the middle of the night and throws the bag over this chicken-wire fence right into the baron's precious bantam hens. In the morning half of them are dead, and the other half don't lay for six months." Cabanis leaned far over the table and whispered conspiratorially, "But that was nothing, I mean nothing, compared to what he did after." He tapped the side of his empty glass significantly.

David went up to the bar to get the drinks. PJ accounting wasn't going to believe how much he had to spend on booze on this case.

As he poured a fresh glass, Casimir said, "Watch out for that one when he's had a snout full. He can get mighty nasty. That's why I don't want him in here."

David smiled, pursing his lips, and shook his head, miming that there was nothing to worry about.

"What did he do next? *Tu veux que je te dise?* Do you want me to tell you?" Cabanis asked when David returned with the drinks. "He started killing us off one by one."

Beneath his level stare, David rejoiced. This was definitely the place to do police work. You didn't even have to ask questions. All you had to do was bring the drinks.

"You don't believe me? Listen up. There were six of us that night with Fanny, right? You know what happened to Jean-Lu. What you don't know is that someone shot Galinette in the head at close range. Then Escartefigue falls down a ravine in the hills up there." Cabanis waved vaguely in the direction of the north with his arm. "That guy was as sure-footed as a goat, running up and down the rocks after wild herbs. Then Jean gets mowed down by a tractor as he's riding home on his Solex. Even the dumb-ass gendarmes thought that was suspicious, but they still called it an accident."

Cabanis looked at David truculently. "And Anou? What do you think happened to him? Hasn't been heard from in years. He probably was the first to get done in. So what does that tell you?"

David said nothing.

"No, merde, I'm not kidding. What does that tell you?" Cabanis almost yelled. Casimir looked at them with alarm from behind the bar.

"It tells me that you think you're going to be next."

"Goddamn fucking right that's what I think. So get me another drink. I need one."

CHAPTER 31

After Chéri left the office, Capucine traced a pattern on the imitation-wood surface of her desk for a few seconds, rooted around in her desk for Brissac-Vanté's card, and dialed his cell phone number. True to Chéri's word, it rang six times before voice mail clicked in. The phone was turned on and had a signal, but no one was picking up.

Next, she called Brissac-Vanté office. A bright, young, perky female voice answered immediately.

"Monsieur Brissac-Vanté, s'il vous plaît. This is—"

"I'm sorry. He's in a meeting right now. Can I take a message and get him to call you back as soon as he's available?"

"Mademoiselle, this is the police. Would you please inform Monsieur Brissac-Vanté that I need to speak to him immediately."

"I'm sorry. He's actually playing golf. He won't be back until much later."

"Golf? No problem. Tell me where he's playing and I'll have him picked up."

There was an awkward pause.

"I can't. . . . . He, well, really, he's gone to England for a golf tournament. I should have said that."

"Mademoiselle, lying to the police is a punishable offense. What if I send a squad car for you and we finish this discussion in my office?"

"Please, madame," the secretary said through an obviously dry throat. "I'm only telling you what Madame Brissac-Vanté told me to say. She called me last week and said that her husband would be going abroad and I was to take messages if anyone called. I only said it was England because he goes there so often."

"And you haven't heard from him since then?"

"No. Not a word. Not even an e-mail. It's really weird. This is the first time this has happened in the whole year I've been working here."

"When, exactly, was the last time you saw him?"

"Last Thursday evening. He was here when I left. He didn't come in on Friday or any day this week."

"Do you know what his plans were for Thursday evening?"

"Of course. I had made a reservation for a table for two at Le Grand Véfour for eight o'clock that night. I don't know who he was taking, but a fancy place like that, it must have been a potential client."

Next, Capucine called Le Grand Véfour and used her married name, which invariably got her further in restaurant circles than her police rank. She asked for the sommelier, who was a close acquaintance of Alexandre's.

"André, can you do me a huge favor? Get the hostess to see if she had a reservation last Thursday for a Monsieur Brissac-Vanté."

He was back on the line in three minutes. "We did, but he was a no-show. He had a guest, a stuffy-looking business type, who sat around for half an hour, drinking a nice Dom Ruinart ninety-eight we have by the glass, and then left in a huff. Chef was seriously pissed off. We *never* have no-shows, and the guest stalked out without paying for his wine. Chef put this Brissac-Vanté on our no-reserve list."

* * *

Twenty minutes later Capucine double-parked in front of the Brissac-Vantés' building on the avenue Henri-Martin. As she approached the door, an extremely well-dressed, silver-haired gentleman exited and held the door open for her with a courtly bow and an engaging smile. Delighted she had been spared announcing herself on the *interphone,* she rewarded the gentleman with an almost imperceptible wiggle of her gluteals.

The door was opened by a maid in a black polyester dress and a white lace-bordered apron, an outfit Capucine had been sure existed only in the movies.

"Madame Brissac-Vanté, s'il vous plaît," Capucine requested with the easy smile of a social call.

"*Madamie pas ici,*" came the answer in a thick Portuguese accent.

Capucine aped a look of alarm and dismay. "But I'm supposed to have lunch with her."

"*Não* here. She *esta* with horses," the maid said on the defensive, convinced she was about to be blamed for something.

It took a few seconds for the penny to drop.

"L'Etrier? We're supposed to be having lunch at l'Etrier? Silly me. I always mix everything up."

The maid's happy smile was as warm as the Algarve sun.

Despite the fact that l'Etrier had enough acreage in the Bois de Boulogne for three riding rings and comfortable boxes for over a hundred horses, the clubhouse was a modest little affair with a small bar, a tiny sitting area, and a twenty-cover dining room.

As Capucine approached the clubhouse, two teenage girls lazily put their geldings over three-foot jumps. They both wore brightly colored ski jackets over riding pants with suede leggings instead of boots, clearly the equestrian must of the season. After each jump they would look into the plate-glass window, presumably at doting mothers.

Yolande Brissac-Vanté sat by herself at the diminutive bar. At Capucine's approach Yolande turned, took a moment to recognize her, jumped off her stool, preparing to run, then realized she was cornered. Her face was a tight rictus of terror, eyes so wide, the white was visible all the way around the azure irises.

"What do you want?"

"I'm trying to find your husband. Do you know where he is?"

Yolande choked back a sob and looked wildly around the almost empty room. The barman could be heard noisily stacking bottles in the kitchen.

"He's away on a business trip. I'll have him call you as soon as he gets back," she croaked. "Now go away."

"Madame," Capucine said, "if your husband is missing, it's potentially very serious. He's a key person in two murder cases. If you don't cooperate, I'll be forced to take you to my brigade for a formal interview."

Yolande cringed as if she had been struck.

"We can't talk here," she whispered. And then, in a much louder voice, "I was just about to go see my mare. Why don't you come with me?"

Wordlessly, they walked down long rows of square, oversized boxes until they reached one that displayed a neat card in a metal frame: *Euthymie*. Yolande leaned over the lower half of the door and peered in at her horse munching hay in the back of the box. An elderly, grizzled groom in blue workers' overalls ambled over and mumbled, "B'jour, m'dame." Yolande started and recoiled, ready to run again. Recognizing the groom, she sighed in relief. The groom apologized for the intrusion, then launched into a patois narrative about poor Euthymie's near foreleg inflammation, which at long last seemed to be responding to the ointment the veterinarian had prescribed.

Yolande smiled at the groom. "That's wonderful. I can't tell you how much I've been needing some good news." Her horse stuck her head out of the box, lips questing for treats in the pockets of Yolande's tweed jacket. Yolande stroked her nose. "The softest thing the dear Lord ever made," she said, more to herself than to Capucine. Her eyes filled with tears.

"It was last Thursday. He told me he was going straight from work out to dinner with a prospective client. But he didn't come home that night. I'm such a bad wife, I suspected he had gone out with a girl and gotten too drunk to come home."

Capucine said nothing.

"He didn't come back the next night, either. I thought he must have run off with someone. I was in a rage. I despise myself for having so little trust in him. Then the call came. It was terrible, but it was as if a ton of bricks had been lifted from my chest. They want money. All I have to do is pay and I'll get him back. Isn't that wonderful?"

Capucine continued to say nothing.

"Don't you see? Mistresses never give men back, but all kidnappers want is money." She bubbled a sound that was halfway between a laugh and a sob.

"How many times have they called you?"

"Once, just that once. On Saturday. The call lasted only a few seconds. They had him. They would notify me later how much I had to pay. But I had to promise I would tell absolutely no one. Especially not the police. If I did, I would never see him again. I'm sure they're spying on me to see if I'm keeping my word. At least you don't look at all like you work for the police."

"And you've had no further communication? No notes? No letters?"

"Nothing. Just that one call." Yolande squeezed Capucine's arm. "Kidnappers always return the victim when they are paid, don't they? Tell me that is true."

"Actually, it is."

Yolande's sigh was so loud, the mare raised her head in alarm.

"But you've got to stay away from me. I don't care about the money or catching the kidnappers. All I want is Thierry back. You've got to promise me you won't interfere. Please!"

CHAPTER 32

In her years at the Crim', Capucine knew Commissaire Jérôme Lacroix only by sight. Still, she had always been slightly in awe of him, a seasoned veteran of the old school, a cop's cop. Lacroix looked like flics used to look: baggy tweed jacket, nondescript necktie, unpressed gray flannel pants, bulky Manurhin MR 73 revolver in a sweat-darkened leather holster under his armpit.

"There aren't enough kidnapping cases in France for the PJ to have a dedicated squad. But I'm the official expert, so all kidnappings come to me, even if I'm already so deep in the crap, I need a snorkel." The crow's-feet at the edges of Lacroix's eyes deepened, and he emitted a smoker's gurgling laugh. His laugh involved his eyes but not his lips.

"Kidnappings are the shittiest job in the police. Both sides hate us. The kidnappers and, most of all, the families. They're almost always well-to-do, so they start out looking down their noses at the police. And then they believe, they desperately want to believe, that all they have to do is pay the kidnappers' ransom and—bingo!—they'll get their loved one back safe and sound. We're only there to fuck it up for them. The kidnappers have explained that to them, but they knew it, anyway."

Lacroix tapped a filter-tipped Gitanes out of a soft pack, lit it, and inhaled deeply without breaking the lock his eyes held on Capucine's.

"When you work in kidnapping, you wind up wanting to join the Italian force. Down there the police are able to freeze the family assets so they can't pay a ransom. They don't give a shit if the victim doesn't make it back home. They want to get their message out on the street loud and clear that kidnapping is not a commercially viable proposition."

Ruminatively, Lacroix shaped the tip of his cigarette in his ashtray until it formed a perfect point.

"So let's see if I have the story straight. Thierry Brissac-Vanté is married to a wealthy woman. His main occupation is as a marketing entrepreneur who represents businesses to hire celebrities to endorse their products. He also invests his wife's money in projects, which are usually very visible and often involve restaurants. That makes him sound like a very good guy to kidnap. His family has plenty of ready cash, and they're used to doling it out in large clumps." Lacroix raised his eyebrows fractionally to elicit Capucine's approval. She nodded.

"The pickup sounds professional enough, somewhere between his office on the Champs-Élysées and a restaurant in the Palais Royal. Most likely it would have been as he walked out the door of his office. All you'd have to do is have a couple of guys hang around in front of his building—easy enough to do on the Champs and not attract attention—and hustle him into a waiting car. No one on the sidewalk would notice a thing. And the wife has only had one phone call, which lasted a few seconds and provided no details other than that 'they had him.' "

Capucine nodded.

"What you've got here is a plain-vanilla kidnapping with two wrinkles—the heads of two of the victim's investments have been murdered, and his wife is good pals with the president's ex-wife. Interesting, but for the time being, we're going to forget about that."

"You are?"

"It's highly improbable that the kidnappers have left any traces, or at least not enough for us to get a bead on them. And kicking up a lot of dust with an investigation is very dangerous for the victim. The last thing we want to do is spook the kidnappers. What we need to know is how and when the transfer happens. That's when we have a crack at nabbing them, or at least picking up enough leads to get a decent investigation going. Of course, the family's going to try as hard as they can to keep us out of it."

"So what are you going to do?"

"The usual. The way kidnappers work is that they let the tension build up in the family until they're ready to cough up serious money. My guess is that the next thing that's going to happen is a phone call where the victim is put on the phone and is made to plead. The call will be cut off before we can get a trace on it. We'll get the number, but it's going to be a stolen prepaid phone, and they won't stay on the line long enough for us to locate where the call came from. The call with the amount and the instructions for the handover won't happen until the family has been left to stew, thinking about how much the poor victim is suffering.

"So all the phones—office, house, wife's cell, and servants' cells—will go on a level-one tap upstairs." He pointed with his thumb to the top floor of the Quai, where the long banks of phone-tapping receivers were located.

"Why don't you add Chéri Lecomte to your list? She claims to be having an affair with Brissac-Vanté and was the one who tipped me off to the fact that he'd gone missing."

Lacroix extracted a small pad from the center drawer of his desk and made a note.

"Then we call the fiscal brigade and get them to start

monitoring the wife's accounts. I'm hoping we'll pick up the kidnappers' calls, but if we don't, I want a heads-up that the wife is withdrawing important sums of money."

"Call Lieutenant Firmin Bouchard. I used to work there, and he's very good. He's already run down the family finances for me, so he has a head start."

"Perfect. If he can get a handle on any offshore accounts the family has, so much the better. That's where we always run into trouble."

Capucine's forehead creased slightly in concern. "That's it?"

"Look, in this game you have to learn to be patient. It's not like regular police work. You have to let them come to you."

"And you think the kidnapping has nothing to do with my murders."

"No, I never said that. I'm just telling you how we're going to try to catch these guys."

CHAPTER 33

Alexandre sat in the exact middle of his study, throned in an ancient leather armchair, holding *Le Figaro* at arm's length and scowling. Clenching a three-inch cigar stub in his jaws, he snapped the newspaper to make it stand up stiffly at attention. Capucine and Jacques, sitting on the sofa opposite, waited for the detonation.

"Risen tezis tzby zat imbefil lusen wowon!"

Capucine got up and gently removed the cigar from his mouth and threw it into the fireplace. Alexandre glared at her malevolently.

When she sat down, Jacques said, "I do believe that was half of a Trinidad Robusto. They're virtually impossible to obtain if your last name isn't Castro. You've committed a serious faux pas, ma cousine. My heart's going pitter-patter, thinking about the spanking you're going to get."

Alexandre glowered at him and gave the paper another shake. "Listen to this. It's by that imbecile Lucien Folon." Alexandre looked up at Capucine to make sure she had understood this time. She smiled sweetly at him. "He calls his piece 'How Bright the Light Once the Bushel Removed.' " Alexandre gave the paper another angry shake. Jacques settled into the sofa, preparing to enjoy himself.

"Now that Chef Prosper Ouvrard has been freed from the stifling yoke of the late, but hardly great Chef Jean-Louis Brault, the genius of his cuisine is blossoming. Freed to add protein to his palette, Ouvrard is creating dishes that are vibrant with life and passion, something never before seen at La Mère Denis."

Alexandre paused, patted the arm of his chair for the ashtray, remembered it was empty, patted again for his glass, remembered that was empty, too, and, with a frown, resumed reading.

"It is high time for the hidebound cabal of critics, led by *Le Monde*'s bumptious Alexandre de Huguelet, notorious vassal of conventional wisdom, to admit that Chez La Mère Denis is now a bird of a completely different feather, a Phoenix risen from the ashes of banality."

Loudly, Alexandre crumpled the newspaper into a ball and threw it in the corner. He got up and poured himself a finger of Scotch from a square cut-glass decanter nestled into a bookshelf.

Unexpectedly, Alexandre calmed. He smiled at Jacques.

"I'll tell you what it's high time for. It's time for me to retreat to my ovens and cook dinner for you two. Trust me, it's going to be entirely vegetarian," he said acidly. "But don't get your hopes up. Amateur hack that I am, the recipes are from those little cards in *Elle* magazine." He left, shutting the door very gently behind him.

Capucine was torn. Alexandre didn't seem hurt, but she knew how sensitive he could be. Of course, a healthy dash of solitude, judiciously seasoned with the herbs and spices of his kitchen, would make the most potent salve. But she still felt guilty not being at his side.

Jacques went over to the bookcase and filled his glass with a good two fingers from Alexandre's decanter. He sniffed appreciatively. "This Yamazaki single malt eventually becomes addictive. Whatever the right-wing press might say about your geriatric gastronome, it's incontrovertible he has excellent taste in whiskey."

Capucine pouted, expecting the other shoe to drop. Jacques's faint praise of Alexandre was invariably accompanied by a barb, usually relating to his ostensible amorous insufficiencies due to his being on the far side of forty. But Jacques said nothing. He sipped his whiskey and examined Alexandre's books, tapping a spine every now and then, either in approval or dismay. It dawned on Capucine that he was stalling about telling her something.

Jacques picked another glass off the tray, put an inch of whiskey in it, and handed it to Capucine, placing his foot, shod in a navy-blue Weston alligator loafer, on the arm of the sofa. He took a deep breath.

Capucine sniffed at the single malt and wrinkled her nose. "How can you two drink this stuff?" She left the room and returned almost immediately with a glass bowl filled with ice and put a handful in her glass.

"If Alexandre sees that, you really *are* going to get a spanking." Jacques brayed his donkey laugh, and most of his confidence returned. "Your name came up again this morning in our executive meeting."

Capucine looked at him quizzically. It was like playing What's Wrong with This Picture? Several things: Jacques wasn't masking the sanctity he felt for the DGSE with levity. It was also the first time he had made this sort of pronouncement without some form of cover against bugging. But most amazingly, he seemed almost embarrassed. Yes, that was definitely it. He was really embarrassed. Would wonders never cease?

"In a word, cousine, the powers on high are skittish— *concerned* is too strong a term—about this kidnapping of Brissac-Vanté."

"Because of the president's ex-wife's friendship with his wife?"

"Pas du tout. They don't give a toss about that. They're in a pet that the investigation will prize open the Pandora's box of your Roque case."

Capucine took a sip of the single malt. Even chilled to the freezing point, it tasted like unwashed socks soaked in rubbing alcohol, with three drops of iodine thrown in for good measure. She set the glass back on the table with a grimace.

"They are troubled that Commissaire Jérôme Lacroix is involved," Jacques added.

"Why? He's extremely competent and zealous."

"Two very dangerous virtues. And, in addition, he has the reputation of being as independent as a deerhound, and it is known he'll be retired in four months. Once he has his pension in hand, he can't be pressured. The concern is that he just might turn into a loose cannon."

Jacques searched Capucine's face for a reaction. She looked back at him expressionlessly.

"One of the ideas aired this morning was that the case be removed from the hands of the PJ and handed to the DGSE. Of course, everyone in the room was opposed. In the end it was decided that Lacroix would be kept on but you would be put in charge. That decision will be communicated to the PJ hierarchy. He's to communicate his findings only to you. Voilà, a significant field promotion for my little cousin."

Capucine's face flattened, and her eyes darkened. "Why me? Because I'm too docile to be a loose cannon? Because they think I'm going to do what you all tell me to do? Because I'm your cousin and that makes me automatically a government toady? Well, fuck you, and fuck your government! I'm resigning in the morning." Trembling with rage, Capucine picked up her glass, drained it, and threw the thick crystal against a wall. It exploded like a mortar burst.

The door opened, and Alexandre peered in.

"Don't worry. It was empty," Jacques said with his all-knowing Cheshire cat grin.

"Good. Dinner's ready. We're eating in the kitchen."

Capucine walked down the hall with her head on Alexandre's shoulder.

The dinner was delectable. It turned out that the tear-out cards in *Elle* had come from a piece about Alain Passard, and the recipes had been considerably simplified for the general public. Alexandre had called one of his pals in Passard's kitchen and had recovered the missing ingredients. The first course was a carpaccio of celery root, sliced paper thin with a mandoline and then sautéed in an obscene amount of butter, a spoonful of Orléans mustard, and a good number of spices and herbs, the precise identification of which, Alexandre explained, he had sworn to take to the grave with him. All Capucine knew was that it was sublime and there was plenty of tarragon in the sauce. Her mood lifted.

Aware that something had been discussed in the study that needed to be forgotten, Alexandre drew them into his own world.

"Of course, Lucien Folon is not entirely wrong. Brault's cooking was often like celestial cotton candy—light, ethereal, but evanescent. Once swallowed, it was gone, like a dream that is instantly forgotten the moment the dreamer wakes, knowing only that he *has* dreamed, but having no recollection of what the dream consisted of."

"You mean like making love to those deliciously androgynous boys in the lycée? So sweet to the touch but with absolutely no substance. You were always left hungry and unfulfilled." She gave Alexandre a womanly look to make sure he knew how things had changed for the better.

Jacques erupted in laughter: clear, tinkling, honest mirth, with not a trace of donkey or cynicism. Capucine couldn't remember him ever having laughed with such abandon.

The next course was something Alexandre called a potato "darphin," which turned out to be a potato pancake made from long, thin needles of potato, crisp and crunchy with finely chopped sage on the outside and soft and starchy on the inside. It was served with an endive and celery salad sprinkled with shavings of parmesan and a lemony vinaigrette. It was so good, they were speechless for nearly a minute.

As Capucine ate, all she could think of was how perfectly informed the DGSE was of the workings of the police. She looked around the kitchen. There must be miniature microphones and video cameras hiding like roaches in all the cracks of the woodwork.

The pièce de résistance was the dessert, a delicate avocado soufflé studded with chunks of Valrhona chocolate, baked in the emptied half shells of the avocado.

Jacques left around eleven. As she watched him ride down in the elevator, Capucine decided she would put on a special show that night for the DGSE cams and see how many junior operatives she could corrupt in one go.

CHAPTER 34

"I have a Madame de Vulpillières on the line," the uniformed front desk receptionist said. "Do you want to take the call?"

"*Oui, madame, je vous écoute.* Yes, madame, I'm listening," Capucine said.

"We have a common friend," a youngish female voice said with a Sixteenth Arrondissement lockjaw drawl so pronounced, Capucine thought it must be put on. For half a second she thought Jacques had put one of his pals up to playing a practical joke.

"Our mutual friend wants to give you something. But extreme care has to be taken. Come to La Coupole tonight at eight thirty, and you will receive instructions. It would look more natural if you came with your husband."

With the accent and the corny 1930s thriller dialogue, this definitely had to be a joke.

"Will you be there?" The timbre had gone up a notch. The throat was clearly dry and constricted. The woman was obviously in the grips of emotion. And there was definitely no snickering in the background.

"*D'accord.* I'll be there." Capucine hung up.

She pulled her keyboard over, logged in to the police database, and punched in "de Vulpillières." Five came up, but only one in Paris. A couple, Bertrand and Sidonie, thirty-seven and thirty-two, seventeen rue de la Faisanderie in the Sixteenth. Monsieur worked for the BNP Parisbasas, and Madame with a relocation agency specializing in easing the moves of foreign senior executives to Paris. They had three outstanding parking violations and were about to be audited for their tax return three years prior. But they didn't know about that yet.

La Coupole had been a hot spot in the roaring twenties, when Montparnasse was the center of Paris nightlife. Nowadays the restaurant was owned by a chain and catered mainly to well-heeled tourists. But the train station–sized Art Deco room had been restored to its original grandeur, and the fillet béarnaise with frites was probably as good as any in Paris.

In keeping with the police precept that it was always essential to use more troops than could possibly be needed, Capucine had stationed Isabelle at a table in a corner of the room and Momo at the bar. She and Alexandre had been shown to a table at the end of a long avenue of high-backed leather banquettes. The din in the cavernous tiled dining room was deafening. Even though Capucine and Alexandre sat side by side on the banquette, they had to yell to make themselves understood.

"The great thing about the chain that owns this place is that they don't attempt to cook above their ability. They let the décor do the work for them," Alexandre said loudly.

Capucine's eyes roamed the room, but the backs of the banquettes were so high that all she could see was the forest of bright green pillars decorated in 1920s motifs and the people down their row of tables.

"Fricassee of Bresse chicken, skate in burnished butter—the great classics. Who could go wrong ordering those?" Alexandre said.

Fifty feet away, on their side of the row of banquettes, a woman leaned forward, her face visible for only a nanosecond as she peeped out from behind the screen of the man sitting next to her. Yolande Brissac-Vanté. Her body motion was a more reliable signature than the glimpse of her profile.

"*Cœur de filet de bœuf au poivre.* They'll flambé the thing in cognac right at our table. I've never been all that fond of those crunchy peppercorns, but let's have it, anyway. It'll be fun, and it's a perfect meal for a place like this. And their *pommes soufflés* will probably be quite decent."

"Not really the sort of thing you want to order on a stakeout." Capucine muttered, keeping Yolande's table in close scrutiny out of the corner of her eye.

Grumbling, Alexandre ordered the filet béarnaise for himself and the skate for Capucine. When they arrived, both dishes were beyond satisfactory, perfectly cooked, sauces above reproach.

Halfway through their meal, a woman with the robustness of a boarding-school field hockey player strode purposefully down the aisle, her heels clicking over the hubbub. She held a bright orange Hédiard bag by its string handles, keeping it as far away from her body as possible.

With a determined smile, she held her hand out to Capucine. "Madame Le Tellier?" she asked. "I'm Sidonie de Vulpillières. We spoke this morning on the telephone."

"Of course." Capucine took her hand. It was dry, strong, masculine.

With obvious distaste, the woman placed the bag on the table. Diners in the immediate vicinity looked on with sympathetic interest. *A gift from the famous luxury* épicerie. *How nice. I wonder what it's going to be?*

Without another word, the woman turned on her heel and marched back down the long lane between the banquettes. Capucine caught sight of Yolande nervously peeping out from behind the cover of her companion.

Capucine tipped the mouth of the bag toward her.

"I'm guessing this is not going to be their famous fruit squares, is it?" Alexandre said.

The bag contained a monogrammed note card tucked into the ribbons of a brown Hédiard box. Capucine removed the card, which contained four lines in a looping, round girlish hand.

I think you need to see this. It was delivered early this morning by someone who came in an Hédiard truck. They still haven't asked for money. I'm at my wit's end. But I'm going to stick to their rules. It's my only hope. Please don't try to contact me. And, whatever you do, don't come to my table!!!!!

Capucine removed the box with her fingertips and pulled gently on one end of the bow. The knot undone, the ribbon fell away. Capucine lifted the top with her fork. Inside was a small self-sealing kitchen bag that contained what looked like a good-size mushroom cap.

Alexandre wrinkled his nose. The bag had been improperly closed and emanated a distinct whiff of charnel house. The couple at the next table frowned at them.

"It's a Chinese delicacy," Alexandre said with a toothy smile. "Actually, we're a tiny bit doubtful about it ourselves."

Capucine put the lid back on the box, returned it to the bag, stood up, and walked to the door of the restaurant. Isabelle rushed up to her. After a whispered conversation Isabelle left the restaurant in a rush with the bag.

As they waited at the cashier's desk for Alexandre's card

to go through, Capucine whispered in Alexandre's ear, "Was that what I think it was?"

"Absolutely. An ear. I've cooked too many pigs' ears not to know one. But no animal I know has an ear that small. I'm guessing it's a human's."

CHAPTER 35

Capucine stood in front of the large, black-painted steel double doors, the only relief in a forty-foot-high flat-stone wall that ran all the way up the long street. After a few seconds a buzzer sounded and a small panel inset in the doors popped ajar and was opened all the way by someone inside.

"Commissaire Le Tellier?" asked a stony-faced warder in a black uniform with an electric blue band across the chest.

Capucine nodded.

"Service weapon please, Commissaire."

Capucine extracted her Sig from the small of her back and handed it to the warder butt first. In exchange, he gave her a white plastic tag with the number 892 in large black numerals. Behind her, another warder, as expressionless as the first, said, "*Veuillez me suivre, Commissaire*. Please follow me, Commissaire."

Following her Virgil, Capucine walked down an endless corridor of steampunky iron cell doors, stacked three stories high, reachable only by narrow parapets. A net was stretched out between the parapets at each level to remove the temptation of an immediate resolution of petty differences among detainees.

Although the prison was located in the heart of the Fourteenth Arrondissement, with its open boulevards and rambling bourgeois apartments, it was a world unto itself, endless, inescapable, situated neither in place nor in time, notorious for its vermin, rats, and enslavement of the weak. Not a wonder that it had the highest suicide rate of any prison in France.

At the end of the interminable hallway they reached a wall of bars that went up to the forty-foot-high ceiling. With an earsplitting buzz the door popped open on a spring and was opened wide by a black-uniformed, blue-striped warder on the other side. She continued down another identical, endless corridor with her escort. The long hall was as still as a deserted church.

Eventually, they arrived in front of a green-painted steel door with a small judas window, riveted like the decks of a ship and held fast with an enormous bolt. Another stone-faced, black-uniformed, blue-striped warder stood in front of the door. He pulled back the bolt, pushed it wide, stepped in, pressing himself hard against the door to make room for Capucine to pass.

Inside, an affable, corpulent man sat at a distressed oak table, sipping tea from what appeared to be an authentic Limoges cup, eating pink *macarons* from a matching plate. Another cup had been set at the table. The warder shut the door and stood stiffly, almost at attention, in front of it.

The man—dressed in a prison uniform cut so elegantly, it could only have been made by one of Paris's leading tailors—rose, smiled broadly, and air kissed Capucine on both cheeks.

"Please sit down, Commissaire. The macarons are from La Durée and the tea from Mariage Frères. I may have to stay here for my allotted time, but that doesn't mean I have to starve while I do it." He smiled warmly at her and poured her tea from a large matching teapot.

"Jean," the man said to the warder at the door, "I'm afraid I'm going to have to ask you to step outside. This may be confidential."

Without a word, the warder opened the door a crack, slipped through, and shut it gently with a barely audible click.

"You have him well trained," Capucine said.

"It's hardly training. Just a case of natural symbiosis. He has a very sick child. The doctors felt his best chance was in a certain hospital in the United States. Of course, the Sécurité Sociale doesn't pay for that. So the Unione does. It seems the boy will be cured." This said matter-of-factly, almost sadly, without a trace of swagger.

Paulu Santoni, a capo in the Unione Corse, had been arrested by Capucine two years before. For some reason, not fully understood by either, they had struck up a friendship of sorts during the case, and it had blossomed during his incarceration. Even though the arrest had been another feather in her cap, Capucine was under no illusion that Santoni continued to be anything but as effective directing his troops from La Santé as he had been from his villa in Ajaccio.

For several minutes they chatted aimlessly as friends were wont. When Santoni lifted the teapot to serve Capucine a third cup, he noticed the tea had become lukewarm. He walked to the door, rapped twice. It was opened promptly.

"Jean, do you think we could have a fresh pot?" The tone of courteous condescension was precisely the one Capucine's mother used with her servants.

"Commissaire, I'm sure you didn't come all this way just to cheer up your old Corsican friend. I'll be out in six months and was hoping you'd allow me to take you out to dinner."

"No, Paulu, I need your advice. A man has been kidnapped, and his ear has been cut off. It relates to a case I'm working on."

"The man's name?"

"Thierry Brissac-Vanté."

Santoni pursed his lips into a tulip shape, shook his head, and shrugged his shoulders. He sat back and caressed his ample stomach.

"A gambler?"

"My husband has seen him play backgammon at the Travellers Club."

"Don't let your husband play there. The stakes are very high, and there is a good deal of sharking. Of course, they are all gentlemen in that club, but some of them have one foot in the *milieu*. It's the first step toward the illegal gambling houses run by the gangs. It's not impossible your Brissac-Vanté found himself over his head with professional gamblers. They prey on that sort."

"And the ear?"

"Cutting off an ear or a finger is the traditional way the milieu punishes someone who has welshed on his debts. They do it whether they've been paid off or not. It's a sign to the others." He scowled with his lips and smiled with his eyes. "I hope you didn't think it might have been us. When the Unione knife comes out, it's put to far better use than cutting off ears."

Capucine laughed. "I was well aware of that. I just wanted to hear what you had to say."

"What I have to say is that your man has been fleeced by some professionals, and there were complications settling the account. This is their trademark. They may have already been paid back, or maybe not." He paused. "But, of course, it's equally possible that someone is just trying to make it look like this is the work of the milieu. I'm sorry I can't be more helpful. I'll let you know if I hear anything about this man, but it's unlikely. The Unione likes to stay away from the Paris milieu."

Santoni stood up. Capucine was well aware that even in prison, he had a very busy day. He went to the door and rapped with authority. The warder opened it and stood politely, waiting for instructions.

"I'll be out in April. I can't resist spring in Paris. I'll stay for a week or so before going home. I insist on taking you—and your husband, of course—to dinner. I always read Monsieur de Huguelet's pieces with great pleasure, but he needs to deepen his understanding of Corsican food. I'm going to take you both to a place that will set that to rights."

With an almost imperceptible nod of his head, he indicated to the warder that Capucine was to be shown out.

CHAPTER 36

Lucien Folon picked up the thousand-page tome of the *Ali-Bab*—the definitive compendium of French recipes—and let the spine rest in his palm. The book fell open to the right page.

Lièvre à la royale. *Hare fit for a king. Even the name of the damn thing inspires respect and fear,* Folon thought to himself. *The acme of French haute cuisine. A palace chef conjures it up for Louis XVI, and the immortal Carême perfects it after pudgy Louis is separated from his head.*

Folon surveyed his kitchen with pride. *A perfect bijou. Everything anyone with talent needs to create perfection.* He'd built it around a still-life oil he had found in the Puces. The splayed legs of a russet hare with blood dripping from its nose rested on the dead body of a broken-necked peacock, the eyes of its enormous tail staring down the viewer. In the background a large classical alabaster urn rose vertically, suggestively, decorated with Greek warriors in bas-relief chasing after pneumatic maidens to claim their reward for victory. *What could be more apropos?*

The still life had been propped up on a long butcher-block counter a few feet away from a four-burner induction range. A stove and a small fridge were fitted beneath the counter, next to a diminutive cabinet that held an entire set of Cristel pots, nested one into the other as elegantly as Russian matryoshka dolls. *Cooking is about insight, not material acquisition. Jean-Lu taught me that when we were kids.*

Folon ran his eye down the recipe. There were over thirty ingredients, and the cooking instructions took five pages. *It's going to take all day to make this, but it's going to be worth it. In theory, it's beyond the capabilities of an amateur cook, but I'm hardly an amateur, am I? Cooking is an art of the mind, not of the hands, another thing Jean-Lu taught me. And I understand haute cuisine better than any chef.*

He double-checked the list of ingredients. *I have everything, but when you get in the heat of the action, something's always missing. Tant pis. You substitute. You improvise. That's how you take ownership of the dish and make it your own.*

He opened the door of the refrigerator and removed a rectangular glass baking dish covered tight with plastic film wrap. *The hare. The one ingredient you can't substitute. The butcher is a genius. I asked him to be on the lookout for the very animal the* Ali-Bab *calls for—male, beyond the stage of infancy, but still an adolescent, with the coat of a redhead, shot in the head so not a drop of blood is lost.*

He slit the plastic film and peeled it off. The butcher had left the skinned, deboned body of the animal intact, head attached, red and raw as if it had been flayed to death. He contemplated the bloody head.

That's what the front of Galinette's head must have looked like. Two shots from a twelve-gauge wouldn't have left much face.

Gratified, Folon got to work. He spread a piece of fatback on the bottom of an enamel-covered cast-iron casserole, decapitated the hare, added a sprinkling of mirepoix diced so fine, it was down to the molecular level, as the recipe called for, and then another layer of linen-white fatback. He smiled. *That's what Jean looked like when they laid him out in his bloody shroud. That was a sight that did my heart good.*

Next came half a bottle of red wine vinegar and two bottles of Clos des Cortons-Faiveley, a premier cru Burgundy. *Expensive, but so what? This is a once-in-a-lifetime dish. And they were only oh-sixes, after all.* He placed the covered casserole on his induction range and tapped LOW HEAT on the keyboard. It began to simmer almost instantly.

Meticulously, he finely chopped the hare's heart, liver, and lungs, a quarter pound of French bacon, six shallots, and a pound of pork he had cooked the night before. He sweated the shallots in butter. *The problem is that I never got to see what Escartefigue looked like after. They only found him when I'd already gone back to Paris. I still wonder if he was as bloody and boneless as the hare or just crumpled and dusty. I suppose it doesn't make any difference. He got what was coming to him, and that's the important thing.*

The shallots sweated, he put all the choppings in a large steel bowl, added torn shards of baguette he had left soaking in milk since he had woken up, poured in a healthy dose of cognac, and then he topped the mixture with an egg, a good sprinkling of fleur de sel de Guérande, fifteen twists of black pepper, and some *quatre-épices.*

He kneaded the ingredients with his hands.

This is the best part of cooking—the feel in your hands and the aroma in your nose. As he kneaded, the milk-soggy bread and chopped offal and pork took on a new consistency: dense, soft, fragrant, yielding. *Fanny's tits.* He made a ball, convinced it was the same size and consistency his sister's breast would have been when she was seventeen. He lifted it out of the bowl, admired it, shaped a flat nipple.

I spent my entire youth thinking about Fanny's tits, and she knew it, he thought. *She wore those little rice-paper-thin dresses, low on the top, short on the bottom. Sundresses, she called them. Every chance she got, she would lean way over to hand me something, showing her boobs hanging free and luscious inside those skimpy dresses. The thing I wanted most in life was to see her nipples. Sometimes I could almost see where the pale-as-milk skin started to become dark. The vision lit up my whole day, my whole week. At night I would do it to myself, thinking about the bottom of her tits, the part I knew was there but could never—would never—see. As far away from me as the far side of the moon. But at least I knew people who had seen that far side. Two of them left.*

And we'll see about them.

He gently extracted the hare from the casserole, spread-eagled it out on a flat dish, poured the cooking liquid in a bowl. With his hands he lathered the inside of the animal with the pork and offal mince. He then unwrapped a large lobe of goose foie gras, cut it into long batonets, which he aligned in the exact middle of the hare. He made a roll of the animal, wrapped it in cooking parchment, and carefully tied it with butcher string. The resulting bundle looked like a dead sailor about to be slid into the sea. But instead of the sea, he buried the corpse in an oven set at exactly two hundred degrees, where it would remain for the next five hours.

He put those five hours to good use, polishing his latest review until his prose sparkled, then taking pains to be sharp and witty answering his voluminous e-mail, drinking two glasses of single-malt whiskey, and writing five more pages of notes for his book, an acid critique of the lamentable philistinism of modern French gastronomic criticism.

He returned to the kitchen and poured the hare's cooking liquid through a funnel-shaped *chinois* strainer into a large stainless-steel bowl. He set the bowl over a pot of simmering water and let it heat gently.

From the refrigerator he produced a glass jar containing a black Périgord truffle the size of a golf ball. *You don't see many this big nowadays.*

When he began dicing the truffle, a humusy, organic, womany aroma permeated the large room. Visions of his sister, naked, permeated his brain.

Next came the tricky part, making the blood sauce. *Careful. If you even look at it wrong, it separates.* He added the chopped truffle into the reduced cooking liquid and slowly added that to the dark blood, warm from the bain-marie, stirring gently with a long wooden spoon. The blood odor merged with the pungent truffle; the sauce came together, slick and creamy, its odor almost impossibly sensual. He wanted to dive into it and never come up.

Like her pussy, he thought. *She made a point of letting me look at it that day, lying there on her back, her legs spread, filling my eyes with her dark thatch. Letting her little pink vulva grin out at me, mocking. It was only when she knew I'd seen enough to remember for the rest of my life that she pushed her dress down. And then she smiled at me. Teased me like a lover. "You should have come earlier. You missed all the fun." When she said that, I had to run away. I couldn't let her see my tears, could I?*

Damn, he'd forgotten something. *What? The port, of course.* Frenetically, he tore through the cupboard where he kept his bottles. *Putain de merde, double merde, triple merde. No port. Tant pis. Madeira will do just as well. Better even. The sweetness will make the dish all mine.*

His stove binged. The hare was done. And the sauce sat

shimmering, shiny beige brown in its bain-marie. He un-
corked a bottle of Château Corton Grancey, 1996, a serious grand cru that was intended to complement its younger
cousin in the sauce. *Breathe, little darling, breathe,* he
thought, encouraging the wine as he unwrapped the hare's
shroud with a razor-sharp deboning knife.

It looked perfect. He cut a slice from the middle and
gently placed it on his plate with a spatula. The slice
looked like a rough-drawn target, dark hare meat on the
outside, a circle of tan pork mince next, and a pale foie
gras heart in the middle. *Perfect.* With a small ladle he
covered the slice with a dark mantle of the slick sauce.

He trembled with emotion. He made sure his first forkful contained the foie gras, the mince, and the hare. He
took a sip of wine to alert his palate and chewed carefully,
concentrating. *Rich, fragrant.* He chewed some more. *Pas
mal. Not half bad.* Another chew. *But something's missing. It lacks the touch.* He assembled another forkful.
*Banal and cloying, when you get right down to it. It must
have been the substitution of the Madeira for the port. No,
that's ridiculous. What's missing is the* main du maître—
*the master's touch. Jean-Lu would have pulled this off
with his fingers in his nose. Merde, he would have raised it
to heights even Carême could never have dreamed of.
Well, fuck him! Let him rot in hell!*

He threw his plate on the floor in a rage.

CHAPTER 37

Capucine's call to Commissaire Lacroix to express her dismay at the lack of progress in the kidnapping case had started out badly.

"Slowly, slowly catchee monkey," Lacroix had quoted with the hint of an edge in his voice. "Our net is spread wide. All the relevant lines are tapped, and we have the servants closely tailed when they're off duty. We have a surveillance unit in the building across the street. Anything more and we risk spooking the kidnapper."

"Chéri Lecomte?"

"She's being tapped, too."

"Why don't we investigate her stand at the Puces?"

Reluctantly, Lacroix had agreed but had insisted that he was so shorthanded, Capucine would have to supply one of the brigadiers.

The next day, a Saturday, found Isabelle and Brigadier Durand meandering up and down the stalls of the Marché Biron, posing as a young, upwardly mobile couple on the lookout for furnishings for their brand-new Seventeenth Arrondissement apartment. When Capucine had briefed them early that morning, she had had serious misgivings.

They were a very unlikely couple. Isabelle had increased the number of piercings in her face, with a particularly conspicuous gold ring traversing the left side of her lower lip. Durand, on the other hand, in his slightly too-tight wool jacket and raincoat, came across as a prissy insurance adjuster.

When they reached Chéri's stand, Durand paused and gripped Isabelle's arm to stop her. She pulled away in irritation and muttered an imprecation.

"Darling, wouldn't that cachepot be perfect in our hallway?"

With the diffidence of the young, they approached the stand that held the Menton rafraîchissoir. Chéri materialized at their side.

"Lovely, isn't it?" she said, flashing her gleaming teeth. "Menton, probably early nineteenth century, a remake of a design that was popular in the eighteenth century."

"Originally for cooling wine, wasn't it?" Durand asked ingenuously. "It really would be perfect in our flat. Don't you think, mon petit chou?" he said, putting his hand around Isabelle's waist. Isabelle looked at him sharply. Enough was enough.

"Exactly," Chéri said. "It's very unusual. Most of them were made to hold several bottles and are much larger."

"Is it expensive?" Isabelle asked.

"It's an original piece that will gain value over time. An investment. I could let you have it for thirty-five hundred euros."

Isabelle looked at Durand with earnest hopefulness. He shook his head.

"I'm sorry. That's out of our range. Give us a chance to look around your stall some more. We love your things. I'm sure we can find something that would fit our little pocketbook."

Isabelle darted another dagger at Durand, frowning in disgust at the corniness.

They wandered to the opposite side of the stand and peered at a series of plates decorated with vegetables in high relief. A woman with an Hermès scarf artfully tied around her neck took their place in front of the rafraîchissoir and entered into earnest whispered conversation with Chéri. After a few minutes, Chéri was heard to say brightly, "D'accord, but you *do* drive a very hard bargain."

The next day, Sunday, two slim, petite young women dressed in sequined jeans, the sort of designer T-shirts that cost well over two hundred euros, and quilted pastel vests, looking for all the world like a Saint-Germain couple, pawed over the stand, making alternatively admiring and disdaining murmurs. They were brigadiers from Lacroix's unit. The two women stopped in front of a Menton rafraîchissoir placed inconspicuously at the very rear of a glass-shelved display case.

"That's just *trop chou,* isn't it, Noémi?"

A dialogue similar to the previous day's ensued with Chéri. When told the price, one of the women exclaimed, "Ooh, la, la! We'll have to think about *that*, won't we, Noémi?"

Five minutes later Noémi was on the cell phone to Capucine.

"It could have been returned."

"Who ever heard of anyone returning anything to the Puces? Buy it," came the order.

By lunchtime the blue and white rafraîchissoir was on Capucine's desk.

The next day, Monday, the Puces were open, but the crowd was thinner. It was a day when most stand owners stayed in bed and let assistants attend to the stand.

When Durand and Isabelle sauntered by Chéri's stall,

they thought they saw the same rafraîchissoir, now on a table close to the entrance. They bent over it, deep in whispered conversation. A tired-looking man with a wilted mustache and a dilapidated old pipe burnt halfway down on one side came up to them with a hangdog smile and proffered the now familiar litany about the piece's provenance. Isabelle had no need to make a cell phone call. She had her instructions.

"Twenty-five hundred. But we'll pay you cash and won't ask for a receipt."

The man hesitated. "Twenty-seven hundred and you have a deal. But it still has to be cash."

It went for 2,650 euros in crisp bills.

An hour later a second rafraîchissoir, apparently identical to the first, was also on Capucine's desk.

Another hour later an INPS forensic unit van was double-parked in front of Capucine's commissariat, and two agents spécialisés were carefully packing the rafraîchissoirs into plastic containers.

"We're only going to take very small chips from under the glaze of the base. The intrinsic value of the pieces will hardly be diminished," explained one of the agents spécialisés.

"You can reduce the damn things to powder if that's what it takes to get results," Capucine said.

"Madame, we're scientists, not philistines," the agent spécialisé said. "You'll have your results tomorrow afternoon at the latest," he added, cradling one of the plastic containers protectively under his arm and walking out the door.

The next day, as she returned from lunch, the uniformed receptionist handed Capucine a thin sheaf of phone messages. The third was from Pascal Challoneau.

"So, Pascal, what have you got for me?"

"Those pieces aren't Menton. They're from Châteauneuf, even though they're made to look like they're Menton."

"Forgeries?"

"That would be the term I'd use, yes. But, oddly enough, made in a well-known faïence and not in some crook's basement."

"How can you know they were made in Châteauneuf?"

"Elementary, my dear Commissaire. These faïences only use local clay. The analysis indicated the clay contained a small amount of extremely fine river sand typical of the Loire Valley south of Touraine. We ran a spectrographic analysis to make sure. Châteauneuf is the only faïence in the region. So one of our agents went to the Printemps and invested a hundred euros—a price that seemed exorbitant to me—in a rather simple-looking flower vase made by Châteauneuf. We took a chip from the bottom and analyzed it—identical to the so-called Menton rafraîchissoirs. It was as simple as that. I'm e-mailing you my report. You'll have it in less than a minute."

CHAPTER 38

The uniformed receptionist buzzed Capucine and announced that Monsieur Brissac-Vanté was on the line. She assumed he had misunderstood and that it was Yolande. It must be something serious if she was calling the police.

"Bonjour, madame," Capucine said, putting as much smile into her voice as she could manage.

A tired and slightly hoarse voice replied, "No, Commissaire, this is Thierry Brissac-Vanté. I'm home, and I'm calling to thank you for being so supportive of my wife. She greatly appreciated your kindness."

"You were released? When?"

"Oh, about ten days ago. I was hospitalized briefly for my ear, and the doctor insisted I rest at home incommunicado for at least a week."

"Hospitalized? Where?"

"At the Clinique Fontini. It's just around the corner."

"Monsieur Brissac-Vanté, this is very serious. We need to catch these people. You should have called us immediately."

"There's no one to catch. I'm not pressing charges against anyone."

"Monsieur, we do need to talk. When would it be convenient for me to see you?"

"After lunch today? Say three o'clock? Yolande will be here. I know she wants to thank you personally."

That afternoon, when the maid opened the door to the Brissac-Vantés' apartment, Yolande appeared behind her, a radiant lighthouse in a stormy night.

"Isn't it wonderful he's back? It's been nearly two weeks, and I still can't believe it. The poor darling was in such a state when he arrived. He had lost a great deal of blood and hadn't been fed properly or allowed to sleep enough. Thank God we were able to get him right into Fontini. The food there is excellent, and they really know how to take care of people. But do come in. Thierry is dying to see you."

Brissac-Vanté's greeting of Capucine was subdued. He sat in a darkened room, the thick velvet drapes tightly drawn, in a black flannel robe with crimson piping and black velvet slippers decorated with an elaborate gold monogram. Even before he spoke, he seemed absent and distracted, not unlike the hero in an English black-and-white movie about a young squire who has been returned severely wounded to his country home after some appalling World War I battle and who is unable to wrest his thoughts away from the carnage of the war. Completing the image, a large white bandage was taped over his right ear.

When Capucine entered the room, he looked up listlessly.

"Commissaire, kind of you to come out here. I should have come to you, but I'm afraid I'm not really up to going out quite yet."

"It must have been quite an ordeal."

Brissac-Vanté did not reply.

"Tell me about your release. How did you get home?" Capucine asked.

Brissac-Vanté spoke in an inflectionless monotone. "There's nothing much to tell. When they cut off my ear, it happened very quickly. I felt almost nothing. I think they must have done it with a straight razor. Then they gave me pills. They must have been some sort of powerful pain-killers. It hurt, but I felt disassociated from my body, as if I was floating. I don't know how many days went by. I had been blindfolded from the very beginning and rubber plugs had been put in my ears. I didn't know if it was night or day. When I had a plug in only one ear, that made me even more disoriented.

"At one point I realized I was in a car. After a long time the car stopped, and I was taken out and left standing. I heard the car drive off. I knew my hands were not bound, but I still stood there for an eternity, not daring to take my blindfold off or take the earplug out. When I finally did, I discovered I was in a vacant lot. I had no idea where. I started walking. It was only when I reached a broad ave-nue with some stores that I discovered I was in Puteaux. There was a taxi rank. I got into the first one and gave my address. I must have looked like hell. The driver didn't want to take me. But I threatened to call the police if he didn't. When I arrived here, Maria do Conceição paid the taxi, and then it was over."

There was another long silence, which Brissac-Vanté seemed to welcome. He breathed rapidly through his mouth.

"How many days were you held captive?"

"I have no idea. I couldn't tell night from day. But Yolande tells me it was ten."

As if speaking to a sick child, Capucine asked, "And how did they capture you?"

"Oh, that was very simple," Brissac-Vanté said at the

edge of exhaustion. "I left my office building to go out to dinner. Two men grabbed my arms from behind and pushed me across the sidewalk. Before I realized what was happening, they shoved me into the backseat of a car, put what felt like a sock over my head, handcuffed me, and stuck the earplugs in. Of course, it couldn't have been a sock. It must have been one of those ski masks turned around backward."

"Did you see any of their faces?"

"No, the men were behind me, and there was no driver in the car. Or maybe he was lying down on the seat when I was shoved in. I don't know. We drove off. I could tell we went up the Champs, because of the incline. Then we went around the Rond Point and down the avenue de la Grande Armée. I knew that because we were going downhill. Then we got on the Périphérique, from what had to have been the Porte Maillot ramp. After a while we were on an autoroute, but I don't have the slightest idea which one. We drove for a long time. An hour, maybe two, maybe even three. You get very disoriented when you can't see or hear. Maybe I dozed. I don't know." He fell silent, exhausted.

With a sigh, he resumed his narrative. "All of a sudden the car stopped, and I was shoved out. I could smell trees and dead leaves, so it must have been somewhere in the country. I was pushed forward and told there were three steps. I guess that means it must have been some kind of house. Then I was put in a room with a bunk with a rough wool cover, and the handcuffs were taken off. I was told that if I got off the bed or took off the blindfold or the earplugs, I would be killed instantly. They brought me food and took me to the toilet when I wanted, but the rest of the time I either sat or lay on the cot." He paused. "Even when—he swallowed a sob—"they . . . they . . . You know what they did."

Utterly spent, he stopped, staring at the floor, lost in his memories. Capucine caught sight of Yolande peering at them anxiously from the door. It was clear she had no intention of allowing the interview to continue.

After the somber gloominess of the apartment, Capucine reeled from both the bright afternoon sun and the enormity of the situation. It seemed impossible that Brissac-Vanté had arrived home, been taken to the clinic, undoubtedly been visited there repeatedly by his wife, and then been brought home again, all unnoticed by the police surveillance team. It seemed equally impossible that a ransom had been paid without being detected by the fiscal brigade.

Capucine sat in her car, flipped the sun visor down, pulled out her cell phone, and pressed the speed dial for Jacques.

Jacques picked up before the first ring was completed. "Ma très belle cousine!" he greeted her coquettishly.

"Isn't this your office number?" Capucine said, confused, having expected to go through two secretaries and wait for ten minutes, if she had been able to get through at all.

"It's my cell. You dialed the office. We have new software that can redirect calls to various numbers when you're out. For some unknown reason, the computer must be aware of your décolletage and decided to bounce you over to my cell phone."

"Jacques, I'm furious with you."

"You're so right. *Bounce* was a poor choice of words."

"No, Jacques, be serious. This is no laughing matter. Bris—"

"Yes, yes. He's at home, feeling sorry for himself, and your policeman is going to have to scold his little scouts for being so inattentive. It's these new little telephones they all have. They probably watch porn all day on those little screens, instead of keeping their eyes peeled."

"Jacques, your people had a hand in this, didn't they? You must have. How else would you have known that Brissac-Vanté was released?"

"Ma belle, I had not the slightest idea. I only guessed that from your tone. Actually, I only picked up your call because I was hoping you were after one of your evening assignations."

"Hardly!"

"Well, then I'm going to have to ring off. I'm in the middle of something rather challenging out in the field, as we like to say."

"Well, did you or didn't you?"

"Silly you. You know the DGSE isn't allowed to interfere in matters on the national territory. I really *am* going to have to run." He paused for half a beat. "But I'll tell you one thing. Those brown tweed trousers you're wearing? They definitely give you a fat butt." His shrieking bray was sliced in half when he cut the connection.

CHAPTER 39

Commissaire Lacroix was even more furious than Capucine about the denouement of Brissac-Vanté's mysterious sequestration. Not only was he frustrated that the case had slipped through his fingers, but he was also resentful at having lost face on the eve of his retirement. Capucine had no trouble at all in persuading him to keep all the wiretaps in place.

The taps proved eloquent. Almost overnight Brissac-Vanté snapped out of his post-trauma depression and shifted into overdrive, embarking on a flurry of phone calls so frenetic that the daily summaries arrived in sheaths almost an inch thick. The gist of it all was that he was scrabbling to pick up the reins of his former life. He had detailed discussions with the executives of all his investments, long conversations with his partner at his agency, and he harangued Prosper Ouvrard daily about the profitability of Chez La Mère Denis. More perplexing were the repeated calls from Chéri Lecomte to Brissac-Vanté's cell phone. He would either ignore them or cut them off by pressing the red NO button. Commissaire Lacroix's interpretation was that the ordeal of the kidnapping had drawn Brissac-Vanté tightly into the bosom of his family to the exclusion of his mistress. Capucine was less sure but could come up with no better explanation.

Despite the cornucopia of information, the days continued to slip by, producing no material leads in either case.

One night Capucine arrived home to the familiar scene of Alexandre sitting in the worn and cracked leather armchair in his study, laptop on lap, cigar stub clenched tightly in jaws, near-empty glass of whiskey precariously balanced on chair arm.

He held up the palm of his left hand in a gesture for silence, pursed his lips, hit the ENTER key.

"*Voilà, pour toi,* you bungling incompetent." He snapped the laptop shut.

His scowl volatilized like the evanescent blue flame of a flambé. He dropped the laptop on a pile of magazines, rose, and took Capucine in his arms. "My day has finally blossomed." He kissed her deeply. "Come into my casbah down the hall and let me ply you with bubbles that will tickle your nose and elevate your thoughts to heights of passion."

"I don't need bubbles for that," Capucine said, kicking off her shoes, extracting her pistol and handcuffs from the back of her trousers, dropping them on a mound of paper on Alexandre's desk. Out of the corner of her eye she caught Alexandre examining her bottom. "Do these trousers make my *fesses* look that fat?"

Alexandre gave one of her cheeks a playful slap. "That's for listening to silly people." He kissed the back of her neck, his hands exploring. "Perfection, as usual."

In the kitchen Alexandre eased the cork out of a bottle of Deutz, filled a flute for Capucine, and kissed her chilled, damp lips once she had drunk. This process continued for a good moment, until Capucine, ravenous, wriggled out of his grasp.

"There's no way I'm skipping dinner tonight, you geriatric satyr. What are you making me?"

"Japanese *ravioles de langoustine.* It's a little dish I invented myself. Brittany prawns in little ravioles made of *gyoza,* on a bed of sautéed cabbage, with a nugget of lemon mousse on top, and a sauce made from the claws and a few spoonfuls of crème fraîche. You're going to love them."

"Gyoza?"

"You know, those thin rounds of pasta the Japanese use for the dumplings you love so much. You buy them ready-made in packages."

Alexandre bustled around the kitchen, preparing his *mise en place.* He ducked his head into an old armoire he had purloined from his parents' attic, foraging loudly, apparently searching for some seldom-used spice. He muttered something largely incomprehensible above the tintinnabulation of bottles and jars. The only fragment that Capucine understood was "hot gossip." This was one of Alexandre's most irritating dramatic techniques, dropping a partially audible bombshell in an attempt to stoke her interest.

Extracting his head, he reiterated. "Bet you didn't know that Thierry Brissac-Vanté fired Prosper Ouvrard."

"Actually, I did," Capucine crowed. "We got it off the wiretap yesterday."

"And you didn't tell me?"

"Police business."

Alexandre ducked his head back into the armoire and resumed his search.

"Well, then, I won't tell you who he's hired to replace Ouvrard," he said, barely audibly over the din.

On her stockinged tiptoes, Capucine walked over to the armoire and kicked Alexandre's protruding posterior. He jerked up, banging his head against a shelf. When he finally extracted himself, she crossed her arms and scowled at him.

"Okay, okay. It's Aiko Kikuchi."

"Who?"

"You know, that very pretty woman who was the executive culinary advisor to Dong. Didn't you tell me you went there with Jacques the other night? It just so happens I interviewed Aiko this morning. As soon as I heard the rumor, I picked up the phone and she was generous enough to share her morning tea with me."

"Brissac-Vanté is turning La Mère Denis into a Japanese sushi place?"

"Not quite. She insists she's going to create true Japanese-French fusion, something she was only playing with at Dong."

"Will it work?"

"Who knows? At first blush, I'd say no. It's obviously aimed at attracting the Saint-Germain glitterati. But that crowd doesn't like to cross the Périphérique to eat. The idea's not bad, but it would have been a safer bet in the middle of the Eighth Arrondissement. But you never know in the restaurant business. Of course, it's bound to be a hot spot for a few months if Brissac-Vanté can get some spin going. Maybe his plan is to sell the restaurant when it hits its apogee. I'll bet Ouvrard and Delphine Duclos are none too happy. They had high hopes for Chez La Mère Denis."

"Actually, we're both *extremely* happy. We're going to America. To New York."

"Why are all French chefs so attracted to New York?"

"I'll tell you why. It's not that complicated. But I'm starving and was just going to make myself some lunch. Will you join me?"

Capucine accepted with a smile.

"The hostess cooking lunch at Chez La Mère Denis. Things certainly have changed, haven't they?" Delphine Duclos asked with a laugh that was nine parts genuine to one part cynical.

Even though apparently nothing had been changed, the

kitchen seemed dead. The long row of burnished copper pots still gleamed over the three piano stoves. The long stainless-steel counter opposite the ranges had been scoured until it glinted. But it wasn't the rosy warmth of a scrub-down after a hard day's work; it was the cold buff-up of departing lodgers.

Delphine went to the center range, turned a dial, pushed a button. The explosive whoosh of a bull coughing was heard. The piano had come alive.

"It'll only take a minute or two to heat up," Delphine said as she went to the service refrigerator in a corner. From her vantage point, leaning over the shining counter, Capucine could see that it was almost entirely empty. Delphine returned to a spot opposite Capucine with a plastic container, a supermarket tub of crème fraîche, a few grassy sprigs of what looked like tarragon wrapped in plastic film, and a half-empty bottle of Sancerre tucked under her arm.

"Don't get your hopes up. I'm really just a novice cook. And when you live in an environment like this, you don't have a hope of learning. The first time you try anything, people start laughing."

She produced a white nylon cutting board and a large kitchen knife with a blue plastic handle from under the counter. The plastic container turned out to contain two large chicken breasts, which Delphine cut into cubes. Then, with a machine-gun rat-a-tat, she chopped the tarragon into fine confetti.

"I thought you didn't know how to cook?"

"Not the way these guys do," she said, waving her arm at the empty kitchen.

She selected a big copper pot from the rack, filled it with water, shook in some sea salt from a box, placed it over the hot central eye of the piano, and came back to lean across the counter from Capucine.

"New York, you said?"

"Yes. It's absolutely amazing. Prosper has three offers to start up restaurants there. And the salaries are unbelievable."

"You're leaving Paris because of the money?"

"Not just that. Prosper feels New York has become the food capital of the world. He thinks French chefs do so well there because they are freed from the crushing weight of tradition. He says it's no longer possible for a chef to be genuinely original in France." She laughed. "He feels sorry for Aiko Kikuchi and her French-Japanese fusion. Even if she succeeds, it will be the success of a dog walking on its hind legs, not very well done but amazing she can do it at all."

"Why did Brissac-Vanté hire her? I thought the restaurant was making money under Chef Ouvrard."

"Your husband is the one you should ask that question. I was just the hostess here." She laughed, this time nine parts cynicism to one part mirth. "Okay. I'll tell you why. Because he's smart. Prosper just doesn't have the name in France to pull people out of Paris to eat here. Even though I'm prejudiced, I'd be the first to admit it would have taken him years to build an image. So the restaurant would have limped along with good days and bad days. Let me tell you, when you're operating a restaurant on a three-star budget, those midweek doldrums will eat you alive.

"Kikuchi has a reputation and will have fabulous profit margins. There will be a lot of talk about cuts of very expensive fish, but her menu will really be all about ramen noodles. Brissac-Vanté's doing the smart business thing. He's hiring a celebrity. He'll kick it off with a blitz of publicity, and when the restaurant takes off, he'll sell it to a movie star or somebody like that, get his money back, and tant pis if there's collateral damage."

"That's what my husband suspects he has in mind," Capucine said.

The plops of vigorously boiling water became audible. Delphine reached under the counter and rooted around. She seemed to have hung on to a rudimentary pantry. She produced a nearly full box of spaghetti. Holding a large sheaf of pasta in the loops of index and thumb of each hand, she lowered it into the pot of boiling water and drew her arms together. The spaghetti fanned out elegantly, forming a perfect circle, the edges sticking out over the rim of the pot. As the boiling water softened the bottoms, the spaghetti sank slowly into the pot until it disappeared altogether. Delphine smiled a secret little smile at the sight. It was obvious that cooking gave her a great deal of pleasure.

"And so you have no financial recourse against Brissac-Vanté?"

"I have plenty. But not with the restaurant. The judge gave him that lock, stock, and barrel because of his convertible debt thing. I hope he won't mind me using his pots and pans." This time the laughter was ten parts out of ten cynical.

"What about Chef Brault's faïence collection?"

"Well, as you say, it was Jean-Louis's collection, not the restaurant's. My lawyer thought Brissac-Vanté might contest that, so he advised me to have it all crated up by professionals and sealed in a bonded warehouse. Brissac-Vanté was absolutely furious. That happened a week or two after Jean-Louis's death. He insisted he had the right to inspect the collection and petitioned the judge to release the bond. He totally lost his temper about it."

Delphine selected a blackened skillet from the rack, trickled a thin lace of olive oil from a large tin over the bottom, placed the skillet a few inches from the eye of the piano, and let the oil heat up until the film shimmered.

"But the judge just laughed at him. He's still examining the situation. My lawyer tells me it's highly likely the judge will accept that I was Jean-Louis's common-law wife and award me everything. So I'll wind up owning all the faïence and the hotel."

"And what are you going to do with that?"

"The hotel? It's still open, and I'm running it until the judge hands down his decision. Now that the restaurant is closed, our clientele seems to be entirely business types having dirty weekends with their secretaries. Actually, business has gone up. I think it's because now there's no risk they'll run into anyone they know coming out of the restaurant. And when Kikuchi gets going, all that raw fish is bound to make the secretaries even hornier."

She placed the chicken cubes into the skillet, shook it vigorously so they wouldn't stick, sprinkled on salt and a few twists of pepper.

"But the minute the probate judge makes up his mind, I'm going to sell it for whatever I can get. That hotel was the millstone around Jean-Louis's neck that drowned him. I loathe the goddamn thing."

"You sound as if you still believe he committed suicide."

"It doesn't make any difference what happened. He was doomed, and he knew it." There was an awkward pause. Delphine filled it by flicking the skillet so the cubes of chicken were tossed in the air, landing on their backs. She was clearly far from a novice chef.

"He took the wrong path at the crossroads. He was brilliant. A genius. All he ever wanted to do was cook. It was all he ever thought about. I tried to talk him into selling this place and getting himself hired at some place like Taillevent. He would have cooked and cooked and won their third star back and become even more famous and certainly made more money than he was making here. But, oh no. He had to own his restaurant, even though he hated everything that had to do with business management and was terrible at it. Can you imagine him trying to run an empire of God knows how many restaurants, like Ducasse? But who was I to give him advice? I was just the hostess."

She scooped the chicken out onto a plate and poured in a good measure of white wine to deglaze the pan.

"And since he was so bad at being a *patron*, he needed something tangible that would prove to him that he held his three stars by the neck. The irony is that Lucien Folon tells me the hotel was never of the slightest interest to Michelin. The people who review the hotels are not at all the same as those who review the restaurants."

"You've seen Folon?"

Delphine spooned some crème fraîche into the skillet, stirred it vigorously into her sauce, added the tarragon, and waited for it to reduce.

"He's here almost every day. He's very supportive of Prosper, almost like a father. Actually, the whole New York idea was his. The people Prosper has offers from are all his contacts." She paused, stirring the sauce vigorously with a whisk. "You know, it seems unbelievable, but I think Folon really misses Jean-Louis. It's not for Prosper that he's doing this, but to hang on to Jean-Louis's memory."

"I thought he hated him."

"So did I. Maybe the fire has gone out of his life now that Jean-Louis is gone. Who knows what goes through the heads of men?"

The sauce was ready. Delphine poured the contents of the pasta pot into a colander she had placed in a sink in a far corner of the kitchen and returned with the spaghetti, which she dumped into the skillet, stirred vigorously for a moment, then added the cubed chicken.

"Voilà," she said, dividing the contents onto two dishes, sprinkling grated Parmesan from a plastic envelope on top, placing one dish in front of Capucine. She rooted around in her trove under the counter and came up with knives, forks, and a handful of paper napkins. "Welcome to the new Chez La Mère Denis!" She poured them both glasses of Sancerre, touched hers to Capucine's, and sipped happily.

"Jean-Louis was a man of contrasts. Everything was both black and white. Take his morbid fascination with faïence. He knew a lot about it. I think he learned that from his father. But he really hated it." Her eyes filled with liquid. "I hope he's happy, wherever he is."

They ate. The chicken was surprising good.

"It's food for children. I used to make this for Jean-Louis. Imagine someone like me cooking for a three-star chef. But he loved it."

Delphine was right. The chicken was food for children. But it was also perfect for a sad grown-up lunch: rich, creamy, just barely escaping blandness with the minty taste of the tarragon.

"And now it's all over. You know, even after he . . . left us, I felt he was still here, because his soul was more in his restaurant than it had been in his body. I'll tell you a secret. As long as his restaurant was here, I felt like a bad girl every time I wasn't sleeping alone in his bed. Of course, I had always been a bad girl every now and then, but not so much, really. And, as the Bible says, you can't live on bread alone, so you do what you have to. But he was always here when I got home. Even after he was gone. I know I'm not making any sense." She blotted her eyes with her paper napkin. "And now there's no longer any home to come home to."

CHAPTER 40

Capucine dropped the thick catalog on the long kitchen table with a clapping snap of finality.

An Important Sale of Faïence
Collection of the Late Chef Jean-Louis Brault
and other select pieces

Commissaire-Priseur Bertrand de Bertignac
Drouot-Richelieu
9, rue Drouot – Paris 75009

"So the probate judge announced his decision?" Alexandre asked.

"Two weeks ago. Delphine got all of Brault's estate."

Capucine opened the door to the refrigerator and extracted an open bottle of champagne. Her friends always complained about their husbands' predictability, but how could anyone find it irritating that Alexandre *always* had a bottle of champagne on the chill?

"The sale's this Saturday. I'm going. Want to come?"

"Wonderful idea. We can have lunch at Au Petit Riche. It's just around the corner."

Capucine and Alexandre arrived at the sale half an hour early, assuming that either Jean-Louis Brault's fame or the notoriety of his death would pack the auction room. But the only occupants were two extremely well-dressed white-haired gentlemen in suede shoes, with brightly colored silk handkerchiefs cascading from their breast pockets. Three of the Savoyards in their black jackets with red collars expertly stacked wooden crates, organizing themselves to lose no time putting the pieces on the dais as they came up for sale.

They decided they had plenty of time for coffee at the café around the corner. It was packed. Squeezing up to the zinc counter, Capucine noticed Lucien Folon at the far end, drinking a glass of white wine and leafing through the Brault sale catalog. He caught sight of Capucine and Alexandre. Clutching his glass tightly, weaving, he pushed toward them through the press of people. Alexandre groaned.

Solemnly, Folon shook Alexandre's hand and kissed Capucine's cheeks. "Sad day." He shook his head like a mournful Saint Bernard. "It feels like a large part of my life is being strewn to the pigs."

Capucine's and Alexandre's expresses arrived. Folon continued on with his *vin triste*.

"Now that the restaurant is gone, when his collection is dispersed, there will be nothing left of Jean-Louis. Nothing at all."

In the cone within the din of the café there was a long awkward silence.

With excessive brilliance Capucine said, "Bertignac did an impressive job putting together such a large sale at such short notice."

"I was amazed at how many pieces Jean-Louis still had," Folon said. "I always thought he'd sold most of his collection off to invest in that silly hotel. But I guess not." He tapped the catalog and then flipped the pages with indifference, trying to hide his emotion. "Did you notice that four pieces have been removed from the sale? The entries are stamped '*retiré de la vente*' in red. Isn't that curious? I wonder why."

Alexandre glanced at Capucine. They shared the strong impression Folon was trying hard to build a bridge over the deep cavern than had opened up between them.

"*Allez, vieux*. Come on, old man," Alexandre said, patting Folon's deltoid, addressing him as an intimate friend. "The auction starts in ten minutes. We need to get a move on."

Once again Capucine marveled at the acuity of auctioneers. The small handful of serious buyers was evenly sprinkled throughout the now packed gallery. The crowd of gawkers, obviously there for the thrill of seeing the last possessions of a famous murder victim auctioned off, gossiped, pointed, exclaimed, totally ignorant of faïence, impressed only by odd shapes, unusual colors, high prices.

Despite the surf of hullabaloo, Bertignac unerringly divined the minimalist telegraphing from bidders: infinitesimal waves of folded catalogs, fingers raised a fraction of an inch, heads nodded a few degrees. With eyes in the side of his head, his singsong litany took account of the bids from the five—not the usual three—clerks at the telephone table. Most impressive of all was his ability to generate spirited bidding wars, sparking offers far higher than potential purchasers had ever intended.

When it was over, the successful bidders lined up at the clerk's desk to write checks and proceed to the window down the hall to collect their purchases. Papers and notes under his arm, Bertignac made rapidly for the door, followed—like a minor rock star—by a small clutch of re-porters and hangers-on. He caught up to Capucine and Alexandre at the door.

"Commissaire," Bertignac said. The reporters pricked up their ears. "I need to talk to you about something." The crowd closed in on them.

"What a pleasant idea, monsieur," Alexandre said. "Allow us to take you to lunch. I have a few cases of wine in my cellar that I've been intending to sell. It would give me the opportunity to pick your brain."

Alexandre and Bertignac discussed the imaginary wine until the reporters and gawkers lost interest and wandered off.

"Au Petit Riche in fifteen minutes?" Alexandre asked. Bertignac nodded, smiling, and dashed off to his office.

The hallway was thronged. Five other sales had just ended, disgorging elated or frustrated bidders seeking lunch to boast or commiserate with their companions. Ca-pucine and Alexandre wormed their way through the crowd toward the front door. Chéri materialized in front of them, haggard despite a jaunty seventies Givenchy *tailleur* with a wasp-waisted jacket and an impossibly nar-row pencil skirt.

Capucine greeted her cheerfully. "Were you at the auc-tion? Did you buy anything? There were some marvelous pieces."

"He won't talk to me!" Chéri's eyes filled with tears.

"Who?"

"Thierry. Someone told me he had been released by the kidnappers, and I called him and called him, but he won't talk to me." She dipped the ladle even deeper into her pool of pain. "And you! The least you could have done was tell me he'd been released and that he was all right. You knew how worried I was. And you call yourself my friend!" Tears trickled down her cheeks.

Capucine hiked her eyebrows microscopically in surprise at the appellation. She had no idea how to reply.

"Have you really seen him?" Chéri carried on relentlessly.

"Yes." Capucine paused, searching for a way to sugar the pill. "It was a legal requirement. It took some doing to get him to meet with me."

"And how was he?"

"He was clearly weakened and in shock from his ordeal, but he recovered quickly."

"That means that you saw him more than once."

"Twice. Once informally. A second time to take his deposition."

"And did he ask about me?"

"As you can imagine, we only spoke about the kidnapping. He tried to say as little as possible about anything."

Alexandre caught Capucine's eye and threw her a life ring. "We need to get a move on," he said, ignoring Chéri.

Chéri's eyes widened in hurt. She sighed deeply and turned on her heel, moving into the crowd. The soles of her Louboutins flashed crimson against the dark tan carpeting.

Au Petit Riche had been steadfastly faithful to the cuisine of the haute bourgeoisie under Louis Philippe ever since the declining days of the good king's turbulent reign. The Belle Epoque interior remained inviolate with its glass-globe chandeliers, floor-to-ceiling fly-specked mirrors, gleaming brass overhead racks for coats and hats, dark paintings in gilt frames, and long rows of red plush banquettes—where diners, squeezed tight, elbow to elbow, would carry on conversations as intimately as if they were deep in the wastes of the Sahara.

Once seated, Bertignac alerted the waiter that the meal would have to be speedy since he had another auction coming up. Alexandre gritted his teeth. *Rapide* and *repas* were not words he liked to hear joined in the same sentence. Bertignac launched into an analysis of his upcoming auction, which consisted of the grandest of grand cru Bordeaux.

"It's a very difficult sale. Yquem and Pétrus now go for several thousand euros a bottle. The buyer who shells out over twenty thousand euros a case is buying a pig in a poke, since we don't guarantee the condition or even the authenticity of the wine."

With great deference the waiter arrived with the menus. Capucine suspected some person in authority had impressed him with Alexandre's influence in the restaurant world.

Their choice was simple enough. To start with, they ordered a selection of pâtés on a communal plate: an intriguing *terrine de pot-au-feu* with a sauce of reduced Bourgueil wine, a terrine of duck foie gras, and a *pâté en croûte* made of foie gras and *trompettes de la mort* mushrooms. After, both Bertignac and Alexandre ordered the beef tartare, vaunted to be made from prime Charolais beef, while Capucine chose a *vol-au-vent de ris de veau*—sweetbreads and their sauce in shell pastry.

When the sommelier arrived, Bertignac extended his hand for the wine list.

"Since you were kind enough to extend the invitation to lunch, allow me to make my modest contribution and invite you to the wine."

He turned to the sommelier and ordered a Chinon Gatien Ferrand 1976.

Alexandre smiled at the idea of one of the greats of the Loire valley. He had found a kindred spirit who wasn't a slave to Bordeaux.

"My head will be full of Bordeaux in three quarters of an hour. Having it in my stomach as well would be too much."

Capucine was well aware that the wine would cost far more than the lunch.

"Was the Brault sale a success?" she asked.

Bertignac was prevented from answering by the arrival of the wine. The sommelier, who had clearly also been made aware of Alexandre's identity, hesitated. With an almost imperceptible inclination of his head, Alexandre indicated that Bertignac would be tasting.

Bertignac, waving two fingers, indicated that the task would be shared. Capucine reflected that her mother would be impressed with his manners.

"Oh yes, definitely. Of course, faïence rarely comes even close to fetching what a case of Pétrus does." He laughed conspiratorially in Alexandre's direction. "But I think Mademoiselle Duclos now has more than enough to make a quite respectable down payment on a lodging in New York."

"Did you really want to talk to me about something, or were you just escaping your admirers?" Capucine asked.

"Actually, I did."

The arrival of the dish of pâtés and a large basket of baguettes cut into diagonal slices interjected a parenthesis into the conversation.

A few minutes later, as he cut off a corner of pâté en croûte, Bertignac asked, "You remember that I had a problem with the authenticity of one of Monsieur Brault's pieces a few weeks ago?"

Capucine nodded.

"Well, as a result of that episode, I had his entire collection gone over by an independent expert. I wanted the sale certified beyond any possible question." He paused for effect, sipping his wine. "The result was surprising. Four of the pieces were forgeries. Very skillful ones, but definitely forgeries."

"Those were the ones you removed from the sale?"

"Exactly."

The main courses arrived. Capucine regretted the departure of the pâtés, which she would happily have nibbled until they were finished.

"And do you know anything about their—what is the word you use?—provenance?"

"No, I don't. But I have two of my assistants looking into that right now."

Bertignac looked at his watch, made an exclamation, took a last big bite of steak tartare, dashed off to settle the tab for the wine, and then headed to Drouot to start his next sale.

The next morning Bertignac called Capucine at her brigade at nine thirty.

"I'm a little embarrassed, Commissaire. As I told you yesterday, I had some of my clerks check to see if we had any information on those four pieces the expert detected as forgeries. I was thunderstruck that Brault bought two of them at my auctions." He paused, at a loss for words.

"I don't really know what to say. It's too much of a co-incidence to believe that he acquired identical pieces from someone else. One was virtually unique, a Nevers vase from the second half of the seventeenth century. The decoration was in white against a dark blue background. The other was a very large terrine, called a *pot-à-oille,* dating from seventeen forty-eight to seventeen sixty, beautifully decorated with a handle on the lid in the form of an artichoke and handles on the terrine in the form of asparagus. It was decorated with very delicate purple and green flowers. The glaze that gave those colors was highly unusual at the time."

"Pot-à-oille?"

Bertignac laughed. "*Oille* is the old term for a soup made with various pieces of meat and vegetables. It's what the modern-day pot-au-feu emerged from. The interesting feature of these extensively decorated terrines is that they show that the hearty pot-au-feu were enjoyed by the upper classes, not just the *paysans*. I'm astonished that two forgeries of such important pieces could have slipped by me and my staff. I distinctly remember the pot-à-oille. It was on my desk for a week, and we all admired it continually. Frankly, I'm more than a little embarrassed."

"There's nothing to be embarrassed about. This is very good news. You've just confirmed all my suspicions."

CHAPTER 41

The following Saturday morning found Capucine and Alexandre in their kitchen, sipping café au lait from the Pasquini and nibbling at croissants while plowing through the three-inch pile of Saturday papers. Capucine had been up for hours; had had a wake-up café au lait; had slipped on jeans and a quilted jacket from Hermès; had gone for a long, fast walk through her neck of the Marais, which she despaired of ever having enough time to explore properly; had bought a large white paper bag of *pur beurre* croissants at a bakery two streets away, relishing the oily butter slicks that appeared in the paper almost instantly; had stopped off at the corner newsstand to buy the thick, magazine-laden Saturday editions of the press, throwing in a copy of *Le Monde Diplomatique* for good measure; had returned home laden, hoping the day would be sufficiently unencumbered to allow her to luxuriate in the bounty of her foraging.

By ten thirty Alexandre was up, regal in a crimson raw-silk kimono he had acquired on his last trip to Tokyo, grunting in irritation at an ebullient review in the *International Herald Tribune* of a restaurant he had detested.

The phone rang.

"Allô, Commissaire? It's Delphine Duclos. Am I disturbing you?"

"Not at all. I'm just sitting in the kitchen, reading the papers with my husband."

"Monsieur de Huguelet?"

"He's the only one I have."

Delphine laughed dutifully. She seemed uncharacteristically ill at ease.

"I've just had an argument with Prosper, well, more of a fight, and . . . actually . . . really . . . I was calling to see if Monsieur de Huguelet could . . . I don't know what." She ground to a halt and then blurted out, "Give Prosper some advice, because he won't listen to me at all."

The thought of Alexandre pouring oil on troubled conjugal waters opened the stopcock of a fit of giggles. Capucine could imagine him advising Ouvrard with the severity of a high-court judge that a shopping expedition to La Perla to buy sexy lingerie was the panacea to any marital problem. Capucine bit her lip to choke back her laughter. The silence intensified Delphine's lack of confidence. Alexandre looked up from his paper and frowned.

"You see, Prosper's had an offer—well, not an offer exactly, but almost—from Chef Labrousse in New York, and we had a fight about it, and I don't want him to do it, so I thought he could chat a little with Monsieur de Huguelet so Monsieur de Huguelet could talk some sense into him, so could we stop by this afternoon for just a moment or two if that isn't too inconvenient?"

"By all means. Why don't you come around five? We have to go out later, but there'll still be plenty of time for a chat."

When she hung up, Alexandre cocked an eyebrow at Capucine.

"What was all that about?"

"Prosper Ouvrard is coming at five so you can explain to him how he should deal with his girlfriend."

"You should have handed me the phone. I could have told him straight off. A good spanking usually does the trick."

Capucine threw half a croissant at him.

"So in your dotage you've decided to come up with new diversions, have you? And who do you think is going to be spanking whom in our relationship?" She twisted Alexandre's ear until he howled. When she let go, he gave her bejeaned left buttock a playful slap. Capucine teetered on the edge between irritation and adoration. She sat on Alexandre's lap and muttered something inaudible into his neck.

Much later they realized it was far too late to go out for a proper lunch, and walked arm in arm around the corner to the Alsatian bistro for *baeckeofe,* which, despite its high-sounding name, was no more than a simple stew of pork, lamb, and beef topped with potatoes and served in a folksy faïence terrine hand painted with gamboling ducks.

Delphine and Ouvrard arrived punctually at five and sat stiffly on the sofa as if they were schoolchildren waiting for a dressing-down by the lycée principal. In honor of his guest, Alexandre produced a bottle of Taittinger Comtes de Champagne, Blanc de Blancs, 1999, rather than his standard Deutz. By the second glass the mood had eased.

"So you've been talking to my good friend Jean-Basile Labrousse?" Alexandre asked Ouvrard.

Ouvrard stood up and hovered. Capucine seized the moment and took his place next to Delphine on the sofa.

"Yes, I have. I understand you know him quite well."

"Are you familiar with Japanese single malts?" Alexandre asked, standing up to face Ouvrard.

Ouvrard shook his head, taken aback by the abrupt change in tack of the conversation.

"Then you have a treat in store. Let me give you a taste of something that you may find life changing." Alexandre led Ouvrard down the hall to his study.

Capucine hesitated. The flic in her burned to discover

whatever it was that was problematic enough to have prompted Ouvrard to solicit an interview with Alexandre; the feminist in her was loath to play the role of the subjugated woman obliged to sit on the sidelines, speculating on men's private conversations behind closed doors; but the diplomat she had been trained to be at Sciences Po won out.

"Are you sad to be leaving France?"

"No. Not at all, now that everything's been sold off. Did I tell you that I found buyers for the hotel? It's a sweet retired couple. I hope they know what they're getting themselves into."

"And I understood that the sale of the faïence went very well."

"Yes, I have more than enough to buy a small apartment in New York. But I understand everyone in New York lives in impossibly small apartments." She laughed happily at the prospect of starting a new life. Then, like a dark cloud covering the sun, her mood changed. "You know the commissaire-priseur decided that four of Jean-Louis's pieces were fakes and removed them from the sale?"

"What did you do with them?"

"I gave them to Jean-Louis's father. Actually, that solved a problem for me. I had wanted to give him a memento of his son. At first I thought I'd give him the best pieces—the baron used to be a collector—but then I decided that would be cruel."

"Cruel?"

"Because he's so broke. It's really awful. Jean-Louis took me to visit him two or three times. Jean-Lu would stuff the trunk of the car full of food. The baron's refrigerator was always filled with horrible-smelling scraps wrapped in greasy butcher's paper. Way worse than what you'd find in the Dumpster behind the restaurant. Jean-Lu would throw it all out. I knew if I gave his father important pieces of faïence, the idea of selling them would torture him. He would want the money, but then he'd feel he couldn't, because it was his legacy from his son. The fakes are worthless, so he won't have that anguish, but he'll still have a memento." She paused, her eyes damp. "It's a good time for me to leave France. I have nothing left here. Nothing at all."

Capucine gently nudged the conversation around to the subject of life in New York, a city she knew relatively well. Even though she found it exhilarating but exhausting to the point of debilitation, the picture she presented to Delphine was of a utopian town where all the cars were yellow taxis, people always ran rather than walked, and food was so important to the populace that even the hot dog vendors on the street offered gourmet delights.

An hour later Alexandre and Ouvrard emerged from the study. Ouvrard looked as abashed as only the voice of reason can abash.

Flowers of French politeness were strewn, and Delphine and Ouvrard took their leave.

"So?"

"So, not so very much. I did my good friend Jean-Basile Labrousse a minor disservice and the worthy Prosper a major service, hopefully reducing my sentence in purgatory by at least a thousand years. And a good thing, too, since I have it on good authority the victuals there are now supplied by McDonald's."

Capucine recognized one of her husband's hobbyhorses arriving at a brisk trot and bridled it before it had the chance to take off at a full gallop.

"What was Labrousse's offer?"

"A rather appealing one, actually. Apparently, Jean-Basile has decided to open a restaurant in New Orleans. He's becoming the quintessential American. They all do, sooner or later, don't they? It's the American virus of ambition. Anyway, he wants to help revitalize the city. It's not a bad idea. Louisiana is virtually French, after all. His cuisine would fit right in, and he'd definitely get the right kind of press on the project. He wants Ouvrard to be the *chef de cuisine*."

"So you told him to take the job?"

"Good Lord, no. Quelle idée!"

"I'm confused."

"Ouvrard is a very talented chef. But, naturally, he was beaten into submission by Brault. His job was to imitate Brault's cooking to such a degree of perfection, no one could tell Brault wasn't in the kitchen. That's what sous-chefs do. Labrousse is ten times more authoritarian than Brault ever was. This is going to be his restaurant where he won't be there all day long, hovering and making damn sure everything is done exactly the way he wants it. He's going to be over a thousand miles away in New York. Can you imagine the pressure he'd put on Ouvrard? His life would be hell. And on top of that, Labrousse would lap up all the glory. The bushel basket would be back over Ouvrard's nascent little flame, but this time it would be a heavy load, one he might never get out from under."

"But you didn't convince him, did you?"

"Nope. But I planted enough seeds of doubt for him to turn it down in the end. In his heart he knows it's not for him, but it's still going to be a difficult decision. You know how it is with children. They're so easily attracted by glitter." Alexandre's smile collapsed into a pout. "Why on earth did you accept Jacques's invitation to go to the so-called brand-new Chez La Mère Denis? You know how much I hate going to restaurants on Saturday night."

"He called this morning and insisted we have dinner tonight. I suggested he come here, but he absolutely wanted to take us out someplace. Chez La Mère Denis was my idea. I wanted to see what it's become, and I thought you might be curious, too, since you're always telling me what a talent Aiko Kikuchi is."

It turned out to be a disappointing choice. The transformation of the restaurant had not been a happy one. The restaurant had been rebaptized Chez la Mère Kikuchi in an attempt at wry sophistication entirely inappropriate to a quiet country lane. The elaborately carved oak paneling—a key prop in Brault's quest to graft himself onto the Troisgros-Bocuse lineage—had been amateurishly whitewashed and decorated with oversized papier-mâché Kabuki masks. Clearly intended to be kicky, the look came across as cheap and tacky.

A long aperture had been cut into the wall between the kitchen and the dining room, and a counter set up for three sushi chefs, who maniacally assembled rolls of fish and rice in an almost frightening frenzy. Beyond, the kitchen, with its long racks of copper pots and three enormous piano stoves, was apparently unchanged. Svelte and shapeless as a preteen boy, Aiko could be seen bending over the stainless-steel counter, her black hair hanging in damp strands, concentrating on arranging a dish with her tiny fingers. She looked up, caught sight of Alexandre, blew a lock out of her eyes, and smiled weakly.

Jacques was perched on a stool at the bar, teasing a bartender who looked young enough to pass for Aiko's niece. The girl giggled, covering her mouth with the flat of her hand and lowering her eyes modestly.

"This is Minako," Jacques said. "She's a mine of information on Japanese single malts." Jacques winked theatrically at Alexandre. "Minako, give this thirsty gentleman some of the nectar you've been plying me with."

The bartender giggled shyly behind her hand but managed to pour a shot glass full of dark brown liquid and place it in front of Alexandre as delicately as if it were a cherry blossom.

"K'm'm'g'gay," she said, rapidly enough to make it sound like a discreet belch.

"Minako is telling you she's giving you Komagatake," Jacques said. "It's a twelve-year-old single malt that is not quite a Yamazaki of that age but is very impressive, nonetheless."

Minako descended into well-screened giggles. Capucine resisted the impulse to check her ID to see if she was old enough to serve alcoholic beverages.

During this dialogue the maître d'hôtel hovered in a suit two sizes too large, oozing passive aggressiveness thinly disguised as exaggerated deference. The instant Alexandre turned to look at him, he brightened like an electric lamp abruptly turned on.

"Table?" he asked hopefully and, almost skipping, led them off to a corner of the dining room. When they sat down, the maître d' shook out their napkins and placed them on their laps.

With a toothy grin Jacques said, "Touch me there again and you'll have to marry me."

Not understanding, the maître d' grinned sycophantically, nodding like an automaton. Two waiters arrived at a trot in high-necked, ill-fitting pajama-like uniforms, one with a tray of house cocktails, a sticky-smelling concoction of sake and mango juice heavily laced with nutmeg, the other with menus. The simultaneous reflex of Capucine, Alexandre, and Jacques was to push their drinks, untasted, to the center of the table.

Jacques stood up and waved in the general direction of the bar. Minako arrived promptly with three shot glasses on a cork-covered tray.

A sense of crushing sadness descended on Capucine. The eradication of Chef Brault was far more complete than if the restaurant had been merely gutted. His oeuvre was like a delicate pencil line drawing that had been sloppily erased by a child and scribbled over with greasy crayons.

Alexandre's and Jacques's chuckles drew her out of her reverie.

"Lobster roll with a sauce of tobiko caviar." Jacques smirked, reading his menu.

"Duck confit spring roll with a hoisin dipping sauce," Alexandre countered.

"Sushi made with wild rice," Jacques riposted.

With a giggle, Capucine added, "And don't forget Valrhona chocolate tempura for dessert."

It took a good number of minutes for their hilarity to subside enough for them to be able to order. But when the food came, it was surprisingly good. Capucine opted for the lobster roll, which turned out to be a complex creation wrapped in a soybean sheet, while Jacques's Kobe beef hamburger was a very rare hamburger steak cooked in a brioche wrapper en croûte with a very gingery ketchup-like condiment made of *shouga* and *gari*. Alexandre pronounced the *confit de canard* spring rolls excellent. They were wrapped in an egg roll wrapper, gently grilled, topped with goat cheese, candied walnuts, and oven-fried pineapple chunks, and served with a glowing chrome-yellow sauce with a Sauternes base.

Just as Alexandre was rising through the clouds of a minor epiphany, Aiko left her kitchen to do a tour of the front of the house. She stopped next to Alexandre.

"What do you think?"

"Your creations are brilliant, genuinely original, inspiring."

For a brief second Aiko's lips turned up in a spindly smile.

"But what about the restaurant? What do you have to say about *that*?"

Alexandre said nothing and took a sip of sake that had been served in a small wooden *masu* box.

"It's the reverse of your success at Dong. There the food

was not so brilliant as what you're doing here, but the décor was out of this world."

Aiko's face turned to stone. She moved her face to within ten inches of Alexandre's. "It's that bastard Brissac-Vanté. He's swindled me," she said in a viperous whisper. "I'd like to skin him alive."

"Swindled you?"

"He sweet-talked me and took me to dinner at his other restaurants and then offered me a two-year contract with an attractive signing bonus. But when I arrived here, there was no money for redecoration. There was no money for anything. It was always going to arrive next week. With all that paneling, the place looked like a funeral home. So I did what I could and painted the walls with some pals and had an artist friend make the Kabuki masks. Since there wasn't even enough money for half the staff I need, I've had to get my family to help out. The bartender is my sister's daughter."

Aiko looked defiantly at Capucine, who, she well knew, was a police officer.

Capucine ignored the hostility. "But you must have enough budget for quality produce," Capucine said. "My lobster roll was out of this world."

Aiko laughed. "You don't need cash for that. I've known all my suppliers for years. I order and pay them at the end of the week from the receipts. The problem is that interior decorators don't work that way."

"So what are you going to do?" Alexandre asked.

"If Brissac-Vanté doesn't cough up by the end of next month, I fully intend to walk out. He can sue me all he wants, but he'll be in here all by himself, rolling his own goddamn sushi." Aiko turned and stalked back to her kitchen.

"That must be why she covers her mouth when she laughs. She doesn't want you to see her fangs," Jacques said.

A damp pall descended on the table.

"Let's go get a drink somewhere that's loud and cheerful. There's a taste I need to get out of my mouth, and it's not from the food," Capucine said.

Half an hour later they were standing at a small horseshoe-shaped bar, sipping cognac in a tiny bistro on the rue Vieille du Temple, not far from Capucine and Alexandre's apartment.

"That was painful," Jacques said.

Alexandre nodded sagely, finished his cognac, tapped his miniature snifter for the barman to pour him another. "It illustrates a truism about food—the vessel often has more impact than the contents. Even the finest grand cru will taste mediocre if it's served in a jam jar."

"You're so right, cousin," Jacques said, smoothing the lapel of his cashmere blazer with gold-plated basket-weave buttons. "The wrapping always provides its own substance."

Capucine ostentatiously examined the ceiling, eyebrows raised, shaking her head in dismay.

Alexandre leaned forward, looking intently at a bar across the narrow street. It was a popular watering hole that sold books—mainly avant-garde poetry and fiction—but also had a thriving bar business. Alexandre peered keenly.

"Look at that. What a godsend. That's Aiko Kikuchi's new book."

Capucine could see that the left-hand window of the bar contained a cardboard poster of a waiflike Aiko in kitchen whites, wearing an endearingly timid smile, an enormous steel skillet hanging limply in her left hand.

"This is going to solve a problem for me. I'm going to read the book tonight and write a review in the morning, making all sorts of comments about her new menu. That way I'll be spared writing a piece on how ghastly that restaurant is. The poor girl certainly doesn't deserve that. I'll be back in a flash." He darted out the door.

Jacques and Capucine turned and put their elbows on the bar. He leaned up against her and bent his head to whisper seductively in her ear, for all the world a young swain courting.

"You came up again in this morning's senior staff meeting."

A sardonic comment formed itself in Capucine's mouth, but she clamped her lips before it could get out.

"It would appear that the Olympian powers are impatient."

"The poor dears," Capucine said sweetly.

"Yes. You see, a decision was taken that the DGSE were not to stick their fingers in the cogs and gears of the Police Judiciaire apparatus."

"And electronic eavesdropping is not the same thing as poking your fingers where they don't belong?"

"Hardly. Not the same thing at all."

"In other words, you're telling me that your poor impatient powers can't interfere with my case until they have something to interfere with. Is that it?"

"Actually, there is hope on high they won't have to interfere at all."

"Well, then, if it's a nice day tomorrow, I might just get around to making an arrest or two."

CHAPTER 42

David sat in his boxy little sit-up-and-beg rental and watched the mechanics walk through the garage door at the back of the Peugeot dealership. They all had exactly the same gait: a "Fuck the world, how cool am I" saunter warring with a desperate "Please don't let me punch in late" trot. Antonin was easy enough to spot. He was the only one who genuinely didn't give a damn. The one who knew for sure he wouldn't be there in a few weeks.

David came back at quitting time and waited. Antonin came out, his shoulders pushed back aggressively, looking like he had just had words, maybe even a punch or two, with someone. As he approached the car from behind, David opened the passenger door wide enough to block him.

"Get in, Anou."

Antonin stopped. His face flattened, and his eyes became slits. David produced his police ID wallet and held it up.

"We can either have a beer at the café or do this down at the brigade. One way or the other, you're going to get in the car."

"How did you find me?"

David lied. "It wasn't all that hard. Records had you working at a Mercedes dealership here in Toulon a few years ago. The dealership filed a complaint against you after you took a wrench to your foreman. I guessed you wouldn't go far and you'd stick to German luxury cars. None of the Peugeot or BMW dealers had a Brault on the payroll, so I figured I'd hang around and see if I could spot a temp who was getting paid cash. And there you were."

"I thought I'd disappeared for good."

"The only way to do that nowadays is to join the Foreign Legion."

Both men grunted a laugh.

A few blocks away David found a café with a terrace that looked out on a dusty, beaten-earth square, vaguely reminiscent of Le Marius in La Cadière. The terrace was nearly empty. A waiter arrived, flicked his side towel impatiently, nodded with indifference, and was dispatched for pastis.

"I'm having a real hard time believing you're buying me a drink because you want to hear all about how I tapped my last foreman a good one on his sciatic with a monkey wrench."

David took his time with the liturgical ritual of adding water to his pastis. "I want to talk to you about Jean-Louis."

"My little brother? Yeah, I saw about that in the paper. Poor little fucker."

"Let's start with Fanny Folon."

"I haven't seen her in nearly twenty years. She lives in Bandol now."

"I understand you had an evening's fun with her just before she left."

"More like she had an evening's fun with me and my buds."

"Now that we've got that settled, you can tell me all about it."

"Not much to tell. I was out cruising with my pals. We didn't have enough money to go to the café, so I decided we'd go check out this little stand of pines on the hill behind the village. A lot of guys would take their girls out there to give them a reaming, and I thought we might have a few laughs. Sure enough, there's Fanny and this dork she was hanging out with, Felix Olivier, going at it. Fanny was giving him a hard time, telling him to be a man and show more enthusiasm. He was arguing back. See, there's the two of them going at it while they're having a fight. Funniest goddamn thing I ever saw. So we're laughing fit to bust a gut, and Fanny hears us and starts to put on an act. She shoots her legs up in the air and starts moaning like she's really coming. All the while she's looking at me and smiling. You know, the big come-on." Antonin fell silent. He had worked himself up to tell the story with all the trimmings but suddenly realized he was telling it to a police officer.

"So then what?"

"So nothing. That's all there is to tell."

"Look, Antonin, I'm investigating your brother's murder. I don't give a shit who you fucked or didn't fuck in your village twenty years ago. As I said before, I'm happy enough to hear what you have to tell sitting in the sun, sipping pastaga, but I'd be just as happy hearing it down at the brigade. Suit yourself, pal."

"All right, all right. Fucking calm down and listen up. So, like it was just too good. Fanny had her enormous boobs hanging out of her dress and was really hotted up, but this wimp Felix just wasn't doing it for her. So I did what a gentleman does. I got rid of pastis-dicked Felix and gave her what she wanted."

"How'd you get rid of him?"

"Went up and whacked him one upside the ear, and he went running off home, howling. No problem there."

"And then you got on Fanny."

"Sure did. Made her moan like a cat in heat. She was begging for more."

"That's when you got your pals in on the act."

"Right. I'd finished. She wanted more. And you have to be fair with your buds. She liked them pretty good. Not as much as me, of course, but pretty good."

"You're a real gentleman. Then what happened?"

"She pushed Galinette off her and said she'd had enough. So we left. That's all there was to it. Fanny was a good old girl. She didn't want any more, and we weren't going to give her a hard time, now were we?"

"And Jean-Louis was with you during all this?"

"Damn straight he was. Listen, that kid had it rough. Our mom died when he was four, and good old dad, the fucking baron, wasn't dealing out of a full deck. All he cared about were his goddamn vegetables and his crazy collection of broken faïence. Jean-Louis would suck up to him all the time. The little fucker was trying so hard to stick his nose up Dad's ass, he was turning into a fag. So I took him with me wherever I went. I wanted to man him up."

"Didn't Jean-Louis have any friends?"

"Yeah. One. He was big pals with Fanny's little brother. What a waste of flesh that little brat was. Always the snide comment. Always rolling his eyes at you. If he hadn't been Fanny's little brother, I'd have popped him hard enough to get some respect out of him. I don't know what happened to that little fucker after, but he sure was a pain in the ass when he was a kid."

"And when you'd had enough of Fanny that evening, Jean-Louis left with you?"

"No. He started to and then turned around and went back to Fanny. Did I tell you he had this puppy love thing with her? So I let him go. I figured he was just going to get his share, you know? Probably his first time. If I'd been a good big brother, I'd have gone back with him to show him the ropes. But then I figured, what the hell. He'll sort it out all by himself, and if he can't, Fanny will give him a hand. She never could get enough, that one. So my buds and I went off to use our last twenty francs to get some beers."

The Boulangerie Barbaroux in Cassis was a far grander establishment than Fanny's parents' shop in La Cadière. Six tall circular tables surrounded by high swivel chairs were bolted into the floor along the long plate-glass window. A row of refrigerated display windows offered, in addition to the usual assortment of Provençal pastry, an array of sandwiches and prepared dishes, all of which could be heated in one of the three microwave ovens.

The boulangerie bustled with chatting office workers on their lunch breaks. David waited in line until one of the eight lithesome counter girls, their summer tans just beginning to fade, favored him with a smile and took his order. He chose a fougasse that was so laden with anchovies, olives, and sun-dried tomatoes, it might almost have been a Neapolitan pizza folded into thirds and slit elegantly by a calligrapher. An attractive, thirtyish, well-figured woman took his five- and ten-euro notes and returned his change. Fanny for sure. A perfect clone of her mother. A little heavier perhaps, but all the more attractive for it. He was the only one who paid in cash. All the others had paid with government-subsidized meal vouchers.

David took his fougasse and a bottle of Kronenbourg 1664 beer to his tiny rental Peugeot and waited.

By two thirty the boulangerie was deserted. Through the plate-glass window he could see the cheerful girls energetically buffing every glass surface with liquid from squeeze bottles.

He pushed the plate-glass door open and walked up to the marble pay counter. Fanny was doing something complicated with the cash register. He assumed she was getting it to tell her what the luncheon revenue had been.

"Are you Françoise Folon?"

She looked him in the eye with a coquettish smile and then let her eyes slither down his frame. "Not for eighteen years. Now it's Barbaroux. And no one's ever called me Françoise. It's Fanny." The smile was her mother's.

"I need to talk to you," David said quietly.

"Police?"

David nodded his head a fraction of an inch.

"Come in back."

The room behind the shop was the boulanger's kitchen, with a long wooden table in the middle and two gigantic stoves along one wall. Fanny pushed two upright oak chairs to the corner of the table. They sat facing each other, the triangle of wood only half a barrier between them.

David studied her, pushing her back into her teens, seeing a full-breasted, lush-lipped, lusty adolescent, impatient with her too-small village, thirsty for the full measure of life's sensuality. It was a common enough story, but the level of piquant in this one was far more intense than the average.

"I'm investigating the death of Jean-Louis Brault."

Her eyes softened. "Poor Jean-Lu, just as he was finally unfolding his wings, they brought him down."

"You were close to him when you were children?"

"I was the closest thing he had to a mother. He was my little baby. He had a terrible home. He lost his mother when he was little, and his father wasn't really right in the head. He and my little brother, Lucien, were best friends, and he was always over at my parents' boulangerie. My parents adored him, particularly my father, who loved to show him how to bake things. And, of course, Jean-Lu was best friends with Lucien, my little brother. The only child in the village that could get along with the little brat." She laughed and shook her head. "He was a real problem, that kid. He mocked everyone. Never happy about anything. And jealous! Let me tell you.

"I'll tell you a story. One morning my father and Jean-Lu were making *pissaladière*. My father would make this special dough for it that he would let rise and punch down four times. Then he handed it over to Jean-Lu, who must have been nine or ten, no more than that. Jean-Lu caramelized some very sweet Italian red onions he'd brought from his father's garden. Then he made a perfect square out of the dough and laid the onions down as a bed. On top of that he made this complicated pattern with anchovies and Niçoise olives. In those days schoolchildren wore these smocks with big pockets, and Jean-Lu's were always filled with all sorts of herbs and wildflowers he'd gather in the hills. He finished off his pattern with all kinds of colored wildflowers and then sprinkled some herbs on top. I tell you, when it came out of the oven, it looked just like a painting. It wasn't just that it was the most beautiful pissaladière we had ever seen. It tasted absolutely unbelievable, too.

"Lucien took one bite out of his piece and threw it on the floor, saying Jean-Lu had put on too many anchovies and it was too salty." Fanny laughed. "My mother was so mad, she slapped Lucien and sent him to his room without lunch."

"Did Anou come to your house, as well?"

"Not really. He was the village hooligan. A tough guy. Sometimes he'd come to pick up his little brother and flex his muscles at me, but he'd never stay."

David fell silent, searching for the words for his next question.

"In the village . . ." He paused. This was not quite right.

"I understand that Anou assaulted you," he blurted out, annoyed at his amateurism.

Fanny exploded in laughter. "Assaulted! As if any of those village children could assault anyone. But I know what you're talking about, though. Let me tell you what really happened. I had a boyfriend. A nice, gentle little boy, the son of the village butcher. He would write me poems, bring me flowers. He was desperately in love with me. Girls at that age like that. Now I realize he must have been a *pédé*—a queer—and didn't really like girls. He would kiss here and lick there, but he didn't really like to get down to it." She gave David a shrewd look, focusing on his long locks, having a hard time deciding which category to put him in.

"So, one evening we were in this little pine copse, and Olivier was getting me really worked up with his tongue but not doing much of anything else. I was starving. I'd had enough of the canapés. I wanted a good, thick, juicy red steak. Can you understand that?"

David nodded sagely, trying hard not to grin at the metaphor.

"And then I heard Anou and his little gang snickering. It was just too much for me. I know I shouldn't have, but my blood was up. So I made a gesture for Anou to come over. I guess you know what happened next."

David said nothing.

"It wasn't as good as I expected it would be. Anou was strong and rough, but he had no sense of rhythm. He was doing it all for himself. One of his friends, Escartefigue, was much better. He really had the knack for it."

"But you stopped them."

"Of course I did. I saw Jean-Lu standing there, crying his eyes out, looking miserable. All of a sudden I realized what a torment it must have been for him. So I shooed the boys away—they left, clucking like chickens—and I took

Jean-Lu into my arms. He cried for a long time. He was such a sweet child. When I looked up, there was my stupid little brother, wide-eyed, jealous that I was comforting his best friend and lusting after me at the same time. He didn't give a shit that his best friend was upset. All he cared about was himself and what he wanted. What a jerk that little kid was."

CHAPTER 43

"This wasn't the easiest case we've ever had, eh, Commissaire?" Isabelle asked.

Hands on the wheel, Capucine turned and gave Isabelle a tolerant smile. They crossed the Pont Marie onto the eternally peaceful Ile Saint-Louis.

"I got worried when you refused to believe I was right about who the murderer was. But I guess you saw the light in the end," Isabelle continued.

Capucine turned left at the rue Saint-Louis en l'Ile.

"Commissaire, I can't imagine why you didn't agree with me from the beginning. The trail of evidence was a mile wide."

At the end of the street, Capucine turned left again onto the quai d'Anjou, drove a few hundred feet, and parked illegally in front of a garage door.

Both women got out of the car and walked up to small, crimson, enameled wood door with a semicircular top, which centuries before had undoubtedly been the servants' entrance to the spacious town house. Isabelle produced a bunch of keys, examined the lock, opened it. Inside, they inspected a row of mailboxes labeled with small plastic numbered squares and, only occasionally, a scrawled paper label with a name.

"It's in the back," Capucine said.

Isabelle opened a second door with her set of keys, and they crossed a tiny stone-flagged courtyard with three cracked clay flowerpots containing shriveled geranium plants. The building in back had been built up over what had once been the stables. There was no lock on the door.

"*Putain*—shit," Isabelle said. "No elevator."

Capucine strictured her to silence with pursed lips. They began the climb up the four flights of worn oak steps on the sides of their feet, making as little noise as possible.

After two flights they paused to catch their breaths. Capucine's cell phone vibrated in her pocket. Automatically, she glanced at the caller ID. David. Calling in the middle of the afternoon meant it must be serious.

Capucine cradled the phone in her cupped hand and pressed the green ON button.

"Not a good time, David. Tell me quick," Capucine whispered softly.

"I just interviewed Fanny Folon. The incident wasn't at all what we thought. It couldn't have been Lucien Folon. He doesn't even come close to having a murderer's profile, and there's no motive at all."

"He hasn't been a serious suspect for weeks. I'll call you later, and we'll tell each other all about it."

At the last landing they stopped in front of the door on the left. Capucine knocked politely. Nothing happened. Impatiently, Isabelle rapped loudly, her knuckles reverberating on the wood. The door opened a timid crack. Isabelle pushed it open violently with her shoulder.

"Police!"

Chéri Lecomte fell back, eyes wide.

When Capucine stepped around from behind Isabelle, Chéri's eyes gaped even wider.

"Ca . . . Capucine . . ." Her voice faded.

"Mademoiselle, you're under arrest for the murders of Firmin Roque and Jean-Louis Brault."

The instant she took measure of the situation, Chéri's confidence popped up like a jack-in-the-box.

"You can't arrest me. I'm an American citizen. Here, just look at this."

Chéri wheeled and grabbed at her handbag on a table by the door.

Isabelle grabbed Chéri's extended arm, twisted it behind her, and slammed her into the wall with a loud thud. She twisted the other arm around and snapped on a pair of handcuffs.

Capucine opened Chéri's handbag, extracted an American passport from a side pocket, and waved it disdainfully in front of Chéri's face.

"As they used to say in New York, 'This and fifteen cents will get you a ride on the IRT.' In France it will get you absolutely nothing. Let's get going."

Back at the brigade Chéri was put in one of Capucine's interrogation rooms, recently redecorated as blandly as a mid-market motel room. Only the black-framed six-foot-long mirror—a fake, intended to raise the stress of the interviewee—and a folding metal chair, painstakingly chosen for its lack of comfort, hinted at the room's purpose.

Chéri was seated in the uncomfortable chair, rubbing her wrists to ease the pain of the over-tight handcuffs. Slate-faced, Isabelle observed her from behind a Swedish blond-wood desk. Capucine paced the room.

"I demand you call the American embassy. You have no right to hold me like this. I need them to appoint me a lawyer right away."

"Don't be silly. This is a police interrogation. You have no right to a lawyer. When I hand you over to a prosecutor for trial, you'll have the opportunity to select counsel and your embassy is free to help you with that. But until then, you're all mine," Capucine said with a malevolent little smile.

"All right, have it your way. What can you possibly think I'm guilty of?"

"I'm going to start by telling you what happened, and then you can fill in the details. You were at the center of a racket that produced and sold forgeries of antique faïence. Pieces from Chef Jean-Louis Brault's collection were copied at the Faïence de Châteauneuf-sur-Loire by Firmin Roque. Then you either sold the copies yourself or had them sold through your contacts."

Chéri raised her eyebrows with polite incredulousness, as if a slightly tipsy friend had made a comically far-fetched allegation about one of her acquaintances.

"Really?"

"But you got greedy. And instead of returning all of Chef Brault's original pieces, you kept some of them and gave him forgeries."

Chéri maintained her tolerant smile.

"But Brault discovered what you were up to and went into a paranoid rage. He was so out of control, you thought he might go to the authorities. So you killed him."

There was a long pause. Pantomiming extreme patience, Chéri made a show of her thin smile.

"And when Roque learned that Brault had been murdered, he immediately made the connection. He knew that if his involvement in the forgeries became known, his halo of Marxist sanctity would crumble. He insisted you come to see him. He intimidated you. You knew he was a consummate politician and perfectly capable of blowing the whistle so he could frame you and Brault and hide behind the smoke screen of your murder trial. So you seized your opportunity and killed him, too."

Chéri laughed happily. "You have a delightful imagination. I can just see you and Alexandre sitting around the dinner table, sipping wine and swapping your fabulous stories. Kudos. But you don't have the slightest shred of proof for any of this."

"As it happens, I have more than enough evidence to remand you to the juge d'instruction right now."

The merest trace of worry dimpled Chéri's brow.

"Let's review the evidence. The tip-off was the outrageous bid you placed on that sixteenth-century Menton rafraîchissoir. The explanation was obvious. You had returned a forgery of the original to Brault after it had been copied at Châteauneuf. A few months later Brault decided to sell it to help finance his hotel. You saw the piece in the auction catalog and desperately needed to buy it before someone noticed it was a fake."

Chéri shrugged her shoulders.

"Next, we have the fact that four pieces in the auction of Brault's collection were discovered to be fakes. As it happened, two of those pieces had been auctioned to Brault by the commissaire-priseur, who was certain that when he sold them, they were genuine. Therefore, someone must have substituted the originals with forgeries. And that someone had to be you."

Chéri shrugged again.

"Our forensics unit determined that you were selling fakes made at Châteauneuf from your stand at the Puces. Since you were selling identical copies of the same piece on successive days, it was obvious you were actively and knowingly perpetrating a fraud."

Chéri shook her head, with an exaggerated frown of tolerant incredulity.

"As to the other murder, the forensic examination of the trunk in which Chef Brault's body was discovered indicated that it had been dragged twice over cobblestones, once empty and once laden. That strongly suggested you had gone down to Arnaud Boysson's Vuitton stand, dragged the empty trunk to your stand, stuffed Brault inside, shot him, and then dragged it back to Boysson's stand. On top of that, Brault's clothing was put on sale at the Puces the day after the murder, another indication he had been killed there."

Capucine paused, eyes fixed on Chéri.

"That's it? That's all the evidence you have?" Chéri said, beaming. "It's all entirely circumstantial. No prosecutor would even think of going to court with that."

"My dear, your knowledge of French criminal proceedings seems to come entirely from American TV shows. In France circumstantial evidence is entirely admissible if there is enough of it. And there is more than enough here to secure both convictions. But even if it weren't, there are also two trump cards."

Chéri's self-assurance wilted slightly at the edges.

"The first ties you inextricably to Roque's murder. The way you did it was clever. After your meeting with him, you hung around until he and his wife left the house—he must have mentioned he was going out to dinner—and jimmied your way back in with a credit card. There were telltale marks on the door frame. Then you went to the basement, figured out which was the fuse for the lights in the front part of the ground floor, took that fuse out, and screwed it into a slot that had held a fuse for double its amperage, probably the one for the kitchen. The fuse immediately blew out, and you replaced it in its original slot. Then you removed all but one of the spare fuses with the right amperage and poured a jugful of water on the floor in front of the fuse box. So far, so good, but then you got far too clever.

"You needed a nice conductive substance to make sure the person who screwed in the replacement fuse would get a lethal shock. So you rubbed it with conductive gel for an electrical muscle toner. You thought you were in luck because you had a small plastic bottle of the stuff in your purse, probably left over from your last trip. I'm sure you always take your toner with you when you travel. It was a clever thing to do, and it worked perfectly. But our forensics group was able to identify the manufacturer of the gel—Slendertone. A brand that's not distributed in France. And you were careless enough to leave the bottle in your medicine cabinet, where my officers just found it a few minutes ago, as they were going through your apartment."

"Utterly ridiculous. You have no proof that I even saw Firmin that day."

"Of course I do. You were so proud of yourself, you got careless. On your way home, you stopped for gas and a bite to eat at the Dordives service station on the A6 autoroute, twenty miles away from Châteauneuf-sur-Loire. It's the first service station on the autoroute. We have your credit card records. You paid for your meal at ten twenty-two and your gas at ten forty-one. Those times are perfectly consistent with the timing of the crime."

The vertical creases in Chéri's brow deepened.

"And your other trump card?"

"That one's even better. Your accomplice is in the next room, signing a confession," Capucine fibbed.

Without a word Capucine and Isabelle left the room.

They went into the big staff room, to a long table populated with TV monitors. From three different angles Chéri could be seen fidgeting, darting nervous glances at the fake one-way mirror, hoping to catch a glance of the people who were examining her. Capucine left Isabelle at her task and stepped into a room identical to the other except that the carpeting was a slightly different shade of blue.

Thierry Brissac-Vanté sat in the uncomfortable folding chair, cowering under Momo's glower.

"I nabbed him coming out of that club on the Champs-Élysées," Momo said. "Funny thing, when I put the collar on him and took out the cuffs, the three fat cats he was with bolted real fast. You see that stuff in the projects, but I've never seen it in the Eighth."

When he recognized Capucine, Brissac-Vanté re-arranged his features into a carefully constructed mélange of upper-class arrogance and a convalescent's rightful indignation, topped off with a gratin of "Do you know who I am?" petulance.

"You're under arrest for the murder of Jean-Louis Brault."

"That's absurd. I demand to see my lawyer."

"It's too late for that. Your accomplice, Chéri Lecomte, is also under arrest. She's in the next room and has just confirmed your guilt."

Amateurishly, Brissac-Vanté mimed incredulity. Acting was not his forte.

"I don't know anyone by that name."

With her foot Capucine pulled a pale blue–cushioned wooden chair into the prescribed position, forty-five degrees and three feet away from the suspect's knee, and sat down.

"Let me share with you what Mademoiselle Lecomte has already confessed. Feel free to correct the details."

Capucine outlined the two murders as she had done for Chéri. Brissac-Vanté was a considerably less skilled poker player than she was. By the end of her narrative, his brow was damp and his eyes were wide with panic.

Still, even though it was done with a lack of conviction, he attempted a riposte. "All you've got is the confession of this hysterical arriviste woman, whom I don't even know. The rest is just conjecture."

Capucine looked at him with a stony face for several long beats. By the end, he squirmed out of her gaze.

"If you don't know her, how do you know she's an arriviste?"

Brissac-Vanté's lips thinned, and the dampness of his brow grew into beads of sweat.

"For openers, Mademoiselle Lecomte alerted me to your kidnapping. She called me, claiming she was your mistress and you had stood her up for a date and then had disappeared. She suspected foul play. She was at her wit's end. It was very moving."

Brissac-Vanté attempted a snort of derision, but it came out as a dry cough.

"We also know that she called you repeatedly after your return, but you refused to pick up for her. Then there's the fact that both of the murdered men had received financing from you. On top of that, our forensics department determined beyond any doubt that the forged faïence was made at Châteauneuf."

His face still contorted by worry, Brissac-Vanté shook his head, either in derision or in an attempt to dispel the nightmare. He started to protest, but his throat was too dry for the words to come out. His eyes dropped to the floor.

"But that's not all. There's also a real *pièce à conviction*. After you were released by your kidnappers, the police kept up its investigation."

Brissac-Vanté looked up sharply.

"Particularly the financial part. Early on we discovered that you have three accounts in the Isle of Jersey branch of the Royal Bank of Scotland. Very conveniently, you can access your account over the telephone using only number codes, no names. While you were being held by the kidnappers, we monitored those accounts only to see if any payments had been made *out* of them. There weren't any. But after your release, we intensified our efforts and discovered that wire transfers for significant amounts had been made *into* them at periodic intervals. We looked into those. A good number came from Sotheby's. We checked with them. You had been auctioning off faïence. Sotheby's was very cooperative. The pieces you were selling were identical to some of the pieces in Chef Brault's collection."

Brissac-Vanté's head fell into his hands, supported by his elbows on his knees.

Capucine knew full well she was at a crucial turning point. She had only the thinnest case. As she had spooled out her pieces of evidence, they had sounded so hollow, Capucine was amazed Brissac-Vanté was so cowed. This was very clear broth for a *procureur*. Obtaining a full confession was critical.

"Your only hope is to cooperate. If you give me all the details, the fact that you have helped the police may dispose the judges favorably toward you. That might make a big difference."

Brissac-Vanté looked at Capucine with almost childlike hopefulness.

"It was all that awful woman's fault. It started because I wanted to help Chef Brault. He was completely neurotic about his stupid hotel. It got to him so badly, his cooking was suffering. He couldn't get bank loans for it, and my wife certainly would have said no to any further investments with him. And then Roque came to see me. He wanted breathing money. The Faïence was doing all right, but he felt he was always a day late and a euro short on everything. He wanted our investment syndicate to cut him another big tranche of debt. But that wasn't going to happen, either.

"I mentioned this to Chéri during a dinner one night. Okay, okay, I did have a short fling with her for a few weeks, but it was no big deal, and she certainly doesn't count as a mistress. Let's be perfectly clear on that. Anyway, she cooked up the idea. Brault was going to supply the pieces, and Roque would copy them in his plant at night. That suited everyone right down to the ground. Brault would keep his collection and get some money, and Roque would get some money while working with his hands and fucking the capitalists. It was great for everybody.

"That is, until that stupid bitch double-crossed everyone. She started keeping a few of Brault's originals and slipping him forgeries. Just one or two at the beginning and then maybe as many as ten or fifteen a year. The problem was the originals. Chéri could only sell lesser pieces at her stand. The quality stuff needed to be sold at auction or in top-quality antique stores. There was a limit to what could be sold in France, so she talked me into taking them to London to put them up at auction there." He paused to look at Capucine to see how she was receiving the story. Capucine smiled encouragingly.

"I'm sorry to say I found that the extra cash came in handy. All my accounts are joint with my wife. It's true I had a girlfriend or two. And I also like to play the occasional game of backgammon. I'm sure you can understand that. Then the inevitable happened. Brault noticed that one of the pieces that had come back from Roque was a fake. He figured the whole scam out immediately and called me, completely hysterical." Brissac-Vanté paused, realizing he'd got ahead of his story. "You see, they didn't know each other. Brault would put the pieces in the trunk of my car when I went to have dinner at Chez La Mère Denis, and then a month or so later he'd retrieve them from my trunk when I went back again. Do you understand?"

Capucine nodded.

"So one day Brault calls me up, berserk. I'd been stealing from his collection. He went on and on, raving completely out of control. So I say, 'Look, the woman who works with me on this and I are going to take you out to dinner, and we'll talk it all over, and everything's going to be just great.' And he buys that, or at least he calms down somewhat. So Chéri and I take him to this restaurant in the Twentieth. This place used to be a hole-in-the-wall, but when we get there, the crowd seems to be more upmarket than what it was, and I'm worried we'll run into someone we know.

"Dinner was not too congenial, to say the least. Brault

starts drinking and getting more and more pissed off and talking louder and louder, and people are looking over at us and staring and all. It was turning into a very bad scene. So Chéri gets this great idea. 'Let's go over to my stand at the Puces, and we can discuss this quietly,' she tells Brault. At this point Brault is already completely sloshed. He'd nod off at the table and then wake up, ranting. I can't tell you how relieved I was to get out of that damn restaurant." Brissac-Vanté paused, exhausted.

"Would you like some coffee or some water?"

"A coffee would be very welcome."

Capucine nodded at Momo, who stepped to the door to mutter at the uniformed brigadier standing guard.

Coffee in hand, Brissac-Vanté looked hard at Capucine. "It all went badly downhill from there. I drove Brault in my car, and Chéri followed in his. When we got to her stand, we sat around, drinking this really shitty cognac she had. Brault got completely out of control, taking out all his frustrations on us—not just the faïence scam, but his worries about his stars, his cooking, his future, his failed life. He was going to turn us in, we were going to do big time in jail, and we were going to pay for what we'd done to him. In the middle of a rant he falls out of his chair, completely passed out. I have to say I was well beyond buzzed myself. I was ready to call it quits.

"But no. Chéri gets up, says she'll be right back, and returns dragging this big Vuitton trunk and a shotgun, which she said she'd found in the trunk of Brault's car. She tells me to take Brault's clothes off, which I do. Then she opens the Vuitton trunk and tells me to grab Brault under the arms while she picks up his legs. We stuff him in the damn thing. I figured it was some kind of joke to teach him a lesson and she was going to lock him in there until he'd slept it off.

"But then she rams the shotgun between his legs. Brault wakes up and struggles desperately to get out of the trunk.

She holds him and pulls the trigger." He paused and shook his head. "It was unbelievable. I couldn't hear, my ears were ringing so loudly. Half of Brault's face was gone. There was blood all over the inside of the trunk. It was a nightmare. Worse than a nightmare." Brissac-Vanté fell silent, horrified by the enormity of the story he was telling.

"She looks at me. 'Problem solved,' she says. 'Help me get this back to where it goes,' she says. So the two of us drag the trunk back down to this other stand, dump Brault's clothes in a Dumpster, and get the hell out of there. Chéri gets into Brault's car and drives off, and I get into mine and go home."

There was a long, flat silence. Brissac-Vanté put his head back in his hands. Capucine said nothing, waiting to see if there was more to come.

"Will I go to jail?"

"Yes, for a while, but with some luck you may be prosecuted only as an accomplice. You need to sign the printout of the confession you've just made, and when you come up in front of the prosecutor, be as open with him as you've been with me. Don't try to outsmart him. Do you understand?"

Brissac-Vanté nodded dumbly. He was clearly far more relieved at the absolution from his confession than at the prospect of a short prison sentence.

CHAPTER 44

The door to Capucine's office flew open. Isabelle stormed in, her face black with rage. She leaned over Capucine's desk, hands braced on the edge, shoulders spread, muscles of her back bunched. The multiple studs in her face glistened. Capucine suspected there might be one or two new ones.

"Half of my files on the Brault-Roque case have vanished off the face of my computer," Isabelle said through clenched teeth.

"I noticed that myself," Capucine said serenely.

Isabelle took no heed. "Roque has disappeared completely. It's all gone. Our case notes. All the *PVs* we collected. Even the part of the transcript of the Lecomte interview that dealt with Roque has disappeared."

"I know."

Isabelle ignored Capucine's comment. "I had a hunch. So I called the magistrates' hall—one of the girls who works over there is a pal—and got them to send me a copy of Lecomte's signed confession, which the procureur is going to submit to the judges when he presents his case. And you know what?" She stopped, demanding an answer to her rhetorical question.

"What?"

"It's been doctored. The part about Roque's murder has been taken out. All that's left is her confession of having murdered Brault."

"We were lucky to get her to confess to that. I thought she'd stonewall us to the end."

"Commissaire, how can this not piss you off? An entire case has vanished into thin air. Poof." Isabelle snapped her fingers.

"I suspected that might happen. I spoke to the procureur yesterday. He intends to prosecute Chéri for the premeditated murder of Brault. The premeditation part struck me as a bit contrived since the murder was obviously a spur-of-the-moment decision, heavily fueled by alcohol. But he's going for a life sentence without the possibility of parole, and he needs premeditation for that."

Isabelle stared at her, throbbing with anger.

"And he's only asking for a very light sentence for Brissac-Vanté, building his case around a picture of a manipulated, weak-willed, dead-drunk playboy who was tricked into becoming an unwilling accomplice to murder. The way he'll present it will make Chéri look even more guilty."

Isabelle thrummed, champing to hear about the Roque case.

"At the end of my chat with him there was an awkward moment, as if the procureur was daring me to ask about the Roque case. Which I didn't."

Livid with rage, Isabelle flexed her shoulder muscles, looking for someone to punch.

"Let it go, Isabelle. You can't serve a life sentence twice. When you get right down to it, what difference does it really make?"

* * *

At eleven that night, as they watched the evening news, Capucine disentangled herself from Alexandre to grab her cell phone as it vibrated its way across the coffee table.

"Salut, Jacques."

"I thought this would be a good time to call. I'm sure you need a break from the strain of applying CPR to your corpulent consort's nether regions. I'll call back later if you were having even a glimmer of success."

"No, Jacques, right now is perfect."

"I'm sorry to hear that. It must be an uphill climb for you. But cheer up. I have good news. You have an important meeting at the Hôtel de Beauvau tomorrow morning at eight thirty. I'm to deliver you myself. I'll pick you up at eight. Now, get back to work. It's the eager bird that catches the flaccid worm. Isn't that the phrase?"

The next morning Jacques refused to elaborate, rattling on with silly facetiousness in the confines of the miniscule Smart Car.

It was only as they swept under the elegantly curlicued gold-plated decoration on the enormous iron gates of the Ministry of the Interior that Jacques made a comment on the upcoming meeting. "If you play your cards right, this could be a big step for you. Who knows, you might even get a little red ribbon to wear on your lapel. Just think how happy that would make Tante Coralie. A Légion d'Honneur medal, just like Daddy's." He was still braying his laugh as he handed the toy-sized car over to the *voiturier.*

A *huissier* in a morning coat, with a silver chain around his neck, showed them into a large office. The emerald light of the elaborate garden poured in through three French windows, rendering the man sitting at the enormous desk, which was dripping with gilt prettification, indistinguishable in the backlight.

It took Capucine's eyes several seconds to adjust. The ministerial toad. She had completely forgotten about him.

Coffee was served with fussy politeness by men in black morning coats. The scene smacked so resolutely of the upper echelons of the French government, the rarified air seemed difficult to breathe.

"Commissaire, I must compliment you on your finesse," the ministerial toad said. "None of the solutions I came up with for our little imbroglio were half as elegant as yours." The toad took a sip of coffee. "It would have been easy enough to bury the Roque case, but the danger would have lurked. There would have always been the threat that one day an inquisitive journalist would do some digging and accuse us of having left a murderer on the loose." He smiled and took another sip of coffee. "But your solution tied up all the loose ends. Not only did you create a culprit, but you put her behind bars, from where she can be produced by this government, or any future government, if she's ever needed. Exemplary."

The toad reclined in his chair, threw back his head, and drank the last, sweetest drops of his coffee.

"Naturally, I've already given the magistrates' hall the gentlest nudge to make sure your culprit will be sentenced to the maximum security ward at Clairvaux Prison, where she will never have the slightest possibility of communicating with the press. And I think we've poured enough oil on the troubled waters of the Faïence de Châteauneuf-sur-Loire that we won't be hearing from them again. Madame Brissac-Vanté was so grateful to hear that the government was making every effort to insure her husband would receive the shortest possible sentence that she's extended a gratifyingly large tranche of credit to the Faïence. Their financial worries are over."

The toad sat back in his chair and contentedly laced his fingers over the considerable tumescence of his stomach.

He looked at Capucine with a long, thin U of a smile, a squat reptile contemplating a fly, waiting for the propitious moment to nab it with a flick of his tongue.

"Commissaire, I really shouldn't tell you this, but last night I received a call from the rue du Faubourg Saint-Honoré." He waved his finger in the general direction of the Élysée Palace across the street. "They are very pleased with you over there. More than pleased, grateful. Particularly about the consideration you showed Monsieur Brissac-Vanté. The feeling is that a short sojourn behind bars will do him a world of good, and—now this really is just between you and me—a certain person was delighted that his former wife will lose a little face. But you knew exactly how far to go. Well done."

He lowered his voice conspiratorially. "I'm going to betray another little secret and tell you that I've been instructed to proceed rapidly in awarding you a decoration that, it is felt, you richly deserv—"

Very quietly, Capucine stood up, walked soundlessly across the Persian carpeting out into the hallway, and slammed the carved oak door behind her as hard as she could.

CHAPTER 45

"Blood. I thought blood was the essential part," Capucine said.

"*Pas à table*. Not at the table, ma chérie. We're eating, dear."

For a half second Capucine thought that her mother had added yet another topic to the long list of things that could not be spoken about at the dinner table. But then Capucine realized her guilt. She had committed the unforgivable: providing fuel yet again for one of her father's interminable etymological lectures. Everyone at the table, except Alexandre, shot her a dark look.

"Not at all, ma petite," Monsieur Le Tellier said. "*Civet* come to us from Old French, which in turn comes from the Latin *caepatum*, signifying a dish made of onions."

"Your Chéri was taken to Clairvaux Prison this morning," Jacques said to Capucine, sotto voce.

"In the Middle Ages civets were dishes of roasted meat, which were then braised in a sauce of onions, spices, and *verjus*. At the end of the process the sauce was bound with burnt bread. It was that liaison that gave it its characteristic black color."

"We were lucky to get a conviction. Chéri only signed

her confession because we had an ironclad case against her Roque murder. It was a play for leniency. She knew that the evidence for the Brault killing was entirely circumstantial. Now that she knows the Roque case has been dropped, she must be fuming."

"Of course, verjus is the juice of unripe wine grapes. Medieval tastes were very different from ours today. They liked their dishes very acid and heavily spiced."

"She's not the only one fuming. As it happens, your pet toad really is in a pet. You've definitely lost a friend there."

"Absolutely," Alexandre interjected. "They only started adding blood to civets in the middle of the eighteen hundreds, when *cuisine bourgeoise* blossomed, ushering in heavy, thick, dark liaisons," Alexandre said, aiming his comment at Monsieur Le Tellier.

"If you're in a dark street late at night and you hear a squishy hopping sound behind you, duck into a doorway quick as you can. There's a very angry amphibian out there, looking for revenge. For his species, a blow to self-esteem is more painful than a kick in the cojones."

"Now, there's a very interesting word—" Monsieur Le Tellier was cut off by the arrival of the much-discussed civet de lièvre, in a terrine Capucine only now recognized was an eighteenth-century faïence pot-à-oille, probably Strasbourg, even though she had seen it all her life.

The room fell silent as Madame Le Tellier ladled out the civet onto beds of flat noodles and a bottle of Charmes-Chambertin 2005 circulated around the table. Madame Le Tellier's matriarchal fork lifted, the four other diners applied themselves with gusto. The hare in the civet had been shot the week before at Jacques's father's château, their gamy muskiness attenuated by a night spent in a wine marinade, their flavor polished by the dense blood sauce. There was a long moment of appreciative silence.

Five minutes into the dish Capucine could see her mother's forehead contract and relax rhythmically. Both

Capucine and Jacques read the signs without difficulty. She was wrestling with a thought.

"Ma tante," Jacques said, the cynicism of his smile stopping only a half step before insolence, "you're dying to ask Capucine how she solved her case but are afraid the question is going to result in inappropriate dinner conversation, n'est-ce pas?"

"I was thinking no such thing." She looked crossly at Jacques for several beats. "But since you bring it up, no doubt to satisfy your own curiosity, Capucine, how *did* you figure it out? I studied the newspapers very carefully and didn't have an inkling."

"Actually, Maman, it was an accident. If the circumstances of Monsieur Brissac-Vanté's kidnapping hadn't been so suspicious, we wouldn't have continued monitoring his offshore bank accounts after he was released. And we would never have discovered he was selling a good number of pieces of faïence through Sotheby's in London. Once I learned that, the whole case fell into place. The rest was just a question of legwork."

Madame Le Tellier beamed. "The kidnapping, of course. I'd forgotten about that. Since there was only the slightest reference to it during that awful woman's trial, I didn't think it was important. Who on earth would do that to such a nice boy? It seems hard to believe he was kidnapped at all."

"Oh, he was kidnapped, all right," Capucine said. "He's an inveterate gambler. He started out gambling in Paris's private clubs and graduated to illegal casinos set up in apartments by the Milieu."

"The Milieu?" Madame Le Tellier asked.

"Organized crime," Alexandre supplied between mouthfuls.

Madame Le Tellier nodded enthusiastically.

"He left markers all over town that he couldn't cover. His problem was that after a few drinks he was convinced he was master of his wife's fortune, which was very far from being the case. So the Milieu made an example of him."

"Imagine that. And did they ask for a great deal of money, ma petite? Did the family have to pay this milieu a fortune?"

"There, Maman, I can't help you. The police was never made privy to that information." Capucine gave Jacques a charged look.

"*Mon oncle,*" Jacques said. "That's an interesting term isn't it, *the Milieu?*"

"Jacques, on est à table! Now, ma petite Capucine, there's something else I don't understand. How did Monsieur Brissac-Vanté meet this woman? What was her name again? Lecomte? Is that it? The press intimated they were lovers. Were they?"

"They met at the Interallié—"

"The Interallié, *voyons!* That woman couldn't possibly be a member of the Interallié." The Interallié was her mother's favorite club, housed in a lavish hôtel particulier with a spectacular garden on the rue du Faubourg Saint-Honoré.

"No, Maman, she's not. She was invited by someone to a reception organized by Brissac-Vanté for one of his sports promotions. She already had the idea of making fakes and was attracted to him because of his financial involvement in the Faïence de Châteauneuf-sur-Loire. He must have found her attractive enough to take to dinner. It was then that they came up with the synergy of Chef Brault's collection and the Faïence's ability to produce fakes and all the participants' need of money."

"So it was all about money?"

"Yes. I don't think they were lovers."

Madame Le Tellier flushed a pink that quickly escalated into glowing crimson. She opened her mouth to protest, but words failed her. Capucine had the tingling sense of having gone too far. She knew she was teetering on the edge of being returned to a status where her position in the Police Judiciaire was no longer admitted by her parents.

Capucine interjected rapidly, "Brissac-Vanté was easily led. My guess is that Chéri Lecomte quickly discovered his urgent need to pay off his gambling debts and lost no time putting a ring through his nose."

"And why was it necessary for these people to kill this chef?" Monsieur Le Tellier asked. Capucine was astonished he had been listening at all. "Alexandre tells me he was truly exceptional."

"The answer to that is simple—alcohol. I see all too much of it in my profession." Capucine cringed, expecting her parents to bridle at the reference to the police. When would she learn enough was enough? But they just nodded, encouraging her to continue.

"From the start it was a difficult evening. Chef Brault, fueled by all his neuroses, was on the edge of hysteria. Brissac-Vanté must have been quaking in his Westons. Lecomte saw a very lucrative business that she had become financially dependent on going down the drain."

Capucine cut a tiny morsel of the civet. Despite her best efforts, the notion of the blood sauce repelled her.

"Committing murder is always easy. The tricky part is getting rid of the body. And all of a sudden Lecomte had a vision of how it could be done. Once she had that epiphany, nothing was easier than to drag her drunk victim and drunk accomplice off to the Puces and commit the deed."

"And the court understood that?" Monsieur Le Tellier asked.

"Oui, Papa. Brissac-Vanté got five years. If he doesn't get into trouble in prison, they'll let him out in two, maybe even less. But Chéri Lecomte will spend the rest of her life in jail."

"She must thank her lucky stars the guillotine is no longer used," Madame Le Tellier said.

"Perhaps not," Alexandre said. "There is a movement afoot that claims that these endless incarcerations in our primitive prisons are far worse than a speedy, painless death."

Capucine staved the digression off at the pass. "Brissac-Vanté has already started to serve his sentence in Paris, at La Santé Prison. I understand his wife comes religiously to the weekly visits he is allowed, and then spends every night on the boulevard Arago with a crowd of Arab women, hoping to get a glimpse or a word from their husbands from a window of the prison."

There was an uncomfortable silence at the table. Even Jacques could not find something irreverent to say. It took Capucine's mother to break the mood.

"Ma fille," Madame Le Tellier said. "Tell me what happened to your charming brigadier. The one with the beautiful hair. I've been wondering if he isn't one of the Martineaus from Quimper. I'd like to talk to him about that. If he is, I'm sure we're distantly related."

Capucine laughed. "I'm sorry to disappoint you, Maman. He's from a small village high in the hills behind Cannes. Since he was from the Midi, I sent him down there to look into Chef Brault's past. It seems the trip rekindled his childhood love of the region. Right now he's back down there, taking his six weeks' vacation, looking for a house to buy, and working on his biography of Chef Brault. I had an e-mail from him this morning. He's standing for election for the town council of the village and seems to think that they might even vote him in as mayor. Apparently, he has a real plebiscite. Even the old former mayor of the village leaves his retirement home once a day to campaign for him."

"Does that mean he's no longer working for you?" Madame Le Tellier asked.

"For the moment he still is. And, of course, he'll be able to commute back and forth between Paris and La Cadière if he's elected. The high-speed train makes everything possible. But I do have a feeling he just might have found his true vocation."

"And so, Alexandre, what about that acerbic food critic? Lucien Folon, wasn't it? What happened to him?" Monsieur Le Tellier asked.

"He was inconsolable about the death of Chef Brault. He's taken a leave of absence from his paper and moved to Tokyo to write a book about molecular gastronomy in Japan."

Madame Le Tellier opened her mouth to ask the obvious question of what molecular gastronomy might be but then shut it with the equally obvious consideration that her son-in-law—who was quite undesirable for reasons she could no longer remember—had already been paid far too much attention that evening.

"You see, dear," Monsieur Le Tellier said. "I told you all along that la petite Capucine's job was perfectly satisfactory. Look how interested you became in her case."

"Hardly, mon ami." When irritated, Madame Le Tellier retreated into a world of the previous century, when spouses were treated as mere acquaintances and addressed by the formal vous.

"She could easily have found a reputable position in a ministry, just like her cousin Jacques." Madame Le Tellier smiled adoringly at her nephew. "*Mon neveu,* shall we take coffee in the salon? I'm sure you need a digestif after your long, demanding day at the ministry."

Jacques rose to take his aunt's arm and lead her into the sitting room.

Capucine and Alexandre were the last to leave the table. Capucine slipped her hand into Alexandre's, buoyed by the sensation that the entire orbit of her existence was defined by the tiny pocket made by their clasped hands.

Turn the page for a delicious preview of the
new book in Alexander Campion's
Capucine Culinary Mystery series

MURDER ON
THE MEDITERRANEAN

A Kensington hardcover coming in July 2014

CHAPTER 1

The cramps seared without mercy. On the lee side of the cockpit she contorted into a fetal twist, feet tight against buttocks, knees hard under chin. Like synchronized dancers, the twin wheels of the helm gyrated back and forth in the grip of the autopilot. Two women sat huddled on the other side of the cockpit, ostracizing her with their whispers. She glared at them, as if their rudeness was the source of her pain.

Another spasm wrenched her lower abdomen in a vise grip. She grunted. On the horizon a static of lightning was followed by a dull bowling-ball rumble of thunder. Greasy, fat drops of rain began to fall out of the sooty sky. She stood up, grabbed a foul-weather jacket from a heap at the foot of the settee, slipped it on, and inched across the sloping deck toward the bow.

Another spasm stunned her. A torrent buckled down, aimed only at her, soaking her to the skin. She couldn't manage to pull the jacket closed. Drenched, her T-shirt stuck to her breasts and stomach. Shuddering, she continued to fumble with the jacket. It wasn't hers. She must have picked up one of the women's. *Great*. Now, on top of everything else, she was going to get an earful when she got back to the cockpit. Even in the downpour, those rich bitches would get their noses all out of joint if one of them had to wear her taped-up, oil-stained piece of shit.

A violent spasm heaved at her bowels. Only one thing mattered, getting to the bow before it was too late. Doubled over, she shuffled along the heaving, sloping nonslip surface of the deck, her bare feet skating through the cascading water. The pain intensified. She wasn't going to make it to the bow.

The top of her head rammed into the wire cable of the forestay. She gasped a sob of pain and relief. The surprise loosened her grip on her muscles, and she felt the contractions of unstoppable peristalsis take charge. She ripped off the foul-weather jacket, threw it down on the deck, shrugged her shoulders out of the elastic suspenders of her foul-weather pants, pushed them down to her knees with the panties inside, gripped the forestay with both hands, swung herself out over the bow pulpit railing. The action unleashed the full force of the eruption. She was sure the explosion of her intestines could be heard in the cockpit, forty-five feet away, despite the din of the storm.

The relief lasted only seconds. She convulsed in pain again. And once again. And yet again. A figure emerged from the sticky darkness. Bound to be one of the two bitches, who'd come to see what was wrong. For a brief second, her embarrassment overrode the anguish of her gut. Hoping to keep from being seen in her mortifying position, she bleated out, "It's nothing. I'll be back in a second. Don't worry about me." Another spasm. Another spurt.

But it wasn't a woman. *Oh God, not now.* He was back. This was absolutely too much. She hurled insults. Strong hands grabbed her naked ankles and shook her legs. Her colon pumped out a weak but satisfying spurt. She relaxed her grip on the forestay, felt herself shoved hard forward, toppled off the bow pulpit, fell butt first into the sea.

She tried to tread water, but the pants around her ankles

held fast. As she squirmed to kick off the foulie pants, she felt the slick hull of the boat rub against her arm. She scrabbled, grabbing for a handhold on the slick gel-coated side of the boat. In an instant the boat was gone, its tiny white stern light no more than a pinprick in the blackness.

She thrashed, but the bagging pants dragged her deeper and deeper the more she struggled. She swallowed a mouthful of salt water, gagged, coughed, swallowed more.

Her last thought was that drowning was supposed to be the most peaceful of deaths. How could everyone have been so wrong about that?

CHAPTER 2

"Capucine, I don't know how I let you talk me into this escapade. The thought of tossing helplessly over the waves of the open sea in your tiny walnut shell has been keeping me awake for days."

Police Judiciaire *commissaire* Capucine Le Tellier smiled at her erstwhile boss, *Juge d'Instruction* Inès Maistre, from under mischievous eyebrows and tilted her head back to swallow the sugary dregs of her demitasse of *café express*.

"The *Diomede* is hardly a nutshell, and she's definitely not mine. She's a bareboat charter. A fifty-five-foot Dufour with four cabins and all the room in the world. Much bigger than my first apartment after I graduated from Sciences Po. Look, you can see her over there."

Capucine pointed at a substantial yacht docked on the other side of the marina. The mainsail furled on its boom was sheathed in a navy-blue cover lettered MEDITERRANEAN ANCHORAGE YACHTS.

Inès peered at the boats over reading glasses perched on the tip of her nose, shrugged her shoulders in Gallic resignation. With an effort Capucine twisted her frown into a smile. The women were almost the same age, still south of their midthirties, and had worked together often in the antediluvian era, a few years prior, when Capucine was still a reluctant hotshot in the fiscal brigade. Capucine had never been entirely at ease with Inès. Her neurotic obsession with putting corporate criminals behind bars was as unsettling as it was captivating.

Capucine had blurted out her invitation two weeks earlier, when an unexpected surge of camaraderie had washed over her during a luncheon meeting. Inès wanted Capucine to work with her on a case. Even though Capucine now had her hands full with her own brigade in the tough working-class Twentieth Arrondissement, the thought of lending a hand on an intricate financial problem had produced a thrill.

A waiter—an eighteen-year-old who was obviously paying for his summer in the sun by working tables—came up with menus. He had a hard time tearing his eyes away from Capucine's décolleté. She concluded she might just have gone one button too far with her white linen shirt.

"Any news on your suspect?" Capucine asked Inès.

"He's a bit more than a suspect. He's guilty as hell. All we have to do is prove it."

"Would you like me to explain about the dishes?" the young waiter asked, eyes still glued to Capucine. Capucine ignored him as if she hadn't heard.

"And he was released two days ago, but that was only to be expected."

The situation was straightforward. The guilty-as-hell man in question was the young grandson of the chairman of a venerable family-owned Paris investment bank, Tottinguer & Cie. The house was so ancient, the name was pronounced differently from the way it was spelled. Nevertheless, Inès was convinced the bank's management, including the grandson, were inveterate financial miscreants. She had been after them for years and had never been able to produce even the slightest simulacrum of a case.

But now she might have found a chink in their armour. André Tottinguer, the grandson, a *gérant* of the bank and also a known philanderer, had been arrested for assaulting his wife. Inès had explained that Tottinguer had arrived home, returning from a tryst, at four in the morning to find his wife pressing the barrels of his Purdey shotgun up against his nose, her finger white tight on the trigger. Fortunately, the silly woman had left the safety on. He grabbed the gun, chased her down the stairwell, fired one shot into the ceiling and another through the lobby's interior glass door after she'd run out. The wife, in her bathrobe and pajamas, managed to find a cab and get to her sister's. The concierge of the building called the police, who arrested Tottinguer.

"And why did the police let him go?"

"That was my idea. No prosecutor would have even tried to present a case of attempted manslaughter. Charges might have been brought for *tapage nocturne,* creating a disturbance in the night, but all you get for that is a fine.

"No, I want to use this incident for an investigation of domestic violence. With your experience in the Twentieth, you're an expert. Once I have him solidly behind bars, the wife will cooperate with me and get me all the fuel I need for the financial prosecution of the whole family."

Capucine didn't know what to say. She twisted her mouth in the tight French frown that could mean either assent or incredulity.

"Capucine, I'm going to get him this time. Believe me. He'll go up for twenty years. And the rest of the family will follow right after. Just watch me." Inès gripped the edge of the table so hard, her knuckles paled.

There was an awkward silence. The tintinnabulation of steel halyards rattling against aluminum masts became audible.

Inès made a valiant attempt to put the conversation back on an even keel.

"Tell me more about this boat trip of yours."

"We leave on the morning tide tomorrow morning and sail straight for Bonifacio. You'll love it. It's the most beautiful town in Corsica, built high up on a white cliff so eroded by the sea that the town overhangs the water and looks like it might collapse at any moment. Then we spend a few days exploring the east coast of Sardinia and sail straight back here."

"And who else is there going to be?"

"There'll be nine of us in all. Six others besides you and me and my husband, Alexandre. My cousin Jacques—he's with the Ministry of the Interior—is coming, too. And one of Alexandre's cronies, Serge Monnot, who owns a number of very popular bars in the Marais, will be the skipper. He's an avid sailor, and he's the one who chartered the boat. Then there's Angélique Berthier and her husband, Dominique. Angélique was a classmate of mine at Sciences Po. She's doing very well as a partner in a head-hunting firm. Actually, we've drifted a bit apart since school, but we used to be very close friends. Her husband, Dominique, is wonderful, a charming marine watercolorist. And there's a woman I don't know, Florence Henriot. She's a friend of Serge's and is in charge of one of the imprints at Hachette. She used to be a famous professional racing sailor. Twice she won the Route du Rhum single-handed yacht race to Guadeloupe."

Inès grimaced and shuddered histrionically. "How could anyone want to do that? God knows how long she was alone on a boat without really sleeping or having a proper bath." She looked up sharply at Capucine. "There are bathrooms on this boat, aren't there?"

"Of course. There's one attached en suite to each of the cabins. Except on a boat they're called heads, not bathrooms."

Inès snorted and shook her head slightly. "That only makes eight people. Who's the ninth?"

"The professional crew member Serge hired. A young girl, apparently. She's on board to cook and clean and help him when he maneuvers the boat, so all we have to do is lie around in the sun and eat delicious meals."

"Good. We'll put the time to good use. We need to brainstorm about Tottinguer."

"And unwind a little. Let's not forget about that part. You're going to be enchanted by Bonifacio, and the Costa Smeralda in Sardinia is the most beautiful coast in the Mediterranean."

"Maybe, but my main objective is to keep you fully in my sights until you're formally assigned to me. If need be, I'll handcuff our wrists together."

Capucine laughed over politely at the joke.

Inès frowned at Capucine over her reading glasses. "Capucine, I need to get this man. Without the quality of the police work you can bring to my team, I'm dead. Just dead."

CHAPTER 3

Five miles away in Saint-Tropez, Alexandre also sat at a restaurant table overlooking the inimitable azure of the Mediterranean. He had asked for the check, and the maître d' had arrived with thimble-size glasses of *liqueur de framboise* and the assurance that the honor of Monsieur de Huguelet's presence at the restaurant Pétrus was far more compensation than the establishment deserved. He was, after all, the undisputed doyen of restaurant critics.

"When was the last time you actually paid for a meal in a restaurant, *mon cousin?*" Jacques asked with a smirk.

Despite himself, Alexandre was invariably amused by Jacques, the son of Capucine's father's brother. The two had grown up together as brother and sister. Jacques never tired of hinting that there might have been something a bit more than purely fraternal to the relationship. Jacques also took unrestrained joy in the fact that he held an ill-defined, but apparently exalted, post with the DGSE, France's intelligence service, which occasionally cast him in the role of éminence grise in Capucine's cases.

Alexandre sipped his bone-chilling *alcool*. He would not allow himself to be baited. The meal had been excellent. They had both had Mediterranean spiny lobster. Jacques had chosen less well and had ordered his sautéed on a door-size teppanyaki grill, while Alexandre had chosen his presented in delicate fresh pasta *ravioles* with a creamy sauce of liquefied fennel bulbs, shallots, mustard, and just a hint of orange juice. Far more than satisfactory.

The restaurant Pétrus had recently opened at the north end of Saint-Tropez's fabled quai Jean Jaurès and was fast making a name for itself not only as a fashionable, *dans le vent* restaurant, but also as the purveyor of reference of prepared meals to the mega yachts that populated the quai. Alexandre decided he would write something upbeat about the Pétrus in his blog on *Le Figaro*'s website.

The framboise downed, hands shaken, promises to return made, favorable mentions in the press hinted at, Alexandre and Jacques set out on their postprandial stroll down the quai Jean Jaurès.

The Saint-Tropez port was immutable, crammed with wide, porch-size fantail decks of gigantic yachts berthed stern to quai, invariably decorated with an ornate vase of flowers on a table, swarming with young, tanned, obsequious, athletic crew in shorts and T-shirt uniforms.

"We have only one boat slave, it seems," Jacques said languidly, aping a disappointed moue. "I hope she makes up in pulchritude what we lack in quantity."

Alexandre harrumphed. "The last thing we need on this cruise is a boat girl. Florence is a world-champion sailor. Serge is very competent. Capucine knows her way around boats. If you ask me, Serge took one look at that coffin-size forepeak cabin and decided it would be perfect for some minion he could boss around like Captain Bligh."

At this point in their *flânocherie*, as Alexandre called it, they reached Sénéquier, the fabled café epicenter of the Riviera. Considering that the vacation ideal of every French person under the age of thirty-five was to spend the month of August with elbows propped up on one of Sénéquier's red, triangular tables, it was not surprising that there were no seats available on the terrace.

Two girls, their long legs at the apricot beginnings of their summer tans, stood up to leave. Jacques pirouetted into a canvas director's chair with the finesse of a dancer, and Alexandre followed suit by spilling into his. A waiter arrived, imperiously flicking his side towel in irritation. There was a queue inside, and he had already received copious tips in exchange for a table. Jacques looked blandly at the man, straightening the crease in his Lanvin white-linen trousers, revealing creamy soft, baby-blue suede Tod's driving shoes. The waiter checked and respectfully stood up straight. Then he caught sight of Alexandre, felt he should recognize him, stood up straighter still.

"Messieurs?" he asked with exaggerated politeness.

"Pastis," Alexandre ordered, glancing at Jacques, who nodded.

When the drinks came, they both fell silent, admiring the high-school chemistry trick of the clear golden pastis turning milky white when water was added.

"Actually," Alexandre said after his first sip, "I really am in a pet about this boat girl of Serge's. I'd planned on doing the cooking myself. Working on those tiny boat stoves is an exciting challenge. I have a whole folder of recipes and a carrier bag filled with basic necessities . . . tins of pâté de foie gras and a few jars of truffles and . . ."

Alexandre had failed to attract Jacques's attention. Alexandre searched the terrace for the source of Jacques's fascination. Jacques seemed captivated by some creature in the very depths of the terrace. This was unexpected, since Jacques never looked at women. A fact that, when combined with his immoderate interest in clothes, made the family wonder if he wasn't, well, just possibly a soupçon fey. Then Alexandre focused on the woman, a translucent beauty with alabaster skin, silken pale blond hair, and ice-blue eyes. Even a woolly mammoth would have stared.

Alexandre caught sight of her companion and jumped up.

"Régis!" he exclaimed happily. "*Toi ici!* You're the very last person I expected to run into in this crass temple of see and be seen. What on earth are you doing here?"

It was the work of a moment to whisk two chairs away from an adjoining table and make introductions. Régis de la Rochelle was a food photographer, well known for his commercials and his illustrations of pricey coffee-table cookbooks; the seraphic creature was called Aude Thevenoux and was, apparently, some sort of lawyer.

"Having an absolutely miserable time," Aude answered for him. Her face revealed not the slightest trace of expression when she spoke. It was almost as if she were a life-size porcelain doll of exquisite delicacy equipped with a sound system operated by a third party.

"The plan was to come down here and charter a boat and go somewhere," Régis said, "but everything is rented, so we're stuck in our drab little hotel room up in the hills."

"And the traffic jams are so bad, it's an hour cab ride to drive the two miles into town," Aude contributed with no more than a ventriloquist's movement of her lips.

"I have the perfect solution," Jacques said. "We have a boat chartered in Port Grimaud. We're leaving for Corsica in the morning. Why don't you come with us? We have plenty of room."

Alexandre hiked his eyebrows. This was a whole new Jacques.

"We could put you up on the settee in the main salon," Jacques said. "It can turn into a double bed. We're going to do an overnight crossing straight to Bonifacio. We could drop you off there, and you could have your vacation away from the crowds, or at least the worst of them."

Aude looked into Jacques's eyes, mute. Even though not a word had been exchanged, the bargain was sealed.

More pastis was ordered.

Régis chatted at Alexandre about his current project as one of the photographers on Alain Ducasse's latest tome. Jacques and Aude looked into each other's eyes.

Lubricated by a series of pastises, they became steeped in conversations as the radiant sunshine bore through the umbrella over the table and the afternoon wore on. When the shadows lengthened, Alexandre's thoughts turned to dinner. It was high time to find a cab and make their way back to Port Grimaud to hatch a plan for the evening meal with Capucine and that odd juge d'instruction friend of hers. He called for the bill, waving away any attempt from Régis to share. As they rose, Aude looked into Jacques's eyes.

"*A demain,*" she said. Alexandre had a strong sense of their complicity.

"We're at the Mediterranean Anchorage Yachts Marina in Port Grimaud," Jacques said. "Our skipper wants to get going by ten tomorrow morning."

Aude said nothing. She shook Alexandre's hand and leaned forward to allow Jacques to kiss her cheeks.